Scoring
Wilder

R.S. Grey

Published: R.S. Grey 2013
authorrsgrey@gmail.com
Editing: Taylor K's Editing Service
Cover Design: R.S. Grey
Cover Photos: Shutterstock ®
ISBN: 1499707975
ISBN-13: 978-1499707977

Monica,

Happy Reading

XO RS Grey

For all the wonderful readers and bloggers in the indie community.

Chapter One

Cheat on me once, shame on him. Cheat on me twice... what the actual fuck is going on? How in the world have I managed to find my last *two* boyfriends cheating on me? No, not *together*. Although, that would have been much more poetic, and at least they could have included me or something.

The reality was much worse.

"Wow. What a treat to walk in on," I noted harshly as I stood in the doorway of Josh's bedroom. Josh and the nameless bimbo screamed and jumped apart on his bed, causing his navy sheets to tumble to the ground. His brown eyes found mine, and for one brief second, I mourned the loss of his warm gaze, but then my field of vision widened and I was slapped with the sad scene before me.

My boyfriend of four months was cheating on me. No, scratch that. *My friend of four years, turned boyfriend of four months,* was cheating on me.

"Oh, no. Please, don't stop on my account. I'm only

his *girlfriend*," I hissed at the bimbo, trying to calm my temper. I was known to be feisty on a good day, so that was hardly brushing the surface for me.

Josh's dark brown hair was ruffled from the bimbo's hands. His sharp features were pitiful, but still handsome. I barely glanced in the girl's direction. Platinum blonde hair was the only feature I noticed. Probably because it was bright enough to burn through my corneas. First, she steals my boyfriend, and then she renders me visionless. Just great.

Is my judgment of character so misaligned that I can't spot the good guys from the bad? No. It's just the fact that I happen to go for guys that can't keep tramps out of their pants. You know the type: young and insanely good-looking.

"Kinsley! It's not—"

"… What it looks like," I finished for him. "Wow, Josh. You know Trey said the same thing, but he didn't have that look of anguish you've got going on right now. Seriously, good work." I applauded him with a hard stare. My claps rang out around the room, and I realized then that it was time for me to leave.

It was a different guy, a different girl, but there was that same twisting sensation in my gut like I was about to keel over on the spot. I spun around and flipped them both the bird before heading back toward the living room to grab my purse.

I heard shuffling and awkward grunts behind me, but I didn't turn around.

"Josh, where are you going? Let her go, we aren't done!" Oh good, she hadn't had her orgasm yet. Maybe my timing wasn't all that bad.

"Kinsley! Wait!" Josh yelled behind me. Did he think

we were in the middle of a telenovela?

"Josh, it's over. Don't bother," I said as I threw my purse over my shoulder.

His hand reached out to clasp mine, and I had to actively fight the urge to punch his dick off. Seriously, is it that hard to stay faithful? Are men physically incapable?

"Kinsley! I love you. I love you!" He spun me around, holding the bed sheet up with his right hand and clasping my arm with the other. His eyes were wild, and for a brief moment, I believed him.

Oh god. He did it. *He went there.* And you know what the sad thing is? I don't even think he was giving me a line. I think the poor schmuck actually thought that he loved me.

"Well, if that's how you show your love I can't imagine the elaborate things you do for your parents."

"Please— hear me out. This meant *nothing*."

I wasn't listening. I was already building a wall between us. "Thank you, Josh. Thank you for ruining my capacity to trust so that any guy that comes after you will automatically have the cards stacked against him."

Josh had stolen another chunk of my heart, my naiveté, my innocence, and smashed it under his perfectly toned body. When I met him I was on my way to feeling jaded to the whole dating process. I'd already been cheated on once by my boyfriend of six months, Trey, who also happened to be the guy that had taken my virginity. (I know, I know. They should make a hallmark card for that experience since it's so cliché: "Whoops, sorry your high school boyfriend can't keep it in his pants… here's a cute puppy wearing a bowtie.")

But now? Now I was about ten miles past jaded. It was time to trade in my designer dresses for patterned muumuus and house slippers. Maybe I could join a support group for divorcées over fifty. You know, those women that decide they don't need men to be happy. They'll just knit, take group trips to the Caribbean, and say things like "I always wanted to go out to eat, but *Jeff* insisted I cook for him. I'm going out to eat every night now, damnit!"

Only problem: I'm eighteen. They'd probably think I was trying to be an ironic hipster.

Whatever, I'd figure it out.

Josh kept calling my name as I walked out of his apartment. A huge part of me wanted to trash everything in my path, but he was moving the next day and I didn't think it'd be right to screw over his landlord. Instead, I just flipped my brown hair over my shoulder and relished in the fact that my legs looked killer in my cut-off shorts.

Keep yelling, Josh, but I'm never turning back.

Chapter Two

"Hell hath no fury like a woman scorned!" I screamed before I downed the fifth shot of the night. The liquor slid over my tongue, but I could hardly taste it anymore. It was my nineteenth birthday, so I was allowed to go a little wild. Not to mention, it was two weeks since I'd walked in on Josh cheating on me, and I was just entering the height of the "guys-can-go-fuck-themselves" phase. Next would be the "guys-can-seriously-go-fuck-themselves" phase, the crucial final step in the cheated-on grieving process.

"I dunno, Kinsley. Tequila 'hath' a pretty wicked fury." Emily frowned as she took the shot glass out of my hand and replaced it with a glass of water. I'd only known Emily for a few days, but I could already tell we'd have a symbiotic relationship. She was the epitome of the shy girl-next-door, and I was the complete opposite.

Emily and I were two out of five freshmen members of the University of Los Angeles women's soccer team. It was the beginning of June and training camp would start

5

bright and early the next morning. I knew I was playing with fire by getting drunk the night before, but the veteran girls assured me that I'd be fine. They said the first day was mostly about technical things; basically lots of speeches and meetings about what the program expected out of us. The real practicing didn't usually start until the second day.

I peered over at Emily and closed one eye so that I would only see one of her. She was pretty with medium-length red hair that was light enough to where I felt like calling her Peach for the rest of the night.

"Em, you're so pretty. Have I told you that you're so pretty? Cause you're so pretty."

She blushed and I made a mental note to get the girl some confidence. Lord knows I had enough for the two of us combined. You'd think having been cheated on twice would ruin that, but it would take a lot more than two dumb guys to undo the amount of leery gazes and unsolicited charm that had been laid on me my whole life.

I took Emily's hand and pulled her to the restroom down the hall. We were about to leave for a house party and I wanted to make sure I hadn't boozed off all of my makeup. Thankfully it wasn't hard to keep on mascara and lip gloss.

"Do you think this is a smart idea? Going to this party before our first practice?" Emily asked, eyeing me in the spotless mirror.

I puckered my lips and wagged my finger like I was about to set her straight. "We'll be fine, and who cares? It's my BIRTHDAY!" I squealed so loudly that Emily scrunched her nose in distaste. God, we were so different. I wondered if our budding friendship would last the summer. She was a small town girl from the Midwest whereas I was born and raised in the LA soccer world.

"Okay. We'll go and have fun and get back in time to get some sleep before practice," Emily said, nodding her head in agreement. I was already corrupting the girl.

"How do you look that good after five shots? Seriously?" Emily asked.

I glanced away from her to eye my appearance. Everything was just as it should have been: heart shaped face, small nose, plump lips, tan skin, and bright blue eyes that looked almost fake against my long mane of dark brown hair.

I was about average height and in great shape from soccer. I had lean, toned arms and legs like a cross-country runner.

"Are you kidding? I'd kill for those little freckles. You look like Little Bo Peep!" I laughed, grabbing her hand and forcing her to spin around in a circle like a prima ballerina. How drunk was I at this point?

Emily laughed and spun around, stumbling over her feet and making me laugh even harder. "What do freckles have to do with Little Bo Peep?"

A thunderous knock sounded at the door before I could answer.

"Let's go rookies! If we don't leave now there won't be any good alcohol left at the party!"

My ears perked up at that. The party was where I needed to be. It was my last hope of having a good birthday. So far it had been a bit depressing. I'd dumped my cheating boyfriend two weeks prior, my parents had ditched me for snow and the Aspen Country Club, and all of my high school friends had moved away for college. I'd bought myself a piece of Italian cream cake and eaten it alone in a cafe, people watching and feeling extremely lonely.

This party was my silver-lining, and I needed to make sure I made the most of it.

"Lead the way, Bo Peep!" I winked and locked elbows with Emily before we left the bathroom.

We walked back into the living room and I surveyed the group of girls that would form my soccer team for the next four years. Most of them I'd met when I was being recruited. They all seemed nice enough and I knew I'd get to know them a lot better once we started training.

The seniors were the only girls that seemed like they might want to cause problems. Tara was the captain of the team and everything about her cried out tyrannical tendencies. Her fellow seniors followed her around like little minions, except less cute. Hopefully I'd end up on Tara's good side, but past experience told me that was less than likely. I was heavily recruited for the team and had been voted rookie of the year by several soccer magazines prior to my signing on at ULA, which is why her radar was already locked onto me. I was a threat to her well-oiled system, which was made perfectly clear when she'd snubbed me at tryouts in front of everyone a few months prior.

Whatever. If I could survive her, then I'd be fine. I just had to do my job and play excellent soccer, that way she wouldn't have anything to complain about.

"Kinsley, Emily, wait for me!" Becca yelled as we pushed our way through the front door. Becca was another rookie on the team. She'd moved into the Rookie house the day before and we'd hardly had any time to hangout, but I could already tell our personalities would blend well together. She was gorgeous; she was only a few inches shorter than me with hazel eyes and bright blonde hair.

I spun around to wait for her as she ran over from the Underclassmen house that was right next door to the Upperclassmen house. We called them the Vet and Rookie houses for short.

"I thought you were ditching us," I said, reaching out to wrap my arm around her shoulder.

"Nope. I had to run over to the Rookie house to grab something." She patted her purse with a proud grin.

"Ahhh," I nodded as we reached the SUV.

The plan was to cram into a single vehicle so that only one person had to be the designated driver. It wasn't the safest form of transportation, but it'd have to work.

"Emily, keep your hands where I can see them," I joked as I laid across the laps of the three girls in the middle row.

"Ew, Kinsley!" Emily protested, and the entire car cracked up. Just to calm her nerves, I reached down and pulled the hem of my tight dress down so that it covered everything.

"Are you having a good birthday so far, Kinsley?" Tara asked from the passenger seat. Funny how we were piled in the back like sardines, yet somehow she managed to get the front seat all to herself.

"Yeah. It's been really great," I lied, tacking on a smile to prove how much I was willing to play the game. I really didn't want to be on her bad side.

"Oh really? Sofie saw you eating a piece of cake all by yourself in that cafe near campus." She shot me a piteous look complete with sad eyes and a small frown. I didn't even glance toward Sofie, the designated driver and co-captain of our team.

"Oh weird... I was there with Leonardo DiCaprio. He

9

must have been in the bathroom when Sofie was spying on me," I quipped, making everyone in the SUV laugh, except, of course, Sofie and Tara. I knew the "spying on me" comment was a tad aggressive, but what kind of bully picks on someone on their birthday?

"Spying on you? We have better things to do, Bryant," she scoffed, and then turned back toward the front window. I didn't mind when teammates called me by my last name but with her, it was almost a little dig, like calling someone "kid" when you're the same age as they are.

"We'll sing you happy birthday when we get to the party!" Becca suggested as she supported the middle of my body on top of her lap. Everyone agreed and promised to sing as soon as we arrived. Their support felt good in that moment and I let Tara's comments roll off my back. It was too early in the season to have an enemy like her.

A popular club mix came on the radio and Tara reached forward to turn it on full blast so that everyone started dancing. Becca gyrated her hips beneath me, making my body bounce up and down. In my inebriated state I couldn't keep my balance. One quite aggressive dance move knocked me forward so that my cheek collided with the middle console.

"Jesus, Becca—your hips should have their own warning label," I laughed, holding my hand to my cheek. I could already feel a bruise forming.

"Oh, crap! Sorry, Kinsley, we'll get some ice at the party," she giggled and helped pull me back up onto her lap. Even though my cheek was throbbing I couldn't stop laughing with Becca. Yup, we'd be a dynamic duo in no time.

When we finally arrived at the house party, we stumbled out of the car and attempted to piece ourselves together. I adjusted my black dress and tried to stand confidently on my heels that were too tall even before taking five shots.

"How does your cheek feel?" Emily asked as we made our way up the modern concrete stairs.

"Now it feels kind of numb from the alcohol, I think... My face hasn't fallen off, has it?"

Emily laughed and tugged me toward the front door. "No, you just have a big red spot on your cheek."

Oh perfect, the first time I see Josh since the break-up and I probably look like I got punched in the face. I moaned and tried to shake out my nerves.

I'd never actually been to one of these legendary parties. I'd heard about them, of course. Every year a few of the guys from the professional soccer team in LA, the LA Stars, rent a giant house together. It was a "work hard, play harder" situation. This year, when Josh had been signed to the professional team, he'd moved into the house— which is why I knew he'd be at the party.

The LA Stars were the top soccer team in the US. Last year, five of their team members competed for the US in the World Cup only to lose in the last few minutes to Portugal. Needless to say, they were some of the top athletes in the world, with sponsorships and frequent spots on the talk-show circuit.

When we stepped into the house, my vision was bombarded with a plethora of beautiful people. Groupies, celebrities, soccer stars. It was hard to see through all the dancing bodies, but at least the chances of seeing Josh were pretty slim.

"Don't go too crazy, girls. Remember that you're

representing our team now," Tara warned before she and Sofie took off and left us in the entryway.

"This is crazy," Emily murmured. I looked over to see her gulping down the scene with quick darting glances. I guess it was a lot to process, especially since LA was already an over the top town to begin with.

"Let's go find some ice for my cheek." I grabbed her hand and started tugging her through the crowd with Becca in tow.

It was hardly 10:00 P.M. and the party was already in full swing. People were mingling *everywhere*. Girls were wrapped around guys on the couches. Three tables were set up for beer pong in the living room and there was a mass of people crowded around them. I waved to some girls I recognized from club teams. Some of them tried to get us to stop and talk, but I pointed to my cheek and told them I'd be back in a bit.

The entire house was a bachelor pad on crack. Open, modern, and filled with every piece of technology imaginable. It was a maze trying to get through the living room, but finally we maneuvered our way into an expansive kitchen. It didn't disappoint. With marble countertops and chic black appliances, it fit in perfectly with the rest of the house. The space was less crowded than the other rooms, but there were still at least fifty people between us and the freezer.

"Here, you just stand there and I'll get you some ice." Emily gently pushed me to the side against the kitchen counter so that she could prepare a little ice pack for me with a bunch of paper towels.

My feet were starting to hurt from my four inch heels, so I reached back to prop myself up onto the counter. I should have inspected the spot beforehand because as I hopped up I heard the telltale sound of alcohol bottles tipping over and crashing into the sink.

"Oops!" I giggled, then covered my mouth with my hands.

"You're a liability," Becca joked, reaching behind me to right the tipped over bottles.

In my drunken state, I didn't seem to care. Sitting on the counter definitely beat standing up on my high heels, and from my vantage point I could see over the heads of everyone standing in the kitchen. The amount of plastic surgery in that room could have rivaled a Miss America dressing room. Everywhere I looked I was greeted with fake boobs and nose jobs, but it was LA and these women had their jobs cut out for them if they intended on landing a professional athlete.

"Kinsley, scoot back, you're about to fall off the counter," Becca said, pulling me out of my people-watching zone. I hadn't realized I'd been swaying so heavily.

I scooted back a little bit so that more of my thighs pressed against the cold granite.

"Oh, here! I almost forgot," she said, reaching down to dig in her purse.

"What is it? What is it?" I clapped my hands together, feeling giddy from the alcohol and party atmosphere. "A vibrator?" I exclaimed loud enough for the few people around us to eye me with suspicious grins. I shot them all a confident smile.

"No, you hussy! It's a birthday crown. It's what I had to grab at the Rookie House earlier," she answered, retrieving a pink, sparkly princess crown out of her purse. It looked like a piece of a costume I'd had as a little girl and I instantly loved it.

"Ooooh. It's beeuuooteefuulll," I drawled with wide eyes as she placed it on the top of my head.

Becca started laughing, making me laugh, and eventually I was clutching my stomach. My nineteenth birthday was definitely getting better. Laughing like an insane person sure beat eating cake alone.

"Here, this should help," Emily said, returning from the freezer and handing me a makeshift icepack with a bemused smile. I'd forgotten my cheek was even injured.

I took the pack and gave her a cheesy grin. "What would I do without you two?!"

"Well you're about to find out because I have to use the bathroom."

"I'll go with you," Becca said, turning toward Emily. "I should find the other freshman girls and bring them in here. They're probably wondering where we went."

"What?" I asked with puppy-dog-eyes. "You're both leaving me?" I actually felt sad about it.

"Yes, just stay there and keep icing your face. We'll be right back!" Becca called as she and Emily disappeared through the crowd. What the hell? Now I looked like a big loser sitting by myself with a princess crown and an ice pack. But I'd be damned if I took it off. I was a birthday princess. I even gave a royal wave to anyone that walked by me.

"That crown looks good on you! Want to do a birthday shot?" A dark voice asked. I looked up to find a group of cute guys surrounding me. They looked a bit older and I knew the one speaking to me was on the LA Stars team. If I wasn't drunk I could have told you his name, but I hardly remembered my name. Kinsley Bryant. Kinsley Bryant.

"Well, since my friends ditched me for the pisser,

er... I mean the powder room... I might as well," I shrugged.

"That's a good attitude," the cute one said as he passed me a jell-o shot. I decided I'd call him Oliver until I remembered his actual name. He looked like an Oliver.

"Skim your finger around the rim so that you can loosen the jell-o from the plastic," he instructed, stepping closer to me.

I shot him an indignant look. "Do I look like an amateur?" I laughed, tipping back the jell-o in one smooth swoosh.

"Mmm, cherry." I smiled and the guys laughed.

I would have paid more attention to them or asked for another shot, but the moment the words escaped my lips, I looked toward the doorway of the kitchen and my breath caught in my throat.

Liam Wilder.

Sex on steroids rolled in pastry crust. Liam Wilder.

I didn't think he showed up to things like this. I thought he jaunted around on yachts and baptized babies all day. Babies that would one day grow up to be swimsuit models, thanks to his touch. No, he's not a priest; he's just a god in the soccer world. (And also in the real world.)

Jeez, he was good-looking up close. Tall, toned, sexy light brown hair, and a face that made you want to cry a little it was so perfect. He was the star of the LA Stars and the resident bad boy of LA. Seriously. Every week there was news coverage of him leaving a bar with some model or actress. He was young, handsome, and could literally sleep with anyone he wanted. Could you blame the guy for taking advantage of it?

From my vantage point on the counter, I watched him walk into the kitchen with people trailing after him like love-sick puppies. I could get so much done if I had people following me around all day. *"You there, make me lunch, and you, fan me with tiny blades of grass."* It's weird that I had no one applying for the job…

His eyes skimmed the crowd until he found his teammate, the one who'd just given me a jell-o shot, and then his eyes looked up and found me. Oh god. I was staring at him as I wore a lopsided birthday crown and held a bag of ice to my face… and it wasn't like I could do anything about it since he was already heading over toward us.

Could I trick him into thinking the ice pack was an elaborate way to get drunk that all the hipsters were using lately? Like I was absorbing alcohol through my pores? Most likely not…

The guys were talking in front of me, but I didn't hear a single word. I was watching Liam as he moved, trying to keep my tongue from detaching from my mouth. He had on a black short-sleeve shirt. Tattoos peeked out from beneath the sleeve on his left arm. The inked design traveled down to his forearm, completing the entire package along with his rugged facial hair and piercing grey eyes.

All right, enough.

"Can I have another jell-o shot?" I asked, shaking myself out of my delirious Liam-filled haze.

"You might want to slow down, birthday girl. You zoned out for like five minutes there," Oliver answered with a sly smile.

"Oliver, c'mon you're going to deny the birthday girl another shot?" one of his friends chimed in. Ha! I knew his name had been Oliver the entire time.

"Yeah! Listen to him!" I laughed and winked at the new guy.

I didn't actually want another shot; I just wanted something to do while Liam stepped closer to us. He'd seen me staring at him and he probably thought I was yet another girl in his growing entourage. I mean I would have been, gladly, but he didn't need to know that.

Oliver moved to go grab another shot just as Liam stepped up to the group.

"Hey Wilder," everyone cheered, reaching out to do that male-handshake thing while I pretended to be interested in my fingers on my lap. Yup, I still had all ten. That's good.

"Oh, I didn't see you there man, you want a shot?" Oliver asked as he returned and handed everyone a small plastic cup.

I looked up just in time to see Liam shift his gaze away from me. He'd been looking at me. His eyes had been glancing in my general direction. I felt hot and sweaty all over, as if I needed to cool my face with one of those paper fans like a 1900s debutant.

"Nah, I'm not drinking tonight. Looks like the birthday girl has had enough though."

What?

"Excuse me?" I asked with a scowl.

"Are you even legal?" he asked with a bemused smile.

What an arrogant asshole.

I prepped my jell-o shot and slung it back, never taking my eyes off of him. The edge of his mouth perked up, and I knew he enjoyed the fact that I was challenging him.

I held the empty cup out in front of me, and as he motioned to take it, I let it drop to the floor between us. His dark eyes followed the trail of the cup's decent to the floor and then came back up to my face. When his gaze locked with mine again, a slow smirk uncurled across his lips.

"I think your posse needs you." I tilted my head to the side and pointed to the gaggle of people waiting for him to see them standing behind him.

He ignored them.

"What happened to your cheek?" he asked, stepping forward and effectively breaking every social code. His teammates had been standing in a circle around me on the counter, so when Liam stepped in front of me, he cut off the circle and pretty much ended the conversation.

The other guys shrugged and laughed, turning to reform their own group and leaving me alone with Liam. I couldn't decide if that was a good or bad thing, but the shots were starting to multiply in my system, so I couldn't be held accountable for my actions.

As Liam leaned forward to inspect my cheek, I remembered his question. "It's kind of a long story, but it involves gyrating hips and a car console."

He smiled at my answer, but he didn't take his eyes off my cheek. His hand reached up and he gently nudged my chin to the side so he could see the bruise better. I tried to keep my breath under control while he touched my skin.

"It's seriously not that bad. I'm just being a baby and icing it so I don't end up with a swollen cheek tomorrow." I needed him to step back. His cologne was practically hijacking my ovulation cycle and I had to fight the urge to let my face collapse onto his shirt and inhale.

"Ah, yeah, I think you'll survive to see another birthday," he smirked as he crossed his arms.

"Oh good. This one's been pretty lame until now," I murmured, realizing how depressing the statement sounded only after I'd already said it. Where the hell were Emily and Becca anyway? Was the toilet some kind of portal to another dimension?

He tilted his head to the side, his gaze unwavering. "What did you get for your birthday?"

I'm still holding out that you're actually a stippergram for me.

"Well," I looked down at my empty hands, "I got this birthday crown?" I said it like it was a question because I wasn't sure that it counted. "My mom always gets me something elaborate, but her package didn't make it here today from Aspen."

Wow, I really did sound pathetic by that point.

He nodded with narrowed eyes, but he didn't respond to the comment. He crossed his arms tighter, forcing my gaze down to his sexy tattoos. They stretched across his bicep on either side, but only the ones on his left arm dipped below his shirt sleeve. It was a tantalizing glimpse, but I wanted to see more. I knew from photos that they drifted up to his chest and back.

"I'll show you mine if you show me yours," I murmured cheekily, referring to his tattoos, of course.

I was seriously playing with fire, but that's what happens when I drink too much and the world puts me in front of the sexiest man alive. No, seriously, I think last year People Magazine named him Sexiest Man Alive.

"I don't think that's a good idea," he said.

Wow. Completely denied. That stung more than my face smashing into the car console. So why was he still standing in front of me, blocking me from talking to anyone else? It was all too confusing for my intoxicated brain to understand.

"That's good. I couldn't show you where mine is anyway," I answered with a sly grin.

Even he was caught off guard by that comment, but

relax, I don't have a tattoo on my who-hah. It's just along my bra line; a simple line of text that runs horizontally under my arm. But wow I was laying it on thick. I glanced down to ensure that I wasn't humping his leg. Nope, but my black dress had ridden up a bit, exposing more of my tanned thighs.

"That's not the reason," he smirked. "Starting tomorrow I'll be one of your coaches at ULA, so I think that would violate the rules, don't you think?"

My heart stopped beating at the word "coach".

Chapter Three

I narrowed my eyes. Had my drunken ears heard him right? *Coach*?

"What are you talking about?" I asked.

His eyes hardened and his jaw ticked once back and forth. "As of tomorrow, I'll be helping out the ULA women's soccer team for a few months."

No. No. No, thank you. That's not possible. He couldn't be my coach. He was too busy licking models to coach a soccer team.

"Kinsley!" Becca called my name from across the room, and I looked up to see her and the sophomore girls waving me over.

I shook my head, trying to clear my thoughts, but my head was too foggy. Why did someone put a fog machine in there? I dropped my ice pack in the sink and slunk off the counter.

"Better get some sleep, Kinsley. You have quite an early morning tomorrow," Liam noted with a smile. I stepped to move past him, but then I thought of something.

"How'd you know I was on the ULA team?" I asked.

He grinned, and for a moment I thought I was going to have to pound my chest to make my heart keep beating. He had slight dimples and perfectly straight teeth. That grin should be tucked away and brought out only for special occasions— where heart defibrillators would be present and accounted for.

"You were the top recruit in the country. There's not a person in the soccer world that doesn't know who you are," he answered with confidence.

I'd been featured in a few magazines in high school, but damn. Liam Wilder knew who I was. He knew me enough to recognize me at a party... and tomorrow he would be my coach.

Oh god. I just almost sniffed his shirt and then I asked him if he'd show me his tattoos.

I'm in major trouble.

With that thought, I nodded and turned away from him to find my teammates. I had to fill them in stat. We had a lot of Googling to do.

"Are you okay? And more importantly, were you just talking to Liam Wilder?" Emily asked with wide eyes as soon as I reached them. Becca was standing directly behind her with her mouth hanging open.

"Yes, and you won't even believe what I have to tell you guys, but I should wait until later." The party was still going strong and I didn't want to squeal about what I'd just found out in front of all these people. Word would probably get back to Liam before I even reached the front door.

"Okay, that sounds really mysterious. Now I'm even more curious," Emily answered.

"You should be," I laughed, and then tugged her and

Becca through the crowd toward the door. "I'm kind of tired. Do you guys want to share a cab back to the house with me?"

"Kinsley!" someone called from across the room just as I'd asked my question.

Josh.

Damnit, with everything going on I'd completely forgotten he would even be at the party. I shifted my gaze just as I saw him pushing through the crowd and calling my name again. He looked cute as always with his dark brown hair and boyish face. Too bad I knew what kind of asshole he actually was.

"Kinsley, wait up!"

Every person in that living room was watching him trying to get to me. Did he have to keep yelling my name like that? I clearly wasn't going anywhere.

Just as he was about to reach me, I saw movement in the doorway to the kitchen and then Liam stepped into the living room. *Oh, great. Let's make it a show. Maybe we could flip the lights on and cut the music so everyone could have a front row seat.*

"Josh, seriously, not now. I'm tired and drunk, and it's my birthday." I stepped closer to Becca and Emily.

"I know. I'm so sorry. I tried to call you and I even sent flowers to the house. Did you get them?"

He meant the roses that I had shredded in the disposal earlier that morning. Whoops.

"Yes. I got them Josh, but I don't want to talk right now." I ground my molars together.

"Just let me make it up to you. Can I come see you later this week? Maybe we can get coffee after you're done with practice one day?" His voice was carrying over the party, and I was painfully aware of everyone's eyes on me.

I couldn't very well make a scene in front of all those people. He deserved to be punched in the face, but seeing as how I had already incurred one injury on my birthday, I decided to give in.

"Fine. Just text me, but you need to realize we aren't getting back together." I turned away from him and started to make my way to the front door. I tuned out everything around me. I didn't want to hear if Josh said anything else as I walked away. I didn't want to know if Liam had heard that entire ridiculous exchange. I just wanted my pajamas and fuzzy socks.

• • •

"Are you serious?!" Becca screamed.

"Dude! If you scream in my ear again I will punch you in the uterus."

Becca, Emily, and I were lying on my bed back at the Rookie House. Four days before, I'd moved into the rookie house where I'd stay for my freshman year of college. It was within walking distance from the ULA campus and a few miles from our practice fields.

"Okay, I'm sorry, but you're not kidding, right? I can't tell if you're joking," Becca laughed.

I rolled over and gave her a dead-serious look, but I was still tipsy so I ended up laughing when she started making faces at me.

"Ugh, okay. Just believe me. He told me at the party that he was coaching us starting tomorrow."

"But why? He doesn't need the money and surely he's already busy enough," Emily protested. I'd been wondering the same thing. I wouldn't have believed it either if I hadn't heard it come out of his own mouth. A perfectly supple mouth, fyi.

"Oh, look at this!" Becca said, pointing to my computer's scene. "This article talks about him volunteering as a soccer coach with the ULA team after a few of his sponsors got onto him for his 'bad-boy' ways. It says they gave him an ultimatum: get dropped from their labels or clean up his act."

"They couldn't drop him! He's the best soccer player in the US!" I argued.

"Obviously. But this article says he's a huge liability," Emily muttered.

"Well, he seemed fine earlier and he wasn't even drinking," I defended him, trying to recall the scent of his cologne from memory. It was probably called Nectar of the Gods.

"Well the night is still young, so maybe he started partying hard after we left," Emily murmured. "He's really hot, though, I have to admit."

"She does have a pulse!" I joked, poking her in the lungs.

"Hey! Yes, okay. I'm not immune to Liam Wilder, but it doesn't matter— he's our coach now."

Ugh, she just had to kill my buzz.

"Not until tomorrow," I clarified.

"How old is he?" Emily asked.

"Twenty-five," Becca answered, having known it off the top of her head.

"Do you think he has a girlfriend?" I asked.

"Well according to Google images, he has about one thousand of them. Seriously, does this man sleep?" Becca clicked through photos, but I didn't look.

"Gross, close it," I groaned, lying back and staring up

at my ceiling.

"He's never been linked to anyone in particular, though. He's photographed with women, but he's never gone public with a relationship. For being a media darling, his life is relatively private. These photos of him with women are mostly at fundraisers and parties," Becca explained.

I wasn't sure what to make of that information. Did he not have a girlfriend because he liked to play the field? Or did the media just not know about it?

"So, what happened with Josh? That was super awkward," Emily asked, trying to broach the subject lightly. There wasn't time to fill Becca and Emily in about what had transpired with Josh, so I'm sure they weren't prepared for the scene back at the party. Emily probably wasn't sure how heartbroken I felt about the whole situation.

"I walked in on him cheating on me a few weeks ago." I paused as Becca and Emily gasped Jerry Springer style. "We'd been friends for a long time, but only dated for a few months. He sucks major cojones, and we aren't getting back together. He still probably has that Bimbo on retainer."

"But he's *really* cute," Becca cut in.

"He's hot, but there's hotter..."

"Liam," Becca and Emily both inserted, and we started laughing all over again.

"You should date Liam to get back at Josh. Could you even imagine?" Becca started rambling. "If there is anyone on the team who even has a chance at dating him, it's definitely you."

"Oh please," I said, rolling my eyes at the idea.

"No, I mean it! Who gets offered sponsorships from

Adidas when they're in high school? Beautiful people like you." She fake rolled her eyes and then I grabbed a pillow and bonked it on her head.

"Hey! What the—"

"I'm not dating Liam to get back at Josh," I laughed, hitting her again.

"So date him to *not* get back at Josh," she suggested.

I bonked her on the head again.

"So help me, you're about to start something you don't want to finish," Becca laughed, grabbing a pillow of her own.

Poor Emily was right in the crossfire.

"Emily, here take my pillow." I paused, eyeing Becca with a small wink. Her smile told me she understood my wicked plan.

"Oh thanks, I thought you guys—"

She didn't get to finish her sentence before Becca and I, how should I say, brought the pillow pain train into the station.

"What the fuck, guys!" Emily screamed and laughed, trying to break free. She eventually did and ended up almost knocking me out with a perfectly timed pillow punch.

"Mercy! Jeez Emily, you're quiet and cute, but then you almost break my neck with a pillow. I am now officially scared of you," I joked as Emily and Becca sat on top of me so that I couldn't move. "But in all seriousness, my birthday would have sucked without you two. I'm really glad you'll both be on the soccer team with me."

Becca answered my sweet declaration by smothering me under my goose down comforter. Girls are vicious.

After they eventually wandered back to their own rooms, I laid awake contemplating what tomorrow would have in store. I knew it was going to be a rude awakening for all of us rookies. We were the top athletes in high school, but starting tomorrow we'd be small fish in a big pond. The workouts would be harder, the practices would be longer, and the coaches would apparently be much, much hotter.

I checked my phone for last minute birthday messages. Every hour on the hour, my mom had sent me a text. Her last one had come at eleven.

Mom: Kinsley Grace, I'm so proud of all that you've accomplished. I really wish we could have flown in to be with you for the day, but I knew you'd want to spend the day with your new friends. I mailed you a care package, and if you didn't receive it today, it'll definitely be there tomorrow. Hope you love it. You're a rock star. Good luck tomorrow. XO

Josh: Kinsley, please text me back. I'm so sorry and I know you need time to process everything, but I made a mistake and I want you back. Please consider it. Love u.

I groaned and dropped my phone back on the nightstand. Did he love me? Could he truly love me? If he loved me so much, couldn't he have spelled out the word *you*? I prayed for his sake, and mine, that he didn't.

The more I thought about it, the angrier I became. There were no excuses. He wasn't drunk or under the influence; his cheating was premeditated and I'd bet my life that it wasn't the first time. The thought of getting revenge by sleeping with Liam sounded good for about thirty seconds, and then I thought about the fact that I didn't really care about Josh enough to go through all of that to spite him. Now if there was some other reason to sleep with Liam Wilder...

• • •

"Hey, wake up or you won't have time to eat before practice. Oh, and you have a giant package downstairs." Becca's voice pulled me out of deep sleep and I groaned loudly. *Hangover, meet brain. Brain, meet hangover.*

"God, this sucks." I groaned again and shoved myself out of bed. I didn't have time to be hung-over. I had to eat breakfast and get hydrated for practice. I followed Becca downstairs where my tired teammates were sitting around in their pajamas eating breakfast and looking like really in-shape zombies. Scary.

The clock on top of the stove read 5:30 A.M. Jeez, this would be a long summer. Practices started at 6:00 A.M. Monday through Friday for the foreseeable future.

"There she is!" Emily called as I wiped the sleep out of my eyes. "Open your package!"

"Is there a stripper in the box?" I asked as I walked toward the kitchen table.

As I bent over the package, Becca caught my eye and mouthed, "It's Liam". I stuck my tongue out at her and started ripping the tape off.

My mom is extravagant and since she can afford it, she usually gives gifts that are way too over the top. That day was no exception. Inside of the box there was enough soccer gear to clothe the entire team. She'd sent me new sports bras, running shorts, leggings, dri-FIT shirts that would fit me like a glove, and some new HYPERVENOM cleats that weren't supposed to be released for another month. Oh, and they were bright pink. My mom knew me well.

"Are those what I think they are?" Becca asked, eyeing the cleats with envy.

"I have no clue how she got these, but somehow I'm not surprised."

Like they would for most girls, getting new shoes and clothes momentarily trumped my hangover. I ran up to my room and put on a new matching set of workout gear before I grabbed my phone to text my mom.

Kinsley: THANK YOU for the birthday gifts. It's too much, but I'll give my teammates some of the gear, too. I'll call you after practice. XX

By the time I finished getting ready, I had to grab a granola bar to eat on the road.

"Here, I bet you didn't remember these," Emily said, handing me two Advil.

"Yes! Thank you, thank you." The excitement of my new workout gear was starting to pale in comparison to my serious hangover. The granola bar and bumpy car ride hadn't settled my stomach, and by the time we made it to the practice field, I felt like I was going to throw up everywhere.

The seniors met us at the doors to the soccer field house with wicked smiles.

"Looking a little worse for wear there, Rookies," Tara laughed, her eyes pinned straight on me. "How you feeling, Bryant?" Her question seemed sweet, but her tone implied that it wasn't meant to be.

"Peachy." I smiled and reached down to grab my water out of my bag.

"Let's go. Coach wants to meet us in the conference room." Tara turned and opened the door so we could file in behind her. But just before she stepped inside, I heard the same sexy voice that I'd heard the previous night— the voice that said, *I'm sexy and I know it.*

"Morning ladies."

Every single girl froze and we turned in unison. Liam Wilder was standing a few feet away wearing workout gear and a friendly smile. Of course his friendly smile could easily be misconstrued for a take-your-panties-off smile, so it's a wonder we all managed to mutter shocked hellos. I guess he'd pulled up in the parking lot a few minutes after we did. I peered behind him and saw a black Mercedes SUV parked in the spot closest to the field house. A photographer was snapping pictures on the other side of the fence. Jeez, they wake up this early to get pictures of him?

"Oh, hi Liam." Tara smiled wide.

I shot Becca a gag-me face.

"You guys should probably call me Coach Wilder while we're at practice," he admonished. I had to fight to keep from cracking up. The shocked look on Tara's face was absolutely priceless, but it still wasn't enough to make me forget the awkwardness of the situation.

I couldn't look up at him. The last time we'd spoken, I'd literally asked him to show me his tattoos, which we both knew really meant I wanted him to show me his *soccer balls.* Hah. I'd have to tell Becca that one later. I tugged her and Emily forward without acknowledging Liam and headed for the conference room. Thankfully, Coach Davis was there already and Liam didn't follow us in.

"Take a seat, girls," Coach Davis instructed with a small smile. The best way to describe our coach would be as... a grandmotherly drill sergeant. On the outside, she had greying hair and kind blue eyes, but when you least expected, she'd make you drop and do fifty pushups. She was one of the main reasons I'd picked ULA. She was the top women's soccer coach in the nation and I wanted her to teach me how to improve my game.

"Morning, Coach." I smiled and took a seat near the front of the small room with Becca and Emily.

After the rest of the team filed in, Coach Davis began to fill us in about practices and what she expected of us throughout the season.

"As you probably noticed, we have a new coach this morning," she began, and I could practically feel everyone's ears perk up to attention.

Coach Davis scanned around the room with a stern expression. "Coach Wilder will be with us for a few months. However, he'll only be with us during the morning drills because he has his own team's practices in the afternoon."

"Why's he here?" one of the junior girls asked.

"Every LA Stars player volunteers. Liam has helped our program in the past, and I didn't hesitate to have him back again this year. Any other questions?"

"Why isn't he coaching the boy's team?" Sofie asked from the back row where the seniors had quarantined themselves.

"One of our assistant coaches is on maternity leave, so when the LA Stars contacted me, I thought it was a perfect time to bring him on. He's a top soccer player and he'll be a source of knowledge for all of you. However, I still feel the need to clarify that he is not here for your personal entertainment. Please use your judgment when it comes to any fraternization away from practice... I have no problem kicking you off this team faster than you can count that man's tattoos."

His tattoos. The same tattoos that I'd asked to see the night before. Okay, the universe was taunting me.

"So I shouldn't tackle him on the soccer field?" Becca whispered behind me, and I almost laughed in the middle of Coach Davis' speech.

"Um, Coach," Tara raised her hand in the air so that she'd be seen from the back, "some of us know Liam *outside* of practice. We're friends with the LA Stars' players, so we'll see him at parties."

Coach Davis nodded but kept her cool facade. "You'll refer to him as Coach Wilder while we're here," she clarified with a hard tone. "I understand that a few of you run in the same circle as Coach Wilder and avoiding him completely would be impossible. However, I'd like you to distance yourself from him in social settings until he is no longer a coach here."

A knock sounded at the door and a second later Liam stepped in quietly. "Are you ready for me?"

Yes. Yes. Yes. We are *all* ready for you.

"Good timing, Coach Wilder. Please come in and introduce yourself. I'm going to go set up drills out on the field. You can meet me out there with the girls in about ten minutes." She headed for the door, but my eyes were trained on the space she'd last occupied. "Oh, and girls, be sure to leave Saturday morning open. We have a team bonding activity. We'll meet here at 7:00 A.M. sharp."

I didn't even register her team bonding comment. I was more concerned about what she'd said before that.

"Drills?" I whispered to Becca. I'd worn my workout

clothes, but it was only because that's what I wore on most days anyway. I thought today was just a learning day.

"Do you still feel sick?" she asked with a wary gaze.

"Like a small toddler is smashing a toy truck onto my head," I answered as Liam took his position at the front of the room.

"Hi everyone. I'm not sure how much Coach Davis has told you, but I'll be with the team for the next couple of months. I'll help you guys with morning drills, and since I've played as a midfielder and striker for most of my career, those are the positions I'll be working with the most."

Oh goodie. He'd be helping me perfect my skills as a midfielder. Unfortunately, about ten other girls also fit that bill, including Tara and Sofie. Becca and Emily were both defenders, so I wouldn't even have them to joke around with.

"Does anyone have any questions for me?"

"Do you have a girlfriend?" Becca whispered beside me, and I kicked her under the table.

Liam must have noticed her whisper because he glanced over toward us. His grey eyes met mine and I almost choked on my own tongue. It was the first time we'd made eye contact since he arrived that morning and I should have given myself more of a pep talk. *He's a normal person. Don't let him take over your brain.* It was no use. He wore his black t-shirt in a way that made me lose focus on everything beyond his reach. His tattoos were just barely visible. His hair was mussed on top like he'd run his fingers through it when he'd rolled out of bed.

And I was expected to concentrate when he was around?

Chapter Four

"Let's get started." Coach Davis clapped her hands after we'd all lined up in small groups. We were starting the day off with sprints. I predicted I would throw up mid-way through my first one. But who knows, maybe I wouldn't even make it there.

"How are you feeling, Birthday Girl?" Liam asked as I stretched out my calves and hamstrings. I was the last one to go in my group, so no one else could hear us.

"This is going to be pitiful. I didn't think we were going to have *actual* practice today." I shook my head and stared straight ahead, trying to take deep breaths to calm my stomach.

"Why would you think that?" he asked with a small smile.

"I realize it seems dumb, but the vets said that usually we just talk and stuff on the first day. Hence, why I went crazy for my birthday."

"That's unfortunate," he nodded just as Coach Davis

blew her whistle for the last group to line up.

Good news, I didn't actually throw up until the fourth sprint, and to Liam's credit, he only grinned after covering his mouth with his hand.

If he wasn't my coach I would have flipped him off.

On the plus side, at least I knew the answer to the did-he-think-I-was-sexy-or-not question. That would be a hard *no*.

I was midway down the field when he had to leave early for his LA Stars practice. He waved to Coach Davis and spun around to jog toward his car. I didn't realize how much I'd enjoyed having him there until he was gone. Even if he was finding quite a lot of amusement in my agony, hearing his words of encouragement had helped somewhat.

After he left, we kept conditioning until my legs were falling off and my stomach was completely empty of all the cake and shots I'd consumed the day before. Still, as I was walking off the field, I contemplated how sad I felt about not getting the chance to talk to him before he left. Even a simple "bye" would have felt good.

What the hell kind of spell did he put me under last night? Snap. Out. Of. It.

"Rough first day, Bryant?" Coach Davis asked as I made my way out of the locker room.

"I swear I'm in good shape. It was my birthday last night and I wasn't expecting to go this hard on the first day."

Coach Davis nodded and clapped me on the back. "Make sure you're more prepared for tomorrow."

"I will, Coach."

Becca and Emily followed me into the ice baths and we relaxed in our sports bras and shorts until I felt completely numb.

"This feels painfully awesome," Becca noted, "but that practice was much more intense than I was expecting."

"I know!" I complained.

"Do you think the vets might have been lying about practice?" Emily mentioned in a hushed tone, as if she was scared they'd overhear us. Most everyone had already gone home or had found another ice bath in the building to heal their aching muscles.

"That would be so bitchy. I think I threw up like three times," Becca groaned.

My stomach rolled in response to her admission. "No more vomit talk. Sheesh... Becca, where are you from?" I asked.

"Dallas, Texas. Born and raised, y'all," she said with an over-the-top wink, and all of a sudden I could *totally* see the Texan in her.

"Oh my god, did you compete in pageants? You have the pageant thing going for you with the freckles and blonde hair."

"Hell no! You've known me for like forty-eight hours and you think I would compete in pageants?"

I recalled the drunken dancing and the inappropriate jokes. "Ah, yeah. I take that back. You'd probably be more likely to sabotage a pageant than compete in one."

She laughed and propped her arms back on the edge of the tub. We could only stay in for a few more minutes before the effects of the ice started to be counterproductive.

"Were you prom queen at your school?" Becca asked me. I snorted.

"I didn't go to prom."

Her and Emily both gasped as if I'd just told them that I was actually a man.

"Oh, jeez. Don't go there. My mom was just as

devastated as you're both pretending to be."

"But, didn't someone ask you?"

I thought back to how Josh and I had skipped out on prom to watch a recorded European football match with a group of friends instead. I didn't even know who'd ended up winning prom queen.

"Josh and I were dating and we both wanted to skip the whole charade."

"Everyone went to prom at my school. I was prom queen," Emily smiled, and her eyes glazed over as if recalling a sweet memory.

"You lost your virginity that night, didn't you?" I smiled.

When Emily started blushing, Becca and I both cracked up.

"There's nothing to be embarrassed about! It's just so sweet," I assured her.

Emily glanced down at the surface of the ice. "It was with my long-term boyfriend and we're still together... when did you lose your virginity, Ms. Los Angeles?"

"What's that supposed to mean?" I laughed, splashing water on her.

"You wear a grungy friendship bracelet next to an uber-expensive Cartier bracelet. You couldn't be more LA if you tried."

"Damn," I laughed. "I should give you more credit, Emily." The three of us were each from opposite ends of the country and had wildly different upbringings. In any other setting we might never have been friends, but as rookies on a team, we were all the other had. Hell, we'd just watched each other barf. If that doesn't form a quick bond I don't know what does.

"Well now you both know how I lost my virginity.

Spill," Emily demanded, bringing the topic back to where it was a few minutes earlier.

I didn't think about Trey often. He was my boyfriend during junior year, and while I don't know who won prom queen, I do know that he won prom king. He was the king of my high school in every sense of the word. When we had sex for the first time, I thought I was in love with him, but it was awkward and over before I'd even felt anything but pain. We did it a few more times, each just as awkward as the first. It was only a few weeks later that I'd found out he'd been cheating on me with a girl from another school.

I tried to tell them the story as best as I could without bringing the mood down or playing the victim card. Just because I'd been cheated on twice didn't mean I'd spend my life exclaiming, "Woe is ME!"

"What? Are you kidding me? Was Josh any better?" Becca asked.

"He was… okay? I think? It looked like he was giving the bimbo a good time." I guess there was no point in being coy at this point.

"What about you?" Emily asked, turning toward Becca. I smiled thinking how good her story would be in comparison.

Becca coughed and glanced toward her arm still resting on the side of the tub. "Oh, well, I've never had sex."

"What?!" Emily and I both exclaimed. I would have bet my life that she was the most experienced out of all of us. I mean, she was gorgeous and funny and what else is there to do in Texas other than fool around? Isn't everyone just banging on barrels of hay?

"It's not a big deal. I was kind of a loser in high school. Soccer wasn't a cool sport at my school and I had braces until the eleventh grade."

"Ouch," I noted. "Well, Becca, you're freaking gorgeous and who cares when you have sex for the first time. Mine sucked anyway, right?"

She nodded, and I knew the discussion was over for the time being.

"Let's get out of here!" I hopped up and out of the ice bath, but when I stepped down, my foot didn't hold my weight and I collapsed onto the concrete.

"Oh my god! Are you okay?" Emily asked.

At least she was worried about me. Becca was laughing hysterically, just as I would have been.

"Guys, I can't feel my limbs. We stayed in too long!" I exclaimed, lying on the cold concrete floor.

We didn't stop laughing until our legs thawed out.

• • •

"Want to shower and then go grab lunch?" I asked the girls as we walked up to the front door of the rookie house. Just before we went inside, Emily noticed a little package sitting at the foot of the porch.

"This has your name on it, Kinsley!"

I narrowed my eyes on the box. It was so small that I'd completely walked past it.

"Oh, I bet it was part of my mom's package from earlier," I said as she handed it over. "All of her gifts have multiple parts."

Becca pulled open the front door before yelling, "Last one to shower buys lunch!"

"Ah!" I shoved past her and ran for the stairs, only to have her take my legs out from under me midway to the top. My knees banged against the carpet as I fell forward and loose carpet fibers found their way into my mouth. Blech. Why did it seem like I would leave this house with way more bruises and scars than I'd brought with me?

"It's not fair! You're a defender! You'll win every time!" I shouted as Becca crested the top of the stairs.

She just laughed and headed to her room. Quiet Emily trekked casually up the stairs after us, clearly uninterested in the competition.

Luckily, we didn't all share one bathroom. The house had been renovated a few years ago so that it felt more like a dorm than a normal home. Each room was connected to a bathroom that two people shared. Emily was my suitemate.

"You can shower first, Em. I'm going to open my gift and call my mom." I smiled and closed the door to give her some privacy.

That was when I finally studied the package. My name was written on the top in hand writing that definitely didn't belong to my mom. She pretty much wrote everything in calligraphy. As a kid, she would send me to school with napkins in my lunch that she'd scrawled long, perfectly lettered notes onto. They'd always tell me something positive about myself: you're intelligent, talented, beautiful, etc. And then she'd add a little joke to make me smile, like:

Question: What did the snail say while he rode on the back of the tortoise?

Answer: *Weeeeeee.*

Have I mentioned that my mom might be insane, but also the most loving person in the world? Too bad she and my dad were living it up without me in Aspen. I guess they deserved it. I'd been a hellion to raise.

But that's how I knew that my name wasn't written in

her handwriting. It was too messy. I turned the package over and ripped open the parchment paper. There was a little box inside, and when I opened it, a small piece of paper fell out along with a gift certificate.

I scrunched my brows and picked up the gift certificate first. It was for a high-end Los Angeles Day Spa and it included an hour long massage and a few other optional treatments. I would absolutely be using the gift certificate at the end of my week. They'd probably need a team of masseuses to work out the knots in my muscles if we kept practicing like we had that day.

I reached down for the note.

"Birthday Girl,
You'll need this after today. Sorry it's a little late, but I thought you deserved one more gift."

No signature. No name. What the hell? My first guess, and the guess from the 5% of me that lived in la-la land, was that Liam sent it. He'd called me Birthday Girl a few times and even once that morning... but then I realized he hardly knew me. Damn. That meant it was probably from Josh. The handwriting sort of looked like his.

The idea suddenly dropped a rain cloud over the entire gift. Did I really want to think about him while I tried to relax in a spa? I reached for my phone and texted him.

Kinsley: Did you drop something at my house today?

Then I closed the text and called my mom. She answered on the fourth ring and hearing her voice instantly made me miss her.

"Kinsley, how was practice?!" she asked.

I sank down on the floor next to the bed and smiled against the phone.

"It kicked my ass. Like literally, my ass is sore as I sit on the phone with you."

"That sounds... painful. Why is your butt sore?" she laughed.

"They made us run a kajillion sprints... aaand I suppose I might have gone a little crazy last night for my birthday, so I paid for it this morning."

"Ahhh, the truth comes out. Did you go out with your new teammates? And if you were drinking, you better not have been driving. Also, you better not have been drinking."

Right, because what US college student wasn't drinking? I chose to just skim by the topic.

"We took a cab, and yes, actually two of the other rookies and I have pretty much formed a little love triangle, sans lesbian tendencies. Becca is from Texas and looks like she could be a Dallas Cowboys cheerleader, and Emily is from Minnesota. She's a little quiet, but super sweet."

"I can't wait to meet them." I could tell she was smiling. "I'm flying in for the first game no matter what, but maybe I'll come to a scrimmage or something? If that wouldn't be too embarrassing?"

I smiled.

"Yeah, you should. I'll let you know when we start getting things on the schedule. But I have to go shower, Mom. I'm going to lunch with Becca and Emily."

"Oh good! Use the credit card I gave you and buy them lunch on me since we couldn't throw you a fun birthday dinner."

I smiled, thinking that since I was most likely the last

person to shower, I owed them lunch anyway.

"Sounds good, thanks. Love you!"

"Love you, too!"

When I hung up, I looked down and checked my phone. Josh had texted back immediately.

Josh: No? Just the flowers yesterday. You said you got those, right? The pink roses reminded me of you. How was practice?

He'd mistaken my question as a peace offering. He was sorely mistaken. But if he hadn't sent the gift card... No, I couldn't even think about it. There was no way it was from Liam, and if it was, then that baby was getting framed and mounted on my wall.

"Shower is free, Kinsley!" Emily called through the bathroom door.

Saved by the shower.

I tucked the gift certificate in my wallet and decided not to tell Emily or Becca about it until I had pinned down its sender.

• • •

"Wake up, Rookies!" a voice shouted just before a fog horn ricocheted through the house the next morning.

"What the hell!" I scrambled to sit up and catch my bearings just as the fog horn rang out again. A glance at my cell phone told me it was barely 5:00 A.M.

"You have three seconds to get downstairs everyone or you'll be running laps around the block!" Tara called. I could imagine the sardonic smile taking over her features. If anyone was power hungry, it was that girl.

I threw the sheet off my legs, which were feeling the effects of the previous day's workout, and slipped out of bed. I banged on Emily and Becca's doors on the way down to make sure they heard the commotion. They both shuffled out after me and we hustled downstairs only to stop dead in our tracks when we saw the upperclassmen lined up in front of the small fireplace. They each had a camo bandanna tied around their head and black stripes beneath their eyes.

They were dressed for war. I was dressed in fuzzy socks and a long sleeping shirt.

"Line up!" Tara yelled. Becca and I exchanged knowing glances. Was this normal or was Tara actually going off the deep end?

Either way, we listened. All the rookies lined up and faced the upperclassmen without saying a word.

"Today is the first day of your initiation onto our team. It's a rite of passage. It was done to everyone that came before you, so suck it up and take it like a champ." Why did that sentence seem so foreboding? Like she was about to ask us to bend over.

That's when I saw the costumes laid at their feet, and I groaned. We were going to have to dress up.

"Excuse me, Kinsley, is there a problem?" Tara asked with a hard stare.

"No," I answered quickly, glancing at the array of colors and fabrics on the living room floor.

"Are you sure? Because you don't seem to want to be here." She was picking a fight and I knew it. She wanted an excuse to go harder on me than the rest of the girls, and I wouldn't give it to her.

"No, I'm excited," I answered, looking up at her with a small smile. It was like looking into the face of the devil and accepting his challenge.

"Good, then you'll be thrilled to see what you're wearing to practice today, Bryant." She reached down and picked up a hideous bright yellow spandex leotard and tutu. Seriously, whoever made it had perfected the exact shade of puke yellow.

"You'll be our *snitch*."

Oh god. My eyes took in the other outfits, suddenly realizing the theme. There were wizard robes and scarves from all of the houses in Harry Potter. Some of the other stuff I didn't recognize, but I'm sure, like my spandex outfit, they all served some kind of purpose.

I was at once impressed with the idea and also dreading having to put that outfit on. I didn't really have a choice, though. I didn't want to be the whiny rookie. I wanted to accept Tara's challenge and up the ante any way I could.

Tara threw the outfit toward me and I had to think fast to catch it.

"Pass out the rest of the outfits," Tara instructed, and her little minions quickly began following orders.

I thought mine would be the worst, but when they handed Becca her outfit, I couldn't help but burst out laughing.

"You'll be a *quaffle*," Sofie explained as she handed Becca a ridiculous outfit made up of a brown tutu that spanned from her chest down to her hips. She'd look like a giant shower loofah.

"What is a quaffle?" Becca challenged as she reluctantly took the outfit from Sofie.

"It's some sort of quidditch ball from Harry Potter.

Who cares, just wear the dumb outfit." Sofie waved her hand and dismissed her.

"Go change and be back down here in five minutes," Tara yelled.

Emily, Becca, and I all ran up to my room so we could change and complain in silence.

"What the hell? Are they allowed to do this!?" Becca asked as she stood in front of my mirror, taking in her ridiculous getup. I couldn't stop laughing long enough to answer her.

"I'm sorry. You guys definitely got the worst outfits. It doesn't seem fair," Emily answered as she finished putting on her fake glasses and wizard robe. The bitch got to be Harry Potter and she looked cute in her fake glasses.

"Emily, you suck," I joked, pulling the spandex leotard up over my sports bra. It was supposed to be my size, but the spandex was tight enough to make it hard to breathe.

"At least they gave you a tutu. You'd look ridiculous just wearing a leotard," Emily offered, trying to show me the bright side. The bright side was that I wasn't dressed as a giant brown loofah.

"How about when we get back from practice, we burn our outfits and use the ashes to put a curse on Tara," Becca suggested as we put on our long soccer socks and running shoes.

"Rookies, thirty seconds to be back down here!" Tara's voice rang out.

The three of us rolled our eyes and hopped up, slinging our cleats over our shoulders. One glance in the mirror was too much. Puke yellow was not my color and the tutu made me look like a nine-year-old.

When we made it back downstairs, it was clear that

Emily had been right. Everyone else was wizards. Well, most everyone. One girl was dressed up as a broomstick. Or maybe just a stick. It was hard to tell.

A senior girl walked up to Emily when we were in line and drew a lightning bolt on her forehead with a fat Crayola marker. Then she moved on to me and Becca. She put a giant "S" on my chest and a giant "Q" on Becca's chest. Seriously, were the costumes not enough at this point?

"We'll give you breakfast when we get to the practice field, but only if you make it there. The upperclassmen will drive next to you guys while you run a designated route that ends at the fields. If you fall behind, the entire team has to run extra, so stay with the group."

I fought back a groan.

"Oh, and everyone will grab a broom on the way out," Tara declared.

"For what?" one of the rookie girls asked.

Tara scoffed at her. "Because you're dressed up as people from Harry Potter, dumbass."

So, yeah, the entire time we ran, we had to carry a broom between our legs. Have you ever had a splinter on your inner thigh? Neither have I. Because that's not where I got them. Think a little higher. *It wasn't pretty, people.* When I got home, I was going to tear apart this itchy yellow material piece by piece.

"At least you both have boobs," Emily pointed out as she ran next to Becca and me.

"What does that have to do with anything?" I asked between breaths.

"Liam will *definitely* notice them in that leotard, believe me."

"Oh shit!" I'd completely forgotten that he would see

us like this. *Crap. Crap.* Crap. Tara had probably done it on purpose. I looked over to where she was driving the car next to us. She was in a cute workout outfit and had even applied a light layer of makeup. That scheming whore.

If only we actually *were* in Harry Potter. I'd totally Crucio her ass. Yeah, that's right, I'd use one of the Unforgivable Curses. Come at me, Ministry of Magic.

Chapter Five

Five minutes before six o'clock, we finally made it to the practice fields. We all fought to catch our breaths while the upperclassmen parked their cars and hopped out looking like they'd just returned from a relaxing vacation.

"Here, Rookies, eat up," Tara said, tossing a box of granola bars onto the ground where we were resting.

"Why am I finding it hard to like her?" Becca murmured. I nodded with narrowed eyes. I wondered how far she'd take the rookie initiation.

We all grabbed a granola bar and our water bottles and trekked into the field house for our morning meeting.

"I'll meet you guys in there, I'm going to the bathroom," I nodded to Becca and Emily.

I splashed water on my face and redid my messy ponytail in the bathroom. There was really nothing I could do to fix my appearance at that point, which was quite a shame because when I pushed the bathroom door open,

Liam was leaning down, getting a drink from the water fountain. The second he caught my yellow leotard out of the corner of his eye, he straightened up and took in the entire outfit.

He had on a dark grey shirt over black sweatpants and somehow he still looked like he was modeling in a GQ ad. I looked like a drugged out ballerina.

"Wow. Is that what girls are wearing to practice these days?" he asked, rubbing a hand across his strong jaw.

I looked behind him to make sure we were alone in the hallway.

"It's part of rookie initiation," I answered. "I'm a snitch from Harry Potter."

His eyes glanced down to the "S" written across my chest, and Emily's earlier mention about my cleavage ran through my mind.

But when he glanced back up, I couldn't discern the emotion behind his eyes.

"I think I liked the birthday crown better," he smirked.

I mashed my lips together and nodded. What was he thinking? Did he remember me flirting with him at the party? Or was he flirted with so often that I was merely a blip on his radar?

"No kidding. I could use a day at the spa when I get out of this thing," I said, trying to sound nonchalant while simultaneously seeing if my comment had any effect on him.

He arched his dark brow as his eyes scanned down my outfit once more. When he looked at me like that it felt *very* inappropriate. Maybe it was just the way my body reacted to him. Damnit, he was distracting me. I was supposed to be Nancy Drew, and instead I was Nancy Draw-the-blinds-and-put-it-in-me. Wait, what?

"Girls are much more creative than guys when it comes to hazing. I think we just had to run a lot and prove we could drink a six pack without puking."

I laughed. "That doesn't seem so bad. I can run for days."

"Yeah, but you're kind of a lightweight," he said with a smile.

"Hey! I had four shots before I got to the party on Saturday."

He smirked a private little smirk that made my knees weak.

"Okay, so maybe I can't handle a six pack, but do you think you could handle this outfit?" I asked, grabbing the hem of my yellow tutu between my fingers.

He cocked a brow, his eyes studying the exposed skin between my tutu and long soccer socks before he pulled his gaze away with a hard expression. It seemed like he was fighting against his urge to look at my body.

Oh god, what were we doing? I gulped and moved passed him toward the conference room before he could reply. Being alone with him was a bad idea, like playing around water when you can't swim.

"There's our snitch," Tara declared as I walked into the room with Liam on my heels.

I glanced up at him as I took my seat beside Becca. His jaw was clenched and he'd furrowed his brows as if contemplating something. A moment later, Coach Davis walked in and Liam stepped back against the wall and crossed his arms.

"Ah, ladies, you're looking ridiculous this morning. I'm assuming this is all in good fun, Tara?" she asked with a hard stare.

"Absolutely! Just a little fun way to welcome the

rookies," Tara answered. *Did Coach Davis actually believe her? I mean, none of us looked like we were having any fun at all. The rookie that was dressed up as broomstick couldn't even sit down.*

"All right, let's just make sure that it doesn't interfere with practice or I'll need everyone to change into other workout clothes."

As if to make the situation worse, today was the first day we split up into position exercises, which meant that Becca and Emily were on the other side of the field and I was left with Tara, Sofie, Liam, and a few other upperclassmen. We were quite a motley crew.

"I think out of everyone, we did the best job making you look ridiculous, Kinsley," Sofie commented with a wicked smile.

Liam was setting up cones and hadn't heard her comment so I was left standing there trying to push aside my temper.

"I completely agree. She looks hideous," Tara commented.

"All right guys—" I began, taking a step toward the dynamic duo.

"Tara," Liam stated from behind me, "my first piece of advice for you is to learn how to be in a leadership role without letting it go to your head."

Oh shit, he'd heard her.

"The team thrives off of your leadership, so if you want to keep treating the underclassmen like shit, that's fine, just be prepared for a long, mediocre season," he paused and his grey eyes met mine, "... after all, having *chemistry* on a team is much more important than people realize."

Woah. Was I imagining a glint in his eye and the sex swing suddenly hanging from a tree beside the field?

When he turned to go set up more cones, Tara locked her eyes on me and I knew that Liam had just made my life ten thousand times worse. That's what guys don't understand. He thought he nipped the problem in the bud, but in reality he had just poured lighter fluid all over me and handed Tara a lit match. Light er' up, boys.

A few minutes later, I was waiting for my turn when Liam spoke, "You should let me know if she keeps tormenting you." I was the last person in line, and the girl in front of me was midway through her drill.

"I think it might make it worse, but thanks," I nodded, moving to take my turn.

He nodded, keeping his lips pressed together in a thin line, before adding, "And you *definitely* don't look hideous."

I paused, trying to think of how to respond. The way his dark tone had emphasized the words made it perfectly clear what he meant— what he was trying to tell me without passing any invisible boundaries.

Holy shit. Liam Wilder, the sexiest and most out-of-my-league man, just told me I was not hideous. I'll take the compliment, thank you very much.

"You're up," he motioned, and before I thought better of it, I turned and gave him a small, private smile.

• • •

"Uh oh, looks like you have another package today," Becca called from the front seat. She'd driven us to get lunch, and

Emily had called shotgun before me (the quiet ones are always the deadliest), so I was in the back, texting my mom about practice and telling her about the ridiculous outfits. The outfit that was now burned to ash in our backyard.

I leaned forward expecting to see another brown box, but instead I found Josh sitting at the foot of our small white porch. We ran a few errands after lunch, so I guess that gave Josh enough time to beat us home after his practice ended.

Which meant Liam was out of practice, too. *Cue dream sequence of Liam running slowly on a beach carrying me in his arms. I love how he's strong enough to carry me with one arm while using the other arm to feed the seagulls. He's such an animal lover like that.*

"Did you know he was going to be here?" Emily asked, shifting her gaze back to me. Oh, right. Josh.

I sighed. "Nope, I actually forgot to text him back yesterday, so I don't know what his plan is."

Becca pulled into the driveway and then she and Emily hurried inside, throwing Josh a quick wave as they passed. Traitors. They abandoned me right when I needed backup the most.

"Kinsley!" Josh smiled, hopping up off the porch and heading toward me.

"Hi Josh," I muttered, stuffing my hands into the back pockets of my cuffed white shorts.

"How are you? Have practices been really hard?" he asked.

Why was he trying to be the nice guy in this scenario? Couldn't he have just moved on and made it easier for everyone? Every time I saw his face I had to battle the urge to punch him— but if he asked me how my day was *and then I punched him*, wouldn't that make me the bitch? *How was your day – punch.*

I sighed and answered him as politely as possible. "It's been a lot harder than I expected, but I like most of my teammates. What about you?"

I knew he wasn't expecting me to answer him so politely. His face broke out into a relieved smile.

"It's been killer. I was used to being the best, but these guys on the team are pros through and through. Wilder really surprised me. I thought he was a party boy, but when he gets on the field, it's all business. The team really respects him." It was strange hearing him talk about Liam like that. He had no clue that I'd even met him.

"He's helping out at our practices in the morning," I offered, mainly so I could keep the conversation in neutral territory.

Josh scrunched his brows. "Seriously? At ULA practices? He must be crazy busy."

I shrugged and moved past him to sit on the bottom step of the porch. "I guess he has some free time."

"Well that's good. I bet the girls love him. You shouldn't let him get to you, though. I've heard he's a serial flirt."

Like a flicking of a light switch, that comment instantly reminded me of why I was sitting outside with Josh in the first place. What the hell was I doing having a pleasant conversation with this guy?

"I'm not so sure you should be handing out advice about that sort of thing. What do you need, Josh?"

He winced. "Yeah, that's true. Seriously, Kinsley, you have to let me explain."

I looked him over, realizing that if he was going to keep popping into my life, and I knew he would because there was already a party planned for Saturday night, then I needed to get this conversation over with.

"Fine, I'm all ears," I answered, and then wrapped my arms around my knees as I watched him pace back and forth in front of the porch. I'm sure the girls could hear our conversation inside, but I didn't really care.

"Kinsley, I never meant to hurt you. That girl, Jenny, means nothing to me. We were friends from camp and she'd been texting me, wanting to hangout. I kept brushing her off, but then she showed up at my apartment."

I wanted to interrupt him and ask how she even knew where his apartment was, but there was no point.

"I let her inside and she practically threw herself on me. She'd heard I made the LA Stars team and I think she wanted to say that she'd hooked up with a professional soccer player. You and I hadn't been doing much of anything lately because we were busy with tryouts, and I just wasn't thinking. I made a huge mistake."

What a lame excuse. The lamest fucking excuse I've ever heard.

"So whenever you're horny, you'll accept the first girl that throws herself at you? You're just an asshole that wanted to get laid."

"I don't love her, Kinsley. It meant nothing."

I nodded, feeling tears burning the side of eyes. I did NOT want to cry in front of Josh. He didn't deserve the satisfaction. He'd been one of my best friends throughout high school. When Trey had cheated on me, Josh had been there for me, telling me what an asshole Trey had been. And when we finally got together almost a year later, he swore to protect my heart. Bullshit. All of it.

"Okay," I finally answered when he wouldn't stop staring at me.

He expected me to fight him on it, but I didn't have

any fight left in me for guys like Josh. Like Trey. Hell, even Liam was probably no better than the rest.

"Okay?" he asked.

I stood up off the porch and took a deep breath. "You said what you needed to say, Josh. We're still not getting back together."

"Kinsley, please don't end this yet. Please think about it. I'd be a fucking fool if I let you go. Do you realize that?"

I wanted to clarify that he wasn't *letting* me go, I *left*, but I held my tongue for fear that the waterworks would start soon.

"I'll see you at the party on Saturday, Josh. We can be friends, okay?" I didn't wait for him to answer; I spun around and ran into the house.

A few sophomores that were huddled at the door tried to act as if they were having a conversation, but all of their sentences were jumbled together.

"Oh yeah, the weather— practice sucked— did you see the last episode of Vampire Diaries?"

I didn't stop to tell them to mind their own business; I ran straight upstairs and fell back on my bed. A few seconds later, there was a light tapping on my door.

"Kinsley?" Becca asked barely above a whisper, like she feared that I would break if she spoke too loudly.

"Will you get your ass in here and grab Emily? I'm not about to wallow by myself."

"Sure thing, punk. PS. If you want me to pretend I didn't hear anything so you can vent, I will."

I propped my head up and smiled. Becca understood me better than most people and she'd only known me for five days.

"Thanks, but I'm assuming you had your ear pressed against the window the whole time."

She scoffed. "I'm not an amateur. I cracked it open a little bit." She winked and then turned to go find Emily.

• • •

The next day at practice, I was stretching off to the side of the field when Liam broke off from talking to Coach Davis and started to make his way over to me. I dropped my head quickly, pretending to be enthralled in my stretches.

"Your drills are looking better," he complimented as he reached me. I looked up just as he crossed his arms in front of his chest and stared off toward the rest of the team.

"Thanks. I'm actually a decent soccer player when my body isn't running on jell-o shots and I'm not dressed in a leotard," I joked, reaching to stretch my other leg.

He smiled and shifted his attention toward me, but he had to narrow his eyes to see me through the sunlight.

"Are you planning on training for the Olympic tryouts?" he asked with a hopeful tone.

"That's the plan," I replied. "I chose ULA because of Coach Davis."

"That was a smart move. The way she runs her practices will be similar to tryouts, I'm sure."

I nodded, unsure of where our conversation would lead.

"Your cheek healed up nicely," he said with a private smile.

I couldn't help but smile back at him as I reached up to feel where the remnants of my bruise were hidden beneath a thin layer of sweat.

We stood there for a moment before I asked a

question that had troubled me for the past few days.

"So are you really as wild as the tabloids make you out to be?"

He didn't answer right away. He rubbed his chin and cast his gaze to the ground, as if scrolling through past memories. "Can I say I'm a reformed bad boy without sounding like a tool?" He laughed. "I started playing professional soccer when I was twenty and I went a little… wild. When I had a few endorsement deals threaten to cut me loose, I realized I had to change my game plan."

"When was this?"

"Three months ago," he answered as he traced a patch of grass with his cleat. "I'm still kissing ass to some of my endorsers."

"Would they really drop you because of your personal life?"

He furrowed his brow before responding. "When Tiger Woods had that affair, he was dropped by most of his sponsors. They don't want scandals associated with their brands."

"Yeah, I guess that makes sense." I narrowed my eyes at him, "Y'know, three months isn't a very long time… maybe you have some residual bad boy left?"

His eyes shot up to mine as a slow smirk unpeeled across his lips.

Leave while he still thinks you're somewhat-charming.

"I gotta get back to practice," I said as I saw the girls running back onto the field from our water break. As I ran toward them, I tried to tell myself the adrenaline coursing through my system was from practice and not from our little exchange.

The next day passed quickly with no sign of Liam at practice and no more attempts at hazing. I was more worried about the absence of Liam than the potential hazing. That is until Becca barged into my room Thursday night.

"Guess why Liam, I'm sorry, *Coach Wilder*, wasn't at practice today," she said, shutting the door and locking it behind her. Her blonde hair was piled in a messy bun and she was wearing some kind of onesie pajama set.

I put my book down. "What? Why?"

She smiled cheekily and plopped her laptop down on my bed.

"Because our dream-of-a-coach was on the Tonight Show just now," she explained with a proud grin. "He's been doing press for the LA Stars."

"That's so awesome! Can we watch it?"

"You're like fifty steps behind me. I'm already streaming it. Scoot over," she said, crawling up next me.

"Should we get Emily?" I asked.

"I just checked. She's on the phone will her lover boy."

"Ah, all right. This is so awesome," I squealed, excited at the idea of watching Liam for twenty minutes without having to worry that he'd catch me staring. "Also, should we talk about the footed pajamas or are we just going to ignore it?" I laughed, eyeing her clothes.

Becca shot me a playful glare. "Don't knock it till you try it. Seriously, I'd wear them everywhere if I could."

"And you wonder why you're still a virgin," I joked, fully prepared for the punch that was about to happen.

Right on cue, she smacked me in the arm. "That is so not cool! If I didn't know I was pretty and awesome, I'd have a major complex about still being a virgin."

"But you're only nineteen. That's still really young."

She narrowed her eyes and then tilted her head away from me so that her next words came out as a jumbled mess.

"Ihaven'toendnehaout."

"What? I can't hear you. Speak up."

"Ihaven'tdoneanythingpashedmaeurh—"

I laughed and cupped my hand around my ear. "Am I freaking deaf or are you mumbling?"

"I haven't done anything past making out, okay!" she shouted, and then threw a pillow at me.

I caught it and tossed it aside, and was about to laugh, but then I realized that she was being way more serious than usual. This freaking gorgeous girl shouldn't feel self-conscious about her experience level. What did it matter if I had a sloppy kiss at fifteen? And horrible, awkward sex at seventeen? I didn't regret it, but it was nothing to write home about.

"Seriously, don't worry about it. It's not like my experiences have been all that great."

She nodded and flipped open her laptop, effectively closing the subject.

Just as she promised, Liam popped up on the screen sitting next to the Tonight Show host. He looked devastatingly handsome in a black suit with styled hair and a cleanly-shaven face. He'd skipped a tie and kept the top buttons of his shirt undone so that every female member of the audience was screaming bloody murder.

"Jeez, I can't believe we actually get to be coached by that guy. How crazy is that?" Becca asked. I couldn't pull my attention away long enough to answer her.

The Tonight Show host was trying to start the

interview, but the girls in the crowd wouldn't stop screaming. It was quite funny, and Liam played it off well, looking humble and charming. Finally the girls settled down and the host and Liam laughed and shrugged as if to say, *what are you going to do*?

"His hair looks good like that, usually it's not styled that wa—"

"Shh!" I cut her off just as the host asked his first question.

"So Liam, I was going to ask what it was like being one of the sexiest men alive, but I think our audience answered that question for me," the host began, and everyone laughed.

Liam looked down and rubbed his chin between his thumb and pointer finger. I'd seen him do the same move a few times before, but seeing it on national television felt strangely surreal. This was the guy that had saved me from Tara on the soccer field. Underneath that body and face, there *might* be a big heart, and I couldn't figure out how that could be possible.

"It's not usually like this, I assure you. In LA I live a pretty private life," Liam answered with a small smile.

"Ah, so I see that you're still with the LA Stars, but you've kind of stepped back from the limelight a bit. My wife, yes even she's obsessed with you, said she hasn't seen you in as many tabloids lately."

"You shouldn't let her read those. They're all fake anyway," Liam joked.

"I'll be sure to pass that along, but she'd kill me if I didn't ask... are you seeing anyone right now?" To his credit, the host looked like he was a bit embarrassed that he was having to ask a question like that.

Becca and I exchanged wide-eyed glances, and she

reached to turn the volume up.

"No. I'm just focusing on soccer and my new role as a coach at ULA," he nodded with a tight smile. Of course the crowd went even wilder when he declared himself single.

"Oh, I'm glad you brought that up. You know there's been a lot of talk about your role with that soccer team this week."

What? What was the host talking about? Even Liam looked a bit confused about where the interview was going.

"Kinsley Bryant is a freshman on that team, right?"

I screamed. "Did he just say my name?! Why did he just say my name?"

"That's crazy! Hold on. What did he say?" Becca asked.

Liam looked surprised but played it off well. "You stay up to date with college soccer, Jim?"

The host laughed and then winked at the camera. "Well, I *do* keep up to date with Sports Illustrated magazine. Have you seen their issue for next month?"

Liam adjusted his position in his seat and shook his head.

"Well, once a year they do a list of the 'Sexiest Women in College Sports'. Are you familiar with that segment?"

Liam shook his head again, and I could tell he was becoming more and more uncomfortable with the topic of conversation. I, on the other hand, thought I might be having a heart attack. The host laughed, trying to salvage the relaxed-interview-vibe, and then flipped to the list inside the magazine.

"Quite a few of the women on that ULA team made the list. Tara O'Connell, a senior, was listed, as well as a freshman, Becca Riley."

Becca screamed and jumped up, almost toppling her computer off my bed.

"Pause it, pause it!" I yelled.

When Becca turned back to me her eyes were wide and she was fanning her face. "What does this mean? How do they even know about us? We were only recruited a few months ago."

I shook my head. "I have no clue, but they definitely freaking said your name! Becca! If they knew you were sitting here in footie pajamas right now, you'd be number one on that list." I started cracking up, picturing her being interviewed in her onesie.

After we'd taken a few deep breaths in an effort to calm ourselves down, we pulled the laptop back into the center of the bed and pressed play.

"But you know who made one of the first spots on that list? Kinsley Bryant. In fact, she was a fan favorite on the web poll."

What the hell? How had I not heard anything about this?

"I'm not sure what you're asking me, Jim. They're all great soccer players, but I'm not there to date them. I'm there to help coach. I've followed Kinsley's career for the past year. She was the top recruit in the country and I'm sure she'll be a contender for the Olympic team when they hold tryouts in a few months."

At that point I'd officially left the planet. Making a list for being pretty was all well and good, but him complimenting my soccer skills on national television made me want to do cartwheels around the neighborhood.

The host yammered on, and then they cut to a commercial so that they could bring on the next guest. I fell back on the bed with a giant grin. "I have officially died. I am now speaking to you posthumously."

Becca laughed and fell back next to me. "I swear he wants you. Seriously, I was watching him at practice and he barely takes his eyes off you."

"That's because he's helping me perfect my drills."

"Or he's imaging you doing those drills sans clothing."

"Didn't you just hear the man? He's not there to date us."

"Yeah, right. We'll see how long that lasts."

I laughed and rolled over. "You are hallucinating, and did you forget about the guy who was waiting on our porch the other day? I'm not equipped to handle any more romance problems."

And that was the truth. If Josh and Trey had been capable of cheating, then a guy like Liam, who had women tattooing his face on their vaginas, was without a doubt a guy I couldn't trust.

Chapter Six

I was getting ready for practice on Friday morning when Coach Davis poked her head into the locker room.

"Kinsley, Becca, and Tara— I need to see you girls in my office for a second," she declared before heading back into the hallway. I finished lacing up my cleats and then glanced up at Becca.

"That sounded ominous," I said as we followed Tara out of the locker room and down to Coach Davis' office. The door was cracked open, but after the three of us stepped inside, Coach Davis motioned for me to close it.

Uh oh.

"So, I'm sure you girls are aware of why I called you in this morning?" Coach Davis asked with an authoritative tone.

"Um, I'm assuming it's because of the show last night?" I answered, eyeing Becca for backup. Were we in some kind of trouble? I could hear Tara's voice in my head, *"Um, it's not our fault that we're pretty."*

"What show?" Tara asked, and I couldn't decide if she was actually naïve or if she just wanted the entire scenario repeated so she could revel in it all over again. My money was on the latter.

Coach Davis sighed and quickly filled her in on the list as well as Liam's interview. Of course, she left out all the fun details… like how hot Liam had looked in all his HD glory. Sigh.

Tara acted like this was the first she'd heard of it. "Oh, wow. They listed me?! I can't believe it. Well, I can. I was on that list last year, so I'd assumed I would be on it again—"

I wanted to stab one of Coach Davis' pencils in my eye just to get out of hearing her finish that sentence. I know that stabbing my eye wouldn't cause hearing loss, but maybe the trauma of the situation would shut Tara up.

"It's important to realize what it actually means for each of you," Coach Davis cut her off, and I had to bite back a smile. "As collegiate athletes at the top soccer program in the country, you are role models for young girls everywhere. You can't help being put on those lists, but I want you to pick and choose any interviews you do in the coming months very carefully. You'll be getting a lot of publicity within the next few weeks and I need you to remember what it is you're working toward.

"I'd prefer if you each spoke with me about any interviews prior to you accepting them. I can't force you to decline, but this isn't my first rodeo and you aren't my first soccer players to make that list. You need to be careful about your image and reputation."

My image. Did I even have any image? I felt a wave of nerves roll through me as her words sank in. Was my life going to change? Was I prepared for this?

Nope. No. No. I was not ready for the limelight.

"So I shouldn't wear my bikini to practice?" Becca asked, lightening the mood.

Coach Davis shot her an exasperated glare.

"Just keep a good head on your shoulders. I think every one of you girls has a chance of competing at the Olympic level if you play your cards right this season."

There it was again.

The Olympics.

I could practically hear a group of chubby cherubs singing behind me as I visualized the Olympic rings with me standing in the very center.

I'd never felt so close to actually accomplishing my dream. Hell, *every* soccer player's dream. It was the whole reason I'd chosen ULA in the first place. Coach Davis had been the assistant coach for the Women's Olympic team for the past three Games, so she could teach me everything I needed to know going into tryouts. However, it wasn't until that moment, when she'd spoken the words aloud, that I actually thought *this could happen*. This wasn't just a fool's dream anymore.

"Thank you so much, Coach. I won't lose focus," I said, clenching my fists and trying to keep my excitement under wraps.

Coach Davis nodded and waved her hand to let us know we could leave. We all hopped up, but just before I was out of the door, Coach Davis called after me.

"Kinsley, could you hold on one second?"

I spun around to look back at her, and then she added, "You can close the door."

I moved to shut it and saw Becca standing in the hall waiting for me. Her brows were raised in curiosity and I shot her a "help-me" face before closing the door so that I was alone with Coach Davis again.

Was it just me or did the baby cherubs just suddenly flee the room? I tried to gauge her mood as I sat back down, but it was impossible. Her mouth was pulled into a thin line, but her eyebrows were relaxed.

"Is everything okay?" I asked.

She sighed and then glanced up at me. "I don't think I even need to be having this conversation with you, but I'd be a fool not to cover all of my bases and make sure you're protected."

I scrunched my brows in thought. "Protected?"

"From the media. I think it'd be wise to distance yourself from Coach Wilder as much as possible. I don't need to reiterate the fact that any sort of relationship between the two of you is off-limits, but the media will do it's best to falsify proof of a relationship if you give them *any* reason to believe it to be true. The media is already having a field day speculating about the two of you, and it's only been one week. You don't need his reputation tarnishing yours before you even have a chance to make a name of your own. Does that make sense?"

She'd overloaded me with information, but the reminder that Liam was totally off-limits felt like a dagger to the heart. To be honest, before that moment, I'd never thought of him strictly as a mentor or coach. He would always be Liam Wilder, bad boy of soccer, and breaker-of-hearts. But that couldn't continue. I knew he was untouchable. So why did it hurt so bad to be reminded of that fact?

"I understand," I responded lamely, keeping my gaze on the edge of her desk. Why didn't she need to warn Becca and Tara about this as well? He could be having a relationship with any of us.

"All right. Go get ready for practice, Bryant. We have lots of work to do," she dismissed me, and I shuffled out in silence. Had she given Liam the same warning? Was he annoyed that the media was trying to pin the two of us together? He had enough negative media coverage as is and he didn't need me adding to it.

I walked out toward the field in silence, weighing the new information in my mind. Would Liam treat me differently now? Should I act like I didn't see the interview at all?

It turns out I shouldn't have worried.

Liam wasn't at practice that day. He was probably flying home from New York, but I told myself I didn't care. I focused on practice and pushed my body until I knew I was playing the best soccer that I could. It felt good to know that my end goal was so close. I just had to stay focused. I had to make sure that for the next few months I was concentrating solely on soccer.

Olympics, watch the fuck out, Becca and I… and sure, *maybe* Tara, are coming your way.

I got my first taste of blood-hungry reporters after practice that day. They were out in the parking lot, hovering around our cars with their clapping lenses and giant microphones. I walked toward them, while simultaneously hitting the unlock button on my car.

"Kinsley!— Kinsley Bryant!— Can we get a quick question—Becca—Becca?!" They were clamoring over one another to be heard, and I knew it wouldn't be long before Coach Davis shooed them away. They were relentless. Even as I ignored them and kept walking to my car, their questions pierced the air, too loud and obnoxious to ignore.

They asked about Liam Wilder and his Tonight Show appearance; I answered quickly with either "yes" or "no" and then pushed past them. They didn't give up, though, and kept pestering us as we hopped into my car and locked the doors.

They were too close for comfort and even as I started my car, they were brave enough to stand directly behind my car's bumper. Little did they know I wasn't above backing over nasty reporters. Spoiler: the rest of this story takes place from a jail cell.

"I can't believe that," Becca said from the back seat.

"When they want to talk about our soccer skills I'll be more than willing to give them an interview," I huffed, clicking my seatbelt into place with a bit too much force.

"Agreed," Becca said with a scowl.

As I backed up out of my spot, I turned around to see Tara still standing with the reporters. I'd forgotten about her during our trek to the car. All of the cameras were trained on her and she had a smile that practically engulfed her entire face. I think the girl had found nirvana.

• • •

"So do you guys want to come with me to the spa?" I asked Becca and Emily later that afternoon. We'd survived the first week of practice and now it was time to celebrate.

"Yes!" Becca yelled, jumping off the bed. I knew she'd be game.

"That'd be fun, but my boyfriend is coming into town for the weekend and I have to go get him from the airport," Emily frowned.

"Is he staying at the house?" I asked as she leaned against the doorway that separated my room from our shared bathroom.

"Yes," Emily began lightly, "if that's okay? I know it sucks to share a bathroom with a guy, but you say the word and we'll go get a hotel."

"Of course it's fine. Becca and I won't be home until late tonight and then there's that party tomorrow, so take advantage. You can have full-on kinky bathroom sex, just clean up afterward." I managed to say most of that with a straight face.

All right, yes, I purposely crossed the line with Emily because it was just too fun making her blush at the mention of sex. I still couldn't believe that out of all of us, *she* was the most sexually active.

"I bet you're a freak in the sheets," Becca said with a suggestive wink.

Emily's face was now officially on fire. "Oh my god, you guys can't talk like that! His dad's a preacher and David is really shy."

Becca and I gave each other a knowing glance. "Yup, they *definitely* have kinky sex. Preacher-son-kinky-sex," Becca said, and we lost it for another minute.

"I bet he's the only boy who could ever teach her," I said with a devious smile.

Becca shot me a sly grin and then added, "yeah... I think that's because he's the son of a..."

"PREACHER MAN," we both sang in harmony before cracking up.

"Guys!" Emily stomped her foot on the ground, making the entire situation ten times funnier. But eventually, I pulled myself together, stood up, and put my hands on Emily's shoulders.

"I swear to go easy on him."

"Yeah. Yeah. See you guys later, have fun at the spa!" Emily called as we tromped down the stairs.

"I'll definitely split it with you," I promised as we pulled up in front of the fancy building.

"Don't worry about it. My mom doesn't mind if I get a massage every now and then. She knows it helps work out the knots from soccer."

"Awesome, then we can splurge on other stuff."

"Let's get Brazilians," Becca suggested with a straight face as we hopped out of the car.

"A Brazilian wax? Hell no."

"What? You don't get them?" Becca asked, clearly surprised.

Sorry, but I don't need my hair ripped out by some rando in the back room of a sketchy waxing place.

"Nope."

"Oh my god, you're getting one! You have to try it at least once and it'll be good to get one now while it's summer. We can even go to the beach tomorrow and show them off."

I gave her a pointed stare. "How do you *show off* a Brazilian wax, Becca? *'Hey everyone, check out my shiny vagina'*?"

Becca burst out laughing. "Okay, that sounded dumb. But seriously, I'm making you get one. If you hate it, you don't have to get another one."

I knew she'd end up getting her way, so I didn't bother fighting it. I was mildly curious about it anyway.

I knew the spa would be high-end, but when we stepped inside, I felt like we were out of place. Soft music played from hidden speakers as water trickled down the side of an intricate fountain built into one of the walls. There was no one else in the waiting room except for a receptionist stationed behind the front desk wearing a calm smile.

"How can I help you two?" she asked with a sugary voice as we crossed the room.

"Oh hi. I have a gift certificate that I'd like to use to get an hour massage and a waxing session, please."

"What type of wax would you prefer: a Standard Bikini, Brazilian, or a French Wax?"

I coughed and swung my head over my shoulder to check if the waiting room was still empty. It felt like I was screaming about getting my anus bleached or something.

"She wants a Brazilian wax," Becca filled in for me with a conspiratorial smile.

"So an hour massage and one waxing session," the zenned-out woman repeated from behind the counter. Her face was stoic and completely pore free. I bet she got a facial twice a day, every day. "Would you like to do the waxing session first?"

"Oh, good idea." I wouldn't be able to enjoy the massage otherwise.

"Same for me," Becca smiled, and the woman worked us into the system.

Since we didn't have appointments, we were told to change into robes and slippers, and then "calm our chakras" in the relaxation room until they were ready for us. I didn't know if my chakra needed calming, but before we headed toward the room, I paused.

"Becca, go on ahead, I'll be right there," I said, holding up my phone as if I had to make a call. She nodded and went on without me. I felt a tinge of guilt about lying to her, but I had one last thing to do before heading to change.

I turned back toward the receptionist with a warm smile.

"Could I ask you for a favor?" I asked gently.

She glanced up from her computer and mimicked my smile. "Of course."

"I was given this gift certificate a while ago and I can't remember who gave it to me. I'd like to send them a thank you card... Could you help me find out the name?"

I'd thought about what the best approach would be while we were heading over, and I didn't think that question set off any red flags.

"Oh certainly, I can give you the last name on the card that was used to purchase the certificate. Would that help?" she asked with her same calm smile.

"That'd be great," I answered, handing it over to her. She typed away on her computer for a minute before smiling.

"All right, it looks like a Mr. Wilder purchased the certificate, but that was only a few days ago. Were you mistaken about when you received it?"

Her voice drifted out after the name "Wilder" passed her lips.

I couldn't even process the second half of her sentence.

Holy.

Mr. Wilder.

Liam-freaking-drop-my-panties-Wilder had taken the time to give me a belated birthday present.

My breathing sounded awkward when I finally muttered a response. "Oh, ha-ha, I guess I was confused about another gift certificate. Thanks."

I didn't even wait for her to say anything else before

darting toward the changing room. I fumbled through the process of changing into a robe and slipping on the spa's sandals. My brain felt frozen in shock; like that bit of information had thrown a cog into my whole system.

When I caught up to Becca, she'd already changed into her robe and was lying with cucumbers on her eyes in the relaxation room.

"Is that you Kinsley?" she asked when the door closed behind me.

"Yep," I murmured, all of a sudden scared that she'd ask me about the gift certificate. I didn't want to tell her it was from Liam because I wasn't sure what his motives were yet.

"These cucumbers burn. Isn't that weird? It's like they're so cold that they're freezing my eyes off."

Leave it up to Becca to make me crack up in the "relaxation room" of a spa.

"Take them off then, dufus."

She smiled but didn't move to sit up. "No. I want my money's worth."

I reclined next to her just as a spa attendant came in and offered us warm towels and jasmine-infused water. To our credit, we acted as civilized as possible until the attendant left the room. The second she was gone, I leaned over and ate one of Becca's cucumbers.

"Ew! That's sick. That had my eye cooties on it."

"Tasted minty," I joked and waggled my eyebrows.

"Hey – have you thought at all about what you're going to major in?" she asked.

I groaned. She'd just asked the dreaded question. "Oh god, do we have to talk about this at the spa? I have no clue. I just want to play soccer."

"Yeah, same."

"We register for classes in a few weeks, right?"

"Yup," she nodded, taking a sip of her water. "We have like three months left to enjoy sweet freedom."

"You mean three months to go to as many parties as possible."

"Exactly. We won't have time once the semester starts."

Just then, the door clicked open and a pretty, petite woman stepped in quietly. "Ms. Bryant, if you're ready, I'll be taking you to your waxing room."

What?! I'd had no time to relax my chakra. If anything, my chakra felt even more panicked. What kind of spa was this?

"Can she come with me?!" I begged, pointing to Becca.

Becca groaned. "I don't need a full-frontal view of your no-no zone."

"Not like on *that* side of the table," I clarified, "I just I don't want to go in by myself."

The petite woman smiled and nodded. "If you'd like your friend to hold your hand that's perfectly fine, but I promise it won't be too bad. I'm very good at what I do."

She sounded extremely confident, which was good considering she was about to be working with hot wax around a *very* important part of my body. Would it be rude to ask to see her degree? She better have graduated from Harvard Cosmetology. Yale Cosmetology just wasn't what it used to be.

I reluctantly followed her toward the waxing room while Becca giggled next to me. She was enjoying my misery way too much.

Once we were inside the room, the petite woman walked me through what to expect and I tried not to break

Becca's hand off in the process.

"You have to ease up. She's not even starting yet and my hand went numb about two minutes ago."

"Okay, sorry, sorry. Just tell me when she's about to go," I apologized, staring up at the ceiling and feeling like I was sweating out of every pore on my body. "Why did I agree to this? I've never had any complaints in that area before. I mean, I'm not like a wildebeest, but I groom myself... I swear. Oh god, do I look like an Amazon compared to the other women that come in here?" At that point I was just rambling to keep myself preoccupied. I could hear the petite woman shuffling around and I automatically imagined the worst. Like what you do at the dentist's office when your eyes are closed and they start up the drill.

I jumped when the woman's hand touched my leg and then a loud crunching sound almost forced me to bolt from the room. "Ah! That didn't sound good."

"Sweetie, that was just me opening the sterile wax strips. We're going to get started, okay? I'm going to go fast—" I could feel her starting to smear on the wax. It was warm, but not too hot. "You won't even feel a thing and it'll be over befo—"

"AHHHHHHHHH! SON OF A," I screamed as she pulled the first strip. The crazy lady didn't even pause. She kept going until I was yelling expletives even sailors would balk at. I was practically in tears while Becca, of course, was laughing her ass off. She could hardly contain her joy and I wanted to put hot wax on her face just to see how much she liked it.

"It's seriously not that bad, Kinsley!" Becca laughed as the woman started smearing on some cooling cream.

"You probably don't even remember! You've

probably done it so many times that you've ripped off all of your nerve endings!"

Once it was all said and done, I'll admit… it wasn't *that* bad. The woman finished and cleaned up quickly, and then I swapped rooms to get my massage. The massage room was larger and the lights were low so that it felt soothing and calm. Finally, I'd get to actually relax.

Yeah, right.

The hour-long massage felt amazing, but I couldn't stop thinking about Liam and the fact that *he* was giving me the massage. Kind of. Well, okay, he knew I would use the gift certificate; maybe he was picturing me on the table.

Every time the masseuse worked out a new part of body, I imagined it was Liam's hands instead of the woman's… I just prayed Liam's weren't quite as delicate and soft. But, whatever, I wouldn't judge him for it.

Needless to say, when Becca and I finally left the spa, I was turned on and walking bow legged. Not a pretty combo.

"You can't keep walking like that or people are going to think your massage had a happy ending. Does it still hurt?" Becca asked.

"No, it just feels so… weird, like something should *be there*. I feel like those smooth lanes at bowling alleys."

Becca shot me a disgusted face. "Oh my god, that's sick. Stop picturing your vagina as a dirty bowling alley."

I threw my head back laughing.

"I wonder if Liam would like it," Becca added so casually that I swear she was trying to get a genuine reaction out of me.

"Who cares," I muttered, putting the car in reverse and trying to push him out of my mind. It worked for half of the way home and then my brain turned into a broken record player, repeating questions over and over.

Did he get me the gift certificate because he wants to be friends?

Did he want me to use it and think of him?

Was I supposed to act like nothing was different between us?

How long will it take for me to get used to this no-hair situation down there?

Does he like hair down there? Do they make hair extensions for that sort of thing... just in case he does?

Was I willing to glue on a vijay toupee for him?

Chapter Seven

Earlier in the week Coach Davis had warned us to keep Saturday morning free for our team bonding activity. I had no clue what she had in store for us, and to be honest, I would have preferred to go relax on the beach, but maybe team bonding would do us some good. Tara and I sure as hell needed it.

When Emily, Becca, and I pulled up to the soccer fields, there was an old yellow school bus parked near the entrance and a few of our teammates were already lingering outside talking with Coach Davis and... Liam.

"What the hell is he doing here?" I asked with furrowed brows.

Emily swiveled to see what I was talking about. "Oh, Liam? I'd imagine all of the coaches are coming since it's a team bonding thing."

Becca turned toward me with a devious grin. "Maybe Liam can show you what 'team bonding' really means."

I threw the car into park and gave her a pointed stare.

"It's too early to decipher what that even means. Bonding as in… having sex?" I asked, grabbing my bag and adjusting my spaghetti strap workout tank.

She waggled her eyebrows. "It means he could teach you some really good bondage techniques."

I shoved her arm. "You're supposed to be a prude, Becca."

She scoffed. "Just because I haven't had sex doesn't mean I'm a prude. I'm repressed, and therefore even less of a prude than other people."

"Well maybe *you* should hook up with Liam then."

She arched a brow. "I don't think I'm the one he wants."

I hopped out of the car before she could say anything else. My face was already flushed from her comment about team bonding, so when I glanced up and saw him slowly perusing me from top to bottom, my heart thumped wildly in my chest. *Stop picturing Liam as a dom. Stop it. Damnit, Becca.*

Liam kept his distance as I went to join the group, but that didn't stop me from peeking at him from beneath my lashes. His soccer shorts hung low on his hips and I could see a sliver of his boxer briefs. Calvin Klein, of course. A shiver ran down my spine and I had to shove my gaze away before I started awkwardly panting.

Dear Mr. Klein or should I call you Calv,

It's me again, Kinsley. Thanks so much for designing your underwear line. If you ever need a focus group for future designs, I'd like to be included. I'm a very good package inspector with excellent attention to detail. Attached you will find my list of references.

"All right, girls, let's load up!" Coach Davis said, clapping her hands. We all shuffled onto the bus, groaning about how early it was. After I took my seat, I tilted my head to the side and watched in horror as Tara took the seat beside Liam in the front. I wanted to slow time and push her away before her bony butt could touch the seat. But, I wasn't a wizard, so instead I crouched low in my seat so that I could no longer see them sitting beside one another.

Did he want her to sit next to him? Why the hell did it matter?

"She's a sleeze-whore," Becca whispered next to me. I hadn't realized that she'd sank lower in her seat as well.

I couldn't help but smile at how ridiculous we looked. Our knees were hiked up against the seat in front of us and our chins were tilted down onto our chests.

"Should we ride like this the whole way there?" she asked.

"I'm not watching *that* the whole way. So yes..."

Just then, Tara's shrill laughter rang out throughout the bus.

"Is he up there making her laugh?" I whispered.

"No. He probably asked her to scoot away from him and she thought it was a hilarious joke," Becca said, trying to make me feel better.

"What if he invited her to sit beside him?"

Becca shot me a pointed stare. "Not possible."

The bus ride didn't take too long after that. Still, Becca and I stayed crouched down, joking and trying to exist in our own world. It was easier that way. Seeing Tara and Liam talking affected me in a way it *definitely* shouldn't have if I thought of him only as my coach.

I was in deep trouble.

The bus pulled to a stop, and I finally sat up enough to see that we were outside of a giant army camp. My eyes widened. Were we going to have to work out with soldiers?

Did people do that?

Coach Davis stood up at the front. Her grey hair was pulled into a high ponytail and she was smiling bright. "Team, we're going to do an obstacle course today. Not an ordinary one. This is a course used to train top-level recruits for the army."

A few girls groaned.

"The goal will be to work together. We aren't done until *everybody* crosses the finish line."

Tara stood up to stand behind her. "That's right, we're only as good as our weakest player," she added, staring directly at me with chilling blue eyes. I made a decision right then to kick her ass at the obstacle course. Team bonding would have to take a rain check.

Becca raised her hand and Coach Davis pointed at her. "Are we allowed to have hunky army guys help us? Like if they wanted to give us a boost over a super tall wall?" Of course she highlighted her point by cupping her hands as if grabbing an ass.

The entire bus started cracking up, and even Coach Davis cracked a smile.

"Becca, this is about team bonding, so no, there won't be anyone around to give you a boost unless it's one of your teammates," Coach Davis said before turning and heading out of the bus. Everyone else started filling out behind her.

Becca sighed as if exasperated. "All right, Kins. Then it's all you, bud."

I acted disgusted. "I'm not touching your butt."

"Oh please, your hand has been itching to touch my ass," she said, making a big show of smacking her butt. I laughed and pushed her forward. She was blocking the middle of the aisle with her ridiculousness.

As soon as we hopped off the bus, the obstacle course

spanned out before us. Although the term obstacle course didn't seem fitting. This was some kind of ninja warrior bullshit.

We all lined up at the very beginning and stretched out so that we wouldn't get injured trying to hurl ourselves over various objects. Becca did her best to spot any available army guys, but they must have cleared the area for the day… probably in anticipation of her arrival.

It started off easy enough; we took our turns going over each obstacle and eventually spread out across the course. Even the coaches were participating, which meant our dear Liam was off somewhere doing something manly. I was too busy trying not to die jumping through tires to notice.

Mid-way through the course there was a mud pit so narrow that only one person could crawl through at a time. The goal was to crawl beneath barbed wire across the entire field without scratching your back.

When it was my turn, I slid down to my stomach, feeling the cool mud slide between my fingers. I was adjusting into a good pose when a heavy shoe dug into my back and my entire body fell into the mud, face and all. Ew. Ew. Ew.

"What the?!" I coughed.

"Oh my gosh, my bad! I must have tripped," Tara's voice rang out overhead.

I twisted my upper body to stare up at her and she started bursting out laughing. "You have mud all over your face!"

Correction: I had mud *everywhere*: my mouth, ears, and nose included. Instead of responding to her, I used a clean part of my shirt to wipe my eyes, but it hardly helped. That's when I saw Liam standing behind Tara looking royally pissed. His sharp features were masked in a furious scowl, and I couldn't help but wonder if he was going to tell her off. I didn't bother sticking around to find out. I crawled through the mud pit imagining an elaborate dream sequence that included Tara falling onto barbed wire while Liam carried me off into the sunset. *Weird, David Beckham was there too and he also wanted to help carry me, and then for some reason they had to take their shirts off...* damn the pit ended before I got to the good part.

After the mud pit, the course wove into a dense forest. Most of the team started to split up even more, but Becca and I stayed close together as the tree canopy darkened over the path. Midway through, I couldn't see anyone near us other than Liam. For whatever reason, he was holding back and keeping pace with us instead of racing ahead. The path continued through the forest until it was blocked by a giant lattice of rope that spanned a few yards above the ground. There was nowhere to go but up, unless you wanted to just walk around the path... but that was cheating.

"Geez, that's freaking tall," Becca huffed, bending forward and resting her hands on her knees. I followed suit and then twisted around to see Liam eyeing the rope lattice. His shirt was covered in sweat and his dirty blonde hair was slicked back and sinfully sexy. I loved seeing that version of him; it made me imagine him hot, sweaty, and naked above me.

Woah. Slow down there, tiger.

I caught his eye and he narrowed his gaze on me, tilting his head an inch to the side. I whipped my head back toward the rope and tried to control how flustered he made me feel.

"I can't go yet. I need to catch my breath," I said to

Becca.

A flash of movement whipped by me as Liam passed us and started spanning the roped web. He made it look effortless, and Becca and I stood there gawking up at him as he climbed foot after foot. The whole process probably took him a minute, tops.

Well. Let's add that to the list of things he can do.

1. Sex-up ladies

2. Play professional soccer

3. Wear Calvin Klein boxer briefs like it was his life's calling

4. Climb tall rope things

"Let's go. The longer you stand there, the worse it seems," he shouted down to us.

Becca cast me an exasperated glance.

"I'll go first," I said, feeling more confident as I moved toward the bottom of the lattice.

"Take it easy and make sure you don't lose your footing. There's no net to catch you if you fall," Liam warned.

His words took whatever morsel of confidence I had and shredded it. Why the hell was Coach Davis making us do this? If I fell and broke my leg, I'd be out for the whole season. Oh, but at least I'll have bonded with my team. No, wait, I haven't done that either.

I pushed aside the thought and started to climb up the web. It was strange trying to get my bearings because the lattice dipped forward and back as I climbed higher. My heart sank every time it shifted. Once I'd moved past the midway point, I knew there was no going back. I couldn't look down, and when I glanced up, Liam's intimidating gaze stared back at me, so I kept my eyes trained on the rope in front of me.

"C'mon, Kinsley. You're almost there," Liam urged me on. I took a deep breath and kept climbing. I was almost to the top when my foot missed the bottom rung of the rope that I was aiming for. My foot met empty air, and I kicked out, trying to stabilize my weight, but I wasn't quick enough. My right arm slipped from where I was holding the rope above my head.

I gasped.

"Kinsley!" Becca yelled from the ground just as my heart kicked into overdrive.

Holy shit.

"Kinsley, reach up. Give me your arm, you're okay." Liam was soothing me even before he'd caught me. I used my core muscles to stretch my right arm to where his hands were reaching toward me. He scooped me up like he was pulling a little kid out of a pool. One moment I was hanging there, feeling my body freeze in panic, and the next I was standing beside him on the plank of wood, breathing quick, shallow breaths.

"Holy shit," I laughed, resting my hands on my head and bending forward. I knew I was fine. I knew I would have been fine even if Liam hadn't helped me, but I still couldn't calm down.

Then Liam made it worse, ten trillion times worse, when his strong hand came to rest on my lower back. HELLO WARM AND FUZZIES. My heart completely stopped, as in took a vacation from my body, and then it kicked into overdrive.

"You're okay, Kinsley," he soothed. "You wouldn't have fallen. I wouldn't have let you fall," he said, soothing his hand back and forth along my back.

I was being slightly dramatic, but heights were not my

forte. Plus, his hand felt so damn good— warm and possessive— running along my spine like he did it every day.

"Yeah, because then the team would have been out a midfielder," I joked.

His fingers pressed into the small of my back as he murmured, "That's not the reason."

Wait, what?

"Kinsley, are you okay?" Becca yelled up to me. "Jesus, don't scare me like that again! You were about to slip and splatter your brains all over me! Not cute."

I smiled. "I'm fine. Now c'mon and please take your freaking time."

The moment Becca spoke, Liam's hand retracted from my back as if he was awakening to the fact that he was touching me *almost* inappropriately. No, it *was* inappropriate. His hand had been resting just two inches above my shorts. Which is about five inches above my vagina. So… yeah, he was basically touching my vagina.

He took a small step away from me and then we watched Becca climb up the rope so slowly that at certain points I wasn't sure she was actually alive anymore. When she finally reached the top, I pulled her into a tight hug and we both started laughing hysterically. Exhaustion and adrenaline were a heady mixture.

"Are you guys good?" Liam asked, eyeing the two of us with a serious gaze. I dampened my lips and nodded, trying to repress the memory of his hand caressing my back.

He's my coach. My *off-limits* coach. He's like chocolate and I'm like pickles. They shouldn't be mixed…

Unless… chocolate-covered pickles?

No.

They shouldn't be mixed. Damnit.

"Kinsley?" Becca asked, drawing me out of my musings. I'd been staring at Liam the whole time, and I felt a blush creep across my cheeks.

"Yup. Good to go. Let's freaking finish this thing."

Chapter Eight

After the obstacle course from hell, there was still some time to head to the beach before the party that night. The weather was just turning warm enough for bikinis, but not warm enough to actually brave the frigid Pacific Ocean. The rookies and I were perfectly content to work on our tans and nap in the sun.

The afternoon zipped by, and before I knew it I was sitting on Becca's bed, waiting for her to finish getting ready.

"What about this?" she said, throwing a dress out of her closet.

"That'd be cute with your blonde hair," I answered halfheartedly. This process was taking way too long, and Becca would look good in any of the three *dozen* dresses now littering the center of her room. I was tempted to lay on them like a pile of leaves, but I was supposed to be focused on helping her find an outfit.

"C'mon, you said that for the last ten!"

I sighed and pushed off the bed. "Exactly! The last TEN. How many compliments do you think my brain can generate? I'm not that creative!" I defended before hopping off the bed and grabbing a form-fitting white dress. "But, seriously, wear this one. It'll show off your tan from the beach." I held it up to her and she eyed it like she wasn't yet convinced.

"You have three minutes before I drag you out of here in your underwear," I threatened, but I couldn't keep a straight face when she started doing a little jig.

"Fine with me," she shrugged, continuing her dance around the room before eventually reaching forward to grab the dress.

While she slipped it on and found a pair of matching shoes, I inspected my outfit in her mirror. I was wearing a light blue cotton dress that was tight around my chest and way too short. I'd thrown on a pair of white converse along with my eclectic mix of bracelets. I'd left my long brown hair down and I'd used styling spray to give it a bit of volume. My light tan from the beach set off my aqua eyes, and I hadn't needed any makeup beyond a little mascara. It took me nineteen years to become equal parts lazy and stylish.

"All right, let's go! You're driving!" Becca declared as she slipped on strappy brown sandals. I could have argued that we should take a cab, but I didn't really mind not drinking. I'd have a beer or something when we first got there and then take it easy the rest of the night. Last week's hangover was still fresh in my mind.

"Bye Emily, my sweet Minnesota gemstone," I called out as we passed her room. For once she was putting away her computer in an effort to hump the real thing. Her boyfriend, David, had arrived last night and they hadn't left the room other than to replenish their liquids.

Becca pressed her hand against Emily's door and shouted, "Tell slutty David that he better wine and dine you after all this Skype sex you've been giving him!"

"GUYS! HE CAN HEAR YOU!" she yelled before something thudded against her door.

We giggled all the way to my car.

"Did you steal that dress from a small baby?" Becca asked as we hopped in and I turned the key in the ignition.

"What?! It's not that short," I argued.

Becca pinched my arm. "I mean… it could fit my big toe, but yeah, it's really cute. Just don't bend over or sit down at the party."

"I thought you wanted me to show off my Brazilian?"

"Touché," Becca laughed. "You look good... I bet Liam will love the dress."

I turned the music up to drown out anymore of her conversation. Her casual hints about Liam were getting more and more constant, and I knew she was trying to eventually wear me down so I'd tell her how I felt.

My plan was to avoid that conversation for as long as I could.

We parked a few houses down and linked arms to head inside. The house was supposed to be less crowded than it was for the previous party. Most of the underclassmen girls were staying in or heading to parties around the ULA campus. Becca and I got invited through my old club soccer friends… and Josh. Blech.

There was music blaring from an invisible sound system, and the second we walked in, I relaxed. I didn't immediately see Josh or Liam, so for now I could pretend like they didn't exist.

"Kinsley!"

I turned toward my name and saw the group of soccer girls that had invited me.

"Hey everyone! This is Becca," I introduced her, and then we stayed in their group for a while, catching up and chatting about practices. A few of them were playing soccer for colleges around the area, so we'd play them sometime this season.

"I need a drink," Becca whispered in my ear.

"I'll come with you," I said to her, and then turned to the group. "We'll be back in a little bit, we're going to go find drinks!"

I let Becca lead me through the crowd as I kept my eyes peeled for Liam or Josh. We hadn't found either of them by the time we reached the backyard, but I was too distracted by the fact that it looked like an adult Disneyland back there. In the center there was a giant pool with couples floating around and a group playing volleyball. To the left of the pool there were half a dozen tables set up for king's cup and beer pong, but the games hadn't started to pick up yet.

We wandered around until we found the keg station. There was a guy manning it that smiled wide as soon as we strolled up.

"Ladies," he said, pulling out two red cups for us.

"Just a little bit for me," I motioned with my pointer finger and thumb.

"Aww, that's no fun," he pouted and started to fill my cup.

"I'm driving," I shrugged.

"Is this your job for the entire night?" Becca asked.

He shot her a confident smile. "I get a break in a little bit. Do you two want to play beer pong?"

I wanted to say no, but I could tell Becca was

interested in the guy. "Sure, why not," I shrugged, giving Becca a knowing glance.

"Awesome. I'll meet you two over there. I'm Jace by the way," he said before filling Becca's cup.

We introduced ourselves and his eyes lit up.

"From the ULA soccer team?" he asked, and I could see Becca blushing.

"Yeah, we're freshmen on the team," I mentioned.

He looked a bit baffled. "Does Liam know you guys are here?"

His question annoyed me. What did it matter? We were allowed to go to parties. He didn't own the place. "I haven't seen him yet, so probably not," I answered with confidence. "We'll be over by the beer pong tables."

He walked away to help more people and I tugged Becca's hand, accidentally sloshing some of her beer onto the front of her dress.

"Oh, oops!"

"Kinsley!" Becca cried, looking down at the spill. "This is a freaking white dress and now you can completely see my boob!"

I tried not to laugh. "Becca! Why aren't you wearing a bra!?"

"I took it off! This dress doesn't need one!" I didn't want to make her feel more self-conscious, but yeah, her boob was on full display. Oh god, people were doing double takes as they walked by. I tried to fan it with my hand, but that only made it worse.

"Welp, now everyone can also see my nipple!" she cried, loudly enough that the people around us peered over to check for themselves.

"Okay, this is okay." I unzipped my purse and dug around inside until I found a leftover bib from a lobster restaurant I'd gone to last summer. Yes, sue me. I don't clean out my purse. What, are you so perfect?

"Here," I said, tearing the package open and handing it to her.

"Why the hell do you have this?" she asked, already tying it around her neck. The front said, "*Wait until you taste my crustaceans…*"

"I think it looks like—like a trendy necklace or something," I said.

She glared up at me with her hands lying limply by her sides, and then I couldn't hold back the laughter any longer… she just looked so pitiful.

"You know, I actually thought Jace was cute!"

I glanced behind her to check him out. Meh, he was decent. Oh no, why was he heading our way? Was his shift already up?

"Ah! Just wear the bib and say that you—"

"Hey ladies, this is Paul, he's going to be my beer pong partner…" His voice started to fade out at the end as Becca turned around and he got an eyeful of her bib.

"What's with the lobster thing?"

Becca's smile was pulled across her face so awkwardly that it made me squirm. "Oh, hah! This is my beer pong bib! Everyone wears them down in Texas."

Paul eyed her wearily. "Seriously?"

She gave a strained laugh. "Yeah, BIG trend down there."

I cringed as each team took their positions on opposite sides of the table. The guys generously allowed us to take the first shot, but it didn't matter. We were about to get our asses handed to us. I was coordinated with my feet, but somehow I'd never fully mastered hand-eye coordination.

"Just to let you know, you guys are seriously going

down," Becca taunted.

I groaned. "Becca, you'll have to drink all of our beer or I won't be able to drive us home."

She eyed the half-full cups on the table. "But, that's a ton of beer."

I winked. "Well we'll have to win so that you aren't completely shitfaced after this game."

"All right, you go first," she motioned, and I turned to prep for my shot. The ping pong ball left my hand and sailed over the table and straight into Paul's chest, right smack dab in the center of his *Beers, Guns & Women* shirt. Lovely. How had I missed that little gem before? Oh right, Becca's boob debacle.

"Sorry!" I laughed, covering my mouth and internally cringing.

"I thought you said 'we were going down'?" Jace laughed, taking his turn and sinking his ping pong ball in the first cup. Becca gave me the stink eye and reached forward to down the first cup of beer.

That's how the game went. Becca and I would sink a ball every now and then, but the boys beat us hands down, and Becca was on her way to being plastered by the time the game ended.

"I wish I could say you guys were good competition, but that was pitiful," Jace laughed, eyeing Becca with interest.

"We should have upped the ante!" Becca exclaimed. "Next round, winner takes all. You guys can have Kinsley's car and my virg—."

"Woah, hold on," I said, clasping my hand over her mouth. "Let's not put my car up for collateral just yet," I laughed, letting my hand slide away only after I was confident she could contain her word vomit.

"Hey, Sofie! Look who's here," Tara's voice rang out behind me.

Becca and I spun around to find the seniors in a line facing us with their arms crossed. I had to blink to make sure I wasn't just making the situation more comical in my head. Who actually lines up like that in real life? Had they coordinated their "mean girl" poses before this moment or was this just all impromptu? *"No, damnit, Sofie. You can't cross your arms, I'm crossing my arms!"*

"Whattup, ladies!" Becca broke the tension with her tipsiness, and I couldn't help but laugh.

"Yikes, Becca. Drunk already? Sheesh." Tara rolled her eyes and I wanted to defend my friend. "And what's with the bib?"

"She's just being funny. She's not drunk." Sure, Becca was tipsy, but Tara was just trying to embarrass her in front of Paul and Jace.

"You know, Becca, drinking problems usually start in college," Tara said with a piteous look. "You should be extra careful. You don't want to get fat from all that alcohol."

Becca stepped forward, and I put my hand up to grab her arm. "We'll be sure to remember that, Tara," I answered with a fake smile, trying to salvage the moment even though I wanted nothing more than to stoop to her level.

"We'll see you guys later," I finished before anyone else could get a word in. I pulled Becca away from the beer pong tables and prayed that the guys would follow after us. I didn't want the seniors to ruin Becca's chance with Jace. He'd been more than interested before they showed up, bib and all. Oh, that reminds me.

I reached over and pulled up the bib. "All right, you're all dry now. You can take the bib off."

She tore the plastic from around her neck and dropped it in a trash can. We were almost inside when I turned to check if Paul and Jace were following us. Nope. Tara and Sofie had already started chatting them up. What the hell?

"I seriously hate those two. They're not nice girls, Kinsley," Becca huffed, pulling open the back door.

"I know, they're bitches. Don't let them bother you. Let's go to the bathroom really quick and freshen up." I threw an arm around her shoulder and gave her a side hug.

We pushed our way to the bathroom, and by the time we got there, Becca was hopping back and forth on her toes because she had to pee so badly. I let her go first, and she swore she'd wait for me outside after she finished. I was inside the bathroom for two minutes tops, but by the time I came out, she was gone.

"Damnit, Becca," I groaned, pushing my way through bodies, trying to spy her blonde hair. The party was starting to fill with people, much more so than when we first arrived. I had a slight panic attack thinking that she could have been shoved into one of the bedrooms, Taken-style, but then when I got to the living room I spied her talking with Jace in the far corner. *Take that, Tara.*

I stood there watching them for a second, trying to assess how drunk Becca was. I'd say she was about a five on the I-might-throw-up-on-your-shoes scale. Watch out, Jace. I shoved over to the side against the wall and looked around for the club soccer girls from earlier, but of course now that I was desperate, I couldn't find them. So I did what any self-respecting person would do, I leaned my shoulder against the wall, pretending to check my phone. The music was loud and there were enough people around me that it sort of looked like I belonged. *Says the lonely girl to herself.*

I thought about wandering back out toward the beer pong tables, but then I felt a warm hand hit the small of my back in a way that made my breathing hitch. I turned to look over my shoulder and found Liam standing behind me wearing a confused scowl.

My heart screeched to a stop and my loins jumped for joy.

I assumed he wouldn't be at the party since I hadn't seen him earlier. But now he was standing right in front of me, in all of his glory, and I could smell his cologne and yes, his hand was still on my back so that he was basically holding me against him.

He bent down so I could hear him over the music. "What are you doing here?" he asked with a hard tone.

Okay. Not the best first line. Something like, *you look beautiful, have my babies* would have been a little bit better.

I crossed my arms over my chest. "I was invited."

He stood back up to his full height and nodded as his eyes roamed the room behind me. What was he looking for?

Liam was intimidating. He captivated a room simply with his presence, and had he not chosen a career in soccer, I could have seen him in a suit and tie, commanding a corporation. His air of confidence was absolute and nonnegotiable.

He sported an afternoon's worth of stubble that blended well with his sexy brows and brooding grey eyes. He seemed like the type that kept people at arm's length, maybe out of arrogance or maybe from personal choice— either way, I wanted to know him. I wanted to possess him so that those eyes were narrowed and focused solely on me.

Oh, wait. Coach. Coach. Coach.

He's my coach, not my lover.

That reminder felt like having a bucket of ice water poured over my head.

"Are we allowed to talk or is that against the rules?" I asked with a note of attitude. Not enough that he could call me on it, but enough for the edge of his mouth to curve up.

"It depends on what we talk about, I guess," he answered, finally returning his gaze to me. I felt goose bumps rise down my arms. I knew he wasn't happy to see me, but I couldn't figure out why.

"Why'd you give me that gift certificate?" I asked, surprised at my own boldness.

His dark eyes scanned down to my body before he narrowed them in thought. "I shouldn't have. I wasn't thinking. It was nothing."

Right.

I nodded and chewed on my bottom lip. He'd been so charming on the Tonight Show; he'd smiled and laughed with the host. But with me, he was nothing but serious. I wished I knew what was going on behind those eyes.

"Have you used it?" he asked just as I heard Becca's voice growing closer. I guess she and Jace had spotted us.

I paled. *Have I used it yet?* Why yes, you paid to give me my first Brazilian, *Coach Wilder.* The idea that he somehow knew what I'd used the gift certificate for made me want to fake amnesia. *"I'm sorry, where am I?"*

Instead, I answered him vaguely.

"Yeah, I went with Becca yesterday after practice," I said, just as Becca threw her arm around me. Speak of the tipsy Devil.

"Ohhh, are you telling him about the spa?" she said with a drunken slur. "Are you going to show him the Brazilian wax?" she asked, and then slowly covered her mouth. Her eyes were the size of saucers. "Oh, oops! I wasn't supposed to say that."

She giggled drunkenly and then looked at me. "I'm soooooo sorry, Kinsley. I thought you wanted to show it off like we were joking about, so that's why I said that. I would never embarrass you like that on purpose." I had a serious suspicion that Becca was acting more drunk than she actually was. She was slurring her speech and talking much louder than she usually did, but her eyes were crystal clear. Tipsy or not, she knew exactly what she was doing.

"I'm going to go find Jace!" she sang, and then danced off before I could even think fast enough to yell at her.

I wanted to strangle her.

No, I wanted to strangle her then bring her back to life, and then strangle her again. I couldn't even look at Liam. I felt his eyes on me, but I was focused on the floor beneath his shoes. This couldn't actually be happening. Rewind. Someone hit rewind!

"You used my gift card to get a Brazilian wax?" Liam asked, and I could hear a hint of a smile in his voice. That's what finally made me glance up. Sure enough, he was sporting a cocky grin and there was a lightness to his grey eyes that hadn't been there before.

I crossed my arms tighter. "She made me do it. It was nothing," I answered, mimicking his own words.

Liam wiped his hand down his sharp cheek bones and strong jaw before he let it fall away.

I could almost see the fight seep out of him.

His jaw clicked back and forth, and I thought he'd say something to dismiss himself from my presence, but instead he murmured, "Come here," as he reached down to take my hand.

I'd like to think that as I glanced down to see my hand

engulfed in his, that I at least hesitated for a moment, but let's not kid ourselves. As he pulled me down the hallway, I had to hold back the urge to yell, "Move it or lose it people." Sure, in the back of my mind I hoped no one spotted us, but that concern was buried deep, deep beneath the rest of my thoughts.

We kept going down the hallway until Liam pushed a random door open and pulled me inside, then closed it and locked it behind him. I was standing against the back of the door, breathing hard and clenching my fists, when he finally turned to look toward me.

"I'm seriously trying here. There's about a million reasons I should walk out of this room right now."

"What are you talking about?" I asked, even though I knew exactly what he meant. I could feel the tension between us. My skin was practically crackling from it.

But until that moment, I thought it'd been one sided. I thought I was pining for something I could never have, *should* never have.

"Do you realize what's at stake for you? If Coach Davis finds out I'm interested in you, we'll be in deep shit. Do you understand how influential she is for Olympic tryouts? That's your future, Kinsley."

He moved up so close to me that our faces were practically touching. His cologne ensnared every one of my senses. Unrestrained emotion radiated off of him; I didn't know if he was about to kiss me or hit me. Liam *was* control, so to see him worked up was both terrifying and exhilarating.

Yes. I knew what was at stake for me, but in that moment I couldn't find the willpower to care. I couldn't see anything beyond him standing in front of me in that dark room. Everything that existed beyond his dark silhouette was hazy.

"I don't care," I answered simply.

Three simple words whispered across a quiet room was all the acceptance he needed. Those words were like the striking of a match.

He moved toward me so fast that I couldn't catch my breath before his lips were on mine. He captured my mouth, wrapping his hands around my waist and pulling me toward him. His arm held my body against his and I could feel every coiled muscle. His kiss was hard and demanding. His tongue swept over mine and I moaned, helpless to my body's reaction to him. My hands clutched his shirt as I tried to take him in, take all of him, and keep it just like this forever.

"Liam," I moaned, trying to understand the emotions ricocheting through me. Now that I was finally allowed to touch him, there was a feeling of immense relief. It was as if my body was inhaling its first breath of air after a long dive.

"Kinsley," Liam responded with a husky moan of his own, and then turned me around and pushed me back toward the bed. My desire flared as his hard body shoved me back. My calves hit the mattress and then we were dipping backward in one clean sweep.

His weight was almost too much, but I liked it. He pinned me down as my dress bunched around my waist. We were speeding 200 miles per hour, not stopping for lights or pumping our breaks. His fingers dug seductively into the flesh of my thigh. I wanted him to leave marks so that I could prove to myself that he'd lost control with me, that this was happening and it wasn't just some lucid dream.

My head fell back as I pressed my body up to meet his. I could feel him against his jeans and I wished there to be nothing between us. Hot skin on skin as his mouth sought out fresh areas of my body.

My hands found his hair and I pulled and yanked just as I'd imagined doing every moment since I first saw him. He responded with small nips on my neck and chest. My dress was tugged down and I could feel his smooth jaw on the swell of my breast.

He had to keep going. I *needed* him to keep going.

But just as his hand skimmed over the top of my thigh to push my dress up, there was a loud crash against the door followed by drunken laughter. Mumbled voices echoed through the door, and in that instant, the magic was sucked out of the room like a giant vacuum. Liam jumped off me so fast that I would have had whiplash if I weren't lying back against his bed.

"You have to leave, Kinsley. Now," he demanded, tugging his hands through the locks of his hair that had been mine only moments ago. Mine to tug, mine to tangle, mine to pull as his mouth kissed me.

He looked like he'd just made the biggest mistake of his life. His tortured expression made me regret everything we'd just done.

Was I a mistake? Did he not want this?

"What? Why?" I asked, propping myself up on my elbows so I could see him pacing around the room.

"Get out, Kinsley," Liam said again, his tone loud and harsh. He wasn't yelling, but he might as well have been. "We can't do this. Leave, Kinsley. Now."

His words felt like a slap in the face, and I had enough dignity to get out before he made it even worse. I had hope that he would come to his senses as I passed him and headed for the door, but I turned the door knob and bolted without him saying another word.

The drunken fool that had ruined our moment was still lying outside against the door. He was now completely passed out with a dopey smile across him face. I stepped over him, held my chin high, and tried not to wonder what would have happened if he'd chosen a different door to pass out against.

Chapter Nine

I was so anxious about practice Monday morning that I woke up an hour before my alarm and was the first one downstairs. I sat in the kitchen, nursing a bowl of granola and fruit, when Becca finally came down, wiping sleep from her eyes.

I'd avoided her like the plague the day before, not only because I was annoyed with her about the wax comment, but also because I didn't want to lie to her about what happened between Liam and I. I tried to push away the memory of his lips on mine. *Stop it. They were not that great. It wasn't the best kiss you've ever had and you are definitely not falling for your coach.*

There, see that's not so hard.

"Morning, Kinsley," she offered gently.

"Hey," I muttered, staring down into my bowl of granola. Yesterday had been terrible. I didn't want to think about Liam, but I couldn't help it. I knew he had feelings for me, and I knew we couldn't be together, but that didn't mean it hadn't hurt when he kicked me out on Saturday night. It felt like a personal rejection rather than a logical one, and I couldn't get that out of my head.

Becca walked around the counter to where I was sitting and gave me her best puppy dog eyes.

"I'm sorry about the wax comment. That was really dumb and I know it was probably embarrassing," she said, wrapping me in a giant hug. "So, I'm not letting you go until you tell me that you forgive me."

I lasted all of two seconds before cracking a smile. "Fiiine. Fine, but you have to promise that I can get you back sometime. Okay?"

"Done! You can pants me at the next party we go to, but just warn me ahead of time so I can plan on wearing really cute underwear," she winked, then headed to the fridge for breakfast.

I laughed and took a bite of granola.

"Now that you're not mad at me, do you think you could fill me in on the whole..." she paused and looked over her shoulder before mouthing, "Liam situation?"

"Wow, that didn't take you long," I joked before finishing off the rest of my breakfast. "If you hurry, I'll tell you in the car."

We gathered our things quickly and I had just enough time to decide that I would be honest with Becca. I felt bad about keeping it from Emily, but the fewer people to know, the better, and Becca already knew something was going on anyway.

Once I parked outside the practice field, she unbuckled and turned to face me.

"Okay, spill," she smiled.

"You first. Did something happen between you and Jace?" I asked.

"You mean before you pulled my ass out of the party?"

After I'd bolted out of Liam's room Saturday night, I'd found Becca and forced her to leave the party with me. She'd passed out as soon as we got to the car, so it saved me from having to yell at her the whole way home.

I cringed. "Yeah, sorry about that. I was mad at you and Liam, and I just wanted to leave, but I didn't want to abandon you there."

Becca relaxed back against the seat, "Nah, I'm kidding. I'm actually glad you found me when you did. I wasn't really into Jace. He was a cute distraction, but I haven't really thought about him since the party."

I envied her. To have the rights to my thoughts back would be a nice change of pace. I'm not sure when Liam had taken root inside of my brain, but he didn't appear to be leaving anytime soon.

"But obviously something happened with you and Liam. Right?" Becca asked, pulling me out of my reverie. "You can tell me. I would *never* tell anyone else."

"Oh, like you kept the Brazilian a secret?"

She mashed her lips together and focused on the steering wheel. "Well, that was actually not so much of a slip in tongue as it was me forcing you and Liam to face your attraction toward one another. I mean, he was staring you down at the party like he was going to strip your clothes off right there. I just thought he needed a little shove in the right direction," she confessed.

I gaped and then narrowed my eyes. "I *knew* it! I knew you weren't that drunk."

"You can't be mad at me. It obviously worked! He dragged you away like he was a caveman about two seconds later!"

I smiled at the memory. His hand had gripped mine so tightly; he hadn't given me the option at all. It's not like I put up a fight.

"It doesn't matter..." I began. "We kissed on Saturday night, but it didn't last long and he instantly regretted it. He pretty much yelled at me to get out of his room."

"Wow, really?"

I frowned and stared out the window. The early morning fog was lifting and soon the rest of our team would arrive for practice. Soon *he* would arrive for practice.

"Yeah. There are about five good reasons standing in the way of my attraction to him. All of which don't seem to be enough to deter me."

"Well, we'll see how he acts today. You can't give up yet. He wants you and you want him. It doesn't have to be complicated."

I rolled my eyes at her for making it sound so simple. He was already on his last warning with his sponsors about his public image. My Olympic dreams were at stake, not to mention my college career and my fragile heart. How could the situation not be complicated?

• • •

I shouldn't have worried. The entire time at practice, Liam completely ignored me, which was quite a feat considering we split up into our position drills again. He gave all the girls feedback after their turn, yet with me he'd do a simple nod or mutter a "good" or "nice form" without making eye contact.

I felt completely invisible.

Tara didn't seem to mind, though. She basked in his attention, making sure to stand extra close to him when she asked about her technique. How many times did he have to describe the same thing over and over again before he realized that she was just manipulating him?

"I'm not sure I've got it. Will you watch me do it one more time?" she asked with just the right amount of needy pout.

Liam pressed his lips into a thin line but nodded for her to continue.

"Oh my god. Enough," I mumbled, tired of watching the Tara and Liam Show.

I must have said it louder than I thought though because Tara looked up at me before she started. "Excuse me?" she asked, taking a step closer to me.

"Enough with this drill, I need a water break," I lied, propping my hands up on my hips and daring her to challenge me. I was in a fighting mood, and in that moment I didn't care that she was the leader and I was the rookie.

"Go take one then. But you really should work on your endurance."

I fought the urge to ask her what the hell needing water had to do with my endurance. I'd beat her at every single one of our sprints and I came in first during our long distance warm up runs every time.

"Okay, c'mon, let's focus," Liam said, staring at Tara. He couldn't even look me in the eye. Fucking coward.

"Did you want to show me that drill?" he asked Tara, but before she turned around, she flashed me a smug grin and flipped her ponytail over her shoulder.

"Sure thing, Coach *Wilder*."

At that point I pretty much blacked out for the remainder of practice. I pushed myself beyond what felt good because I wanted to work out all my annoyance and anger. Coach Davis joked about me being an overachiever at the end of practice, but I couldn't even muster a smile.

• • •

"Finally, you answer!" my mom said as I fell back on my bed. I'd had lunch and showered after practice, but now my muscles were starting to ache and an afternoon nap was calling my name.

"I know, I'm sorry. I've been busy lately. I just got back from practice and I'm exhausted."

I held the phone between my ear and shoulder as I pulled the covers up to my chin.

"Ah, I won't keep you long. I wanted to talk to you because there have been quite a few companies calling us lately with endorsement deals for you. I know you can't take them up on their offers while you're playing for the NCAA, but there's Adidas and Nike, as well as a few other big ones."

That was the last thing I was thinking about at the moment, but she was right. I had to consider my career beyond college at some point. After all, if I made the Olympic team college would be put on hold.

"Would you mind just saving them for now?"

"Sounds good."

After we hung up I rolled over and plugged my phone into charge. Then I grabbed my calendar off my nightstand and flipped through the worn pages. Last time I checked there was exactly ten months until the Olympics tryouts. Now there was nine months, two weeks, and one day.

I threw off my blanket, ran down the hall, and barged

into Becca's room.

"C'mon, let's go," I demanded.

She was sitting at her desk, scrolling through Facebook. "What? Where? We just got home."

"Let's do some strength training. We didn't do much of that at practice today."

Becca groaned, but stood up and closed her laptop. "You're a freaking drill sergeant."

"Don't you want to stand a chance at tryouts?"

"Yes, but I also really want to not move for the rest of the day," Becca laughed.

"Rest is for the dead, Becca!"

We ended up working out hard, and then crawling onto the couch and not moving the rest of the day. Despite what Coach Davis and Liam said, the chance of me making the Olympic team was really slim. They scouted girls from every college and every professional team in the country, and then they selected the top players and invited them to tryout. My goal for now was to play the best soccer I could at ULA and hope to get that invitation in nine months.

It was the perfect distraction from the thoughts about Liam trying to weasel their way into my consciousness.

• • •

"He completely ignored you at practice yesterday?" Becca asked.

"Not even a peep in my direction. I think he's done with me," I answered as Becca and I headed to my car Tuesday morning.

"I assure you, he is not done with you. He's clearly doing it on purpose... maybe you should make it impossible for him to ignore you."

"How? Attacking him at practice?" I laughed.

"No. More subtle than that." She squinted in thought. "It'll be hot today... I think practicing in your sports bra would be completely acceptable."

I grunted. "Oh, yeah, really subtle. Maybe you should have given me that advice before I put on a neon pink sports bra this morning."

Becca cheered, practically hopping off her seat. "That's even better! I'll do it too so he doesn't think you're doing it on purpose."

"Whatever. Let's see how the practice goes first."

Becca groaned. "Fine, but all I'm saying is that if you want him to stop ignoring you, you should make it harder for him."

"That just feels so... calculated. Not to mention I shouldn't be concentrating on him during practice."

"There's not a girl on that field that isn't concentrating on him during practice. You've been kicking ass lately, so you deserve a little fun. A little Liam-filled fun. You deserve to fill your fun bits with Liam."

I laughed and put the car in park, trying to prepare myself for seeing him in a few minutes.

"Operation Brandi Chastain has officially begun," Becca declared.

"Why her?"

"Remember when she scored the goal in that shoot-out for the World Cup title and she ran across the field and ripped her shirt off?"

"So... you want me to rip my shirt off?"

"That'd be awesome, but I think people would assume you were on drugs. Better just take it off like a normal person."

The first hour of practice went as usual. We didn't split up into positions, which was unfortunate for two reasons: 1. Liam could ignore me much easier when we were in a big group, and 2. Becca was in my ear telling me to take my shirt off every five minutes. She really was a bad influence. I should reevaluate my friendships.

"Okay, seriously. It's hot as hell and even if we weren't doing Operation B.C. I'd want to take my shirt off," Becca said.

We were taking a five minute water break and it was the perfect time to get rid of our shirts if we were actually going through with the plan.

"You can't abbreviate the operation to B.C. or I'll just think of Spartacus the whole time."

Becca cracked up and I chanced a glance toward Liam. He was standing off to the side, chatting with Tara and Coach Davis. He hadn't looked in my direction once that morning and I was getting tired of it. One glance from him and I would have forfeited the dumb "operation", but I was sick of being ignored. Not to mention he looked even sexier than usual with his light grey t-shirt and workout shorts. His legs were toned and I wanted to throw myself at him every time my eyes lingered to where he was standing.

"Ugh, fine. Take your freaking top off," I whispered, tossing down my water bottle and reaching for the bottom of my shirt. There wasn't a cloud in the sky and it *was* hotter than usual. No one could blame me for wanting to rid myself of extra layers... right?

I laid my shirt on top of my soccer bag and straightened back up.

Becca giggled wildly and I hissed for her to be quiet.

She'd ruin the plan for sure.

"He's watching you and scowling."

"Scowling?" I groaned. What was with him and scowling? It was his default expression whenever he was around me.

"Yeah, full on angry scowl. God, he's so hot. I'm not sure if this plan will work, but at least he's looking at you."

"Cute sports bra, Kinsley," Emily said, coming up to us. I hid my mouth behind my hand, trying to cover up my laugh with a cough.

"Thanks Emily," I finally mustered. Telling Emily about Operation B.C. was completely out of the question. She had a much better moral compass than Becca and I, and I'm sure she wouldn't have agreed with our logic.

Coach Davis blew her whistle, drawing our attention over to where she was standing with Liam and Tara. "Okay, girls! Let's line up on the sidelines and we'll form teams for a short scrimmage."

Liam was still scowling and now Tara was joining him. Oh good, I was pissing everyone off. Yippee.

We hurried to line up and I ended up at the end of the sideline with my hands on my hips, waiting for Coach Davis to call my name for a team.

"Do you really think that's appropriate?" Liam asked behind me, his volume soft enough that the sophomore standing beside me didn't hear.

His tone was veering toward asshole territory and his question pissed me off, so when I turned toward him, I narrowed my eyes. "What are you talking about? I workout in a sports bra all the time."

Liam scoffed. "There are paparazzi standing over there with their lenses trained on you and your lack of clothing."

I rolled my eyes, not even glancing to where I knew the paparazzi were stationed. They were there every day and I'd mostly forgotten about them. After all, they were only there for Liam.

"No. They're trained on *you*. They wouldn't be here if you weren't here."

"It doesn't matter. Put your freaking shirt on, Kinsley."

Yes, he was *technically* my coach, but in that moment he was talking to me as Liam, not Coach Wilder, so I chose to test my limits.

"You know, I think I'll workout in my sports bra for the rest of the week." I stretched my arms over my head and even he couldn't help his eyes from drifting down to my chest for a fraction of a second. Ha! Wait, did I want to be this girl? Using my body to get his attention? It's not like I had a choice. The only way to get his attention at that point was to piss him off, so that's what I'd do. Very mature, I know.

"You're acting like a child," he hissed, his grey eyes flashing darker than usual.

I leaned in close and narrowed my eyes. "Funny. When you were *on top of me* on Saturday you didn't think I was a child."

"Kinsley!" Coach Davis called, and I realized she'd been trying to get my attention for the past few minutes. "Listen up! You're on Tara's team. Let's go."

I flashed Liam a sharp smirk before jogging to the center of the field to stand beside Tara, who was still scowling at me. Whatever. I glanced back toward Liam. His hands were clasped together behind his head and he looked like he was about to punch something. I guess that was a good sign?

• • •

"Are you kidding? That's a GREAT sign!" Becca cheered when we were alone in my room later.

"Remind me why I'm taking advice from you? You could be completely leading me astray."

Becca shook her head. "No, I assure you. I have yet to have a relationship in real life, but I've read lots of Cosmo and I used to take a ton of those quizzes about love."

"Wow... that's really reassuring. NOT."

Becca laughed then stated her case. "Listen, yesterday he didn't even talk to you. Today he sort of yelled at you— tomorrow, THE SKY IS THE LIMIT. You should really be *thanking* me right now."

She sat there staring at me as I moved around my room, picking up dirty clothes.

"What? What do you want?" I asked.

"A thank you," she said with a giant smile.

I laughed despite myself. "I'll thank you when he's waiting for me in my bed when I return home from practice."

Becca groaned. "Oh my god. I want tickets to that show."

"Ew. You're sick."

"Oh, please. You'd want tickets to that show, too."

She was right. I wanted front row seats.

Chapter Ten

I should have realized something was brewing. Tara and her cronies had been much too quiet since the Foghorn-Wake-Up last Tuesday. So, when Tuesday of the following week came and went, I thought the hazing thing might have been a one-time occurrence. Oh, how wrong I was. Tara and the other upperclassmen were creative. (Much too creative to not have had proper training from some kind of terrorist organization. I was going to have to look into that.)

"Wake up, Freshman," Tara yelled Wednesday morning, jarring me from my sleep. I blinked my eyes open to find Tara, Sofie, and a few other seniors in my room, standing around my bed.

"What the hell? Get out of my room!" I scrambled to sit up.

"That's no way to speak to your captain, Bryant," Tara answered with a sadistic grin. "Get up, get dressed, and meet us at the fields with Becca and Emily in fifteen minutes."

I held my tongue as the seniors left my room to go wake up the other two girls. I wanted to throw my shoe at Tara's head, but by then she was down the hall and my aim wasn't that great. I had no clue what they were up to, but it's not like I really had a choice in the matter.

I threw on my workout clothes and went downstairs to fill three water bottles and grab some granola bars. Emily and Becca came down a few minutes later and the three of us silently headed to my car.

"I have no clue what their problem is, but last week seemed like a team hazing thing. Now it's just the three of us. That can't be right, can it?" I asked as I put the car in reverse.

"It's bullshit. I have no clue what we did to be put on Tara's shit list, but I'm not letting her walk all over us," Becca added from the passenger seat.

It was Emily that tried to defend the seniors. "Maybe it won't be that bad, guys. Maybe they'll have breakfast or something for us at the practice fields." Becca and I rolled our eyes.

"And then maybe we'll gab about boys until practice starts," Becca added sarcastically.

The seniors were waiting for us when we pulled into the parking lot, and I felt like I was about to stand in front of a firing squad.

"There are our three favorite rookies. So kind of you to show up," Tara oozed with her arms crossed in front of her chest. I'd never met someone whose personality clashed with their looks as much as Tara's. She was gorgeous and sweet looking with perfect features that seemed to morph into a girl-next-door appearance. Yet, her true nature was *anything* but sweet. What had her childhood been like? Was she bullied or was she the one doing the bullying? I'd bet my left boob it was the latter.

"Let's start with some laps, girls," Tara instructed. My first instinct was to protest, to call her out on her bitchiness, but at that point I still hoped that if I played her game and proved to her that I was a willing subject, then she'd back off.

We did laps, sprints, up-downs, and push-ups until Emily threw up and begged to stop.

"Seriously, I feel sick and we still have practice later," Emily begged.

Tara's hard eyes shifted to Emily. "You're right. Emily, since you're obviously the weakest link, you'll do double what the other girls do."

No. That was it. Picking on Emily was taking it too far. Emily didn't deserve any of this. At least Becca and I talked shit about Tara behind her back. Emily was the unassuming victim.

"I'll do Emily's stuff. I'll do double."

Emily's warm eyes flitted to me and I saw hope flash behind her gaze.

I could handle Tara. I'd handled girls like her my whole life. Today wouldn't break me, but Emily looked like she was at the tipping point and I wouldn't let Tara force Emily to quit the ULA soccer team. It wasn't worth it.

Sofie stepped forward with an odd expression on her face. "I think that's fine. Let's let Kinsley take both of the girl's spots since she's so generous."

I stared daggers at Sofie. Did she and Tara get off on being cruel? How did they sleep at night? Oh right, standing up in their coffins, because they were fucking vampires.

Tara's eyes lit up. "Oh, great idea, Sofie! Becca and Emily, you've done enough. Kinsley will keep going for the both of you. Start doing up-downs, Bryant. We'll tell you when to stop."

My middle finger was itching to flip her off. I would have done it, too, but then I saw relief flash across Emily's face. If I fought them, they'd make her keep going.

"You can do it, Kinsley. Just imagine how sexy you'll be in a bikini," Becca called with a defiant air. She couldn't do anything to Tara, but she could cheer me on.

I smiled at Becca and started doing up-downs. I didn't protest once. I thought about the Olympic tryouts, I thought about how hard I'd worked to get to where I was. One bully wasn't going to stand in my way of achieving my goals. Especially not when I had Becca and Emily cheering me. A second wind came over me and I pushed myself harder, accepting Tara's challenge and meeting it head on. If she wanted me to sprint, I'd sprint faster than I ever had before. If she wanted me to do crunches until I threw up, I'd do it with a giant smile on my face. Bullies never win.

"What the fuck is going on here?" A dark voice yelled, and I looked up from where I was doing push-ups.

Liam walked up to the group, dressed in a black t-shirt and black workout pants. The dark clothes combined with his sharp, angry features made him look seriously dangerous. What was he doing here? Was it already time for practice?

The seniors were all lined up, looking confident with their arms crossed. Becca and Emily had been crouching down next to me, trying to keep my spirits up.

"Oh, nothing, Coach Wilder. Kinsley and the other rookies wanted to join us at the fields for an early workout." Tara shrugged.

Bullshit. God, the way she could manipulate people was truly scary. I would have loved to have a chat with her parents, but something told me they were locked in a basement somewhere.

He never once took his eyes off me, and I pleaded with him to see through her lies.

"That's enough. I don't care what's going on here. Practice is starting soon and you all need to head into the field house." Did he believe her?

I pushed back onto my heels to catch my breath. I was exhausted. I felt like I'd just finished running a marathon and I knew I wouldn't last through practice without passing out.

The seniors turned to head inside but not before throwing me threatening looks. Did they think I was going to rat them out?

Emily followed after them, and then Becca finally moved when Liam gave her an impatient glance.

It was just he and I staring at each other over a field of worn grass. He still looked so angry and I was scared he might take it out on me. But when he finally spoke, there was only empathy in his voice.

"I'm not going to make you rat out the seniors, but this shit can't continue. That's not the way teams work and Coach Davis would be pissed if she knew this kind of thing was happening."

As if I didn't know that already.

"I'm not an idiot. I know, but I'm not going head-to-head with Tara this early on in the season. If she wants to wake me up and force me to work out, then I'll let her. It'll make the victory of making the Olympic team all the sweeter. It's the fact that she's picking on Becca and Emily that makes me mad."

"Becca and Emily weren't doing push-ups when I pulled up," Liam noted with a frown.

"That's because Emily barfed. The seniors thought I should keep going for everyone."

Liam wrapped his hands behind his head and then let his clenched fists fall back to his side. I met his hard stare, and for a moment I thought everything between us was about to finally explode. I thought *he* was about to explode.

"I won't let them treat you like that, Kinsley."

"Why do you care?" I asked, daring him to tell me the truth.

"I'm your coach," he answered too fast.

I pushed off my hands and stood up, staring straight into his dark grey eyes. "Well then consider your job done. Thanks for the help, *Coach*."

I moved to walk past him.

"If it doesn't stop, I'm bringing it up to Coach Davis," he said, reaching for my arm.

I paused as our body's stood side by side. I was facing the field house and my impending doom. He was glancing out toward our field where the early morning sun was highlighting each of his chiseled features.

Coach Davis wouldn't kick Tara off the team for something like this, not if it was Tara's first offense. Most likely it would just be another nail in my coffin when it came to Tara. Of course he didn't see it that way.

"I can fight my own battles, *Coach Wilder*," I hissed at him. "But you can do whatever *you* want. You always do. I'm going to go get ready for practice." I brushed past him and as my arm grazed his, the tension simmering between us buzzed through me, igniting my blood and awakening my senses like a shot of caffeine.

I knew I was being hard on him, but the entire situation pissed me off and he was the only person I could take it out on. Whatever was going on between us was fighting to surface, and that was the last thing I needed to worry about at the moment.

• • •

Later that night, Becca and I sat in my room while I tried to simultaneously *think* and *not think* about Liam Wilder. I felt bad for being harsh with him earlier, but the situation was frustrating to say the least. I never knew how he would treat me or how I was supposed to treat him. I needed to get my head straight and that's what Becca was there for.

"So, let's recap," Becca announced, pulling my dry erase board off my wall and erasing the list of Game of Thrones characters ranked in order of hotness. Not my fault I have a thing for Jamie Lannister… hand or no hand.

"Hey! I needed those," I protested.

"Yeah, right. We both know you have them memorized. Besides, you can't think he's hot. He bangs his sister."

"Yeah, whatever. Start your recap so we can simplify my life, please."

Becca nodded before shutting both of my doors and turning on music so our voices were drowned out.

"Let's start at the beginning," she said, starting to write at the top of the white board.

Reasons Kinsley SHOULDN'T think about Liam:

1. Cheated on by two ex boyfriends. Conclusion: guys

are dicks. Don't date them.

I took the marker out of her hand and started writing number two and three.

2. GOALS: Olympics and ULA training schedule – NO TIME FOR GUYS!

3. He's COMPLETELY off limits. (Kicked off team off-limits.) BACK AWAY FROM HIM STAT.

Becca nodded and then grabbed the marker again.

4. He's a badboy. (Reformed or not) Refer back to #1 and multiply it by ten.

Then, finally, I wrote number five.

5. He doesn't like me. And/or actively hates me.

"Good work," Becca said, recapping the marker and propping the list up next to my dresser. "Doesn't it feel better already? I mean those are five solid reasons you should just forget about him altogether."

"Exactly," I agreed, but my voice didn't seem very convincing. What the hell was wrong with me? Did he need to also be a crazy puppy killer before my libido finally said, *all right maybe he's not for you?*

"So, we can go to the costume party on Saturday and you don't even have to worry about him being there. Remember how he didn't show up until really late last weekend? I bet he won't show at all this time."

Becca was just floundering at this point. She wanted to go to the LA Stars' costume party because a) how many times in your adult life do you get to wear a costume? And b) she already planned on us dressing up as Superman and Batman... only the girl versions. We were going to get our costumes the next day.

I couldn't tell her no just because I was scared Liam would show up. I'd just avoid him like he'd avoided me the entire week and we'd be fine.

"Do you want me to erase the board?" she asked.

I thought about it for a second. "No, just erase his name. I might need the reminders."

• • •

Friday after practice, Coach Davis called me into her office. Sitting on the opposite side of her desk was a handsome guy dressed in a suit with thick, black-framed glasses. I instantly recognized him. It was Brian King, an ex-professional soccer player that worked at ESPN as a news commentator. He had a face for TV, which is why the network had snatched him up as soon as he'd retired from soccer at the ripe age of 24. He'd torn his ACL for the second time and no amount of surgery could put him back in the game.

"Kinsley, this is Mr. King," Coach Davis introduced

us, and I reached forward to shake his hand. I was conscious of the fact that I'd just showered, so at least I didn't smell, but I was dressed in Nike shorts and a t-shirt while he was in a fitted suit. I felt out of my element to say the least.

"It's nice to meet you, Mr. King."

"Oh, please call me Brian," he smiled.

I took a seat next to him and turned my attention back to Coach Davis.

"Brian is here because he'd like to do an interview with you about the upcoming season and your Olympic aspirations."

I glanced quickly to Brian, who was offering me an easy smile. He really didn't seem like a bad guy, but I had no clue why he cared about me when there were probably hundreds of other girls in my same position.

"Ohhkay," I nodded, waiting for more information.

"I tried contacting your parents, but I thought since I was in the Los Angeles area, I might as well come down and meet you face to face," Brian explained.

"So, are you interviewing other people from the team?" I asked.

Brian shifted in his chair so that his body was aimed toward me rather than Coach Davis.

"At this point, you'll be the only person being interviewed from ULA. We'll be covering five young Olympic hopefuls in the months leading up to tryouts. Our audience really enjoys getting to know athletes like yourself. It makes the Games much more fun to watch if fans know some details about their favorite athletes."

"But I haven't made the team yet," I tried to argue. "Why do you want to interview *me*?"

"You haven't Googled yourself recently, have you?"

Brian asked, clasping his hands on his lap and leaning toward me.

"No," I answered truthfully, looking to Coach Davis for backup. She offered me a supportive smile and a small nod.

Brian chuckled and then reached down into his briefcase.

"Here's my card. I think we should schedule a time to get coffee sometime next week and we can discuss the interview in more detail." Then he stood, effectively ending the meeting.

"Thank you for your time, Coach Davis. And Kinsley, I look forward to meeting with you next week." He smiled, a wide camera-ready smile, and then exited the office. His cologne lingered on the chair next to me and I sat for a moment, trying to let everything sink in.

Coach Davis hopped up from her seat and came around her desk to sit beside me.

"Kinsley, this is all up to you. If you don't want to do the interview, then I can send a polite rejection, claiming a busy practice schedule as an excuse."

I shook my head and flipped Brian's business card over in my hand. His cell phone number, email, and office number were printed in bold black letters.

"I just need to think about. I'm not sure if I'm ready for the spotlight." I wanted to add that I'd never be ready for public scrutiny. I was a private person when it came to most things. Not to mention, I still felt like I hadn't proved myself in the soccer world. I didn't want to have everyone expecting great things from me, especially not when I was already putting so much pressure on myself.

"I think I'm going to go run for a bit," I declared, pushing off the leather seat and giving Coach Davis one final smile.

"Don't push yourself too hard, you've already had a hard practice week," she answered.

Not hard enough.

When I got home after my run, Emily was in our bathroom washing her face.

"Hey, Em," I smiled, sitting down and pulling off my running shoes. My shins hurt from running for so long, but I felt a thousand times better than I had after practice. Nothing cleared my head like running.

"Hey, Kinsley," Emily said, moving into my room and sitting down against my door.

We sat there in silence for a moment. She looked like she was thinking about something but was too scared to bring it up.

"How's it going?" I asked with an encouraging tone.

She chewed on her bottom lip and then finally looked up at me. "It's good... I just wanted to thank you for what you did on Wednesday morning. I know that you were just as tired as Becca and me."

"It's not a big deal, Emily. Truth be told, I think the only reason you were involved is because Tara hates me and you and I are friends." I shrugged, trying to determine if that revelation upset her.

"Yeah. I sort of put that together myself. It's worth it, you know. I mean you and Becca are really close, but I'm really glad we're friends, too, and if that means having to deal with Tara, then it's still worth it," Emily said with a small smile.

Her words caught me by surprise and I couldn't help but feel a little bit emotional. Sure, Becca and I were closer, but Emily was the type of friend that you could always count on. Quiet, loyal— the type of friend that lasted through the years.

"Can I hug you even though I'm super stinky?" I asked, already crawling toward her and leaping onto her lap.

"Ewwww! You *do* smell!" Emily laughed, shoving me off her.

"Sorry! Friends have to deal with stinky hugs. You asked for it!"

A pounding came on the other side of my door.

"Are you two in there having fun without me? What the hell! Open up!" Becca called. Emily and I moved forward and pulled the door open wide enough for Becca to sneak through.

"Ew. What are you guys doing? It smells like rotten feet in here!"

Becca scrunched her nose and pretended to pass out.

"Oh, get over it! I'll go shower, okay? But don't leave! We have to plan our costumes for Saturday."

Chapter Eleven

I was getting ready for the costume party on Saturday night when my phone vibrated with an incoming text.

Josh: Heading to the party tonight?

I'd completely forgotten about Josh in the recent days. My thoughts were spread thin, with Liam taking up nearly 99% of them. So naturally, Josh had been one of the first things to go. Now that I was confronted with the idea of seeing him at the party, my first instinct was to ignore him all together. I didn't want to be friends with him. I wanted to move on and concentrate on better things. But since ignoring people is generally frowned upon in our society, I shot him back a one worded reply. Compromise.

Me: Yep.

I dropped my phone and glanced down at my outfit.

Becca and I had found matching SuperGirl and BatGirl shirts that cut off a few inches above our belly buttons. I'd paired mine with a red lycra skirt that was tight around my waist but then flared around my thighs. A short red cape and my white converse completed the look. I was glad Becca had enforced operation B.C. earlier in the week because my toned stomach now sported a healthy tan which made the outfit a little more sexy. Compared to what the other girls would be wearing tonight, it wasn't *that* bad.

Becca was going for the full shebang. She looked awesome in her BatGirl shirt and black skirt. She had on black heels and a black cape and kept striking a super hero pose every time she entered my room.

"Who's texting you?" she asked, doing a high kick and then pretending to punch my dresser. The costume was starting to go to her head.

"Jeez! I'm glad you're wearing spanks or I would have just seen way too much of your bat cave!" I laughed as my phone buzzed again. I glanced down.

Josh: Cool. It'll be smaller than last week's so I should be able to find you.

"It's just Josh asking if we're going to the party," I answered.

I didn't respond to his second text.

"Ah, gross. That reminds me, should we review the five reasons that *L* is not worthy of your attention?" Becca asked, already bending down to retrieve the white board that I'd stashed under my bed the other day.

"Nope!" I hopped up. "No. We're good. Honestly, I want to forget about soccer and everything else on my plate and just have fun. Okay?"

Becca smiled and then spun around with karate hands. "Tonight we'll be SuperGirl and BatGirl and no one will even recognize us! We can do whatever we want!"

I started laughing and pulled my dresser open to get some spanks for myself. I could already tell Becca and I would be spin-kicking the entire night and I didn't feel like flashing everyone my Lois Lane.

Becca's phone buzzed just as I finished pulling them on.

"Cab's here! Wait, I mean, the BATMOBILE AWAITS!"

"Okay, okay!" I ran over to open my bathroom door and shouted for Emily. "Em, are you sure you don't want to come with us? We can put together a cute costume really quick!" I knew the answer would be no. She'd told us yesterday when we invited her to go shopping that she was going to stay in and Skype with her boyfriend. We had, of course, made fun of her for having Skype sex, and she blushed for an hour straight. Seriously, it was just too easy.

"Yeah, I'm sure. Call me if you guys need a ride or anything!" Emily answered, already sitting at her computer with Skype open.

"Fiiiine, but don't forget to use protection... you don't want your computer getting a virus," I joked with a corny grin. Emily shot me the finger. *Thatta girl.*

"You guys better be glad that I'm not on a call with him yet or I would have killed you!" she yelled as I started to back away.

"Yeah, yeah. We're leaving. Adios!" I said, trailing after Becca.

Before we ran downstairs, we checked ourselves out really quick in my mirror one last time. My long brown hair was hanging down my back and framing my delicate features. Not bad at all. Becca's cropped blonde hair was sexy and cute.

"Let's do this!" I shouted, grabbing Becca's hand and pulling her down the stairs and out to the cab. We piled in and gave directions to the cabbie.

"So are you going to hangout with Jace again?" I asked.

"Who?" Becca quirked a brow, and for a second I really didn't think she remembered him.

"You're kind of the definition of a tease, Becca. You flirt with guys and then you leave them high and dry."

"It's not like that! I have to test the waters first."

"But you thought Jace was cute, right?"

"He was fine, but I tried to make jokes and he didn't get a single one. He did that awkward thing where he'd chuckle slowly with a confused expression. I wanted to smack him in the forehead and walk away."

I laughed. "Okay, so you want someone cute *and* funny? That's not so hard."

She scoffed. "You'd be surprised."

"We're here, ladies," the cabbie offered politely. We tipped him well and then hopped out of the car. The house was quiet from the street, but as we walked closer to the front door, you could hear the bass from the music growing louder and louder. We pushed the door open and stepped inside. Immediately I was greeted by a group of girls I didn't recognize. They were all dressed up as the same theme: M&Ms. But let me clarify: they were actually wearing skin tight spandex dresses with tiny "M&M's" printed over their boobs.

"Great, now I want some M&Ms," I said while throwing my hands up.

"No time for sweets whilst crime runs rampant!"

Becca declared dramatically.

"C'mon, let's see who all is here," I said, which we both knew was code for: let's find out if the seniors and/or Liam are anywhere in sight so we could strategically avoid them the entire night.

We continued into the party, stepping into the living room that had been transformed into a techno-infused dance floor.

"Now the age old question: do we want to get a drink now or wait until we find the seniors and then drown our sorrows while they scheme their next plan to take us down?"

"Now," I answered, heading in to the kitchen. There were costumed people everywhere. The usual suspects were present: pirates, ninjas, even a weird clown, but then there was a group of guys dressed up like princesses. I'm pretty sure some of them were even wearing heels.

Becca and I located the table of liquor. In the very center there was an igloo with a sombrero and mustache haphazardly glued on.

"I guess they even dressed up the punch?"

"Hah. Funny," Becca answered, grabbing two cups. A little card next to the punch clarified that we'd be drinking "El Puncho".

Once we were armed with drinks in hand, we started the hunt for the seniors. We checked outside first. Just like last week, there was a keg and beer pong tables. We wandered through the crowd and then looped back around toward the house.

No seniors.

Then we went back inside and checked in the kitchen and living room again. Still, we didn't spy them.

Could we have lucked out?

"I don't think they're here," I shrugged with a sly smile.

"I can drink to that!" Becca exclaimed. We hit the lips of our solo cups together in a "cheers" and then downed the rest of the punch we'd been nursing during our search.

"Let's go easy on the punch," I warned, but Becca was already busy refilling our cups. Welp, I can't say I didn't try to warn her.

"Kinsley!" My name rang out behind me, and I spun around to find Josh heading toward us. He was dressed as a race car driver in a bright red jumpsuit with patches up and down the arms. The front of the jumpsuit zipped all the way down his torso and he'd left the first few inches open at the top so that his tanned chest shown through.

"Hi Josh," I offered politely, reaching for my cup of punch and taking a big sip. I didn't think going easy on it was such a good idea anymore.

"You guys look great," he smiled, taking in my SuperGirl outfit with blatant lust.

"This is Becca," I said, motioning to where she was standing.

"Hey, nice to meet you, Becca. Do you play on the ULA team as well?" he asked with a smile, ignoring her obvious disdain. Josh was a charmer. He could stand there and pretend like we were just friends, like nothing had even happened between us. It was almost eerie.

"Yup," Becca answered brusquely, and then turned away. I had to fight to keep from laughing.

Josh nodded his head, his smile falling a fraction of an inch. "Well, I'm going to go say hi to some teammates, but will you stay in here? I'll come back and find you so we can dance."

I couldn't form words because I was busy tipping back

more of my punch, so I just gave him a thumbs up.

When he walked away, Becca turned toward me with a quizzical brow. "We're not actually staying in here, right?"

I smiled. "Hell no. Let's go dance."

It was perfect timing. I'd had just enough punch to make me feel silly and loose, but not enough to where I thought break dancing was a good idea. That usually came after about one more cup. Becca pulled me through the kitchen and back toward the living room. More people were dancing now and somehow we got sucked into a random group of girls that were dancing in a circle.

I had no clue who any of them were, but at a party it seems like names are less important than showing off a badass dance move. I'd just finished what I assumed to be a flawless rendition of twerking á la Miley when I looked up and saw Liam across the room.

My gut clenched.

He wasn't there when we'd done our initial search of the party. Oh, but now the bastard was *definitely* there and he was *definitely* standing against the wall chatting with a girl. I couldn't pull my focus away even as the dancing continued around me. I was frozen as I watched him with her. They weren't standing close. He was leaning his shoulder against the wall, and she had her arms crossed over her chest. She was dressed as a slutty pirate or maybe a slutty penguin. I couldn't tell the difference from where I was standing. Anyway, she looked gorgeous and I couldn't help but feel a tight twist in my gut. It was the same feeling that I had when I'd walked in on Josh cheating on me, but this was worse. More visceral and out of my control.

It seemed insane. After all, I'd made a joke when I walked in on Josh. Hell, I hadn't even shed a tear. But now, as I stood there watching Liam just *talking* to another girl, I had the urge to do something crazy like fight her or yell at him. I hadn't even yelled at Josh. I'd spoken to him harshly. But if Liam had walked up to me then, I would have thrown blows.

Did they put steroids in the punch? Was that why I felt like fighting someone?

"Hey, Kinsley! Why'd you stop?" Becca caught my attention over the music. I tilted my head to where Liam was standing and her eyes followed the trail.

"Ahhh," she nodded. "Looks like it's time to swap these girls out for a pair of super hot guys." Becca grabbed my hand before I could protest and then pulled me over to where a small wooden coffee table sat in the center of the room. It was a cheap, IKEA knock-off, so I didn't really protest when Becca pulled me on top of it.

We were raised a foot above the rest of the party then and my first instinct was to find Liam again. I wanted to know if he was still talking to the girl or if he'd spotted me, but then Becca pulled my hand, throwing me off balance for a moment.

"Here!" she said, handing me her cup of punch since I'd set mine down a while ago so that I could dance with free hands. I downed the contents of her punch like I was taking a shot and then set the empty cup down on the table.

A seductive pop song started playing through the speakers and I lost myself in the movements of my hips, my arms, and my swaying body. It didn't take long at all for guys to start shifting toward the table. Like moths to a flame, they could sense how tipsy Becca and I were. I moved as if Liam was dancing with me, as if he could feel my hips gyrating from side to side.

"Wanna dance?" a guy asked as he sidled up next to

me. He was tall enough that we were almost level while I stood on the table. I glanced toward Becca and she gave me a thumbs up. A guy was already approaching her as well.

"Sure," I shrugged, hopping down from the table with his help.

And so it began— a string of guys that were bold enough to ask a random girl to dance. I didn't let any of them stay past one song. I'd smile and twist out of their grasp, reaching for Becca and pretending to be too drunk to care when they asked for another dance. They weren't actually into me; they just wanted a pretty thing to grind their dicks against. Seriously. I'd rather just dance with a group of girls than have random guys dance with me.

Becca ditched her last partner as well so we were back to dancing by ourselves.

"Can you do the Stanky Leg?" Becca asked, trying to show off the move. I tried to copy her, but I ended up just looking like my leg was cramping up.

"No! That's so terrible, Kinsley. You should stop before someone calls an ambulance," Becca laughed, putting her hands on my shoulder and forcing me to stand still. We were standing like that when I spotted Liam moving through the crowd. His dark eyes were locked on me as he slid through the dancers. His presence threw my balance out of whack, like I needed to hold onto someone or I might fall into him. Good thing I had Becca.

"Kinsley," Liam murmured when he stepped up to us. He was forcing me to acknowledge the situation and his pull over me. I wet my lips and shifted my gaze toward him. He wasn't alone. His teammate, Penn, stood alongside him. I hadn't seen him at any of the previous parties, but he was Liam's best friend. They'd played together on the LA Stars for five years and they were often interviewed together on various talk shows.

If there was anyone on the LA Stars team that could give Liam a run for his money in the looks department, it was Penn. He was just as tall as Liam, with dark brown hair and a Crest commercial smile. That smile was currently aimed directly at Becca.

I peered from him to her and almost jumped for joy. She was staring at him too, visibly caught in his trap with her mouth slightly open.

Complete goner in 3…2…1.

"This is Penn," Liam said, more so to Becca than to me.

Penn nodded and took a small step closer to Becca. If I'd ever experienced instant attraction, these two had it in spades. Becca usually had a funny comment on hand, but in that moment she was completely quiet, just nodding gently and staring up into Penn's brown eyes.

"You guys should dance," I offered, and Penn shot me a confident smile before raising a brow in question.

"Becca?" he asked, stepping toward her.

Becca peered at me for a quick second and I knew she was a melting at the very thought of getting to dance with him. Her hazel eyes were practically clouded over in lust for this guy.

Penn offered his hand to Becca and tugged her through the crowd. I watched their bodies disappear behind dancers until I couldn't see them anymore. That's when I realized how awkward it was that everyone around us was dancing, but we were standing still. Silent, brooding, and with so much hanging in the air between us I could have reached my tongue out and tasted it. What would buried attraction taste like? *Rich dark chocolate.*

We were both being immature, waiting for the other

to speak first. I couldn't meet his eye; I wasn't sure I'd keep it together if I did. I wanted to ask him who the girl was. I wanted to ask him what he wanted from me *that day*.

We were in dangerous territory, in a crowd of people that shouldn't know Liam and I had any sort of relationship beyond coach and player. Both of our reputations depended on it.

"I just came out here so that Penn could meet Becca. He was interested in her," Liam explained, finally breaking the silence between us with a harsh tone.

I glanced up to see his brows were furrowed, and I knew he was in his standard brooding mood.

"Oh good, you can leave then." I narrowed my eyes on him, challenging him to say something.

Instead he took a step toward me and wrapped his hand around my waist, gripping it in his palm. His fingers dug gently into my skin and I bit down hard on my bottom lip.

He pulled me toward him as he bent lower. Our faces inches from one another.

"You look good dancing with those guys, Kinsley. You should keep letting them touch you," he said with a harsh tone. He was pissed. Beyond pissed.

"At least they're not afraid of what they want, Liam," I murmured, trying to step out of his grip. He tightened it and then twisted me around so that my back was pressed against his chest. His arm wrapped around my waist, and suddenly I was a victim to my body. I wasn't going anywhere, even if I wanted to fight him.

"They don't want *you*. They think you're sexy, but they don't know you," he clarified, pressing his lips to my ear. I closed my eyes and turned my hips in a slow circle. If someone had glanced over they would have thought we were dancing. Our bodies were moving slowly against one another, but in reality we were waging war. When I pressed my hips back against him harder, he groaned angrily in my ear.

"And what about the girl you were talking to earlier? Does she know you or does she just think you're sexy?"

"You don't get to be jealous, Kinsley. We aren't together," he bit back, gripping my waist in his hand and pulling me harder against him. I leaned my head back against his chest and he tilted his head down so that I could see his eyes. Our lips were so close he could have bent down just a few inches and kissed me. It would have been so easy.

"Then same goes for you, *Liam*. Why don't you let me go? Besides, you aren't *allowed* to touch me, or have you forgotten that I'm off-limits?"

That's the first time I thought about our situation from his perspective. If I was being tortured, he was right there with me, except he had it worse. He was in the position of power. If he took advantage of me— the young, naïve student— he'd take the fall for it.

His expression darkened and his gaze shifted from my eyes down to my lips. We were going to keep throwing digs at one another because that's all that we could do. We weren't allowed to be together. Hell, we shouldn't have even been dancing, but we were both helpless to the moment.

I should have pulled away, he should have left me alone, but then something happened that served as the final catalyst for our illicit romance.

The lights cut out.

It was already dim before, but then the room turned pitch black. Someone must have hit the light switch.

Who knew how long it would last, but Liam didn't wait to find out. He twisted me around, pulling me to his chest, and kissed me so hard that I let out a little yelp. I recovered quickly, opening up for him, tilting my head and letting him slide his tongue over mine. It sent lust swirling through my body. I picked my leg up, twisting it around his hip. One of his hands left my waist and he helped pin my long leg around him. He groaned into my mouth and I completely lost myself in him.

"Leave them off!" someone yelled, and I smiled against his mouth. It was like the world had given us a momentary break from the rules. A hall pass. We were in the dark, in the middle of a crowded dance floor, but no one could see us. One hand drifted higher up my skirt while his other hand pulled me against him so I could feel him against my spanks.

"God," I groaned, dragging our hips together. Would the lights stay out long enough for him to take me right here?

"You're so fucking sexy, Kinsley," he moaned into my ear. "Do you know what I want to do to you? What I *imagine* doing to you every time I see you?"

His words were fueling the fire between us. I responded by skimming my hands under his shirt, feeling his impossibly toned abs. His skin was hot and smooth, and his muscles were coiled, as if he were restraining himself from what he actually wanted to do to me.

We were just on the edge of falling... and then the lights flicked on and we flew apart.

Chapter Twelve

Our breathing was erratic and heavy as we tried to piece together the last few minutes. We were standing a foot away from each other and the lights kept flickering on and off as someone continued to play with them.

I pressed my palm to my stomach, feeling my diaphragm spasm in response to our secret kiss.

Everything in life was a hazy mess. In the past few days I'd had ten million decisions fall across my lap: Fight Tara or deal with her crap? Do the interview with Brian King or keep my life as private as possible?

But that cloud of uncertainty didn't reach Liam.

He was the northern star. I had no choice but to become enveloped in his brightness and let it coax me toward him. Wanting him was an unconscious impulse, like taking my next breath.

And now, without a doubt, I knew he wanted me, too.

"You're not in costume," I murmured, glancing over his faded jeans and black shirt that fit him so well I swore they'd been designed with his proportions in mind.

The edge of his mouth curved up. "I'm not a costume type of guy."

Everyone around us was still dancing and the girl behind me kept accidentally knocking into me. I was about to turn around and ask her to get a hold of her flailing elbows, but then I'd have to look away from him. I wasn't ready for that yet.

"That's not fair," I lamented.

"I don't think I mind costumes so much when you're wearing them," he smirked, letting his gaze fall to my bare stomach. I don't think I minded them either, especially since his hand had been on that bare skin only moments earlier.

"C'mon," he motioned. "I'll go put one on." He tilted his head toward the hallway and I knew we were heading back to his room. I scanned behind me, but didn't see anyone I knew. Becca and Penn were dancing off to the side of the room. His hands were on her hips and her head was tilting up to him. He bent down to say something in her ear and she smiled into his neck.

Half of me wanted to interrupt them and mention Becca's wax or cash in my "one free pantsing" that she'd promised me, but I couldn't do that to her. Best to wait until she was more sober, that way she'd remember it. Hah.

"Coming?" Liam asked, and I realized I'd stopped following him.

He was standing confidently in the hallway, cloaked in darkness. His facial hair was more grown out than usual, like he'd forgotten to shave earlier that morning. But the thing that got me the most, that I couldn't wrap my head around, was his strong hand outstretched and beckoning for me to catch up and grab hold. He was putting himself on the line.

Someone could see us sneaking away from the party, but I told myself the chances were slim. Everyone was too busy concealing their own secrets to worry about discovering ours.

Instead of grabbing his hand, I sidled past him, never breaking eye contact until I turned and walked toward the room he'd pushed us into last week. He chuckled under his breath behind me and I hid my smile as he opened the door.

Not much had changed in one week. Our relationship was still forbidden. He still had to lock the door behind him, but there was a slight sense of hope in the air... maybe because he flipped the light on and gave me a glimpse of his world, his room. It made me feel less like a secret and more like a welcome addition to his life.

It was only one room with an attached bath and closet, but it was huge and decorated well. His bed had a tall black headboard with a crisp, black trimmed bedding set. The room was entirely too clean for a normal 25 year old guy.

There were two framed photographs sitting on his desk. One was of him when he was younger, smiling and smack dab between what looked like very doting parents. I could tell they were his parents because he looked like carbon copies of each of them. The other photo was of him and his team winning silver in the last Olympics. He was smiling up at the crowd, wrapped in an American flag, and holding his silver medal proudly.

"You look so young in this photo," I smiled and stepped closer. I could feel Liam's presence behind me. What was I doing in his room looking at old photographs? Five minutes ago we'd been attacking each other in the living room surrounded by hundreds of people.

"I was young. Young and wild," he smiled and shook

his head clear of thoughts before heading toward his closet. I crossed my arms and moved back against the bed. I sat on the end, in what felt like neutral territory, but I could still see him moving around among his clothing.

He grabbed a light blue shirt off a hanger, and without thinking, started tugging his black shirt over his head. He was facing away from me, so of course I watched his back muscles pull and stretch. I could see the tattoos that wrapped around his left shoulder blade. They extended down the back of his arm to his elbow in a half sleeve. I wasn't close enough to make out any of the content, but they were beautifully done. The forms were sketched perfectly and the black ink stood out against his tanned skin. I guess he went shirtless at practice most of the time.

Lucky teammates.

I didn't find the will to speak until he pulled the light blue shirt over his head and his bare skin was out of view. I mourned the loss. It was like getting a glimpse of the David. A tan, tattooed David.

"I saw your tattoos," I joked, pushing off his bed and stepping closer to the closet. He peered over his shoulder at me and smirked. Then he turned fully and I saw the emblem on the front of his shirt. Superman.

He'd chosen the shirt on purpose. He was now Superman. SuperSuperHotMan… and I was Supergirl. We were the freaking cutest thing I'd ever seen. Okay, mostly he brought the cute factor. I was just the sidekick.

"Then it's only fair that you show me yours. Unless you were bluffing?" He raised his brow. He was referring to my tattoo.

I couldn't believe he remembered my line I'd used on him the other week. The night we'd officially met.

"I wasn't bluffing," I smiled gently, taking another

step closer to him. "Do you actually want to see it?"

The right side of his mouth quirked up in confidence. "If you can show me without taking that skirt off."

I'm sorry, did my uterus just call out to him or am I hearing things?

I cocked a brow and bit back my smirk as I twisted to the side. My fingers found the hem of my SuperGirl shirt and I pulled it up along with the bottom of my bra. My small tattoo was hidden beneath it in small black calligraphy. I'd had my mom write it in her perfect scrolly handwriting, and they'd transcribed her words onto my skin. The whole thing was barely two inches, running horizontally along my ribcage a few inches below my breast.

Liam stepped forward and bent down to get a closer look. His warm breath hit my skin and I realized he could see the very bottom of my breast from his angle.

He reached out and dragged the pad of his finger gently beneath the tattoo. "*She believed she could, so she did.*" Goose bumps bloomed beneath his touch and I shivered as his dark voice read my tattoo.

He nodded, lingering on the text for a moment longer before standing up.

"I've heard that phrase before, but it really fits you."

I bit my lip and nodded.

"I think I like that more than all of my tattoos," he noted with a small smirk.

I disagreed, along with all of the U.S. female population, but I held my tongue.

"You don't seem like a tattoo type of girl."

I tilted my head to the side. "Why?"

He pulled his bottom lip into his mouth and then a second later shook his head. "You're young." Bullshit. That wasn't the reason, but he wasn't going to give me the real one.

"It's my mom's handwriting."

He nodded thoughtfully, glancing down at where my shirt now covered up the ink.

"You have to show me at least one of yours. I didn't get a good look while you were changing."

His dark eyes pierced me for a moment before he reached around and pulled the back of his shirt up. Without thinking, I reached to help, pushing the soft fabric over his skin. I had to fight the urge to push it all the way off the top of his head.

At the center of his left shoulder blade, depicted in black ink, were the words "Veni Vidi Vici" entwined within the Olympic rings.

"Ah, of course you had to get an Olympics tattoo. I like it," I said, tracing my finger over the words. Before I finished, he stepped forward, out of my grasp, and pulled his shirt down.

"C'mon. Let's go get something to eat."

"I'm not hungry," I protested, not ready to leave the privacy and simplicity of his quiet room. In here we were just two people talking. Out there we were two people the world wanted to condemn.

"I am," he winked, and then walked past me. "And you should be. You're working out too hard and it's starting to show. Have you upped your diet?"

Oh god, what was it with guys and proper food intake? We had a nutritionist on the team and I ate healthy enough.

I didn't answer his question. Instead, I flexed my arm and grinned. It was toned but still pretty skinny. Liam laughed, stepped forward, and wrapped his fingers around my arm, pretending to feel my muscle.

"Does this look like the arm of a girl who doesn't eat enough?" I winked like Popeye.

"Good thing you aren't a defender," he laughed.

"What!" I argued, dropping my arm. "Becca is a defender and she's my size!"

He nodded and moved toward his door. "True. But I'm not making out with Becca in dark living rooms, so I don't have to worry about her well-being," he challenged, flicking the light off in his room and leaving me standing in the dark. I had no choice but to follow him out. The bastard.

"She'd never have you!" I yelled, running to follow him. Then I blushed when I saw him already standing at the end of the hall with Penn and Becca.

"Kinsley!" Becca exclaimed, jumping forward onto me. I wasn't prepared to catch her weight, so I toppled backward, landing with a thud on my ass and jamming my elbow into the ground.

"Ouch! Get off me, you mongrel." I couldn't decide if I should cry or laugh, so I just yelled with a smile on my face like a weirdo.

Penn shook his head and reached down to grab Becca, who had obviously had another cup of punch after we'd finished ours a while ago.

"You're supposed to be SuperGirl! You were *supposed* to catch me!" Becca stomped.

I pretended to spin kick her. She laughed and spun around and soon we were kicking and punching down the hallway away from the boys. Becca brought out the weird in me.

"My elbow seriously hurts," I laughed as we paused to catch our breaths.

Penn and Liam were standing a little ways down the hallway, laughing and nodding their heads in agreement. They were probably agreeing that they should ditch our asses for sexy, worldy, models that didn't pretend to be tipsy super heroes. Pfft, no. That sounded boring, who would want that?

"Is *Peen* cool? He's super hot," I joked, unable to stop the laughter from spilling from my lips.

Becca *actually* karate chopped my arm after that. We needed to get out of these costumes stat.

"His name's Penn," she corrected, loud enough for the boys to hear, which made me laugh harder.

"That's what I'm saying: Peen."

Becca shook her head but couldn't conceal her smile. "You suck, but yes, he's awesome and super funny. Cute and funny! Can you believe it?"

I high-fived her. "I'm going to go get something to eat with Liam, I think. How weird is that? Do you guys want to come?"

We started heading back to the boys.

"Nah, I think Penn is going to take me home." By the tail end of her sentence we were in range for the boys to hear our conversation.

"Yup," he confirmed, rocking back on his heels.

"Can I trust you with my friend, Penn?" I asked, putting my hands on my hips and pretending to puff my chest like a superhero would. I imagined my cape floating in the AC draft behind me for added dramatic effect.

"I got her," he winked. "Have no fear."

Liam laughed and stepped forward to grab my hand. "Let's go, SuperGirl."

I let him drag me through the front door toward his car but not before yelling goodbyes to Becca. All the while,

I smiled about the fact that I actually got away with being Liam's date at a party. Sort of. Okay, hardly. We weren't together around anyone, and when we kissed it'd been pitch black. He also didn't ever refer to me as his date.

But we were in matching Superhero costumes.

Sooo, it seemed pretty *official* to me.

"My elbow really does hurt," I said, finally sobering enough to realize that it was throbbing.

Liam reached inside his jean pockets and unlocked his SUV. He came around the passenger's side and opened to the door to let me in.

"Let me see," he said after I'd hopped up onto the seat.

I showed him the back of my right elbow.

"You're always injured at my parties." He shot me a playful frown.

"Because of Becca! She bruised my face with her gyrating hips last time." Damn Becca. She's worse than Shakira.

He laughed and stepped back. "If it still hurts after we eat, I'll take you to get it looked at. And I think I should hear more about the gyrating hips story."

I laughed and buckled up. "All right, I'll explain it on the way."

• • •

I was expecting to go inside the restaurant like most normal people, but Liam ordered from the car and then a waiter ran out with our order a few minutes later. Liam tipped him handsomely before handing me the bag of food.

"Sorry that we can't go in, but the press would have a field day, especially now that you're 'The Rising Star in

Soccer'."

"What? Is that printed somewhere?"

"It was the title of an ESPN article the other day. Did no one mention it?"

I shook my head. Who would have mentioned it? My friends didn't check ESPN, my dad was busy working, and my mom was busy sending me care packages.

I didn't really mind not knowing about articles like that though. I didn't need anything else going to my head.

"I don't want to read it, but you should save it for me so I can read it when I'm like sixty," I laughed. "When I need to cling onto my glory days."

"Will do... but you're okay with eating in here?" he asked, eyeing me cautiously.

His question almost shattered our happy moment. When we were at the party things started to feel normal, but that was because we were secluded in our own tiny world. There were no seniors, no press, and no adoring fans. Now it was a completely different story, and the reality of our situation was starting to sink in. We couldn't leave his car for fear that someone would recognize us and leak the story to the press

But we still had a little while to live in lala land. When I got home I'd worry about the consequences of my actions, but for now I'd just appreciate being with him.

"What'd you order?" I smiled, tucking my thoughts away for later.

"Chicken and waffles. You'll love them," he answered with confidence.

"Oh, I don't like chicken *or* waffles," I joked.

"Humor me," he winked, preparing a bite and handing it over to me.

"You don't mind if we eat in your fancy car?" I asked,

eyeing the nice leather upholstery.

"It can be cleaned and this meal is more than worth it."

Because it was with me or because he really liked chicken and waffles?

After I tasted the bite I feared it was the latter.

"Holy shit, that's good!" I exclaimed, stealing the next two bites after that as well.

"Well, I guess I know where to take you to fatten you up," he laughed before finally taking a bite of his own.

We ate in silence for a bit. Well, he was silent. I moaned and groaned in bliss about the maple honey butter they'd used to coat the waffles.

"You know it's probably not a good idea for us to be seen together at those house parties anymore," Liam announced, catching me off guard.

I chewed the rest of my bite. "You're probably right." I agreed with him even though his announcement made me feel sick. Was he regretting everything, *again*? No. He was being smart.

"I don't really enjoy them much anyway," he continued, staring out his front windshield.

"Why do you live in that house then? I don't get it, not to be rude, but it seems like you have enough money to move out of the Animal House."

Liam smiled. "I own that house and let some of the guys from the team pay rent. My other place is being renovated, so I'm staying there for now. It's usually a lot of fun, but they've been throwing a ton of parties lately."

He *owned* the house? It was massive.

"Do you mind that they throw parties in your house?"

"It's not so bad, and that's kind of the point: Party hard now before settling down."

Of course. They were all young, attractive athletes. Liam was still in the partying hard phase.

I dropped my fork back into the bag and cleared my throat. "I'm kind of tired," I said, sitting back against my seat.

He concentrated out through the front window as his eyes narrowed. Finally he spoke. "Yeah, it's getting late anyway."

I thought I could push my negative thoughts away until I got home. I'd been wrong. The feeling had sank in as soon as he brought up the fact that we shouldn't be seen together. And it only hurt worse because he was absolutely right. We'd been careless, trying to push the bounds without weighing the consequences.

When we got to my house, Liam put the car in park a few houses down so that no one could see us. We sat facing out through the front windshield, completely silent as the night crept on around us.

When he turned his head toward me, I could *feel* it. I could feel his eyes rake over my skin. I swallowed and stared at the black dashboard, trying to get my head on straight. This was all so confusing. I knew Liam wasn't good for me, so why couldn't I get out of his car? It was no use; feeling his eyes on me was like feeling his fingers glide over my skin. I bit down on my lower lip, trying to quell the desire flowing through me.

One second I was in my own world, and the next Liam had unbuckled my seatbelt and pulled me onto his lap. Every consequence that had been flitting through my mind only seconds ago no longer seemed relevant as our lips melted together. His mouth tasted sweet from the syrup as I wound my fingers through his tousled hair.

With us it was always 0 to 60 in three seconds flat.

His hands dragged up under my skirt to the edge of my spanks.

Everything has a consequence.

I bit down on his lip, spurring him on.

Everything has a consequence.

His finger skirted the material, making my spine curl.

He pulled back, separating us by an inch, just enough to stop the chemical reaction ricocheting between us.

"You need to get some sleep," he murmured so that his breath fell across my lips.

"No."

The edge of his mouth curled up.

"Yes."

I swallowed, trying to regain my composure.

"I'm sorry this isn't easier," he murmured, lessening my worries enough that I could answer his apology with an edge of playfulness.

"Nothing to apologize for… that was the best goodbye kiss I've ever had."

When I was with him, there were no consequences.

Chapter Thirteen

"What did you and Penn talk about last night?"

"Marriage mostly. Where we wanted to buy a house and raise kids," Becca answered flatly. We were lounging around after she woke me up by jumping on my bed a few minutes earlier. I'd pulled the comforter out from under her and she'd fallen back and hadn't gotten back up.

"Oh, that's cool. Don't forget me when you're toting the kids to soccer practice."

Becca rolled over and propped her head up on her hand. "Ew. No. Stop. We didn't talk about anything important. I was pretty tipsy, so I'm sure I tried to make a lot of jokes, but he didn't seem to mind."

I smiled. "Any hankypanky when he dropped you off after the party?"

Becca frowned. "Nada. Nothing. He was really sweet and he walked me to the door, but he went in for a hug, which is almost as bad as a high-five. No, a high-five is better because then we could have laughed and he would

159

have thought I looked so charming while I laughed that he would have wanted to kiss me."

"Hmm, he's definitely into you. That's what Liam said when they joined us on the dance floor. So, maybe he's just trying to take it slow, or maybe he thought you were still tipsy and didn't want to take advantage of you."

"Is it taking advantage when I would have willingly helped him attack me? I would have taken my BatGirl outfit off *for* him."

I laughed. "I'm not sure, but he is super hot. Can't blame you there."

Becca stared at the comforter and nodded as if thinking the same thing herself.

"I want some chicken and waffles," I demanded.

"You just had them last night. I can't believe you ate in his car. I would have handcuffed myself to the console and never left."

"I'm trying to stay away from the psycho-killer approach..."

Becca laughed. "To each their own."

A small knock sounded at my door, and then one of the sophomore girls stuck her head inside.

"Hey, Kinsley, there's a delivery guy downstairs asking for you."

I glanced over toward Becca, but she just smiled and declared, "Strippergram. I thought we should start our Sunday morning off right."

I laughed and hopped off my bed to follow the girl back downstairs. Just as she'd promised, there was a middle-aged delivery man standing on our porch holding a clipboard and a big box.

"Kinsley Bryant?" he asked when I pushed open the screen door.

"Yes, sir!"

I signed, thanked him, and then ran back upstairs at lightning speed. Becca hadn't budged an inch. Lazy cow.

"My mom seriously needs to relax with the care packages. I fear that it's her main pastime these days."

Becca hopped up to help me open the box. "Pfft, don't knock her gifts. If she wants to order random things from Amazon and ship them here, let her. I now have a year supply of deodorant thanks to her."

I rolled my eyes and peeled the tape off the box. Inside, beneath a lot of colorful tissue paper, there was a hot pink bicycle helmet, elbow pads, knee pads, band aids, and ice packs. At the bottom of it all there was a simple piece of white card stock with what I'd learned to be Liam's handwriting.

For your protection whenever you're around Becca. Hope your elbow is feeling better. - L

"No he *did* not," Becca laughed, pulling the card out of my hand. "Damnit! He doesn't get to be funny, too. That's not fair."

In five minutes flat I had on all the gear and was traipsing around my room like a five year old about to go out on my first bike ride. Well, either that or someone that just escaped from an insane asylum.

"C'mon. Let's go wakeup Emily," I said, walking awkwardly to the door of my bathroom.

"Ok, but you have to do it since you're the one in that gear. I don't have anything to deflect her punches if she attacks me."

"You realize we're talking about Emily, right?"

Becca paused and held up her hand. "The same Emily that almost broke your neck in that pillow fight. I think she may secretly be a boxer or a fighter. I swear."

"Good point," I laughed. "Stay behind me."

• • •

Unknown: Come to practice early tomorrow.
Kinsley: Who is this?
Unknown: Liam.
Kinsley: Prove it...
Liam: She thought she could, so she did.
Kinsley: Okay. You pass the test, lover boy. How early are we talking? And is that a good idea?
Liam: You're supposed to be the young and reckless one... 5:15.
Kinsley: What if there are photographers?
Liam: I'll make sure there aren't any.
Kinsley: Did you just make me an accomplice in their murders?
Liam: My bad. Delete this text.

I scanned through our text exchange three more times before dropping my phone onto my chest. I had no clue what he wanted from me, but I knew I had to see him.

After telling Becca that she'd have to drive herself to practice because I was going early to meet with Liam (to which she squealed in my ear for thirty minutes), I picked out a cute workout outfit and attempted to shut off my brain to no avail.

At 5:00 A.M., I rolled out of bed, pulled on my clothes, and threw my hair up into a messy ponytail. If he wanted me to be *anywhere* at 5:15 A.M. other than in my bed, then he better not expect me to have actually brushed my hair. No way, Jose.

When I got to the practice field there was a white Toyota parked where Liam's car usually sat. There wasn't anyone behind the windows, but when I checked my phone, I saw a text from Liam that he'd sent a few minutes prior.

Liam: I just got to the field house.

Before I went inside, I turned around to make sure there weren't any lurking photographers. The fields were completely abandoned, so I ducked inside and made sure to close the door securely behind me. I hadn't realized I'd been holding my breath until I exhaled slowly.

We were officially sneaking around.

I'd never been to Liam's office before. It was down the main hall, past Coach Davis' office and the conference room. When I walked up, the door was open a little bit and I could see Liam sitting behind a desk scrolling through his phone.

I tapped on the door before pushing it open gently.

"Morning," I said, suddenly feeling nervous.

"Morning," he answered with a small smile, dropping his phone onto the desk and giving me his full attention. "Are you hungry?"

I nodded and pushed the door closed behind me. The room suddenly felt tiny. Well, it was actually really small, but Liam filled the space and made it so I couldn't take a breath without catching a whiff of his bodywash.

"Nice office," I said, glancing around. Clearly he hadn't changed a thing since the other assistant coach had left for maternity leave. "My favorite part is your ovulation calendar." I pointed to the wall beside his head and he shifted his gaze toward it and cracked up.

"I guess I should have actually looked around, but I'm

hardly ever in here," he laughed, then shifted his focus toward me. It was too much. Standing across his desk with his dark eyes pinned on me made me fidget in my running shoes. I dropped my cleats and water bottle on the chair in front of his desk, and then for one brief moment, I felt bold.

Bold enough to walk around to the back of his desk where he was sitting. "I'm kind of nervous. This is a weird situation and you seem much too calm."

While he was sitting, I had the height advantage and I liked it. He was the one in control of our situation. He was the one in the position of power, but right then I felt like I had the upper hand.

He reached his hand out and wrapped it around my waist. He didn't pull me toward him, he just rested it there. My power evaporated as quickly as it had arrived.

"You should eat. Give your body time to digest a bit before practice starts."

I hadn't even noticed the plethora of food sitting on his desk. There was fruit, protein bars, two smoothies, and some granola. I reached for one of the smoothies because it seemed like the easiest thing to eat. I wasn't that hungry. My body was focused on other, more important things.

"Is that your truck out front? The Toyota?" I asked, turning gently toward him so that his hand pushed up the top of my workout tank by default.

His gaze followed his hand and he narrowed his eyes before answering me. "It belongs to one of my roommates. I let him borrow my car for the day so that I could travel without people following me."

So that's why there weren't any photographers outside.

"Good thinking," I answered, letting my focus fixate on the smoothie in my hand.

"Kinsley, I know this isn't a normal thing, what we're

trying to get away with. I know I'm putting you in a terrible position," he began, but I turned and cut him off.

"We're both in terrible positions."

He nodded, but his brooding expression didn't change.

That was the moment where I either had to say *"I want this, but we shouldn't"* or *"I want you, despite the consequences."*

I chose to ignore both decisions. I set my smoothie back down and pushed his chair away from the desk. *Time to try a different approach.*

"How about you put me in a *better* position?" I asked, placing myself between his chair and the desk. The wood hit the back of my thighs an inch below my thin running shorts. He followed a path up my body before our eyes met. He uncurled a wicked grin and then stood up. The wheels on his chair screeched against the linoleum floor, giving a sound effect to the shifting positions of power. He stood taller than me. His body eclipsed mine as he leaned forward, pushing me back against the desk even more.

"This isn't why I asked you to come here this morning," he clarified, but he wasn't backing off.

"I didn't lock the door," I muttered as his lips found the base of my neck.

"Then I'd better be quick," he answered, trailing kisses down toward the top of my tank. Holy hell. Where had my confidence come from? I wasn't this girl. But Liam was enough of a man to coax my boldness out of me. Sometimes it felt like he owned my body more than I did. I was nervous about what he'd do with that power, how far he'd take it, how much he expected of me.

One of his hands found the hem of my shorts while the other one cupped the back of my neck. He pressed my head back so that when he bent down, his mouth found

165

mine at the perfect angle. Our lips pressed together and I knew he could feel the desire emanating from me in the same way I could feel it from him. It was apparent in the way he pressed himself toward me like he wanted to seal our bodies and inhabit the same airspace. In the way his tongue delved into my mouth, tasting me and demanding more.

His hand never left my neck as his other one drifted down the waistband of my shorts, beneath my underwear. The second his fingers trailed into new territory, I opened my mouth to him even more. I was completely at his mercy. He couldn't stop. I needed him to keep kissing me, to keep drifting his hand farther down.

I whimpered as his hand found my wetness. I couldn't believe this was happening. We were being so careless, but I was too helpless to stop him then. When he whispered my name against my ear and his finger sank into me, I collapsed back against the desk and let him work my body up into a tight ball of desire.

It didn't even take long. His fingers touching me were too much for my psyche to try to control, and soon I was coming. Hard. I was smart enough to stay quiet, but still a small whisper escaped my lips. He captured it with his mouth, sucking my bottom lip until I finally found the ground again.

He pushed off of me and I knew he was instantly regretting our carelessness, but I wasn't going to let him off yet. He'd taken care of me and I was sure as hell not leaving that room until I took care of him as well. I needed it as much as he did. So I pushed off the desk before he could get the chance to protest. I sank down to my knees and he inhaled a sharp breath.

"Kinsley, no."

I glanced up at him with a wicked gleam. "Yes."

His eyes flashed toward the door and I knew I was flinging myself into danger, but I couldn't stop. My desire didn't belong to me anymore. It belonged to him. It had belonged to him for longer than I cared to admit.

I pulled the hem of his workout shorts down, taking his briefs with them. I couldn't believe what I was about to do, *in his office*, but I wanted to. I wanted him to lose his mind. My fingers wrapped around the length of him, appreciating his size. I knew I'd enjoy it when we finally had sex.

"Kinsley, no," he was still trying to protest, but he was rock hard in my hands and I knew he wouldn't be able to find any more words when my mouth finally touched him.

I stroked up and down and glanced up, meeting his eyes just as I started to take him in my mouth. His eyes rolled back and he gripped the edge of the desk behind me.

"Fuck," he groaned, spurring me on so that I knew I had him. I kept running my hand up and down his smooth length in rhythm with my mouth. He was moments away from coming and I had to know what it looked like, what it felt like, to make Liam Wilder lose his mind.

I begged him to come with my mouth and hands, and then he was, so fast and so hard that I lost myself in the moment. Watching him come was the single hottest moment of my life and I wanted more. It was addicting, and if we didn't have practice soon, I knew we wouldn't have left his office all day.

He reached down and grabbed the back of my arms, lifting me to a standing position. Then he reached down to pull up his briefs and shorts.

"Kinsley, fuck Kinsley, that was the sexiest thing I've ever experienced, but you are in so much trouble. Do you realize what time it is?" I glanced at the clock behind him. It was 5:50 A.M., which meant Coach Davis and some of the girls were definitely in the field house.

I tried to look guilty or remorseful, but I wasn't. What was wrong with me? Did I need to get caught before I realized how serious this entire situation was?

Liam reached around me and grabbed a protein bar and my smoothie. "Here, you need to eat before practice." I wasn't hungry, but I took the items anyway.

Once his hands were empty, he tugged them through his hair and headed toward the door. He pressed his ear to it for a moment and then pulled it open.

I'd expected to see a group of people waiting for us with accusations in their eyes, but the hallway was empty.

He motioned for me to hurry, so I grabbed my cleats and water in my hands and was about to walk past him and out into the hallway when he grabbed my arm and pulled me back.

"I'm not playing around with you, Kinsley. I want to be with you," he whispered in my ear before releasing my arm. I stumbled into the hallway, trying to gather my wits.

What was I supposed to do now? Go wash my mouth out and get ready for practice? I could still feel him sliding his hand over my skin. I needed a nap and a cigarette. Too bad I didn't smoke.

Becca was the first person to see me standing there motionless in the hallway. Her eyes went wide. She grabbed my arm and pulled me into the locker room. I didn't say a word to her, but she knew what happened. She knew I'd tell her about it later.

She unwrapped the protein bar and untied my cleats like I was her little kid.

"Thanks, mom," I joked as I bent down to lace them

up.

"Dude, I *cannot* wait to hear about your morning," she whispered before pushing up off the ground and moving to finish getting ready herself.

That's when reality first sank in. What the fuck was I doing? We couldn't be so stupid as to think we could meet up in the field house again. I'd wanted to see him so badly— to prove there was something *real* between us— that I hadn't stopped to consider what would have happened if Coach Davis had walked into that office while I was on my knees.

I'd be cleaning out my locker right now and kissing my future goodbye.

Practice passed surprisingly quickly. We didn't split up into our positions, but Liam still stuck close to me. I'd get a drink of water and find him watching me, finish a drill and look up to see a heart stopping smile aimed right for me. That smile was quite a good motivator, but I couldn't push past the fear sinking into the back of my mind.

Just before he had to leave to head to the LA Stars' practice, he came to stand by me on the sidelines while I rested.

"Any regrets, Bryant?" he asked, crossing his arms and looking out onto the field. "About this morning?" I asked, keeping my eyes on the field.

"About us," he clarified.

I laughed nervously under my breath and shook my head. "Ask me that again in a few weeks," I said before jogging back into practice.

• • •

"You gave him a blow job!? When I was like two feet away

in the locker room?! EW!" Becca exclaimed when we were in my room later. Emily was downstairs eating dinner so she wasn't able to hear Becca squeal.

"Oh my god, keep your voice down," I warned, pointing to the door.

"Sorry, sorry. But seriously, was it hot? I've never given one, and I can't even imagine doing it to Liam Wilder. You should get access to an exclusive club or something."

I groaned. "Can we not highlight the fact that I'm now part of a *very* large group of women that have gone down on Liam Wilder?"

"Oh, crap. Yeah, I'm sure it was special to him though." She tried to recover from her slip up.

"Yeah, right." I rolled my eyes, recalling his words as I'd slipped past him into the hallway. "He said he wanted to be with me though, and he sounded really serious. I'm not sure what that means, but it felt good to hear after everything we'd just done." *Even if he didn't mean it.*

I really wanted him to mean it.

Becca nodded. "You should give him the benefit of the doubt. The media has painted this playboy image of him, but so far he seems like a surprisingly grounded guy."

"Wow, Becca. That was wise."

"Thanks, I feel smarter than usual today. Now can you tell me all of it again?"

She was referring to the events from that morning in Liam's office.

"No perv, go get your own secret affair."

She scrunched her nose. "Ugh! I haven't heard anything from Penn since Saturday. Not a peep!"

"Well does he have your number?"

"No..."

"Give it time. He's probably just as busy as Liam."

"So he's probably also getting blow jobs before practice?"

I gave her a pointed stare. "You know what I mean."

She laughed and then rolled off the bed. "I'm going to order pizza. Do you want some?"

"Yes please, you know how I like it," I answered, reaching for my laptop.

"With a side of Liam's coc—"

I cut her off. "Becca! That's just crude!"

She laughed the whole way out of the room.

Chapter Fourteen

As the rest of the week passed, I realized just how complicated our situation was. Liam couldn't come to my house and I couldn't go to his unless there was a party or something. We couldn't chance fooling around in his office again; we'd barely gotten away with that the first time. We couldn't go out to eat or really go anywhere in public because of the paparazzi.

As the rest of the week passed, I waited for the inevitable, *"this isn't worth it"* speech. He would have worded it perfectly, explaining that it wasn't me, it was the *situation*, but the idea still wore me down. I'd lay in bed at night, exhausted from practice, but I still couldn't fall asleep. I'd wonder what he was thinking, if he was moments away from sending the text that would break my heart.

I was getting ready for bed Friday night when he called.

"Come outside," he said as soon as I picked up.

I peered through my window but didn't see his car.

"I'm around the block so your teammates won't see me," he answered as if clarifying my train of thought.

"Okay, hold on, I'm in my pajamas," I explained, unable to wipe the giant smile off my face.

"You can stay in your pajamas..." he suggested, and I felt a shiver run down my spine.

"Pfft. Yeah, right. I'll be down in a second." I hung up and threw my phone on my bed.

"Becca!" I shouted, knowing she was down the hall watching an episode of Parks and Recreation. She had a love for Amy Poehler that was deeper than most normal human relationships.

A second later, she was standing outside my door. "What is it? Amy and I were bonding."

I gave her a pointed stare. "First. You are *not* on first name basis with Amy Poehler. She actually doesn't know you exist. Second, help me get ready." I paused and whispered the next part. "*Liam* is downstairs waiting for me."

"God, that's romantic," she mumbled, stepping into my room with her standard onesie on. This one had penguins and a hood with a penguin beak.

"Have I told you yet how awesome you are today?" I asked, stepping over toward my closet.

"Yeah, whatever. This penguin onesie is going to waste since Penn hasn't bothered to contact me."

"Want me to ask Liam about it?" I offered, throwing my pajamas off and grabbing a purple t-shirt dress that was soft from too many washes. I threw on some brown sandals and pulled a jacket out just in case it got cold in his car.

"Only if you can do it without him thinking I'm desperate. Just a casual mention, okay?" she asked, grabbing my bracelets off my night stand and bringing them to me.

"All right, I promise I'll make it seem casual."

She smiled. "You look like a bazillion dollars, but you didn't even need my help."

"You helped. I feel less nervous now," I promised.

"Don't let him keep you out too late. I want to go to the beach in the morning."

"Deal!" I shouted as I ran down the stairs. "Don't wait up for me though!"

Emily and a few of the sophomore girls were sitting in the living room watching a movie. They paused it as they saw me running down.

"Where are you going?" Emily asked just as five pairs of eyes swooped toward me and waited for an answer. I didn't want to lie to Emily, but I couldn't tell all of them the truth.

"Out with some high school friends that are in town. I'll be back in a bit," I answered without meeting Emily's eye.

The night air was cool, and I reveled in the crisp wind blowing strands of my long hair. It felt intoxicating, like even the weather knew how hard my heart was beating at the knowledge that I was about to be alone with Liam for the first time in five days. I spun around once to ensure that none of the girls were watching me from the windows. When I didn't see anyone, I picked up the pace and flew down the street before turning the corner.

Liam's black SUV came into sharp focus beneath a street lamp. His dark silhouette was barely visible inside.

In that moment, I felt truly criminal. I'd just lied to my friend, and now I was sneaking out late at night and checking behind me for witnesses.

I inhaled a shallow breath, pulled the door open, and hopped in quickly.

"This feels wrong. Should it feel wrong?" I asked, tossing my jacket onto the ground and peering over at him.

"No, it's not wrong," he clarified simply in his controlled tone, but he could tell I wanted more. "It only feels wrong because we're having to sneak around. We aren't breaking any laws and it's not like we have spouses that we're lying to."

"I'm lying to my friends, to my teammates," I brought up, wanting to push the subject. It felt good to have it out in the open. I wanted to know how he felt.

"I know. I am, too." Then he hesitated. "But to be honest, I'm not lying to everyone. Penn knows the truth. I mean it was pretty obvious when he saw you leaving my room at the party."

I'd already assumed Penn knew about us. He and Liam were close.

"Becca knows too obviously, but she can be trusted. She's my best friend on the team."

"What about Emily?" he asked.

I couldn't meet his eye. That was the one person I felt shitty about lying to. "No."

He reached over to clasp my hand. "We can end this. If this is too much, we can end it."

There it was. The sentence I'd feared the entire week.

"Do you want to end it? I mean, it's not like there's even anything to end."

"No," he answered quickly. "I want to keep seeing you. I *have* to keep seeing you, but I don't want you to feel like you don't get a choice in all of this."

I took a deep breath, inhaling his words and letting them wash out the last few days of doubt.

"You just like pretending to be a spy. You like sneaking around and waiting on dark streets for me." I turned toward him and gave him a playful wink.

"I'm not after you because it's a challenge, but I'd be lying if I said the sneaking around wasn't a little fun. That morning in my office will be burned in my memory as one of the hottest moments of my life."

I wanted to squeal at his confession, but instead I bit my lip and nodded to keep my excitement from brimming over.

"What do you want, Kinsley? Do you want to end this?" he asked.

What did I want?

"I want to have it all," I answered vaguely, staring out through his passenger side window for a moment.

I broke up the silence that followed by changing the support to something lighter. "Hey, I'm supposed to casually and *not* desperately bring up the Penn and Becca issue. Is he a player? Because seriously, there's no one cooler than Becca. She's funny and smart. And she's been a really good friend since I started the team."

Liam chuckled, "You have nothing to worry about. Penn's interested, but he's a reserved guy. He just got out of a serious relationship and I don't think he was expecting to meet someone like Becca so soon."

Ah, that explained a few things.

"Well, tell him to hurry up because Becca won't wait forever."

He smirked and leaned closer. "Are those her words or yours?"

"Mine. She'd kill me if she knew I was telling you all of this. I was supposed to be really subtle about it."

Liam reached over and ran his hand behind the back

of my neck. "I'll mention it to Penn and see what he thinks."

I nodded as his fingers started to dip beneath the hem of my dress and drag along the top of my spine.

"What about you, Kinsley?" he asked, tilting his head toward me a few inches. "Are you going to wait for me?"

He made himself seem vulnerable asking a question like that. It was so un-Liam like; he exuded confidence and control, even the way that he held my neck felt like a dominant touch. But, he was hanging on a ledge waiting for me to answer that question and I let myself relish the moment.

"Do you think you're worth waiting for?"

What a loaded question. Liam and I were playing house. We were living in lala land where no one else existed but us.

"I think *you're* worth it, and that's all that matters. Hang in there with me through this craziness and then we'll be together openly. I promise."

I nodded. "Okay."

"Okay?" he asked, dipping his head toward me. His scent took over my senses. I leaned forward over the console and we met somewhere in the middle, pressing into each other until he finally looped his arms around my waist and dragged me on top of him.

"Is that your gear shift or are you just excited to see me?" It was a corny joke, but I couldn't resist.

Liam squeezed his eyes shut and laughed despite the cheesiness factor. "I am *definitely* excited to see you. Especially in this dress," he answered as both of our gazes fell to his hands on my thighs. I was straddling his lap, my knee was jamming into his seatbelt buckle and my other leg was sandwiched between the door, but I couldn't feel the

177

discomfort of the space when his hands were on my legs, slowly drifting upwards.

"It's like they didn't know people would be using the front seat for hardcore make out sessions. They could have at least added a little more leg room," I smiled.

The edge of Liam's mouth tilted up in a confident smirk. "Weird. When I was purchasing a car I didn't take into account the amount of make out space afforded by the front seat. I should have asked the salesman to climb on my lap during the test drive."

He was being playful, yet the whole time his hands were moving seductively over my skin.

"I like your dress," he complimented as his hands drifted upward. A shiver ran through me and Liam noticed.

"I've had it forever. It's probably too short now, but oh well."

"I like the length," he noted as his fingers found the edge of my underwear. It felt strange to be having a conversation as my breathing quickened and Liam's eyes dilated and shifted toward a dark smoldering grey.

My cell phone rang from the passenger seat, but we both ignored it. He tilted his head toward me and gently skimmed his lips along mine. It wasn't a kiss, it was an invitation. He wanted me to make the first move, so I pressed against him, the force of my kiss pushing his head back against the seat. He moaned just loud enough to drive me crazy. I pushed my hands under his shirt feeling hard, coiled muscles beneath my touch. I'd never been with a guy like Liam. He made Josh and Trey look like boy scouts. My hands kept drifting higher over his abs and I could feel his chest tightening in response to my touch. I loved it.

Then my cell phone rang again and I broke the kiss with a heavy sigh.

"What the hell?" I reached over and grabbed my phone. **BECCA** flashed across the screen and I instantly stilled.

"What's up?" I asked as soon as the call connected.

"Jeez! Answer your phone quicker, lady. Are you guys still outside? You need to move or duck or something. I just saw Tara leaving the house a second ago. She walked past my window, but I'm not sure where she went after that. Maybe she got into a car or something."

"Crap," I said, quickly scrambling off Liam's lap and sliding down in the passenger seat so that my head barely met the base of the window. "Do you think she saw me leaving?"

"I have no clue, but you need to be more careful. This isn't a game." I know she was watching out for me, but her warning made me mad.

"I'll be back in a second," I answered, and then ended the call abruptly.

"What's going on?" Liam asked with concern. His eyebrows were drawn together and his brooding expression was back.

I explained what Becca had just told me.

"I haven't seen her," he answered, quickly glancing around his car.

"Well, we were *occupied*. She could have already walked by. Shit," I mumbled, trying to stay calm. Becca's words kept replaying in my mind. *This isn't a game. This isn't a game.* She was right, so why couldn't I bring myself to stop playing?

"It'll be okay, Kinsley. I'm sure we're overreacting. There's no way she followed you. No one is that insane."

I nodded but stayed silent. Was this worth it? Was the anxiety worth the ten minutes that I could sneak into Liam's car and be with him? What kind of relationship is that?

But then I glanced toward him. He was facing me, his hands were clenched into fists, and everything about him was wound tight. He was absolutely breathtaking with the streetlight seeping in through the window behind him. I could just barely make out his smooth jaw, the disheveled hair, the piercing eyes. I realized in that moment that I was helpless in deciding my fate. There wasn't a single cell in my body that would let me walk away from Liam Wilder without a fight.

Even if I ended up fighting myself.

"I'd better go," I mumbled.

He nodded and I could see his jaw tick back and forth. "Are you okay? I can walk you back?" I knew the situation was killing him as much as it was killing me. What kind of guy wanted to take a girl on a *date* in his car and then watch her walk home by herself?

"You'd better not," I said, shaking my head.

"I'm going to drive by in a minute to make sure you got inside okay," he stated. I knew he thought I was upset with him still.

I pushed off my seat and leaned forward to give him a goodbye kiss. It caught him off guard at first. Maybe he wasn't expecting one. My lips pressed against his and then in an instant his hands were in my hair, my hands were gripping his neck, and we were both ensuring the other didn't pull away. We poured all of our worry and angst into the kiss. His tongue demanded entrance and I tilted my head to get a better angle. He sucked my bottom lip into his mouth until I whimpered and kissed him harder.

When I pulled back my lips felt swollen and tender. We stared at each other, our desire written across our faces, but neither of us said a word.

It felt like I needed to say something, something to confess how I felt for him, but we both knew. It was apparent in everything we did.

"I want to tell you I like you, but that seems dumb, like it's not enough," I admitted before turning toward the handle of the car.

Liam reached over and touched my hand to stop me. "I know," then he paused, thinking it over, and repeated his words, "I know."

• • •

The rest of the weekend passed quickly. Liam had a photo shoot in New York so Emily, Becca, and I stuck close together. We went to the beach Saturday morning with a few other girls from the team. Everyone laid their towels in a row and pulled out a magazine or book. Becca was the only one brave enough to test the waters. I stood on the shoreline, dipping my feet and ankles into the icy water.

Josh texted me a few times over the weekend. I never responded to any of them because I knew that he wouldn't move on if I didn't nip it in the bud. I'd tried to be nice to him in the beginning, but the longer he tried to win me back, the more I realized I couldn't give him an inch or he'd take a mile.

Saturday night Becca got a text from Penn.

It was the holy grail of texts. We squealed over it for twenty minutes before realizing that she had to formulate a response back to him. He was taking it slow and steady, asking her about her day and how her week of practice had been. I'd explained his situation, that he'd just left a long-term relationship, and Becca seemed more than happy to take it slow.

After twenty minutes of pleasantries, he invited us to a get-together at his house the following weekend.

Cue another half hour of squeals highlighted by a few crazy somersaults from Becca that resulted in her knocking my lamp off my bedside table. Luckily, the glass didn't break.

"I feel like I'm getting my hopes up about him," she said as she placed the lamp back on my nightstand.

What an understatement. She was definitely getting her hopes up, but it was too late to change that.

"You're allowed to be excited, but I'm glad you know that things with him will have to go slow."

She nodded. "I need to keep reminding myself that he just got out of a long-term relationship and doesn't need me complicating things."

"He wouldn't be texting you and inviting you to his house if he thought you were complicating things. Just take it easy and we'll figure it out. He seems like a really good guy though."

"What if he just wants sex?"

"Then you have sex with him and lose your virginity to one of the hottest professional soccer players in the country," I laughed. "But no, seriously, we'll figure it out. I'll try and get more intel from Liam. On the bright side, if he just got out of a relationship that means he's capable of commitment."

"Should I Google his ex?" she asked, already leaning toward my laptop.

"No! Don't search crap like that. It's not fair to them or us. I've wanted to Google Liam a million times, but I know how much he hates when the media makes up fake stories about his life. He'd be so pissed if I was getting my information about him through TMZ."

"Okay, okay. You have a point. I'll treat Penn like he's a normal person... for now."

"Good, *Peen* is a normal person."

That earned me a pillow smack.

Later that night, just as I was about to fall asleep, Liam texted me.

Liam: Finally home from New York.

Kinsley: Welcome home! Bring me anything? ;)

Liam: I had a miniature Empire State Building but this little kid stole it in the airport lounge and I felt guilty about taking it back.

Kinsley: Are you serious?

Liam: Yeah, so some kid is walking around with your gift.

Kinsley: Haha, oh well... Are you glad to be home at least?

Liam: Yeah, it was a long trip. All work and no play.

Kinsley: I can't relate. I lounged around on the beach all day.

Liam: Show me some proof...

I smiled down at his text, trying to decipher if he was being serious or not. Either way, I decided it wouldn't hurt to remind him of what he was missing while he'd been away in New York. I pulled my shirt up while I laid in bed and then tugged my sleeping shorts down a bit so that he could see my tan torso and the curve of my hip bones. It was just enough to get his imagination going without showing anything too risqué. I skimmed the top of my shorts with my fingers and snapped the picture with the other hand.

I attached the photo with a message that said, "Can you see the tan line from my bathing suit bottom?"

Not two seconds later, my phone rang in my hand and his name flashed across the screen.

"It's late, Liam," I teased after answering the call.

"I don't care. Are you alone?"

My room was pitch black and I couldn't hear anything in the hallway. I glanced over toward the bathroom to see the light off, so Emily was already asleep.

"Yes, everyone is asleep."

"I wish I was there right now."

I hummed into the phone. "Oh really? And what would you do if you were here?" I asked, trying to play the role of the seducer.

"I'd put my hand exactly where yours was in that photo," he began, and without thinking, I put my hand back where I had it, letting it rest on the hem of my thin sleeping shorts.

"And then?" I asked, hearing the evidence of lust in my voice.

"I'd skim my finger on top of your shorts, dipping it gently inside to feel the soft skin underneath." My finger followed his trail. "And then I'd tug your pants and underwear down and toss them to the side."

"You're not wasting any time," I murmured, fingering the top of my shorts before pushing them down my long legs.

He chuckled dark and low. "You wouldn't mind. You'd beg me to speed up."

"Mmm," I hummed, stroking my fingers back and

forth along the seam of my panties before gently pushing them aside.

"Kinsley, I want you to touch yourself."

I inhaled sharply and let my fingers drift lower, along the sensitive skin of my upper thigh.

"Maybe I already am."

I could hear his slow smirk through the phone when he hummed in approval. "Stroke yourself like I would if I was there." His tone was dark and more seductive than I'd ever experienced. I'd never been bold enough to do something like that while someone listened, but I didn't hesitate for one moment.

I let my fingers glide between my thighs, stroking slow at first, and then faster and faster as he spoke dirty thoughts through the phone.

"I wish I could feel how wet you are right now."

His heavy breaths spilled through the phone and I sped up my pace even more. I dipped my finger inside and pulled my wetness up toward my bundle of nerves, reveling in the sexy moment.

"I'm so close, Liam," I admitted with a weak voice.

"I bet you taste so sweet, baby. I'd slide my fingers in and out, and then lean down and taste you for myself."

"*Liam...*"

"Come for me, baby. Let me hear you."

I stroked faster, arching my back and feeling the beginning of tingles spread through my body.

"I can't wait to sink into you, Kinsley. Promise me you'll spread those thighs wide for me."

Those sexy words pushed me over the edge and I lost myself in the bliss of the moment. It rolled through me in a seductive wave and I liked knowing he could hear my moans. I purposely made sure he knew just how much I was enjoying my orgasm.

When I stopped shaking, Liam spoke, "Fuck, baby, I loved listening to that."

I tugged a pillow to my chest and smiled up at the dark ceiling, suddenly feeling embarrassed for getting so carried away.

"I'll see you tomorrow, *coach*."

I hung up the phone before he could answer and squeezed my eyes shut. My phone buzzed in my hand and I looked down to see he'd sent one last text.

Liam: Don't make any plans for tomorrow night.

Liam Wilder brought out a side of me that no guy had seen before. It was a little wild and a little reckless, but with him, there was no other option.

Chapter Fifteen

Monday morning I was positively giddy on my way to practice. Becca and Emily said that I looked loony, but I ignored them.

"It's just a beautiful day!" I joked, pulling my car into my normal spot at the fields. Since Liam got back from New York the night before, he'd be at practice. We had plans to meet up later, but I wasn't sure where we were going yet.

"You're so annoying," Becca laughed, sliding out of the passenger seat. As soon as her feet hit the pavement, she paused and I watched her smile fall.

"What's wrong?" I asked, leaning forward to see around her. From my seat I couldn't see what she was staring at, so I quickly hopped out of the car and ran around to find a sight that made me tighten my fists.

Josh was waiting for me at the front of the field house with a bouquet of flowers and a giant sign that said, "I'm sorry, Kinsley".

"Oh my god," I murmured under my breath. This was not appropriate. One glance around the packed parking lot and I knew that everyone on my team, my coaches, and Liam had already seen him. I couldn't believe he was doing this.

I walked straight up to him, trying to stay calm. He smiled wide when he saw me approaching and for a very, very brief moment I felt pity for him… but then I remembered the Bimbo naked on his bed.

"Josh, what are you doing here?" I asked with a tired tone.

He unraveled a lopsided grin. "Isn't it kind of obvious?" he joked, pointing to the "I'm sorry" sign.

I nodded slowly, trying to conjure up the right words. Emily and Becca walked past me into the soccer field house but I couldn't look at them. I wished Josh knew me enough to realize that something like this was truly embarrassing for me. I wasn't a public person. I didn't want my entire team knowing the sordid details of our relationship. This was too much, and if anything, it pushed me away even more.

"Josh, you can't do this. We're not together and it's for a very good reason. I freaking swear that I'm not trying to be coy and lead you on. I mean it when I say that we aren't getting back together. You have to leave me alone."

His face fell slightly and his dark brown eyes studied me with curiosity.

"You don't give up on things that matter to you, Kinsley. That's not the way love works," he said, pushing the flowers into my hand and heading toward his car.

I wanted to shout after him, to tell him he didn't know how love worked, that you don't cheat on someone that you love, but I just pushed through the field house doors and headed to practice.

My worst fear would be realizing that love actually *did* mean what Josh thought it meant: you could do whatever you wanted to your partner as long as you said you were sorry and looked charming while you said it. Nope. I respected myself too much for that.

I dropped his flowers in the locker room just as I realized that I needed to find Liam. I had no clue if he'd seen Josh's display, but if the situation were reversed, I would have hated seeing his ex-girlfriend standing there waiting for him. I didn't want him to misread the situation.

I didn't get the chance to see him until we lined up outside for drills. I purposely stood on the end so that if he wanted to, he could talk to me. When I smelled his body wash behind me, I sighed. At least he wasn't so angry that he was going to ignore me.

"Are you okay?" he asked, taking me by surprise.

"I'm fine. I'm sorry that happened," I began just as one of the junior girls inched closer to me. Her innocent action didn't go unnoticed and I realized I had to guard my speech.

"That was really *unprofessional*," I said, looking up at him and pleading with him to understand my veiled words. His eyes weren't angry or brooding, instead he was studying me with a wistful smile.

"I'm not afraid of a little competition, Kinsley," he whispered. "I play to win."

A smile spread across my lips, but I did my best to hide it. He moved behind me, heading toward Coach Davis to help her with drills, but his hand skipped along the base of my back as he walked by. The casual touch made goose bumps bloom across my body, and I knew I was making the right decision. Liam could disarm me with a single touch, and I'd never felt that way about either Trey or Josh. I was officially in over my head.

Once I'd showered and changed after practice, I laid back on my bed and checked my phone. There was a text message from Liam that I decided to check first.

Liam: I'll pick you up around 7. Don't eat dinner.

I texted him back right away.

Kinsley: Any hints? What should I wear?
Liam: Pajamas.

I laughed and swapped screens to check the missed call and voicemail I also had waiting for me.

"Hello Kinsley. This is Brian King. We spoke in Coach Davis' office last week about a potential interview opportunity for you. I know this is last minute, but I've been called away to Europe and my editor would really like this interview set up before I leave. That puts you in a tight spot, but if there's any way I could convince you, would you be willing to meet me for the interview after you're done with practice on Wednesday? I realize this is very late notice, but unfortunately the magazine has left me with very few options. We could meet at a coffee shop in West Hollywood. I'll be coming from downtown LA. Also, I've sent Coach Davis a list of possible interview questions that you can run through with her. Let me know what you think."

The voicemail cut off and I was left momentarily stunned. I hadn't thought about Brian's offer in a few days and now I was suddenly forced to decide one way or the other ASAP. I wasn't 100% sold on putting my personal life out there for everyone to see, but if I looked over the interview questions and thought they seemed okay, I'd agree to the interview. Brian seemed like a nice person, and I didn't want him to get in trouble with his editor if I turned down the interview.

I glanced down at my phone and hit "call" before I even fully realized what I was doing.

"Hi Brian, this is Kinsley."

"Kinsley! Hi," he answered, shuffling papers.

"I listened to your message and I think I'd be able to meet with you on Wednesday. I could be in West Hollywood around 5:00 P.M.?"

"That's great. 5:00 P.M. works for me as well. I know this is hardly any notice, but it will be a short interview, mainly about your position at ULA and your training for the Olympic tryouts. If our readers enjoy it, we'll do a more in depth interview in a few weeks. That is, if you agree to it."

I laughed politely. "Let's get through this one first. Could you forward me the interview questions you sent to Coach Davis?"

"Sure thing. I'll also text you the address to a coffee shop where we can meet."

I rattled off my email and thanked him for his time. I had a good feeling about the article. I still had no clue what to expect, but at least I'd have the questions beforehand.

As soon as I hung up, I called my mom and filled her in. She promised she'd run through the questions with me tomorrow after practice, just to make sure I didn't make a fool out of myself.

Five minutes before 7:00 P.M., Liam texted me that he was waiting around the corner. I hopped off my bed and threw on a jacket and my Converse. Then I shouted bye to Becca on my way down the stairs. I rounded the corner at top speed, jumped into Liam's car, and planted a kiss right on his mouth before I'd even realized my shoes were untied and I'd put my jacket on inside out. Details.

"Well hello there," he laughed against my lips after I pulled away to catch my breath.

"Hi," I murmured, then sat back and adjusted myself in my seat.

"That was a good greeting."

I smiled and shrugged. "I was just excited to see you, I guess. Where are we going?"

"It's a surprise," he answered, putting the car in drive and heading away from my house.

"Ah, fine, but I wore my pajamas. I couldn't tell if you were kidding, but I decided I'd take you up on the offer anyway." I unzipped my jacket to show him my faded "Made in the '90s" shirt that was on its last leg and my sleeping shorts.

"I wasn't bluffing. You'll be glad you wore them."

I smiled and watched him drive. I had no clue where he was leading me, but the uncertainty was half the fun.

"I think I'm doing my first interview on Wednesday," I mentioned as he exited the highway.

"Really? With who?"

"Brian King. I met him the other day with Coach Davis."

"Ah, I know Brian. He's a decent guy." His eyes were focused on the road and I couldn't tell if there was more he wanted to say about the subject.

"Have you ever done an interview with him?"

"No. We played soccer together for a year, though."

I didn't have time to ask more, because Liam was pulling into a small Drive-in Movie Theater. Who knew they even existed in LA still?

"I figured since going to the movies is out of the question, we could at least sneak into a drive in movie and pretend like it's a real date," Liam explained with an earnest expression.

A giant smile spread across my lips. "It's an awesome date. I'm in pajamas… it doesn't get better than that."

He laughed at my joke as he pulled his SUV into one of the middle parking spots. It was a small theater with room for twenty or thirty cars at most. It was filling up fast around us and I knew we'd gotten there just in time.

"How will we watch the movie if the screen is behind us?" I asked, twisting my head to look through the back window.

He smirked and hopped out. "C'mon, we're sitting in the trunk."

I had no choice but to follow him to the back of the car, and when he lifted the back latch, I was glad I did. He'd set up a picnic of sorts. Well a picnic made up mostly of candy, does that count? He had it all lined up perfectly. Twizzlers, Skittles, Sour Patch Kids, Snickers, Butterfingers, and M&Ms… to name a few. There was a little cooler of drinks pushed off the side next to a tub of popcorn that he'd put a lid on for our drive over.

"Did you raid a small candy village to get all of this stuff?"

He smirked. "I have a sweet tooth. It's my one flaw."

I rolled my eyes and shoved his arm playfully.

"I think they're showing Sixteen Candles tonight. I've never seen it," he said.

I gasped. "What! How have you not seen it? It's on TV like once a week.

He shrugged. "Okay, so I have *two* flaws."

I smiled. "I can't believe you did all of this."

"I hate not being able to take you on real dates, so I wanted to make it special," he admitted, then followed with, "I also just really like candy."

He flashed me a wicked grin and helped me up into the back of the car. Once we'd stuffed our faces, we pushed the food and drinks to the side and laid down on the blanket Liam had brought.

Somehow we ended up shifting around until he was leaning against the back seat and I was leaning back on his chest with his legs on either side of me. Okay, it wasn't exactly an accident; I kept shifting back until he pretty much had to accommodate my body in his space. Oh, oops, how'd we get into this adorable position? *Strategic planning, my friends.*

His arms were wrapped around me, holding the blanket in place. As easy as it would have been to turn around, kiss him, and forget about the rest of the movie, I really enjoyed just sitting there together. It felt good to feel his chest rising and falling against my back.

Every now and then he'd ask me if I was comfortable or if I needed a drink, but I just shook my head, not wanting him to move a muscle for fear that the magic would be lost.

Chapter Sixteen

The blissful feeling of lying in Liam's arms was long and forgotten when I woke up to someone ripping the blankets off my bed Tuesday morning.

Tara's voice invaded my consciousness.

"Get up and get dressed. You, Becca, and Emily have a special job this morning."

What the hell? Was I going to have to start barricading my door every night to ensure she couldn't Edward Cullen me? It probably wouldn't work; she'd just climb in through my window like the angsty vampire did.

I groaned and sat up, trying to blink away my sleep. Tara was joined by Sofie and another one of her evil henchmen. They all stared down at me with cunning smiles that made me wish I slept with a rifle beneath my pillow like an old southern veteran.

"Get up," Tara ordered again.

Her tone was wearing on me, not to mention I thought we were moving beyond the whole high school bully situation. It seemed like she'd maxed out her asshole card, but apparently she needed another shot of evil to tide her over for a few more days.

Were we positive that she didn't have any serial killer relatives?

I pushed myself off the bed and moved toward my dresser without saying a word.

"Meet us downstairs when you're ready, Bryant," Sofie muttered before she burst through the bathroom door to get to Emily's room. I cringed when I heard them yell Emily's name to wake her up.

As I pulled on my workout gear, I dreamt about bringing the hazing issue up to Coach Davis, but I still wasn't sure it was worth it. Everything would change if I ratted out the seniors. They'd make my life living hell, but they'd do it more subtly and twice as vicious as they already were. If I was going to tell Coach Davis, I had to be sure that it was worth the trouble.

So I made myself a deal. Today would be the last day. If they weren't done after whatever they had planned for us this morning, then I'd bring the issue up to Coach Davis.

Becca, Emily, and I were shuffled into the back seat of Sofie's car in silence while the rest of the underclassmen were still asleep in the house. This was the second time they'd gone after the three of us, and I wasn't dumb enough to think it was a coincidence. I guess Tara really did hate me.

The last time I'd been in Sofie's car was on my nineteenth birthday. I knew Tara wasn't going to be my friend that night, but I'd had no clue just how crazy she would actually turn out to be. If I could have gone back in time, I would have warned former-me to get the hell away from Tara as soon as possible... and maybe also to warn my

Mom away from the front-bang trend. They don't work for everyone!

There was a sense of dread lingering in the air as we headed to the field with the seniors. Tara had said they had a "special job" for us, but they couldn't *really* do anything to us, right? I mean if they even came close to breaking the law, I'd go to the police immediately. I wasn't about to start digging graves for all of her victims.

"Since you three were so compliant this morning, I think we'll go easier on you than we were planning to," Tara said with a foreboding smile.

Oh, how *sweet* of her, I thought, staring out the window and wishing the day was already over.

When we got to the practice field, Sofie parked the car and the three of us scrambled out of the back seat.

"All right, rookies. Today we thought you three should learn the art of hygiene," Tara began, pulling three unopened toothbrushes out of her purse.

What was she talking about?

"Those field house bathrooms could be a *lot* cleaner," she continued, handing us each a toothbrush. "So we'd like each of you to clean a stall, and then when that's done, you can tackle the bathroom floor."

Becca groaned. "I'm sorry, do you think you can get away with this? The costumes were funny, ha-ha. You had your fun, but this is ridiculous and you know it."

Emily just stood there gaping, like she couldn't believe the circumstances she'd stumbled into. I felt guilt hit my stomach. She wouldn't be here if it wasn't for me.

"Becca is right. I'm not doing this. You guys have watched too many 90's movies," I said, tossing the toothbrush to the ground. Tara could kiss my ass.

Tara's gaze traveled from the toothbrush sitting on the

ground, slowly up to my eyes. The sardonic grin eclipsing her features was a warning of things to come.

"Come talk to me for a second, *Bryant*," Tara said, wagging her finger and turning to walk away so we could talk in private. I followed after her, mainly so I could tell her how crazy she was without being overheard by anyone else, but the next thing out of her mouth stopped me dead in my tracks.

"If you don't pick that toothbrush up and follow my orders as your *captain*, I'll have no choice but to go to Coach Davis with some disturbing news."

I rolled my eyes. "What are you talking about, Tara?"

She ran her finger back and forth across her lips, and in that moment, I realized how truly cold-hearted she actually was.

"Let me tell you what I'd be *forced* to tell Coach Davis," she began, making sure to keep her voice soft enough that no one could overhear her, "I went to a party the other night and saw both you and Liam there. That wasn't a big deal considering it was an LA Stars party, but then to my *horror*, I saw the two of you go into his room, and when you came out it was *very* clear that the two of had been having sex. Now, because I'm not sure how intelligent you are concerning this matter, I'll spell it out for you." I bristled at her harsh tone. "Liam makes most of his money from endorsement deals— Endorsement deals that are completely contingent on his public image. The LA Stars might not drop him, but you better believe those companies wouldn't want him as a liability. He was supposed to be volunteering not trying to get laid. And you, our sweet little rookie, would be kicked off the ULA team so fast you wouldn't even have time to clean out your locker. Coach Davis made it perfectly clear that any relationship between a coach and a team member was off-limits."

In case that wasn't enough, she just kept adding layers of icing to the cake as the blood drained from my face.

"Can you even imagine the headlines they'll run? LA Stars player takes advantage of ULA freshman…"

I stood there, gaping and trying to piece together just how conniving one person could be.

"Oh, and I have quite a few witnesses that can back up my claim. I mean, how stupid could you be to have sex at a freaking LA Stars party? Really, Kinsley, you made it all just too easy."

I looked up into her narrowed eyes. "You're such a bitch."

Her smile told me she took that as a compliment. "I hope you like cleaning toilets, Bryant," she said before turning on her heel and heading back to the group. I didn't say a word. There was nothing to say. In that moment, Tara held all the cards. But soon the tables would shift. I wasn't going to let her get away with it. There was a way to beat her at her own game, but not until I had time to think over my options. With my chin raised, I walked back over, bent down, grabbed the toothbrush off the concrete, and headed to the bathroom without a word.

When Emily and Becca followed me after a moment, their gazes bored into the side of my head.

"I'm really sorry, guys," I muttered, opening the toothbrush. This was freaking ridiculous. How did Tara have time in her day to mastermind shit like this?

"It's not your fault," Emily answered with a frown. Poor Emily, she had no clue what I'd brought her into.

Becca caught my eye and I sighed. "I'll explain it later," I mouthed, and she nodded solemnly.

It was the worst morning of my life and it was hardly 5:00 A.M. I reluctantly tore open my toothbrush and got to work in the bathroom, letting my mind wander toward ways of torturing Tara to death. I was thinking that old fashion method where the four horses pull your body apart would fit nicely for her.

To ensure that we were actually cleaning, Tara would check up on us every few minutes. She'd poke their head in, mutter a snide comment, and then leave again. After what felt like hours, she finally came in and told us to stop.

"That's enough. We're going to go run some laps before practice."

The three of us followed behind her and I could hear Emily sniffling behind her. Tara was making her cry. *I* was making her cry.

"Emily, it's okay. I'll run for you like last time."

Tara laughed. "No, Bryant, I think you three should all run. I think your friends should realize how selfish you really are."

The word selfish struck a chord as Emily's tears ran down her cheeks. Was I being selfish for pursuing a relationship with Liam? I didn't think it would hurt anyone.

Tara might have disliked me before, but the fact that I had some kind of relationship with Liam pushed me toward the top of her enemy list. Unfortunately, my friendships with Becca and Emily meant they were getting dragged alongside me.

"I'm so sorry, guys," I pleaded as we began to run. Emily wouldn't look at me, but Becca shot me a stern look.

"Do not apologize for anything. It's Tara that should be apologizing. She's trying to ruin your life by turning us against you, but she has no clue the kind of enemies she's making," Becca bit out.

"We have to be smart about this. We can get her to stop, but if we go about it the wrong way, we'll be taking ourselves down with her," I answered.

"Kinsley, I know about Liam," Emily said out of the blue.

Becca and I both turned sharply toward her. "What are you talking about?" I asked.

"We share a bathroom, and you and Becca seriously talk way too loudly about personal matters. Like I know that you made Becca come look at a freckle on your butt last week because you thought it was shaped like a giraffe. I mean, I get it. You guys have a really strange relationship." She realized she was veering off topic. "Oh, right. Anyway, no one else in the house knows about you and Liam, I've made sure of it, but I just wanted to let you know that I know," she shrugged.

I had no clue how to approach the subject. "Are you upset that I didn't tell you? I'm really sorry I lied to you, Em. I just wanted to keep it as private as possible, and I didn't want to drag you in as an accomplice."

Emily furrowed her brows. "I'm not mad. I know why you didn't tell me. I just felt a little left out. To be honest I was kind of glad not to be included in the beginning because I would have told you it was a beyond terrible idea."

I cracked a small smile. "And now?"

"Still a terrible idea, but I can't blame you. If he were interested in any of the rest of us, we would have done exactly what you're doing. You're just the lucky... or maybe unlucky one."

Relief settled over our small group. It felt good to have my secret out in the open and I trusted Emily not to tell anyone.

"I swear this is the last time guys. I feel disgusting from washing the bathroom. We'll take her down. We just need to figure out how..."

The three of us were focusing on pushups when I heard Liam's harsh tone ring through the air.

"Tara, I thought I warned you about this last time? What the hell do you not understand about treating your teammates with respect?"

I paused mid push-up to see Tara turn to him with a conniving grin.

"Liam! Just the man of the hour..."

It didn't escape my notice that she called him Liam instead of Coach Wilder. She was proving how in charge she was in that moment. She held all of our fates in the palm of her pretty little hand.

"Excuse me?" Liam asked, standing to his full height. He looked lethal. He'd never looked at me the way he was looking at Tara. Unabashed rage masked his beautiful features, and for one moment I was scared something very bad was about to happen. I tried to shoot him a weary gaze that could somehow sum up how fucked we were now that Tara knew about us.

"We've got to go get ready for practice. Excuse me," Tara said, waving sweetly and walking away without bothering to answer him.

Liam eye's followed her movements for a moment and then tugged his hands through his hair. He looked helpless and in a sense, he was. Going to Coach Davis was his only option.

Would he do that?

If he did, would Tara tell Coach Davis about our

relationship?

"Are you guys okay?" Liam asked, bending down to where we were all sitting.

Emily nodded, but stayed silent.

"Oh yeah! We had a *wonderful* morning. I'll let Kinsley fill you in though," Becca said as she pushed up off the ground with Emily so they could head into the field house after the seniors.

"Kinsley, why the hell are you letting her treat you like this? I'm taking this to Coach Davis."

The last sentence spurred me into action.

"She knows," I began, but I could hardly get the words out through the emotion building behind my eyes. I was in way over my head and I couldn't see which way was up anymore.

Liam nodded, slowly grasping the seriousness of the situation. His hand reached down for mine so that he could help me up just as Coach Davis pulled into her parking spot. She hopped out of her car and eyed us warily for a moment before heading inside. Just fucking great. Her suspicion was the last thing we needed.

"I've got to go to practice. We'll talk later," I promised, turning on my heel and running inside before he could say anything else.

Our relationship was poison for my career. The media would spin us into whatever sold the most magazines and "happy soccer couple" wouldn't sell shit compared to a soccer bad boy going after a naïve girl that he was supposed to be *coaching* at the time.

We were royally screwed.

• • •

Liam: Is everything okay? Can you meet me tomorrow before practice? Call me.

"You're going to talk to him, right?" Becca asked after having read the text over my shoulder. We were in my room later that night trying to come up with a plan on how to handle Tara.

"Yes. Of course. I just need to think about it for a second. If I go to Coach Davis myself she'll pull Tara into the office and Tara will throw Liam and me under the bus. But if I tell Liam, maybe he'll have a better plan?" I chewed on my bottom lip like I'd been doing all afternoon.

"I think you should tell Liam because he has the right to know about what's going on."

"Yes, god, I know that. I just don't want to get him involved if I don't have to. He has enough on his plate without adding this, too."

"What about you?" Becca pointed out. "You have just as much on your plate."

She had a point, but then I glanced at my clock. 11:00 P.M. Too late for a phone call considering I had practice at 6:00 A.M. the next day, right? That's what I told myself.

Kinsley: Yes, but we shouldn't meet before practice. Don't want to be suspicious.
Liam: What about after?
Kinsley: I have that interview.

He didn't bother texting back. A moment later, his number illuminated my screen and I panicked. I swiped my finger across the screen and flew into my closet, shutting the door behind me. I felt like a secret agent. Albeit a very amateur one.

"Hello?" I asked, not even bothering to turn the closet light on.

"Kinsley, tell me what's going on. How did Tara find out?" He sounded tired.

I sank down onto the carpet and pushed back behind the clothes so that they fell in front of me like a curtain.

"She and a few other people saw us go into your room at one of your parties and she said it was clear we'd just had sex. Coach Davis told me to stay away from you and I didn't listen."

Liam didn't speak right away. I could hear his steady breathing and then he finally groaned. "I've dealt with assholes before, but she's cunning."

"Yeah, well you can tell her how 'cunning' she is when we're both kicked off our teams."

"I won't let that happen, Kinsley. Tara is the not the end-all be-all. She can't do shit to me, and I won't let her touch your career. Let's just cover our bases at practice. Act normal and try to deal with Tara's shit for a few more days. I'll get everything figured out."

I nodded in the darkness.

"Sounds good, Coach."

He laughed. "I'm sorry our relationship is such a fucked-up mess."

"Hey! It's *our* fucked-up mess, okay?" I joked.

"Do you remember when I asked if you regretted us?" he asked.

I smiled at the memory. "Yes. I said I'd let you know in a few weeks."

"Have you made your mind up?"

Of course, I'd made up my mind. I didn't regret us for a single moment— not even when my hand had slipped into some *questionable fluids* in the field house bathroom that morning.

"Nah. I think I need a few more weeks to think about it still."

"You're just stringing me along, Kins."

I laughed. "Gotta keep you on your toes." Then I thought of something that had been bothering me all day.

"You know, I don't really understand what Tara has to gain from all of this. I'd understand if I was vying for her position or something, but I'm not. She made Emily cry today."

He sighed. "She hit on me last year at a party. Well, she did it a few times, but she finally came straight out and laid her invitation on the table. Obviously, I turned her down. I don't know if she's still pissed about that or not."

"Ew. Ew. Ew. I do not want to picture you and Tara together."

"There was no *together*."

"She's like the villain in a Disney movie."

He laughed. "Worse."

I smiled for the fiftieth time since I'd answered his phone call, which brought my grand total of smiles for the day to fifty-one, because I was smiling then thinking about smiling.

"Can we talk about something else before I go to bed? I don't want to dream about her."

"My mom is visiting in a few weeks," he said.

"Oh really? Where does she live?"

"England. My dad relocated for work when I was young."

"Ah."

"She is coming in for one of my games. I'd like you to meet her."

I sucked in a breath of air. "Oh god, that was your way of calming me down before bed? Casually dropping the fact that I'll have to impress your mom in a few weeks?" I laughed.

"My mom is awesome and laid-back. You don't have to earn her approval. You'll already have it if I like you."

"Ooohh, so you like, like me?"

"I like you, like you."

"Do you like me more than M&Ms?"

"How do you know I like M&Ms?"

I laughed, thinking back to the drive-in movie. "Last night you inhaled the entire bag before I could even take some."

He chuckled into the phone. "Ah, my M&M blinders were on. Excuse my poor manners."

"You didn't answer my question."

"Kinsley, I've never liked any girl more than I like M&Ms."

I laughed and let my head fall back against the wall. "Am I getting close?" I joked.

"I'd say I like you more than regular M&Ms, but you're going to have to really step it up if you want to beat out peanut M&Ms."

"I have a tough road ahead of me."

"I think you can do it," he joked, and I smiled against the phone.

"Challenge accepted."

Chapter Seventeen

The coffee shop was crowded when I arrived for my interview with Brian King the next day. I ran my hand down the front of my pencil skirt and tried to appear confident as I traversed the table looking for a smile that was bright enough to catch my reflection. Brian King would be attached to it.

Becca had helped me pick out the perfect outfit. I was wearing a pretty silk blouse tucked into a modest skirt that was tight but fell just above my knee. My kitten heels clapped against the hardwood floor until I came to a stop in the back of the coffee shop.

Brian was sitting there at a table with a photographer, but I couldn't process the fact that *Josh* was also sitting at the table with him in a nice button-down shirt and slacks.

"Oh, hello?" I muttered with a soft scowl as I made my way over to them.

Josh looked up at me and beamed while Brian gave me a hesitant smile.

"Hi, Kinsley. Please, please take a seat. As you can see, there's been a slight change in plans."

I shifted my gaze back and forth between Brian and Josh.

"What's going on?"

"The editor at the magazine called me this morning and informed me that Josh would be joining us for the interview. The magazine wants to go in a different direction with the piece."

I dropped my purse onto the ground next to my chair and took the seat that Brian offered me.

"What direction are they wanting to go in exactly?" I asked, eyeing Josh skeptically. His smile was a little too wide for my taste… like he was the cat that finally caught the canary.

"Oh, just having two rookies spotlighted instead of one," he began as if the whole idea was fairly innocent. "Josh is a rookie on the Stars and you're a rookie at ULA, but you'll both be trying out for the Olympics in the coming months. It makes for a more well-rounded piece." The way Brian explained it, the article seemed harmless enough. If they wanted to include us both, I didn't have a problem with it.

Both men sat there waiting for my reply. "Um, okay, I suppose that's fine?" What was I going to do? Storm out over a slight change in plans? Josh was a good soccer player; he deserved the spotlight, too.

"Okay, great!" Brian clapped his hands together and pushed some paperwork toward me. "There are just a few things we need you to sign before we get started. It basically states that any photographs the photographer takes during the interview may be used by the magazine and that we'll post your words verbatim so that you're protected in the editing phase."

I chewed on my bottom lip as I scanned over the documents, suddenly wishing I had my mother here with me. Signing contracts of any kind feels intimidating.

"Did you already sign yours?" I asked, glancing up at Josh.

"Just before you got here. It looked fine to me," he shrugged and offered me a small smile.

"You take your time, Kinsley. I'll go get you both some coffee."

Brian wandered off and I tried my best to read the details of the contract. It was brief and simple enough, so I signed on the dotted line and then pushed the paperwork back toward Brian's side of the table.

"How have you been?" Josh asked, leaning toward me. I saw the photographer's camera shutter open and close in quick succession. I guess the photographs started immediately upon signing the contract.

I leaned away from Josh so that it'd be harder to get us in the same frame.

"Fine. Just really busy."

He smiled and reached out to touch the back of my chair. "You're obviously doing well if the magazine wants to interview you."

I smiled tightly and nodded. Thankfully Brian returned right then, saving me from anymore awkward small talk.

"Here you go, you two," Brian said, handing us our coffee and flashing me his giant smile. He'd blind people with those teeth if he wasn't careful.

"Thank you." I smiled tightly and concentrated on pouring cream and sugar into my mug while Brian fiddled with the paperwork and set out a recorder.

"I'm going to start recording now, if that's all right?"

Josh and I both agreed.

The interview passed quickly and I learned early on that I didn't have anything to worry about. The questions were similar to the ones that Brian had sent the other day. I answered them the way that Coach Davis and I agreed upon. Toward the end, Brian started asking questions about my relationship with Josh. I answered simply, routing around our messy breakup and focusing more on our friendship. Josh, thankfully, followed suit.

"That was great, you two. Thank you so much. Let's get a few photographs and then we'll be all done here."

• • •

As soon as I left the coffee shop I texted Liam to let him know about the last minute change.

Kinsley: Josh was at the interview.

Liam: What? Why?

Kinsley: They wanted to highlight two rookies instead of one. It seemed okay. I read the contract before I signed.

Liam: You should have called me or Coach Davis.

Kinsley: Why?

Liam: I don't trust reporters – I'm about to have dinner with my coaches. We'll talk later.

For a split second I was angry with Liam for being dramatic… but then his concerns set in. He'd been a part of this industry for years, so maybe I should have run the new interview style with him or Coach Davis first, but I hadn't even thought about it.

The worst part was that Liam was absolutely right. Later that night, Emily ran into my room with wide eyes and her computer cradled in her arms. Becca and I had been watching Bridesmaids, but we paused it when we saw the look on her face.

"Did you have that interview today?" she asked warily.

I sat up off the bed. "Yes, earlier. Why?"

She twisted her computer around and showed me the front page of a popular sports website.

"*Romance Between Olympic Hopefuls*" was spelled out in giant letters across the top of the screen. The photo that accompanied it made me want to throw up. Josh had his arm around the back of my chair and we were both smiling wide. The worst part of all was that he was glancing toward me affectionately. While at the time, I'd wanted to kick the legs out from under his chair, to the untrained eye, the photo was damning evidence.

"What the hell!?" I shouted, hopping off my bed to get a better view. I had to hand it to the magazine. In less than four hours they'd started putting up teasers and photos to promote the article that would run sometime in the next few days. Those scumbags were timely.

"That fucking reporter! This article was supposed to be about *soccer*, not about me and Josh."

I wound my fingers through my hair and squeezed my eyes shut.

Shit. Shit. Shit.

Liam was right. Reporters were not to be trusted. On top of everything else going on, I could now add this article to the top of the list.

I snatched my phone, called my mom, and filled her in.

"Can we fight it?" I asked, pacing back and forth as Becca and Emily watched on with shocked expressions.

"We'll have to wait and see what the article talks about. Perhaps they wanted to play up a potential romance in the teasers so that the article will be more popular. Don't worry about this. The photo was harmless and you look beautiful. Try and get some sleep and we'll deal with everything once we know more."

"I just feel so used, Mom. They said it would be about soccer and my tryouts. I'm beginning to realize that no one actually cares about my soccer career. They're making me famous the same way reality stars are famous. Kim, Khloe, Kourtney, and Kinsley!"

"Don't you think that's all the more reason to focus on the Olympic tryouts? Remember this when you're pushing yourself to train harder. I think it's best if we steer clear of any more articles and I'll have your father's PR people release a statement explaining that you're single and your main focus right now is on soccer and nothing else. We'll clear this up."

I sighed, already feeling better. "Okay, thanks Mom."

"Love you, hang in there. It'll get better."

When I hung up, Becca and Emily didn't say a word. They were both looking for me to make the first move.

"Let's pretend that this isn't happening and go back to watching the show."

"Sounds like a plan," Becca nodded and hit play. I went back to my bed, grabbed the covers, and huddled underneath them. For the rest of the night, I pretended that my life was very simple, like all that I had to focus on was laughing at the jokes on Bridesmaids and hanging out with my two friends.

I would not become Kinsley Kardashian.

• • •

The full article was released the next day and was plastered across every website I could find, from TMZ to the New York Times. I didn't bother reading it. I knew it would be bad based on the accompanying photos. They'd cropped and manipulated every single one to make it appear as if Josh and I were together. A happy, Olympic couple. Gag me. Or better yet, gag Josh.

I'd let my father's PR team take care of it from my end. They'd release the statement about the false claims and I'd worry about the things I could actually control, which at that point was one thing: soccer.

I went to the fields early and ran sprints. I did some weight training and tried to use all my pent up energy on something productive. By the time practice started, I was pensive and tired.

Liam was in a terrible mood as well, worse than I'd ever seen before. When we split up into positions, he was snappy with all of us. His mood was distracting me and I kept mixing up the formations.

Finally, he snapped at me. "Kinsley, get your head in the game. This isn't that hard, and you've had all summer to work on it." His tone was harsh and a few of the girls stood watching him with a gaping mouth.

Tara, who was only a few feet behind me, muttered, "Uh oh, are the lovers fighting?"

A few of the upperclassmen snickered, and in that moment I lost it. There was only so much I could take and getting yelled at by Liam in front of my enemies was the straw that broke my freaking back.

I spun around on my cleats and pointed directly at Tara. "You know what? I'm so sick of your shit. What kind of captain tries to sabotage their own team? Do you even realize what you're doing? What's the fucking point of it all? So you can snicker about me with your friends after practice? Newsflash, Tara: No one fucking likes you. I bet Sofie and the other seniors are only friends with you because you've blackmailed them as well—"

"Stop," Liam yelled, grabbing me around the waist and pulling me back. I hadn't even realized I was in Tara's face until suddenly I was being dragged away.

"I would start cleaning out my locker if I was you, Bryant," she spoke with an eerie calmness, but I could practically see the wheels spinning in her head. I'd just awoken the beast and I was about to pay for it. Her eyes were sharp and her lips were twisted into a calculating smile.

Thankfully, Coach Davis was on the other side of the field so as soon as the incident began, it was over. For the moment. Tara and the seniors went over to grab water, and I stood there cooling off and appreciating the fact that I was sitting in the eye of the storm.

Liam and I were completely silent until it was time for him to leave, and for the remainder of practice, Tara and I kept our distance from each other. My heart was beating like a hummingbird's as I tried to process how I could somehow stop the avalanche about to take place.

This was it. The proverbial shit was about to hit the fan and I wasn't ready. I was a nervous wreck the rest of the day. I couldn't get in touch with Liam after practice, but I couldn't go to Coach Davis before talking to him first.

There was no more time to wait though. If Tara was going to go to Coach Davis, we had to beat her there. For all I knew it was already too late; Tara could have gone to her directly after practice.

"What are you going to do?" Becca asked. She was sitting on the edge of my bed and I was standing up, pacing back and forth across my carpet. I felt like a caged animal. My heart wouldn't stop pounding and my hands were clenched into tights fists. I'd realize how tense I was and try to relax, but then Tara's face would materialize in my thoughts and I'd tailspin back into tense anger.

"I have no freaking clue."

"Kinsley, this is serious... if Tara goes to—"

"I know. I know that," I cut her off and reached down to grab my running shoes. It was late, maybe eight or nine, but I needed to run.

"I'll be back in a little bit," I muttered, heading down the stairs and out the front door without a second glance. I jogged down my front lawn and turned right down an empty street. Hearing my feet pound against the asphalt was like waking up from a foggy dream. Until that moment I'd thought I was invincible. But in reality, I had put my dreams, my future, and my career on the line for a guy that I only had known for a few weeks. In the big picture of my life, Liam was a dot on the timeline, yet he was capable of wiping away everything that could have come after him.

And to make it worse, I had no one to blame but myself. *I'd* chosen to take the chance. I'd chosen to live in the moment and test fate. What if Coach Davis called me into her office tomorrow and told me I was off the team? What if she told me she wouldn't be inviting me to the Olympic tryouts? What would I have then? Liam? How could I look at him without seeing my failure?

I kept running until the fear had sunken deep into my bones. This was a wakeup call. A wakeup call that I feared was happening too late. Maybe if I explained everything to Coach Davis she'd give me another chance. I had no other option. I wasn't prepared to give up my dreams.

I was contemplating that fact as I rounded the corner back to my house and saw Liam's SUV sitting out by the curb. It was parked directly outside of the Rookie house rather than hiding around the corner. My stomach sank even lower and I slowed to a walk as I got closer to his car. My heart hammered in my chest, but I couldn't control its rhythm. The run and this surprise were too much for my nerves to handle.

I passed by his SUV and peered inside, but it was empty. The front door opened behind me and I spun around to find Liam heading outside. His hair was disheveled. His eyes were sharp and narrowed on me. A few of the sophomore girls peered through the thin gap before closing the door behind him.

"What are you doing here?" I asked, frozen in place.

"Letting the team know that I won't be coaching them anymore."

My breathing stilled. "What?"

He kept walking closer to me, his expression indiscernible. "I spoke with the LA Stars and Coach Davis today," he explained, running his hand along his jawline.

I felt my world screech to a stop. Holy shit, he'd done it. I reached up to cover my mouth with my hand, waiting for the other shoe to drop.

"Everything is out in the air now. Tara can't blackmail you and Coach Davis will deal with her separately."

He wasn't telling me what really mattered. What actually mattered. Did I have my dreams still or not?

"What happens? What happens now, Liam? Am I still on the team? Are you still on the team? Do you still have your endorsement deals?" Suddenly I felt just as close to exploding as I had before my run. I couldn't handle the stress. It was too much.

Liam came to stand in front of me, taking my hand in his. I let him because it was easier, but I wasn't sure I wanted him to touch me.

"The LA Stars were upset about the potential for bad press, but they wouldn't kick me off the team for something like this. A few of my sponsors were pissed and yeah, my most conservative sponsorship dropped me. They don't know how the media will spin the story and they didn't want to take the chance on me. I'll be able to talk the others down. This afternoon, I told Coach Davis a toned down version of the truth— that Tara was interested in me and that I was interested in you. She was hazing you and a few other rookies and threatening to use false facts to get you kicked off the team."

"They weren't really false facts," I whispered.

"Technically, they were. We never had sex," Liam corrected. He was splitting hairs at that point, but I didn't care to argue. "Coach Davis and I agreed that it'd be best if I stopped coaching the team so that the drama could die down."

"But aren't you in trouble with the LA Stars?"

He shook his head. "I wasn't ever in trouble with the LA Stars. That was all just media bullshit. I've been playing better in the last few weeks than I have in my entire career."

Had I just heard that right? He talked to Coach Davis and the LA Stars. He was telling me everything was okay. He was telling me that the worst of the storm had passed, but my brain wasn't catching up yet. My heart was still pounding and I just needed a few moments to absorb everything.

"Kinsley, it's settled now. We don't have to hide—"

I shook my head, once and then twice, trying to clear everything out. Five minutes ago my worst fears had been bubbling over. I'd had a taste of what it would be like if my soccer career was pulled out from under me and it'd been the scariest moment of my life.

I took a small step back from Liam.

"Kinsley?" he asked warily.

After everything he'd just explained, I should have felt relief, but instead I felt like I was hung-over from the day.

"I just need a few moments to think. I'm exhausted..." I answered honestly. "I'll talk to you tomorrow, okay? Thank you for fixing everything. I know it was probably scary having the face everyone by yourself."

"Hey— I told you I would take care of it. I didn't want you to worry. I would have done anything to make sure that none of this touched you— that your career wouldn't be jeopardized."

His words felt good to hear, but I couldn't let them settle in. I was a full glass of water and life kept trying to pour more liquid in. The excess was pouring down the sides and spilling out. I just needed five freaking minutes of swallowing some of today's events before I thought about adding more.

I squeezed my eyes shut and nodded before stepping around him. I think I had to block his appearance altogether; his dark eyes, his creased brow, his pouty lips. If I didn't, I wouldn't have been able to move past him.

"Thank you, Liam. But today I realized how close I

came to losing everything I've worked for and I feel like a royal idiot... like the loser that chooses a guy over the Olympics." I spun around and headed into the house.

"That's it? You're going to give up?" he yelled out behind me. I paused, staring down at the grass, too fearful of look back toward his brooding eyes. "I just put a lot on the line for you, Kinsley. I was out there fighting for you, fighting for us, the same day you and Josh were plastered all over the fucking internet. But I did all of that because I wanted to be with you, I wanted the whole package—not the sneaking around, not the forbidden romance. I wanted to take you out on a real date and show you off because I wasn't afraid of starting something real with you... so what are you scared of?"

His shoes crunched on the gravel, and I turned just in time to watch him hop into his front seat and slam the door closed. His engine roared to life, and in a moment he was gone, speeding down the street and leaving me with remnants of whiplash.

What was I scared of?

Chapter Eighteen

"I brought you dinner. Are you hungry?" Becca asked, placing a bowl of soup and a sandwich on my nightstand.

"No, I'm just really tired," I answered, "but thanks."

It was Friday night and a few of the girls were heading to go see a movie. I'd opted to stay in my room and wallow. All I'd done the past 36 hours was eat, sleep, and breathe soccer. It was refreshing and just what I needed—to remind myself of my true love in life.

Becca pulled my comforter down so she could see my face. I think she expected me to be crying; instead she found unwashed hair and smeared make-up. There might have also been some melted chocolate on my chin that I'd been trying to lick off for the past half hour.

"I realize why you're doing what you're doing," she began, and then paused until I met her hazel eyes. "It's a sort of self-punishment. You almost feel *guilty* that you got away with everything, so now you're punishing yourself. It's bullshit."

Her words struck a chord. "What are you talking about?"

"You feel bad because you broke the rules and didn't get caught. And then when you did, nothing really happened. Life continued on. Well, you know what? Maybe that was a dumb rule in the first place. Would you be pushing Liam away if you were allowed to be dating him this entire time?"

I chose to assume that was a rhetorical question.

"I'm going to the movies with the girls, but tomorrow, you and I are going to that get together at Penn's house. I already told him I would go, and you owe it to me to come with me."

I'd completely forgotten about those plans. It'd be Becca's first time seeing Penn since they met and I knew she was excited about it.

"I don't kno—"

She held up her hand to stop me. "I cleaned a toilet with a *toothbrush* for you. You're coming."

She had a point.

"You're my best friend, Becca. Thanks for everything," I called just before she left.

"You're welcome, but you're still coming to Penn's," she laughed, and then closed my door behind her.

• • •

Saturday morning I had plans to meet with Coach Davis for breakfast. There were still a few pieces of the puzzle that hadn't been cleared up and she'd requested to meet with me so we could clear the air. Even though I didn't think she was kicking me off the team, I still felt nervous about being reprimanded by someone I looked up to as much as her.

"Morning, Coach Davis," I said as I took a seat across from her. She looked up from her coffee and smiled. It was strange seeing her outside of practice. She looked so nice in her scarf and jeans. Like a real person and not just a soccer coach. If we were meeting under different circumstances, I would have complimented her outfit.

"G'morning, Kinsley, how're you doing?" she asked.

"I'm fine. I feel good after the last few days of practice. I think the team's really coming along."

She nodded at my response, but the edges of her eyes crinkled as if she were trying to see something I wasn't showing her. Her hand gestured to the seat across from her and I quickly shuffled to sit down and get comfortable.

When I was finally settled, I looked up and took a deep breath.

"I asked you here today for two reasons. The first was that I wanted to apologize to you specifically. I put Tara in a position of power on the team and I wished I had paid more attention to the way she was abusing that power. The things that she put you, Emily, and Becca through are inexcusable, and it's not the way I want to run my program."

"Coach—"

"I'm not done yet. I strive to create a program where you girls can come to me with any problem."

I nodded and took a quick sip of water.

"Second, we both know your behavior with Coach Wilder was extremely inappropriate. You chose to put yourself over your team and went against rules that I had in place for a reason." I winced at her words. "Now, that being said, I understand that this particular situation was a little unorthodox. Liam was volunteering with our team, and technically, he wasn't on staff at ULA. The rule was put in place so that you girls would stay focused, and to be honest, I didn't want any of you getting hurt. When Liam came to me and explained the situation, his feelings for you were very apparent. I'm not so cruel as to break up young love. I'll leave you all to do that for yourself."

I smiled at her joke and then glanced up from my water. "So where do we go from here?"

"Well, Liam is no longer with ULA, so your relationship with him is no longer of my concern."

"So, I could *technically* date him?"

Coach Davis smiled gently. "You'd have to ask him that question."

Oh, right. There was the *slight* problem concerning Liam's probable hatred for me. He'd left the ball in my court Thursday night, and there'd been 48 hours of radio silence between us since then. I thought that's what I needed. I was feeling overwhelmed and I wanted to take the time to get my thoughts in order. Well, my thoughts had definitely cleared and the only thing I cared about was the fact that Liam and I were no longer off-limits.

I paused before asking the next question. "And what about Tara?"

Coach Davis took a sip of her coffee and narrowed her eyes, as if collecting the pieces of her thoughts.

"Tara spoke with me yesterday and gave me an ultimatum: 'Either you go or she goes'."

My heart started pounding in my chest. "Ah."

"But the last time I checked, Tara was not 'Coach Tara.'" Coach Davis sat back and crossed her arms over her chest.

"Thank god," I murmured under my breath.

She smiled. "I told her to pack her things and leave. I

was prepared to offer her a second chance, but the fact that she was so blinded by her hate for you that she would want to kick off one of the best players on our team shows how little she truly cares about the program."

Holy hell.

"Wow."

"There will be some adjustments, but I feel good about the decision and I think the team will really benefit. We'll vote for the new captain on Monday."

"I don't really know what to say."

Coach Davis eyed me for a moment and then leaned forward, as if she didn't want me to miss a single word.

"You have a good head on your shoulders, Kinsley. In the few weeks that you've been with the program, you've had quite a few challenges thrown your way, yet no matter what, you haven't let it affect your practice or your commitment to the team. You've had multiple opportunities to shove yourself into the spotlight, but I think the way that you're going about your career is very wise. All too often, athletes shoot themselves in the foot by reaching for celebrity status before honing their skills."

Her warning reminded me of Liam.

"Do you think it's a bad idea to be with Liam? If I'm supposed to stay away from the spotlight?"

"I don't think you could find a better match than Liam. He has a reputation, as I warned you about, but now you've seen firsthand how the press likes to embellish their stories about young athletes. He's a damn good soccer player and I think you could learn a lot from him."

Wow. I couldn't believe the way the conversation was going, but I'm really glad I agreed to meet with her. The haziness around the last few days was beginning to settle and my options were right in front of me, ready for me to take them.

"Thank you so much, Coach Davis. For everything. I promise I won't take my second chance lightly."

"Good. Now, let's order. I'm starving." She winked and handed me a menu.

• • •

"Penn said his house is on the beach so let's wear bathing suits under our dresses in case people are swimming," Becca declared as we pushed off the bed to start getting ready.

"Okay, I have this cover up that's kind of fancy enough to be worn to a party," I mentioned, heading toward my closet. It was an icy blue silk material that wrapped around my body and crossed in the front so that it stayed closed when I pulled my arms through the spaghetti straps.

"Hmm, I'm not sure what I have. I could just wear a nice top and shorts?"

I found the cover-up hanging in my closet right next to an identical one. I'd forgotten my crazy mother had ordered me the dress in multiple colors. One blue and one fuchsia. I think they'd been a part of a "Maui" themed care package. I'm not kidding, the woman is dedicated.

"Oh, I forgot my mom bought me two! If it's not too 'sister-wives' of us, we could both wear these?"

Becca ran to the closet with a giddy smile. "That's perfect."

"You should wear the teal with your blonde hair," I said, pushing the cover-up toward her.

"We'll look like we're fourteen-year-old best friends that have to match wherever we go."

I pushed her out of my closet so I could change into my bathing suit. "We kind of are."

"Hey wait, are you nervous to see Liam?" she asked as I started to shut the door on her face.

"Nope. No. Zilch. Nada. Who's that?" I lied before squashing her out of the door way.

I was as cool as a cucumber.

"The lady doth protest too much!" she called before cackling her way toward the bathroom. As long as I live, I'll regret not putting that hot wax on her face.

An hour later we were leaving the house in our bright, silky cover-ups. Becca's hair looked sleek and sexy and she'd curled mine so that it hung down my back in beachy waves. Penn's house was all the way out in Malibu, but I didn't mind the drive down Pacific Coast Highway. You'd think after having lived in Los Angeles my whole life I'd be sick of the ocean, but most of the time I was just too busy to take a trip out just for fun. It'd been almost a year since I'd been out to Malibu, and as we pulled up to his beach house, Becca and I exchanged impressed nods.

Penn had a modern home with lots of windows and sharp, clean lines. We could see people mingling around inside already, so we pushed through the front door and were greeted by music and laughter.

"This isn't so bad," Becca nodded. The party was intimate compared to the last few weeks and the crowd appeared to skew a bit older than the LA Stars parties. There were people mingling around with cocktails and beer, but I didn't recognize anyone right away.

"Good call with the bathing suits," I nodded, noticing a few of the guys were wearing swimming trunks and t-shirts.

"Should we go get a d—"

Becca was midway through her sentence when she was interrupted.

"Kinsley! Becca!" Josh called just as I turned to see him approaching us.

He'd taken his shirt off so that his broad chest was on display. I could tell from his awkward walk that he was already tipsy.

"Hi Josh," I answered simply, unsure of where we stood. Surely he didn't know the article would be spun around on us, so I couldn't blame him for that. But it still left me with a bad taste in my mouth.

"You two look like twins," he smiled, casting his gaze from me to Becca, then back again. Becca stifled her laughter by covering her mouth.

He was just tipsy enough to be harmless and I think I liked him better that way.

"We should party, c'mon," he reached out for my hand, but I pulled it out of his grasp.

"Actually, Becca and I were going to use the bathroom," I lied, giving him a simple smile.

He bought it. "Okay, come find me when you're done." We watched him walk away and get swallowed up by the crowd of people before us.

"He must have started drinking early," Becca noted, and I glanced down at my phone. It was only 7:00 P.M. He'd be well on his way to plastered if he kept the same pace.

"Not my problemo anymore! Let's go find drinks."

I strung my arm through hers and we walked through the party. Quite a few people paused to watch us walk by, but I think it was the matching dresses that pulled them in.

Penn's house had an open-concept layout. The dining room opened up into the living room and then it expanded into another sitting area. The entire back of the house was composed of floor-to-ceiling windows that showcased a pool and a perfect view of the ocean.

"Wow. This place is amazing," Becca murmured as we both stopped to watch the sunset for a moment.

"Glad you guys like it," Penn answered behind us. Becca's body stilled and then she unwrapped her arm from mine. When she spun around to face him, I could tell she was trying to mask her elation behind a cool facade, but there was no hiding it. She was thrilled to see him.

"Hi!" she beamed up at him, and I shifted my gaze to Penn. His dark hair was styled back and his brown eyes held a little twinkle in them as he smiled down at her. His head was tilted a bit to the side like he was trying to take all of her in but couldn't quite figure out where to start.

He was wearing a white plaid button down that he'd rolled to his mid forearms. Beneath that he had on dark red board shorts.

"I'm so glad you guys made it," Penn said, finally glancing for a brief moment at me. It was like he had to remind himself that I was there standing beside Becca. Wow, this guy was falling hard.

"Hi Penn. You have an awesome house," I complimented him, sweeping my hand around the room. "How long have you lived here?" I felt as if I had to carry the conversation. Becca couldn't wipe the smile off her face long enough to actually speak.

He ran his hand along the bottom of his chin in thought. "I think two years now. Liam and I wanted to invest in some neighboring properties so we nabbed these two places right when they went on the market."

Neighboring properties?

"I thought Liam owned the house that the LA Stars live in?" I asked.

"Ah, yeah, he has that house as well as the place next door," Penn clarified, pointing out through the window. I followed his gaze to the house in the neighboring lot. *Liam's* house apparently. It was beautiful. It looked just as beautiful as Penn's, but the styles were completely different. There was a giant wraparound porch and white siding. Navy blue shutters hung perfectly from each window and light flooded the bottom floor, as if drawing people toward the house.

I wondered if he was there now instead of enjoying the party.

"He was having a few sections completely remodeled, so he was staying at the other house while they finished up."

Ah, I remembered him mentioning that, and it also explained why he never took me there when we were trying to sneak around.

"We wore our bathing suits. Do people usually swim?" Becca asked, drawing me back to the conversation.

Penn smiled. "Yes, but not until later. Usually when the bigger crowd dies down. It's more fun that way…"

Oh yeah, I bet it is.

Becca bit her bottom lip and nodded. I could tell she was nervous. Her hand was holding her opposite elbow and she only held eye contact with Penn for brief moments.

"Do you guys want me to take you on a little tour?" Penn asked, eyeing Becca. I figured it was probably my time to bow out.

"You guys go ahead. I'm just going to grab a drink and I think I saw a friend of mine over there." There was no friend, but they wouldn't have left me otherwise. Becca's hazel eyes locked on mine, and for a moment I couldn't tell if she was thanking me or pleading with me not to leave her. Either way, I shrugged and gave her a thumbs up when Penn turned. As he waited for her to catch up to him, I wondered if their tour would include a special viewing of Penn's *downstairs*.

After they were out of sight, I wandered over to the drink station where a well-dressed server was whipping up cocktails. Technically I wasn't old enough to drink, but it's not like the guy was going to card me at a party like this.

"What can I get for you?" the server asked with a polite smile. He was mixing a drink for another guest while he talked to me, and for a moment I just watched him in action.

"I'm not sure actually. I don't think I want a beer, but I don't know many cocktails."

"Have you tried a greyhound before?" he asked, finishing off a drink and handing it to the person beside me.

"No, what's in that?" I asked with a timid smile.

"It's one part vodka, one part grapefruit juice, and then garnished with a bit of lemon or lime," he explained with a friendly tone.

"That sounds awesome. I'll take one of those," I said, reaching into my purse for a tip.

We chatted casually as he mixed my drink. I loved the dark pink hue of the final concoction, and the moment I took a sip, I knew he'd pegged me right. It was delicious. The grapefruit cut the vodka so that the combination was just sweet enough to be deadly.

"I think this might be my new favorite drink," I complimented.

"You come back when you're done and I'll make you

another."

I smiled before turning back toward the party.

I took another sip of my drink and surveyed the scene before me. The crowd had grown a little bit since we'd arrived, but his house was big enough that there were little cliques of people rather than a sea of bodies. I was eyeing each of the groups, trying to spot someone from the club soccer world, when I laid eyes on Liam speaking with a pretty woman near the back windows. The sunset illuminated him from behind and he was breathtakingly handsome. He had on black swim trunks and a black LA Stars shirt. His hair was a bit longer on top, tousled more than usual, and I knew he needed a haircut soon. He was wearing a confident smile and sporting a cleanly shaved look that made it impossible not to notice his strong jaw. I could practically feel him dazzling the entire room. Women would regard him with interest as they walked by, but he was focused solely on the woman in front of him.

It was clear they knew each other well. They were laughing and talking with their hands. Before I knew it, I was bee lining straight toward them instead of heading in the opposite direction. I couldn't help it. I was moth to a flame when it came to Liam.

As I stepped closer, his grey eyes landed on me for the first time in three days. There was a flash of something behind his gaze: surprise, lust, hatred— I couldn't tell, but I took a deep breath and willed my legs to carry me closer. His cool expression gave nothing away and I felt my heart rate pick up, hammering inside my chest, as he watched me approach.

I stepped up behind the woman he was chatting with, who was still oblivious to my presence, and gently tapped her shoulder. She spun around with a residual smile on her face from whatever she'd been discussing with him. It was friendly, even as she aimed it on me, and I wasn't sure if I appreciated that or not. If she was his date, I didn't want her friendly smile.

"Can I help you?" she asked after I stood there like a simpleton. I hadn't planned out a single word so I let my mouth take over. It seemed like the best option.

"Hi... um, do you mind if I cut in for a moment?" I asked, purposely keeping my gaze on her instead of Liam. I wasn't sure what his reaction would be and I was floundering enough as it was.

She tilted her head in surprise and offered me an amused grin. "Sure, thing." She turned back toward him. "We'll talk later, Liam."

"Thanks," I murmured, but as she walked away, I called to her. "Actually, you might get him back in like five minutes... depending on how much he hates me."

She grinned and I heard Liam chuckle behind me. It was dark and smooth like I'd imagine a glass of bourbon to be. When I spun to face him, he was regarding me with enough heat to start a fire. And not a wimpy fire... a giant, smoldering bon fire. His right brow was dropped just a tad, his grey eyes were narrowed, and he was wearing a secret smirk that said he had me exactly where he wanted – hook, line, and sinker.

"I'm all ears," he murmured, crossing his arms over his broad chest.

I took a moment to gather my wits that he'd stolen in a flash. "Were you going to hook up with her if I hadn't interrupted?" My voice held more curiosity than jealousy.

"No," he grinned with a twinkle in his eyes. "That's my agent. She would bill me extra for services like that."

"Ha-ha. She's pretty," I stated, matter-of-factly.

"Not my type."

"What's your type?" I asked, crossing my arms protectively over my stomach, careful not to spill my drink.

"Long legs, brown hair… the kind of girl that pretends I don't exist for three days and then has the confidence to cut in at a party when I'm talking to another girl."

I bit back my smile. "Not another *girl*, your agent."

He smiled and his features relaxed into pleasant repose as if he were chiseled from stone. I studied the way his cheek bones sloped into his sharp jaw. It was hard to focus on anything else when I hadn't been this close to him in days. It was like my body's resistance to his sheer magnetism had faded and now I was starting again from zero.

Yes, brain. He's still the most beautiful thing in the world.

"You didn't know she was my agent."

I looked down at the floor and shrugged.

"I spoke with Coach Davis earlier."

"How'd that go?" he asked.

"Tara got kicked off the team."

He raised his brows. "She needed to be, but I didn't think they would actually do it."

"She made it pretty easy for Coach Davis to give her up from what it sounded like," I murmured and glanced down his body. His tattoos were peeking out from beneath his left shirt sleeve and I blushed remembering the image of him changing in his closet.

"It'll be better for the whole team with her gone," Liam said, taking a small step toward me. I swallowed past the lump in my throat.

"She also told me that this," I pointed between the two of us for fear that I was being presumptuous saying the

234

word *relationship* out loud, "wasn't off-limits anymore."

He crossed his arms and skirted around my statement completely. "I wasn't sure if you'd come," he admitted, taking another minuscule step toward me. Each time I inhaled I was overwhelmed with a mix of bodywash and cologne. My breathing picked up so that I could get another intoxicating whiff as soon as the last one faded.

"I couldn't let Becca come by herself. She took a ton of crap from Tara because of me… and she really wanted to see Penn."

"Are you here just to support Becca?" There was a touch of anger in his voice that hadn't been there a moment before.

I mashed my lips together and shook my head, unable to form the actual word, *no*.

"Are you going to swim later?" I asked, changing the subject to neutral territory.

"We'll see," he answered with a confident air. He wasn't going to give in easily. I clearly had some groveling to do.

I peered behind him toward the pool and his hand reached out to touch my arm gently. "Hey, you should go find Becca and Penn for a minute. I've gotta finish that conversation with my agent or I'll have to set up a meeting with her this week." His tone made it clear that he was less than enthused to leave my side, and I took it as a good sign.

"Okay... the agent that you *definitely* don't think is pretty?" I quipped, only half joking.

He smiled as if my jealousy amused him, then he bent low and enunciated every single syllable of his next sentence.

"She's not Kinsley Bryant."

Damn. A witty retort involving another girl named

Kinsley Bryant he might have known was on the tip of my tongue, but he kissed my cheek and went to find his agent before I could utter a word. I watched him walk away, realizing that my attraction to Liam Wilder was back in full force. I'd pushed aside the addiction for the past few days, thinking that if I focused on soccer I could pretend that he didn't exist. Yeah, no. My brain took that as some kind of reverse psychology crap, and instead, I thought about him all day every day.

The time for bullshit and games was over. I wanted him and now there was nothing stopping me.

Chapter Nineteen

I stood there for a moment, absorbing the last few moments, before realizing I was standing in the middle of the party by myself. I was supposed to be mingling and enjoying my youth, not looking like a mute loner.

I raised my Greyhound to my lips, letting the bitter grapefruit flavor roll over my tongue as I scanned the crowd. Let's see, there was a group of well-dressed yuppies sipping on craft beer, two models wiping white dust off each other's nostrils, and a group of socialites texting on their phones instead of looking at one another. I didn't recognize anyone around me, and Becca and Penn must have gotten lost on their tour because they still weren't back yet.

Just as I was about to give up hope and head back to the bartender (who was essentially paid to be friendly to me), I spotted a pair of Liam and Josh's teammates. They were the guys that gave me jell-o shots on my nineteenth birthday, and when I made eye contact with one of them, they waved me over. Just like that, I went from the president of the wall flower club to standing in-between two hot guys. Ha! Life was looking up.

We all reintroduced ourselves even though we had hazy memories of one another from the night a few weeks ago. Cole was the goalie for the LA Stars and he was a beast of a man. He wore his hair much too long for my taste and he had a long beard that looked like he'd grown it out on a dare. Oliver played defense for the Stars and looked the part. He was tall and toned enough to resemble the hulk.

"This is such a nice house," I said before taking a sip of my drink.

"Yeah, Penn always throws the best parties here," Cole said.

"Although none of them could top your birthday celebration," Oliver said with a friendly wink.

I groaned. "Can we forget about how drunk I was that night?"

Oliver laughed. "Well at least your cheek healed up nicely."

The group laughed and I started to relax. They really were nice guys.

"We heard the ULA girls are coming to watch one of our games soon. It's a preseason game, but it'll be a good match," Cole mentioned.

That was news to me, but it made sense. Coach Davis probably wanted us to watch how a professional team worked together.

"That'll be fun."

"Did you come here by yourself?" Oliver asked with a curious expression.

I glanced around me, trying to spy Becca so I could

point her out to them. Finally, I spotted her and Penn chatting with a group across the room. She noticed me pointing and sent us a little wave.

"No, I came with my friend, Becca. She's on the team with me."

"Ah, Penn's girl," Oliver nodded before taking a swig of beer.

I smiled at his assessment. Becca would love to know that's how the team referred to her.

"Does he talk about her a lot?" I asked, sounding passably casual.

Oliver eyed me with a curious grin. "No more than Josh talks about you."

I froze. The idea of Josh saying anything about me to these guys was incredibly frustrating.

"He and I aren't together," I clarified, trying to conceal the annoyance in my tone.

Cole nodded. "Don't worry, we know. The guy needs to move on."

I sighed and nodded, wanting to change the subject.

"Where are you guys from?" I asked.

"Kansas," Cole answered, just as I felt a hand touch the base of my back. The smell of liquor stung my nostrils as I glanced up to find Josh standing behind me.

"I've been looking for you everywhere, Kinsley," Josh commented with a slur.

Cole and the guys shuffled awkwardly.

"I've just been hanging out, Josh," I answered with a tight smile. His attention was veering toward uncomfortable territory and I wasn't sure how much more I could handle before I snapped.

His hand snaked around the side of my dress so that he could pull me closer toward him. The movement jerked my body so that my drink sloshed over the rim of the cup onto the floor.

"Josh, seriously, cut it out," I demanded, putting my empty hand up to his chest to try and push him away from me.

"Kinsley, relax. Let's have some fun." He started to tug at the base of my dress and the guys stirred around us. Aggression filled the air and I knew they were itching to get involved.

"No, Josh. Enough." I pushed him away again, harder this time, and his brown eyes clouded over in hate. In a matter of seconds his entire demeanor changed.

"You're such a fucking ice queen, Kinsley," he spat, finally releasing me with a shove. My drink spilled out over the front of my dress, but I couldn't break my eye contact with Josh. "I never loved you, bitch. I just wanted to get in your pants—"

Liam's fist connected with Josh's jaw midsentence, and I gasped and stumbled back. Liam was standing directly in front of me, blocking me from Josh.

"Don't you ever fucking talk to her again. Do you hear me?" Liam grabbed Josh's shirt and pulled him close again. Their sharp features clashed against one another. Josh's boyish handsomeness was muted next to Liam's sheer dominance.

Josh struggled out of Liam's hold and then lunged forward and punched Liam in the side. It was a weak hit, he was too drunk to get a good shot in, but it was enough to get the entire group of men involved. They sprung into action and the entire scene was a blur of punches and groans. I watched in shocked horror as Liam landed a solid punch to Josh's face right before the guys pried them off one another.

"Don't kid yourself, Wilder," Josh said as his dilated eyes connected with mine. There was so much hate sitting behind them. "She won't love you either. She's incapable of love. She's fucking cold-hearted."

Josh's words were like sharp, poisoned arrows. He was clearly speaking thoughts that had been swirling in his head for weeks.

"Maybe she didn't love you because you were too busy fucking girls behind her back, asshole. Don't ever fucking touch her again or so help me—"

Penn's voice broke in. "Guys. Enough. This is a party, not an underground fight club. Josh, get out of here and go clean yourself up."

Cole stepped forward and grabbed Josh by the back of the neck. "I'll take him home. Let's go, rookie." Cole pushed Josh forward and he stumbled a bit, trying to stay standing. He was shitfaced, no one would have argued that fact, but that was still no excuse for the things he'd said.

"That kid needs to learn some respect," Oliver mumbled gruffly as he let go of Liam and stepped away.

Liam was still riled up; he shook his arms out and exhaled sharply as he watched Josh head toward the front door. I could feel the energy burning off of him and I was stuck between wanting to move closer and wanting to run away. Everything had happened so fast and the only thing my brain could process was the fact that Liam had stood up for me. He'd put himself between me and Josh, his teammate.

He slowly spun around to face me. He surveyed my expression and then dragged his eyes down my body to assess the damage. His shoulders dropped and his hands unclenched. His brows unfurled ever so slightly and he swallowed down the last of his anger.

I wanted to reach out and touch him, to feel the residual warmth on his skin and feel where Josh had mistakenly attempted to fight back. Was Liam injured?

I stepped forward a microstep just as Becca propped herself in front of me and blocked my view of him with her golden hair and concerned eyes.

"Kinsley, are you okay? Did Josh hurt you?" she asked, pulling my arms away from my sides so she could inspect them. My body was fine; it was my nerves and pride that were frayed.

I shook my head as if realizing for the first time that I was still standing in the middle of a party. Every single person in the room had heard Josh shouting about me being an ice queen. I could feel everyone's eyes on me, and suddenly I wanted to be anywhere but there.

"Becca, can we get out of here?"

Before I knew it, she was pulling me away from the living room.

"This is one of Penn's guest rooms," Becca said as she pushed open one of the doors down the hall. It was decorated sparingly, but the bed looked comfortable and there was a photo of the Los Angeles skyline framed on one wall.

"Thanks. I just needed some air for a second." I sat on the edge of the bed and ran my hands up and down my arms.

Becca sat next to me, angled so that she could inspect my body for any remnants of Josh's grabby hands. "I can't believe he said that stuff. But he was drunk, Kinsley, he didn't mean any of it."

I held up my hand to stop her. "It doesn't matter. Josh sucks ass. He was fun to have around as a friend, but he's a truly terrible boyfriend."

"And a lousy drunk," Becca added.

I nodded and sighed. "Do I look like crap? Should we just cut our losses and leave?"

Becca's face fell. She pushed a few strands of her golden hair behind her ear and furrowed her brows. "Not yet. Seriously, Josh is gone and no one else will bother you."

"I know, but everyone heard that fight. There were so many people out there."

She set her mouth in a thin line and her hazel eyes locked onto me. "You shouldn't feel embarrassed because Josh is an asshole. No one will judge you. Besides, they're probably too busy talking about how cute me and Penn are. The Liam, Josh, and Kinsley love triangle is so 20 minutes ago."

I couldn't help but laugh. I hoped she was right, but I still frowned thinking about having to resurface in a few minutes. For someone who hates having their personal life in the public eye, that was about as bad as it could get. One hundred strangers looking on as my ex-boyfriend verbally assaulted me and then having two men grapple over me. The latter sounded semi-romantic, but it actually made my skin crawl. I felt like I was on display and I could just hear everyone buzzing about the fight for the rest of the party.

I groaned and pushed off the bed to investigate the damage. My bright blue eyes stared back at me in the bathroom mirror as I tried to piece myself back together. It could have been worse, I told myself. Liam was relatively unscathed and Josh was the same ol' jerk. Nothing new to report there.

Becca came to stand next to me and wrapped her arms around my shoulders.

"I'm glad I curled your hair. It still looks really good,"

she complimented, trying to turn my mind toward something else.

I smiled at her in the mirror. "Let's go ruin it in the pool. No one was outside earlier, and that way we can stay at the party but avoid having to listen to the gossip."

Becca grinned and then spun around to grab two towels from a rack behind her.

"Let's do it!"

We linked arms and left the guest room. People could talk all they wanted, but I wasn't going to let them ruin my night. When we headed back into the living room, I was surprised to find the party was starting to dwindle. There were still a few people there, milling about, but the bartender was breaking down his setup and the music wasn't streaming through the speakers anymore.

"Isn't it kinda early still?" I asked Becca as we passed through the living room. I didn't see Liam anywhere, but I felt the hair rise on the back of my neck thinking about the fact that he was still in the house somewhere.

Becca shrugged and we kept heading out toward the pool. Just as I'd hoped, there was no one outside.

The view of the house hadn't done the pool justice. It was actually made up of three separate pools, each at varying levels. Where we stood, level with the back of the house, there was a long lap pool. To the left there was a set of stairs that Becca and I followed until we found another pool that was much larger and shaped like a kidney bean. Palm trees rimmed the edge, concealing it from the house and beyond.

We followed the stairs as they continued to slope down around the edge of the pool. They led us to a round Jacuzzi at the very bottom that was almost level with the beach so that you could step from the last stair onto the warm sand. The light from Penn's house illuminated the shoreline so that you could still see the rolling waves crashing against the sand. It really was a spectacular house.

"I guess one pool wasn't enough?" Becca laughed as she and I started to head back toward the top, satisfied with our search.

"Penn is a greedy bastard, but I'm not complaining. Should we go to the middle pool?"

"Yeah, I liked that one best."

We dropped our towels and cover-ups on the small lounge chairs surrounding the pool. I adjusted my blue triangle string bikini, and without a second thought, I ran and jumped into the water.

When I surfaced, Becca was standing at the edge and smiling.

"Remember when Tara was hazing us and I told you that it'd be worth it because you'd look killer in a bikini? I was totally right."

I cracked up. "Revenge is best served *skimpy*," I joked before lying back to float on the surface. It was impossible to see the stars with the light pollution and smog from LA, but I imagined that they were overhead and it was still nice to stare up into the blackness.

I heard two pair of footsteps descending the stairs and glanced behind me to find Liam walking beside Penn. My heart kicked into overtime and I realized that it'd be really nice if my body would become habituated to seeing him. I swear every time he stepped into a room, or in this case a pool, my body had to come to terms with his existence in the world all over again.

"The party is officially over," Penn said as they came into full view.

Becca shrugged. "It looked like it was heading that

way. I can't believe Josh ruined it for everyone."

Penn smiled as he walked up to her. "Y'know, I think it might have been a good thing. I was wanting to kick everyone out the moment I realized you'd brought your swimsuit."

Even I blushed at his comment, so I wasn't surprised when Becca bit down on her lip and averted eye contact. She looked irresistible in her dark blue bikini and I knew she had Penn wrapped around her finger.

"Hey Liam, can I borrow your phone?" Penn asked as they stepped closer to the pool.

"Oh, I left it inside," he answered, patting his swim trunk pockets to confirm. Not two seconds later, Penn reached out and shoved him into the pool before he could realize his fatal mistake.

"Asshole!" Liam yelled between laughs after he surfaced.

"I can't believe you actually fell for that. We learned that when we were like twelve!"

"I was distracted," Liam shrugged with an adorable grin.

"Yeah, whatever. Let the record show, Penn: 1, Liam: 0," he gloated before spinning toward Becca's direction. "Want to walk down to the beach with me, y'know, since we're the only dry one's now?" Penn asked, extending his hand out to her.

The longer I watched their interaction, the more I became aware of the fact that I was avoiding Liam's gaze. He was still standing near the far edge of the pool, and I could see him watching me out of the corner of my eye. I let my body sink back into the pool, suddenly appreciating the veil of the water surrounding me. I never heard Becca's response, but a moment later she and Penn were both heading down the stairs toward the beach, and I knew Liam and I were alone.

No more hiding.

The silence settled between us. The light from the bottom of the pool cast his handsome features into shadows and I tried to swallow past a lump in my throat.

His predatory eyes were a warning of dark, wild things to come.

I didn't realize I was backing up against the edge of the pool until he stood in front of me, trapping me against the wall. His hands gripped the edge on either side of my body just as his hips touched mine beneath the surface of the water. It was liquid seduction, the way my smooth legs entwined between his as if we were taking a bath together.

"Are you upset with me?" he asked, bending forward and nuzzling my neck with his pouty lips.

I bit my bottom lip to keep from moaning. "No."

He dragged his lips up to my ear.

"He doesn't get to touch you anymore. I've listened to him talk about you around the house for the past month and I've had enough. I know you aren't leading him on, he needs to realize that it's over."

I shivered against him, but nodded. His words sounded like the law and I was all too willing to comply.

"I'm sorry I did the article with him," I murmured, needing to get it off my chest.

He shook his head and I closed my eyes to gather my wits. "You didn't know."

He bent his elbows, leaning in dangerously close, but not touching me with his hips and chest yet.

"I'm sorry I've been distant the past few days. I just had to get my bearings, but… I want you. I don't want this to end," I whispered.

I ran my hands down his sopping wet t-shirt and then began to collect the material at the bottom. I pushed it up over the toned ridges of his abs, revealing more and more of his skin as I went. He reached to the back of his neck and helped me pull the shirt over his head before tossing it out of the pool.

I sighed as my eyes scored down his bare chest. My hands drifted from the base of his arms, up over his broad shoulders and neck. My eyes met his and I smiled seductively, challenging him to kiss me.

His body pressed closer to mine and the water parted to accommodate his movements. I anticipated his touch as if his skin would shock me, but instead, when his hard stomach pressed against mine, I felt like he was setting my skin on fire.

"Then be with me. Be mine." He kissed my neck, just below my jaw, and I tilted my head back slightly to give him better access. His fingers traced a valentine heart against my neck, as if emphasizing his request.

"You don't know what you're getting yourself into. I'm jealous and untrusting. The last two boyfriends I had were scumbags."

"So you've traded up. I'm not a scumbag."

I laughed. "I bet your ex-girlfriends would beg to differ."

He pulled back to look me in the eye and gently cupped my chin.

"Yes, I have a past that you wouldn't care to hear about, but my parents have a marriage that has survived thirty years. I know what it means to value the person you're with."

When I appeared to be absorbing his words, he started to let his hands drift down the back of my neck, just over the knot on my bikini top. I could feel the strings starting to loosen and I flashed him an amused grin.

"Is that you *valuing* me?" I teased.

His eyes danced with desire. "One of the ways."

He looked devious as he bent to kiss the swell of my breast. It's not as if my small bikini was really keeping us separated, but it gave me the illusion that there was still a barrier between us. As his fingers released the strings and the small triangles fell away, I felt desire overtake my entire body. It was slow and seductive, but it had all the makings of a wildfire.

His hands followed the strings as they tumbled down the front of my body, and then he brushed them aside and cupped my breasts in his firm hands. I moaned and tilted my head back just as his mouth pressed against mine. He kissed me and sucked on my bottom lip until I was whimpering for more. His fingers caressed the skin around my breasts, memorizing their form, and then his lips left mine and he strung kisses down the front of my body. I let him, tugging my hands through his damp hair and encouraging his exploration.

Just as his lips found my nipple, his hand found my bikini bottom and I trembled. I was trapped against the pool's wall, but the feel of concrete gently scraping against my back spurred on my desire. I liked knowing I couldn't get away. Not when it was Liam ensuring my imprisonment.

He didn't try to untie the strings on my bikini bottom. As his tongue teased my nipples, he pushed my bikini aside and pressed two long fingers inside of me. My moans filled the air, encouraging his movements.

"You're so sexy, baby. Let me feel you come," he encouraged, moving his fingers in and out while rubbing me with his thumb. Oh *boy*, was he good at that. He played my body like it was his own creation and I lapped it up willingly.

When I came a few moments later, I had one leg wrapped around his hip and my mouth was biting down on his earlobe so that my soft moans fell right into him. He didn't stop fingering me until I'd felt my orgasm wane into sweet aftershocks, and even then it felt as if he wanted to stay connected to me forever.

When he finally pulled back and looked down at me, his gaze dragged over my skin, slowing taking in my heaving chest and full breasts.

"It's a pity Becca and Penn are walking up those stairs," Liam teased with a wicked look in his eyes.

I flew into motion, trying to conceal our foul play, but it was Liam that stepped forward and deftly retied my bikini top. He bent down and gave me a soul stealing kiss before wrapping an arm around me and picking me up, away from the wall.

I squealed as he spun me around, splashing water up around us. I liked the playful side of him, and it was the perfect cover for when Becca and Penn crested the top of the stairs.

"How was your walk, you two?" I asked, noticing Becca's tousled hair. Hmm, was it from the ocean air or was Penn to blame? I didn't get time to call her out on it before Liam spun me around then tossed me across the pool. It took me by surprise, but I held my breath just in time. When I pushed back to the surface, I shot him an evil stare.

"I will so get you back for that," I threatened, already swimming toward him.

"Oh really?" he cocked a brow and dove under the

water. He swam closer to me and then picked me up just as I was starting to swim away. He threw me through the air again and this time when I came up, I held my hands in surrender.

"You win! No more tossing me around! This is precious cargo," I joked, waving to my body.

He scoured down my bikini and it was clear he was picturing every single dip and contour he'd just seen. I licked my lips and tried to contain the building lust. With him around it was nearly impossible.

"How do you guys feel about watching a movie? I have tons of popcorn and candy," Penn asked as I swam closer to them.

"Sounds fun. You had Liam at candy, I'm sure," I teased, eying him over my shoulder. He was still standing in the middle of the pool, where'd I'd left him, probably trying to contain his erection that I knew was hiding beneath the surface.

Hah. Looks like I won after all.

"Only if it's peanut M&M's, baby," Liam winked, with an over the top southern accent.

I shook my head and swam toward the edge of the pool. I was wrapping a towel around myself when Becca got my attention with a small wave. Her eyes were wide and she kept trying to mouth something at me.

"What?" I whispered.

She widened her eyes and mouthed it again. I think she either said "Weeds in the wok" or "We need to talk". Knowing Becca it *could* have been the first phrase, but I chose to go with the latter. I nodded and then mentioned something to the guys about needing to check my phone. Becca scurried after me, her movements falling at about negative one-thousand on the secretive scale.

The second we were alone she grabbed my arm.

"I think Penn wants me to stay here tonight," she admitted with a pale face.

"So? That's good, right?"

She frowned and wrung out her hands. "I don't think I'm ready for that. I definitely want to be with him, but I need you guys as a buffer. What if we suggest something like a big sleepover? Are things with you and Liam heating up? Maybe we could all stay at Penn's house?"

Even though her idea seemed childish, it also sounded really fun. I knew Penn wouldn't mind considering how into Becca he was. And what guy doesn't want to build a blanket fort with two chicks? Answer: They all do. It's probably one of the top watched porns: sex in a haphazardly constructed blanket fort. Every guy's wet dream.

"That sounds like fun. We'll play it my ear, but I have your back. No worries."

All right, I sort of just wanted to build that fort.

Chapter Twenty

When we came back out, the guys were sitting on the lounge chairs chatting, probably about soccer. What else did two professional soccer players discuss?

Liam looked up as we were making our way over.

"Kinsley, let's go to my house and change clothes and then we can come back to watch the movie," he said, standing up and heading over.

I nodded, and when he was close enough so that I didn't have to announce it to everyone, I whispered, "Do you think I'll be staying here tonight?" I couldn't meet his eyes but my cheeks were burning.

His small smile said it all. "Of course, I won't let you drive back to LA this late, and besides, I want to sleep with you."

Sleep with me! I practically squirmed on the spot.

"I have an idea," I announced to the group, suddenly agreeing with Becca's plan. "What if we have a giant sleepover? We can go grab stuff from Liam's place and then head back over..."

Liam's smile widened and he shook his head slowly. Not as if he was saying no, but because he seemed amused. "We can do the sleepover at my house. I have a movie room with couches that are comfortable enough to sleep on."

I didn't expect him to buy the plan so easily, but I suspected he was trying to make it easy on Becca and me.

"Sounds good," Penn answered. "We'll meet you guys over there in a little bit."

Becca shot me a grateful smile and then she followed Penn up the stairs.

"C'mon, we can get to my house from the beach," Liam said, taking my hand and the cover-up so that I couldn't put it back on.

"You don't need this, we're only walking a short ways," he declared as I arched my brow.

"Mhmm, I'm sure that's the reason," I teased as his gaze drifted down my body.

"All of my fantasies did not live up to the real thing... I think I need a few more minutes before you put clothes back on," he teased confidently, making me feel even more exposed.

I laughed and shook my head. Fantasies, my ass.

"Did Becca want you to suggest the sleepover thing?" he asked gently.

I bit my lip wondering if I should throw her under the bus. Maybe he would tell Penn. "Well technically it was her idea, but I thought it would be fun. Are you upset?"

He watched me explain and then narrowed his eyes. "It's probably for the best. I want to spend time with you, but if we were alone, we'd be going straight to my bed right now."

His words coated me like honey and I tried to shake off the allure.

"Well you can take me to your bedroom," I winked, "...for a change of clothes."

He laughed and tugged my hand as we ascended the stairs to his house. It was even more beautiful up close. The design was open and inviting. Warm white hues and bright blue accents filled the living room and kitchen.

"This is where I like to spend my time when I can get away from the LA house," he said as he tugged me past the kitchen that looked straight out of a magazine. "I was having a few things fixed so they had the water and electricity cut off for the past few weeks."

I guess we were passing the tour all together. I was getting a glimpse of each room as he continued pulling me toward his bedroom.

"I completely agree about it feeling like a home." I smiled up at him and our eyes locked for a moment. I think he was glad I appreciated his house. But to be honest, anyone would.

When we got to his room, he pulled open his drawers and handed me a t-shirt and some boxers.

"This should work. Sorry I don't have bras lying around. Guess you'll have to go without." He smiled as if he wasn't actually *that* sorry.

I glanced down at the boxers to find that they had little snowmen on them. They seemed very un-Wilder-like.

I held the waistband up between my fingers. "Stylin' duds you have here, Mr. Wilder."

"Hey, don't knock the boxers. They're my Christmas pair." He laughed as he pulled out a pair of boxer briefs, sleeping pants, and a shirt for himself. I thought he was going to head into the closet to change, but as soon as he had his clothes pulled out, he dropped his swim trunks right then and there and headed to the shower.

My mouth fell open at the sight of him. Every single inch of his body was toned and tan. His tattoos fell in perfect congruence with the movement of his muscles. I knew it took years to mold a body into that perfection and I appreciated every single inch of it as I watched him head to his bathroom.

"Come shower," he demanded just before his body disappeared from my sight.

I stood there motionless as I heard him turn the water on and then step inside. Shampoo bottles clanged against the glass as I tried to make a decision. Were we moving too fast? Should I wait and shower separately? Did I even need a shower? There was chlorine in my hair and the longer I let it dry, the more damage it would cause... Welp, that's settled.

His form was partly hidden by the fogging glass, but puffs of intoxicating steam were already rising from the top. I popped open the glass and sneaked in after him without taking my bikini off. I thought I could shower just fine in my bathing suit. Liam disagreed. His eyes lit up as he took me in and then in no time at all, he'd untied my top and bottom and my bikini fell to a pile on the shower floor. Damn, those hands could really move when he had a goal in mind. He kicked my bikini aside and brought me toward him. My hands splayed out against his chest, feeling his smooth skin as he started to soap up my body.

We were naked, so blissfully naked together, that I felt giddy and turned on all at once.

He squeezed a dab of body wash onto his hands; it was *his* body wash and it smelled clean and manly. He was going to wash me with it and I didn't mind one bit that I'd come out of the shower smelling just like him. I wanted to use that body wash from now on.

My eyes fell closed as his hands drifted over my skin. He skimmed over my shoulders, down my back and spine. It felt like he was slowly driving me insane under the pretense of cleaning me off. When his hand fell between my legs I thought I'd collapse onto the tile, but he didn't let me. One hand wrapped around my waist while his fingers brought me to another orgasm.

"You're so responsive to my touch," he said, nipping my ear as my hand found him hot and hard.

I grabbed the soap from behind him and returned the favor, but honestly it was more pleasurable for me than it was for him. Getting free access to run my hands across his skin was like getting to gorge myself on the most decadent desert. I reveled in the way he tensed when my hand drifted lower, past his waist. I gripped him tightly and stroked him up and down as his head fell back under the stream of water. I loved making this man moan. If I could only hear one thing for the rest of my life, I would choose that moan— hearing him make those low groaning sounds as pleasure overtook him. He came fast and hard, spilling out onto my hand and belly. It was a deviously sexy sight and I almost mourned the loss as the shower washed it away as quickly as it had appeared.

We both left the shower wearing sated smiles, but I still felt his eyes on me as I pulled on his shirt and boxers. We'd yet to completely have our fill of one another.

"You realize that the entire time we're watching the movie I'll be thinking about the fact that you aren't wearing panties or a bra underneath your clothes," he commented, pulling on his pants.

I winked over my shoulder, feeling bold and beautiful

after his constant stream of compliments in the shower. "Technically, they're *your* clothes." I said, moving toward the door.

He grinned wickedly, ditched his shirt, and made to chase after me. Damn his soccer training. He was much faster than I was. I ran down his hall laughing as I dodged his hands, then I hid behind the couch, faking to dodge left and right. He called my bluff and caught me as I tried to run away.

"Mercy!" I squealed as he wrapped his arms around my waist and picked me up.

He was setting me back down to my feet when Becca and Penn walked in. Becca eyed us curiously, but Penn just laughed and shook his head.

"What the hell have you two been doing while we've been changing?" Becca laughed.

I winked. "Playing chase. I'm much faster than Liam."

He wrapped his hand around my waist and squeezed. "Maybe you should train me then."

I laughed and pushed him away with my hand. "Yeah, yeah. Did you guys bring any movies?"

Penn held up three DVDs. "I brought Shawshank Redemption, 300, and Boondock Saints."

Becca and I both cracked up. "You are such a guy, Penn."

"I don't think my options are any better," Liam admitted, rubbing the back of his hair with his hand.

"C'mon Becca, let's go check out Liam's stash while the boys make the popcorn."

"Did you guys bring your own candy? Because I'm not sharing," Liam called behind us.

The second we rounded the corner toward Liam's movie room, I put my hands on Becca's shoulder and silently squealed up and down. She joined in and soon we looked like two crazy people jumping and spinning in a dark hallway.

"This is a dream, right? We're going to wake up tomorrow in the house and I'm going to be wearing my onesie," Becca whispered as we kept walking.

"No. This is definitely happening, my friend." I smiled so wide my cheeks hurt.

"Sorry we took so long changing. Penn was a little distracted. We may have rounded a few bases."

I threw her a shocked glance as we pushed through the door to the movie room. He'd pointed it out to me earlier, but of course we hadn't actually been inside. No detail was forgotten inside the room. There were giant plush recliners in the first two rows and then two rows of couches behind it. They were wide and overflowing with fluffy pillows. The screen was obscenely large and there was a fancy-looking projector mounted on the far back wall.

Beneath the projector there were shelves upon shelves of movies.

"Wait, *how* many bases did you guys skip?" I asked as soon as the door was closed.

Becca couldn't wipe the smile off her face. "Well, let's say he knows what I taste like."

I started cracking up. "BECCA!"

"What?! You did it to Liam... in his *office* no less!"

"I know, I know. I'm just... wow. Has a guy done that to you before?"

She bit her lip. "No, but now I'm wondering why the hell I waited so long."

We started cracking up again and I couldn't stop with the giddy squeals. Eventually we tried to look through

Liam's movie collection, but it wasn't very successful.

"I'm not sure how long we have until they get here, but the second we get home tomorrow, I have about one million questions for you," Becca whispered. We could hear the boys laughing down the hall and it sounded like they were heading our way.

"I'll try and help, but seriously I'm not much more experienced than you are," I shrugged.

Becca nodded. "We'll break out 50 shades. It should give us some answers."

"Yeah, like how to get flogged while wearing a ball gag," I joked.

"True. Maybe we should stick to Judy Blume's books."

I shoved her arm playfully just as the boys strolled in. Their arms were filled with drinks and snacks.

"Did you guys find something to watch?" Penn asked.

Becca and I glanced from each other, down to our empty hands, then back to the shelf. "Ummm..." Becca mumbled.

I reached forward and grabbed the first movie I touched: Wedding Crashers.

"Oops… haven't we all seen this one?" I asked, holding it up. Everyone nodded, but Liam grabbed it out of my hand and went to pop it into the spaceship-quality projector system.

"That's good, we'll probably end up talking through it anyway," he shrugged. He had a point. With four people that were all hyped up on sexual tension, we probably wouldn't be paying attention to the movie for very long.

All four of us could have fit comfortably on one couch, but Becca and Penn took the couch closest to the screen and Liam and I scooted onto the back one. The previews started to play as I adjusted on my seat and spread a blanket that felt like a cloud over my lap. Liam narrowed his eyes on me playfully and tugged the blanket onto him as well. It wasn't that big, probably because it was made of virgin baby sheep's wool, so I had to scoot closer to him. Thank you, tiny blanket.

We had popcorn resting on our laps and candy spread out in front of us.

"Hey, do you guys have anything good up there?" I asked, leaning forward to see their stash. Becca tossed me back a handful of Swedish Fish and one of them hit me in the eye.

"Hey! I only caught like three of those," I complained, popping one into my mouth.

"I caught the other one," Liam proclaimed proudly. A little red fin was sticking out of his mouth and I reached over to bite it off. He nibbled on my lower lip, and for that brief second I forgot where we were. When Becca cleared her throat, I pulled back and found her leaning over the couch, holding out the bag of candy.

"Should Penn and Kinsley switch? You guys can't have sex while the movie's on," she joked. All at once Penn, Liam, and I shouted, "No!"

Becca laughed and shook her head before turning back around to cuddle next to Penn. When the movie started playing, we all made a good faith effort to actually watch it, but not even ten minutes in, Liam held out a bag of Peanut M&Ms in front of my face. I eyed him warily. Chances were if I reached for them, he'd gnaw my hand off.

"More than Peanut M&Ms," he whispered, and it took me a moment to realize what he meant. When it clicked, I bit down on my bottom lip to try and conceal the cheesy grin fighting to break free. I took the bag, leaned into the crook of his shoulder, and one at time, we ate the entire thing.

Don't judge, it was a small bag.

Sometime during the movie I must have fallen asleep because when I woke up the lights were off and I had to pee like a racehorse. I was lying horizontally on the couch with a pillow tucked under my head that hadn't been there before. Liam was tucked behind me with his arm wrapped around my waist. I could hardly breathe, let alone move, with his grip wrapped securely around me. I gently peeled his arm off and then shuffled in the dark until I found the door.

When I came back from the bathroom, I peeked over the front couch to find Becca and Penn cuddled in the same position Liam and I had just been in, and I couldn't help but smile. I would have snapped a picture of them if I could have done it without waking everyone up and looking like an intense creeper. They looked so perfect together and Becca was sleeping with this tiny smile on her face. It was pretty hilarious, but still adorable.

I tried my best not to wake Liam when I crawled back onto the couch, but I could feel my heart racing beneath my shirt. I lifted the blanket and slid down next to him so that my face was pressed against his chest. I took a deep breath and inhaled a whiff of his deodorant and body wash, letting my eyes flutter closed.

"Where'd you go?" he whispered, wrapping his arms around me. I hadn't realized he was awake.

"Went to look at your baby pictures and tax returns."

"I thought you were ditching me."

"Not after you shared your candy with me." I smiled

against his chest and he wrapped his arms around me tighter.

"I really like you... you should be my girlfriend."

My body stilled against his chest. Was he really asking me that or was he talking in his sleep? Maybe he'd never actually woken up and I was talking to his subconscious.

I played along as if he was *actually* asking me.

"It's late and asking me to be your girlfriend makes me feel like we're in high school."

He chuckled softly and bent to kiss the edge of my mouth. "Go steady with me. Be my date to an event I have to make an appearance at next week."

"Yes."

"Was that a 'yes' to being my girlfriend or a 'yes' to being my date?" he whispered.

"To both. Now let me sleep, you fool, before I change my mind."

He laughed and I snuggled closer to him until I felt warm and cozy enough to drift back to sleep.

Chapter Twenty-One

I woke up the next morning to the smell and sounds of crackling bacon. I rolled off the couch, wrapped myself up in the soft blanket, and then peered over to find Becca still asleep with no sign of either Liam or Penn. They must have been the source of the bacon smell.

"Wake up, Sleepyhead," I said, yanking off her blanket. She groaned and started spouting out some very colorful names, one of which was something like: Wheat-Thinned Slut Monkey. I'm sorry, but what does that even mean?

"Is that any way to talk to your bestie?" I laughed as she tried to pull the blanket from around me.

"This is mine! Get your own!"

"Kinsley! Becca! C'mon, breakfast is ready!" Penn called out. We sprang into action and raced to the kitchen, slipping and sliding in our blankets and socks. I almost wiped out when we rounded the corner to the kitchen and Becca couldn't stop laughing for five solid minutes.

Liam quirked his eyebrow at us. "I thought I got you Becca-proofing supplies."

I held up my leg and arm, which were both sporting bruises courtesy of my best friend aka spawn of Satan. "I keep forgetting to wear them. Maybe we should just wrap Becca up in bubble wrap. She packs a lot of punch for a small package."

The boys laughed. "I veto the bubble wrap," Penn joked.

I waggled my eyebrows as I stepped up to inspect the meal they'd cooked. "You'll rethink your decision after she karate chops you in the stomach."

Becca bonked me on the arm as a warning.

"I hope you guys like bacon and waffles."

My eyes lit up. "Waffle for me please!" I grinned and took a seat at the table. Becca followed suit.

"What, we cooked it *and* we have to serve you?" Liam teased, already preparing a waffle on a plate. I shot him my best puppy dog eyes.

"Oh, please. Turn those off. They don't affect me." Yeah right, in two seconds flat I had a waffle, orange juice, coffee, and maple syrup placed in front of me.

I winked up at him. "We'll do the dishes."

We spent most of Sunday lazing around on the beach. Liam rubbed sun block into my skin, taking extra time to get every surface he could find. I smiled over my shoulder at him and he bent forward to kiss me.

"Do you remember our conversation last night?" he asked.

"The one about the relationship status?" I asked, biting my lip and looking back out toward the ocean.

"Mhm. Just wanted to make sure you were conscious of what you were agreeing to."

I laughed and admitted I'd worried about the same thing. "So you're my boyfriend? Liam Wilder is my boyfriend?"

He chuckled. "Well I don't refer to myself in the third person, but yes, Liam Wilder is your boyfriend and... he's a lucky guy." He ran his hand beneath the strings of my bikini and I feared he would untie them as quickly as he had the night before. I slapped his hand away playfully.

After that conversation was over, I felt much less stressed about the situation. Being around him was easy and fun. Sure, when he pulled out a soccer ball and the four of us were playing around I could hardly concentrate from the way he looked in his swim trunks, but maybe I'd get used to that eventually. A few times I caught him watching me in the same manner and I had to stifle a laugh.

All four of us tried to prolong the day as long as we could. I was loading my plate in the dishwasher after dinner when Liam wrapped his arms around my waist and nuzzled my ear. "You don't have to go home. You can stay and I'll take you to practice tomorrow."

God, that was tempting. The feel of his arms around me blocked out most of my functioning brain cells, but I still had enough sense to shake my head. Liam was a force of nature in my life. If I let him, he'd breeze in and turn everything upside down until all that was left standing were my feelings for him. I had to put some healthy distance between us, just for a night.

I spun around in his arms and wrapped my hands around his neck. When I popped up onto my tiptoes, I was almost level with his face. "I should go home and call my parents... check my email, you know, wrap my head around what normal life is like again."

He chuckled, "This could be normal life."

I shivered at his insinuation. "Don't try and convince me. My desire to leave is already dwindling."

"Sounds like I should *keep* trying to convince you then." He dipped his head and kissed my neck. My eyes fluttered closed and I let out a small sigh.

Then I snapped back to reality. "Nope. No. No. Liam!" I pushed away from him and he held up his hands, trying to contain his laughter.

"You play dirty! Becca, let's go!"

She felt the exact same way I did, which is why we all but sprinted from the house, waving goodbye to the boys and not letting them get near us. We hopped into my car and I locked the doors behind us just for good measure. The second we were inside and safe from our hormones, we started cracking up.

"Those boys are dangerous," I accused as I started my car and backed up out of the driveway.

"Good thing you were there for moral support or I wouldn't have left. Penn probably would have had to kick me out three weeks from now when I'd barricaded myself in his room."

I laughed. "I just can't believe how fast everything is happening. Liam asked me to be his girlfriend last night."

Becca spun to face me in her seat. "What?! When?"

I bit my lip and tried to focus on the road ahead of me. "Well, sort of *in* the middle of the night, but then he confirmed it again this morning on the beach."

I could see her gaping from the corner of my eye. "What did you say?"

"Yes! Of course. Do you think I'm insane?"

"Yes, a little bit. But, that's unrelated to this situation.

Wow, he's such a catch." She nodded as if imagining him for a moment.

"What about you and Penn?" I asked.

Becca narrowed her eyes and stared out the front window. "I'm not sure yet. He just got out of that relationship and he's told me he wants to take things really slow. I don't think he wants to disrespect his ex by jumping into a new relationship so soon."

"I guess that makes sense. How long ago did they break up?"

"A little over a month."

"Hmm..." Honestly, I wasn't sure what the rule was on the appropriate amount of time between relationships. I guess it depends on how long they were together and the way they broke up.

"I think it's obvious that he has serious feelings about you, you guys were practically attached at the hip today. Just hang in there and I'll try to get info from Liam if you need it."

Becca smiled. "Yeah, I'm trying to just go with the flow, but I'm not very good at it. I think my body's too stiff."

• • •

Monday morning, Coach Davis sat everyone down and explained that Tara was no longer a member of the ULA team. We voted for the new captains right away, opting to bump Sofie up and then replace her spot with a junior that everyone loved. I expected more commotion about Tara's leaving, but as soon as Coach Davis said the announcement, it was almost as if you could hear an audible sigh pass through the group.

After practice I was heading into the locker room when Sofie caught up to me.

"Hey, could we talk for a second?" she asked. Her eyes were fleeting from me, to the ground, then back again, and she was fidgeting with her hands.

"Sure. Of course," I said, preparing myself for the worst. At certain moments during the past few weeks, Sofie was just as bad as Tara, but now that her leader was gone, it was as if Sofie almost seemed shy.

"I just wanted to apologize for everything. Tara and I were really out of line, and while we both should have probably been kicked off the squad, I realize now that I was given a second chance and I won't blow it. I should have never treated you like I did and there's really no excuse..."

I put my hand on her arm.

"No worries. Let's forget the past few weeks ever happened and we'll just move on. Sound good?"

Relief flashed across her face. "Thanks, Kinsley." To my surprise she reached forward and gave me a tight hug. It was awkward. So very awkward. I patted her back and then kind of squirmed out of her hold eventually.

Throughout the rest of the week I tried to stay in the moment. At soccer, I focused on soccer. Coach Davis pushed us hard and it felt good to keep my mind occupied on something other than Liam.

We had a scrimmage scheduled against another area college the following week, so we were gearing up for that. I was nervous just thinking about it, but Coach Davis assured me I would be starting in the game. Unfortunately, that only made me more nervous. It would technically be my first college game and I wanted to impress everyone that was expecting me to excel. No, I wanted to *exceed* everyone's expectations of me. I wanted them to say, "*I thought she'd be good, but that girl is on fire.*" They'd have no choice but to compare me to Katniss.

On Thursday, we were huddled up and Coach Davis was filling us in on last minute things before practice ended.

"Don't forget that this Saturday we'll be going as a team to watch the LA Stars play. This will be a good learning experience for all of you that are coming off of high school teams. The level at which these professional athletes compete will give you a taste of what we need to aim for during our practices and games. I won't make everyone ride together, just meet outside the stadium at 5:45 P.M. Wear your black ULA shirts and jeans."

With everything else going on, I'd forgotten about going to watch Liam play.

"You're going to get to see your *boyfriend* play in a professional soccer game," Emily teased as we drove home. We'd filled Emily in on most everything that had happened over the weekend when we got back Sunday night. She had her mouth hanging open for most of the explanation, but by now I think it was starting to sink in.

"Penn will be there, too," I pointed out. Even though they hadn't made it official, Penn and Becca talked every day, just like Liam and I did, so they were technically together. Labels be damned.

"Doesn't count!" Becca clarified from the backseat.

"Um, yes, it definitely counts," I corrected.

"So Kinsley and I will go to that industry event with the guys on Friday, and then I can drive the three of us to the game on Saturday," Becca offered.

"Sounds bueno," I quipped.

"Mmm, that reminds me... let's go get tacos for

dinner!" Becca exclaimed. Emily and I agreed on principle alone. You don't turn down tacos in LA.

Chapter Twenty-Two

Liam and I had schedules that didn't sync very well during the week. I practiced in the mornings, he practiced until late afternoon, and then it seemed like he usually had some meeting or interview to attend after practice. We'd met for dinner on Wednesday and chatted every night, but by the time Friday rolled around, I couldn't contain my excitement about seeing him.

Becca and I had spent our afternoon primping and shopping for the perfect dresses to wear to the industry event. It was being held at a ritzy hotel downtown and Liam warned me that there would be all sorts of agents, media, LA socialites, and celebrities in attendance. Basically people that I had about zero in common with, so if all else failed, Becca and I could hang out with the coat check crowd.

We'd searched the mall until we found dresses that fit our body types perfectly. My silk mini dress was slinky and loose and looked like a modern take on a flapper dress. It hit just below my collar bone in the front, but it had a plunging back, see-through long sleeves, and gold sequins sewn in beautiful designs over the entire thing. The hem cut off at an almost indecent length, but because the dress was loose, it allowed me to show off my long tanned legs without making everyone wonder if I moonlighted as a lady of the night.

I'd spun my hair into a loose, silky twist at the base of my neck so that my toned back was completely exposed.

"I'm starting to get really nervous," Becca proclaimed as she finished touching up her makeup. I was buckling the thin ankle straps on my nude high heels when I glanced up. She had on a sparkly white dress that fit her body like a glove. It was tight, with cap sleeves and a short hemline. She'd paired it with some fuchsia heels that were perfect for summer. Her short hair was straight as always, but she'd pumped up her eye make-up.

"Nope. No. If you start to be nervous than I'll be nervous. You look awesome." I stood up and saw my reflection in the mirror behind her. She'd helped me with my makeup so that my blue eyes popped against my tanned skin and dark hair. I felt *good*.

She dropped her makeup brush and started scrutinizing her appearance, winking one eye and then the other and then smiling from different angles. All right, she wasn't even getting ready anymore, so I waltz into the bathroom, spritzed us with perfume, and pushed her out the door.

"Stop winking at yourself, psycho. It will be fun. We'll meet the guys there. They'll hand us drinks, we'll mingle with celebrities, and then be on our way," I tried to assure her as we headed to the hotel.

I didn't admit it, but I was glad that Becca was taking

the role of Nervous Nelly because it forced me to be the confident, cool one for the both of us.

"Oh my god, if Amy is there I'm going to talk to her."

"Amy?" I asked as we headed toward the hotel.

"Poehler aka my best friend. Keep up, Kinsley."

My cell phone started ringing and I had Becca answer it so I could keep driving.

"Kinsley's secretary speaking, she's driving... we're on our way... probably twenty minutes in this traffic... okay I'll tell her... oh my god, no. Gross. I'm not telling her that... (laughter)... okay we'll call you when we get there."

Becca ended the call and dropped my phone back into my little clutch.

"That was your boyfriend. He can't wait to see you and he wants us to call him when we get there. He'll come out with Penn and get us."

I nodded. "What else did he say?"

"You'll have to ask him. You guys are gross."

I laughed and started to feel my shoulders relax. I think Becca was feeling better, too. We turned the music up and sang along the rest of the way to the hotel.

When we arrived, I pulled up in front so the valet could take my car. We both gaped as we pulled up into the driveway. I'd been to the Hotel San Louise once or twice for brunch with my parents, but seeing it lit up at night was breathtaking. The hotel was fashioned after the roaring 1920's. The facade was white with beautiful lights leading us toward the valet. Becca had texted the boys when we were about to pull up, so when I handed my keys to the valet and rounded the car I wasn't surprised to find Liam and Penn waiting for us outside of the hotel doors.

Boy did they look good against the backdrop of the hotel. I felt like I was stepping into a scene from The Great

Gatsby.

I paused to take Liam in from head to toe, admiring the way the black Armani suit was tailored for his body. He'd skipped a tie and wore his crisp white shirt with the top two buttons undone. His usually unruly hair was styled back, reigning in his rugged good looks, but he'd left his five o'clock shadow to balance out his features. I wanted to take the lapels of his jacket between my fingers and tug him toward me for a kiss, but we were still a few feet away from each other.

As Liam and Penn stepped forward to greet us, I held back a smile. Their tongues were practically hanging from their mouths. It felt good to know that I, Kinsley Bryant, nineteen year old soccer dweeb, could bring Liam Wilder to his knees... almost.

He reached forward for my hand and spun me around slowly. He whistled low and sexy when he saw the back of my dress.

"Kinsley, I think you forgot your jacket in the car," he teased as I finished the spin.

I shrugged innocently and inhaled his cologne. He wore his signature scent and I let it wash over me as he bent to steal a chaste kiss from my lips. Before he pulled completely away, he whispered, "You look so beautiful."

I smiled up at him, trying to take in the magical moment before getting swallowed by a giant crowd of people.

"Thank you," I said, patting my palms against his suit jacket and feeling his hard chest beneath the layer of fine cloth.

"I should have warned you, but there's a Step and Repeat in the hotel lobby before the entrance into the event."

"A what?"

Liam smiled. "A red carpet. They'll want to snap a few pictures of us before we head in."

A wave of nerves instantly crashed over me. Woah, wait. Was I ready for this? Coach Davis and Liam's sponsors knew a *little* bit about our relationship, but what would happen when the story broke to the media?

"So what are we going to do?" I asked, peering up to try and decipher what he was thinking. His features were sharp, but relaxed.

"I'd prefer to have you on my arm, but it's probably safest if I walk in with Penn and you and Becca walk in together after us."

I reached up to kiss his cheek. "Thank you." I knew he was trying his best to protect me from the media.

We explained the plan to Penn and Becca, and then made our way to the front door of the hotel. I could see the photographers through the frosted glass and my nerves were building upon themselves until I could feel my hand shaking inside Liam's.

He gave me a reassuring smile before letting go and heading inside with Penn. I tried to listen to the paparazzi, but it was impossible to hear them through the door. A few moments later, when Penn and Liam had exited the carpet, the front door swept open so that we could enter next. I reached back for Becca and took a deep breath as the staff held the door for us.

The moment we passed through the threshold, flash after flash started illuminating the ritzy hotel lobby. They'd set it up so that the event's guests were funneled down a long red carpet. Photographers were on one side of a red rope and there was a giant banner running along the back of the carpet with various brands' logos repeating all the way down.

I smiled and tried to look normal, but my features felt tight and fake. Was I smiling or just opening my mouth really wide? Becca squeezed my hand and I squeezed back as we walked toward the center of the red carpet. Once we hit a certain mark, a publicist insisted that the two of us turn and pose for a photo. The flashes multiplied as we angled toward one another.

"Kinsley, are you attending the event solo tonight?" one reporter asked, and the moment the question was out, everyone else joined in, one after the other, as their voices clamored to be heard.

"Kinsley, who are you wearing tonight?— Are you seeing anyone?— Do you know why Liam stopped volunteering with ULA?— Are you planning to take your relationship with Liam public?"

I just kept a fake smile plastered on my face as if I couldn't hear a single word. Even still, my head was spinning by the time the publicist gave us a thumbs up. I tugged Becca off the red carpet as quickly as possible and looked up to see Penn and Liam waiting for us at the entrance to the event. The sooner we stepped into the party and away from the media, the better.

As soon as my heels stepped from the red carpet back onto the sleek marble floors, I thought I was in the clear, but then I heard a familiar, shrill voice behind me. At first I didn't believe it, but when I spun around, I saw Tara posing with a handsome guy that I didn't recognize.

"I'm wearing Versace and these shoes are Louboutins, obviously," she answered one of the paparazzi's questions while fluffing her hair and striking the perfect pose.

"Your teammates just passed us on the carpet. Are you going to be hanging out with them at the event?" a reporter asked, pointing in our direction.

Tara's gaze followed his finger until our eyes locked and my stomach dropped. She should not be given microphone privileges. There was no way to know what was about to come out of her mouth next.

"We're actually *not* teammates anymore," she clarified with an air of attitude as she turned her attention back to the cameras.

That comment sent the paparazzi into a flurry of questions, and I was left clutching Becca's arm with a vice-like grip. Becca shot me a pleading look as Liam started pulling me toward the entrance of the party. He didn't want me to be subjected to her drama, but I had to know how she was going to answer.

"I actually left the team for some quite *interesting* reasons. I had a problem with a certain individual on the team. There was tons of juicy drama, but I have to go to the event now, boys! Maybe we'll get to the bottom of the story another time!"

My jaw ticked as I listened to her plant the seed of my impending demise. She was bypassing the gritty details of our drama for now, but she and I would have to clear the air soon. We both had too much ammunition on one another and I knew she was just waiting to use it to her advantage. Liam squeezed my hand and shot me an apologetic frown. I wrapped my other hand around his arm so that he knew I wasn't upset... just overwhelmed. I hadn't factored Tara into my evening attire. If I knew she'd be at the event, I would have tucked a flask into my sequined clutch. Or maybe a glock.

The red carpet led the four of us toward a set of double doors where a PR person was checking people off the list and admitting them as they arrived. When she glanced up at Liam, she smiled and waved us through quickly.

My heart rate started to slow down as soon as we were inside the majestic ballroom. In here, we were just another guest at the party.

The event organizers had spared no expense. The colors of the event were black, gold, and white and they extended to every single detail. Black cocktail tables were positioned throughout the room. They'd covered the walls in ornate black and gold striped wallpaper. White orchids sat on every table and black balloons covered the center dance floor. It was already packed by the time we arrived. People were milling around by the bar stations and the dance floor. I was relieved to see that it wouldn't be a sit down type of event.

Right away I recognized quite a few celebrities chatting with their friends and entourages. I was used to seeing them, having grown up in LA, but I'd never attended a party with so many of them in attendance. That's when it struck me that I was here as a date to one of those people.

The second we walked in, people started buzzing around Liam, waving hello and patting his arm as he passed by. He was clearly well-liked by everyone in attendance, a little *too* well liked by some of the women, but I did my best to ignore it. And by ignore it, I mean staring them down and praying they were actually men in drag.

Liam placed his hand on the small of my back so that his fingers touched my bare skin. We were greeting one of his friends as he ran his hand slowly up and down my spine, just enough to make my skin tingle. A backless dress was definitely a good choice.

"Would you like a drink?" Liam asked.

"Sure. It'll give me something to do with my hands," I

joked as he led us over to the bar.

"This place looks amazing," Becca noted, scanning up over our heads toward the coffered ceiling illuminated by gold stars. I couldn't tell if it was a lighting trick or if they'd actually stuck stars to the ceiling.

Liam leaned in. "Champagne or a Greyhound?"

I smiled at the luxuriousness of champagne, but I had to resist. "I should probably stick with a diet coke since there's media here."

He and Penn stepped up to order us drinks, and Becca and I stepped aside so we'd be out of the line.

"You look gorgeous. Are you still nervous?" I asked, putting my hands on her shoulders like I was giving her a pep talk.

She laughed and puckered her lips. "No, dahhling, *you* look gorgeous." I laughed. "Not really. Now that we're inside it isn't so bad."

I agreed and let my hands drop back down to my side.

"I thought those reporters were going to jump across the rope and tackle you," Becca laughed.

I rolled my eyes just as Liam and Penn walked over with drinks. Liam kissed my cheek and handed me a glass of soda.

"Why thank you," I winked. Penn handed Becca her drink and we all clinked glasses before taking a sip.

"Were you guys talking about the reporters?" Penn asked.

"Yeah, they were vicious," Becca answered.

As the group chatted, Liam placed his hand on my lower back once again, drawing me near his body. It felt intimate to have him claiming me like that. It was as if he couldn't stand near me without touching me somehow. I rested my body weight against his chest and I felt his hand dip just past the plunging hemline on the back of my dress. The one downfall to the flowy garment was that there were no barriers to keep Liam out. He easily slid his fingers an inch lower than they should have been. If he kept going he'd hit the top of my lacy underwear.

I eyed him warily, but he was talking to Penn and wearing a confident smile. The guy had one perfected poker face. I smiled to myself and took another sip of my drink, but when I slid the glass from my lips, I looked up to see Josh and the blonde bimbo.

Yes, the one I found in his bed while we were dating. They were heading in our direction from the entrance of the party.

I almost couldn't believe it at first. Surely, he'd have more class than that. Or maybe he didn't know Liam would bring me? Either way, my stomach clenched and I wanted to flee the scene immediately. Liam's fingers pressed into my back gently, letting me know he saw Josh approaching as well.

"Hey everyone," Josh offered with a small smile. I was almost surprised that he even came up to our group, but then I remembered that he and Liam had practiced together all week. Liam had told me that on the field they pushed all the bullshit aside and played as teammates. I wasn't sure what the rules were for this situation though.

We all offered simple hellos and I thought Josh would slink away, but no. He actually had the nerve to introduce his date, Jenny.

Penn and Liam nodded and Becca murmured a hello. She didn't know that Jenny was the girl that Josh had cheated on me with, but she had enough sense to realize that anything concerning Josh was bad news.

Jenny didn't glance up at me once. She averted eye

contact as her gaze flitted around the room. I could feel Liam tensing more and more next to me. I was sure my anger was a tangible thing floating around the entire group.

The silence was growing more and more awkward and eventually I just couldn't handle it. "All right, Josh, you have sufficiently made this awkward as hell."

The moment the words were out, Liam let his arm drop from my back and stepped forward, angling himself in between Josh and me. Thankfully, Josh wasn't completely plastered by this point and realized that fighting wasn't the best idea.

"Yeah, okay. You're right. I'll see you guys at the game tomorrow." He smiled tightly and walked away. Jenny trotted after him trying to keep up.

Our group was stunned into silence at first, but then Becca spoke. "I realize that he is beyond, beyond foolish, but we'll eventually have to be able to have a conversation with him since he's Liam's and Penn's teammates."

I scoffed. "Yes, I completely agree, but I'm not about to let him introduce me to the girl I found him in bed with when we were dating."

Becca gasped. "That was *her*? He had the freaking gall to bring her as his date and introduce *her* to *you*?!" She was fuming and I couldn't blame her. If I wasn't standing next to Liam, I would have been much angrier about the situation myself. But the moment Josh was out of my sight, Liam's cologne wafted around me and I remembered the guy I was actually here with. Liam trumped all.

I glanced up, making eye contact, and rested my hand on his forearm. "I hardly care. I'm here with you and there's no one else I'd rather be with. I just would love to not have to pretend to like her if I don't have to."

His sharp features started to relax as my words

washed over him. He took a deep breath and leaned in. "If I didn't have to keep up appearances at this event, he wouldn't be standing right now."

I shivered at his words. "Don't. Please. He doesn't mean enough to me for you to waste your energy. I don't even want to be his friend. I'll be polite to him whenever we're forced to be near him, but please don't let him ruin our night."

Liam kissed me square on the mouth, stealing my breath and replacing it with all of his feelings for me. When he pulled back I knew he was in control of his anger. My lips had replaced the need to beat up Josh. Kinsley's lips: 1, Josh: 0.

I glanced over to see Penn wrapping his arm around Becca and tugging her in close. She was smiling at him, and for a moment, everything felt at peace.

"I still have to say hi to a few people. Do you guys want to meet us on the dance floor in a little bit?" Liam asked Penn.

They agreed and soon he was whisking me through the party, never letting his hand stray from my back. He introduced me to his agent, the sweet woman who gave us a moment to talk the week before. She smiled knowingly when she shook my hand and I knew she'd been rooting for me all along. I realized then that she looked to be in her mid-thirties and was wearing quite a beautiful wedding ring.

"It's such a pleasure to meet you, Kinsley. You seem to be a good influence on Liam," she gushed, eyeing him like an old friend.

I grinned. "Oh really?" I wanted more details.

"He's been more focused on the important things lately. It's making my job quite a bit easier."

Liam chuckled. "Maybe I should make you work harder for that cut."

She gasped jokingly. "Don't even think about it."

We chatted a bit more and then he led me toward another group.

"I promise this won't last much longer. I just have to get it over with in the beginning, and then it'll just be you and me for the rest of the night," he promised. He took me in from head to heels and I swatted him playfully with my hand.

"I'm not sure that look you're giving me is appropriate for public," I warned with a teasing smile.

He smirked before pulling me in for a kiss. "Oh, it wasn't. You don't want to know the thoughts that have been playing in loop through my mind since I saw you in that dress."

"It's the back, isn't it?" I joked, trying to quell the heat between us.

His hand traced down my spine, landing just above my ass. "I've never considered myself a back-man until I saw you wearing this."

I laughed and he kissed me one more time before tugging me into another group. At least this time I saw a familiar face standing next to me. Albeit, not a truly welcome one. Brian King, El Reporter McLiarpants.

"Oh, hello Brian." I offered him a terse smile as Liam struck up a conversation with another person in the group. Brian turned to me and I could tell he was a bit shocked to find me standing next to him.

"Kinsley!" his eyes lit up with shock. "I didn't know you'd be here. I've been meaning to get in touch with you since the article went live, but I've been so busy."

"Ah, I'd imagine so," I said, taking a sip of my soda.

"How are you doing?" he asked, scanning briefly down the front of my outfit before meeting my eyes.

"I've been okay," I answered honestly.

"I'm actually glad to get to talk to you in person," he said, angling toward me. "I wanted to apologize. When I first asked you to do that article my intention was for it to be about soccer. My editor pushed for that romance nonsense because we needed ratings. He ended up spinning the story and I had to fight him tooth-and-nail. Obviously, he had the last word." His apology seemed so earnest, and my gut told me that he wasn't a bad guy. I knew he was probably under a lot of pressure to deliver certain kinds of stories to the magazine.

"I mean, I went to school to become a sports writer, not a contributor to a gossip rag." He ran his hand through his hair and I felt compelled to ease his conscience.

"Brian, no worries. I know you had good intentions," I said, patting his arm. His entire body seemed to relax and he unveiled a small smile.

"But truly, I'm happy to see you. Are you here with your team?" he asked. I guess he hadn't seen me walk up with Liam.

"Oh, no actually I'm here with friends." I trusted that he'd meant well with the article, but I wasn't about to blabber about attending the party as Liam's date to a reporter, even a friendly one.

"Oh," he nodded, eyeing Liam behind me, "I see. Well I hope you enjoy yourself. Maybe I'll find you on the dance floor later?" he asked with a hopeful glint in his eye. At that precise moment I felt Liam's hand wrap around my back, even as he continued his conversation with the other guest. The man was dominant and ready to piss all over his territory to say the least. I decided to push his limits.

"Of course, Brian. We'll dance later." I could feel Liam shifting toward me just before he cut in.

"Actually, I was about to take you there right now, Kinsley," Liam answered, taking my champagne glass and depositing it on the nearest table.

Chapter Twenty-Three

"You wanted my attention, and now you have it." Liam smiled handsomely as he twirled me onto the dance floor.

"Hmm, maybe I wanted a dance with Brian," I teased with a devilish stare.

"Over my dead body, baby," he joked as he wrapped his arms around my waist. A slow song played over the speaker system.

"I thought you guys were old teammates?" I asked with a quizzical brow.

Liam's gaze swept over me. "That has nothing to do with him dancing with you while you're wearing that dress."

"It's not *that* bad," I challenged as he spun me out gently and then rolled me back in. He was an experienced dancer and I found it impossibly easy to follow his lead.

His hand fell back into place on the skin just at the base of my spine.

He smirked confidently and shook his head. "My hand

is two inches above your thong. This dress should be burned."

"It's loose!" I laughed and he tipped me back, placing a warm kiss on my neck before dragging me back up.

Liam shook his head playfully.

One song transitioned into another and a few more guests joined us on the dance floor.

"I'm excited to see you play tomorrow." I smiled and wrapped my hands together behind his neck.

"It'll be a good match. Am I allowed to come to your scrimmage next week?"

I drew my head back so that I could look up into his eyes. "How'd you know about that?"

He cocked a brow. "I checked the ULA schedule. I'm not going to miss one of your games if I can help it."

I mashed my lips together and let my head fall against his chest. I don't know why the idea of him checking my soccer schedule seemed romantic, but it was. It showed how supportive he was of me and my team.

"Yes. You can come," I murmured.

We enjoyed the next few songs and I stayed in that world with him. Every now and then he'd spin and dip me, and I couldn't help the laughter that overtook me at his playfulness. As each song passed, the space between our two bodies seemed to lessen. His hands drifted up and down my back. His lips would skim my mouth, my neck, and my cheek whenever he could get away with it. I was slowly crumbling to pieces and he was the orchestrator of my demise.

"So much for keeping a low profile," I murmured, not truly upset at all.

He shrugged. "I have no problem with everyone in this room knowing that you're with me."

"Mmm, we'll see what they write about us in the papers tomorrow," I teased just as I saw Becca run by the dance floor. She was blocked by dancers, but I followed her path, and when she almost disappeared around the corner toward the restrooms, I finally saw her face was red and splotchy.

"Oh, no. Becca's crying," I murmured, pulling out of Liam's hands.

"Did you see her?" he asked, spinning toward the direction of my gaze.

"She was heading toward the bathroom. I should go check on her." I turned back toward him, resting my hand on his arm. "I'll come find you after. Okay?"

He nodded, but his eyes were narrowed. "Go see if she's all right."

I spun through the other dancers and rushed to the bathroom. At first I thought the room was empty, but then I saw that the last stall was closed, and when I stepped closer, I heard muffled crying.

I tapped on the door. "Becca?"

"Kinsley?" she asked, hopeful.

"Yes, open the door and let me in."

A moment later, the latch slid across and she propped the stall door open enough for me to slide in behind her.

"Becca, what's wrong? Are you okay? Did Penn do something?" I asked as she leaned back against the wall and hid her face in her hands.

Becca tried to take a deep breath, but a small sniffle broke through.

"Penn's ex is here."

I sucked in a sharp breath.

"Okay… that's okay," I answered, stepping toward her and bending forward so I could try and see her face. "Did you see her? Did Penn point her out to you?"

I wasn't connecting why she was crying yet. Was she just upset about the fact that his ex was here? I'd hate to see Liam's ex, but this seemed like more.

"She came right up to where he and I were talking and introduced herself. I knew it was her because he'd told me her name and he clearly looked distraught."

I nodded and bit my bottom lip.

"She asked to talk to him in private. He didn't follow her right away. I don't think he wanted to leave me, but then she latched onto him and practically dragged him away. I tried to stay positive. I thought maybe she just needed to talk to him, but when I came back from getting a drink, I saw them wrapped up together in the corner making out."

"Oh shit." I cupped my hands over my mouth and stood there silently. I couldn't believe it. Penn seemed really into Becca and to kiss his ex right in front of her was so blatantly disrespectful. I felt rage wash over me.

"I'm so sorry, Becca," I offered, reaching to touch her shoulder. She just shook her head and stepped toward the stall's door.

"Can we just leave? I don't want to be at this party anymore, and I definitely don't want to see Penn and his ex again."

I nodded continuously, pulling her out of the stall and out of the bathroom. There was no way to exit the party without heading back through the main ballroom, so I directed her through the crowd while she kept her head down. We were almost midway through the room when Tara blocked our path.

"Leaving so soon, ladies? Is Becca already plastered?" she asked, shooting Becca a pathetic glance.

I completely ignored her question and tried to shove past her. Unfortunately, she sidestepped again, and as I moved forward, my foot got caught on her leg. I tripped and tumbled forward, catching my upper body with my hands and banging my knees hard on the ballroom floor. I'd managed to catch myself as gracefully as possible, but I couldn't help bringing Becca down with me and the small commotion was causing a scene.

"Oh my god, these two are completely plastered," Tara oozed with a feigned concern. "Can someone call them a taxi? Or maybe we should notify security?"

"I'm fine. I just tripped," I answered just as a random bystander reached down to help Becca and me to our feet. I shot Tara a death stare and was met with an identical one from her. The threat was clear: *game on.*

"Kinsley, you don't have to get drunk at a party to get attention. I have a feeling you'll be getting *plenty* of attention from the press in the next few days," she promised with a glint in her eye.

I scowled, trying to determine if that was a direct threat or not. "What are you talking about?"

"Let's just go, Kinsley," Becca huffed, already moving through the crowd toward the entrance. I ran after her, trying to catch up before she saw Penn. *I'd have to deal with Tara later.*

I caught up to Becca and we were almost at the entrance of the ballroom when we saw Penn, Liam, and a woman I assumed was Penn's ex. They were a few feet away from the door and had already spotted us approaching. I wrapped a protective arm around Becca and tried to ignore the urge to yell at Penn.

That urge only multiplied when my eyes scanned over his ex. I wanted to stomp her beneath my heels. I didn't care what her story was. She symbolized Becca's sadness and for that, I hated her. She was pretty, of course she was, but she was the type of pretty that guys like, but that women can see right through. Fake, orange tan, false eyelashes, and a plastic surgery nose. She had long dark blonde hair that was piled up on her head and a skintight dress. Her eyes were focused dangerously on Becca and I felt my predatory side flare up even more.

Liam stepped forward and fell into step on my other side.

"I had your car brought around just in case," he whispered. "Were you just talking to Tara?"

I gave him an appreciative glance. "Yes, but it doesn't matter right now. Thank you for bringing the car around. We're gonna go."

He closed his eyes and nodded as if that was for the best. "I'd leave with you, but I have a few last things to handle. Can I come to you after I leave?"

I glanced toward Becca. There was no telling what kind of mood she'd be in, but if she needed me, I didn't want to bail on her to be with Liam.

"Call me first and we'll figure it out," I explained as we brushed past Penn and his ex. Becca turned her head away from them and hurried out. I shot Liam an exasperated shrug and followed after her quickly.

That car ride home was hard to endure because 90% of me wanted to turn the car around and seriously lay into Penn. What was he thinking playing with Becca's feelings like that?

"I feel like an idiot. He never told me we were exclusive. Yes, we've been spending time together, but he hasn't asked me to be his girlfriend. I should have expected something like this."

"No!" I protested. "He asked you to be his date tonight, which means that he doesn't get to make out with another girl right in front of you. He's not a fool; he knew that he was playing with your feelings."

"I told myself not to get my hopes up, but I did anyway. I really like him Kinsley, but he's off-limits. He's not ready for a relationship. God, obviously he's not even over his ex."

I didn't know what to say, so I just kept muttering, "I'm so sorry."

She didn't say anything after that. She stared out of her window the rest of the way home, and when we got there she went and washed her face and changed into her pajamas.

"Want to come in my room and we can watch something?"

She frowned. "I don't know. Maybe I should just sleep."

"C'mon. I seriously can't let you go to sleep like this. Come watch a Parks and Rec with me and we'll laugh and curse boys to the depths of hell."

She laughed pitifully, but followed me nonetheless.

I propped my laptop on my bed and kicked off my heels.

"Aren't you going to change?" she asked as I crawled onto the bed in my dress.

I shrugged. "It's oddly comfortable and I feel pretty in it."

She smiled and shook her head, and I leaned down to press play on the show. It felt good to make her smile after the day she'd had, but I couldn't concentrate on the show. I kept replaying our conversation and her tears in the bathroom. Becca deserved more than that, and I couldn't understand what Penn had been thinking. Why would he have done that to her? Maybe his ex-girlfriend was still an unfinished story. Did Liam have an ex like that? We hadn't even talked about it.

Becca interrupted my thoughts. "I don't think I'm going to give up on Penn," she murmured with her eyes still locked on my computer screen. She'd obviously not been really watching the show either.

I twisted toward her and nodded. "Not until you know the full story. I'd be the first to tell you to leave him and find someone better, but I honestly think you should hear Penn's side of it. That ex-girlfriend was staring daggers at you so she clearly feels threatened by his new interest in you. Maybe she kissed him and you saw it at the worst time?" I paused and reached to touch her arm. "But seriously, Becca, he has some groveling to do. He can't expect to treat you like that and get away with it."

She chewed on the side of her lip, thinking it over. "We'll see."

Just then I heard a small tapping on my door.

"Come in," I said, expecting to see one of our teammates pop their head through, but instead Liam pushed the door open and cautiously took a step inside. He looked nervous about being there and I instantly shot off the bed.

"Hey! What are you doing here?" I asked, unable to mask my surprised grin as I scanned down his suit. He was holding a plastic bag in his left hand.

"You weren't answering your phone and I wanted to make sure you were okay." His eyes scanned to Becca, who was lying on the bed in her footed pajamas, and then back to me.

"Is this a guy-hating zone? Should I leave?" Liam asked with a timid smile. I wanted to kiss it right off him. He looked so handsome standing in his suit in my bedroom, even if he did look out of place.

"Depends on what you have in that bag, Wilder," Becca called out.

He laughed and held it up to look inside. "Ice cream, candy, and some alcohol. I wasn't sure what you guys would want." He shrugged and I leaned forward, kissing him on the cheek.

"Thank you *so* much," I murmured into his ear before pulling back and taking the bag out of his hands.

"Should I leave?" he asked as I took the bag over to Becca and let her peek inside.

"Well I'm assuming you bought these M&Ms for yourself, right?" Becca joked.

He rubbed his hand along the back of his hairline, flashing us a sheepish grin. "There's another bag for you guys."

We laughed and Becca waved her hand. "C'mon. We're pretending to watch TV while we actually consider how I should slowly murder Penn."

Liam kicked his shoes off and then placed his suit jacket on the back of my desk chair. I watched him, completely enamored by his movements. He rolled the sleeves of his shirt up and then finally came over to the bed. It was a perfect sandwich in my opinion. Becca on one side of me, Liam on the other, and candy spread across my lap. What more could a girl want?

"Am I allowed to ask you about Penn and his ex?" Becca asked cautiously as she tossed him his bag of M&Ms.

"I don't like her," he muttered, tearing the package

open.

"Well that's good. You're on our team then." I smiled toward him and bumped his shoulder playfully.

"I forget how they met, but they dated for a year and she messed with his head the entire time. She'd string him along and tell him how much she loved him and then treat him like shit. I told him to leave her countless times, but eventually she left him and I thought he finally could see her for the bitch that she was.

"He hasn't seen her since the split, but I'm not surprised that she showed up tonight. She probably heard that he'd moved on and felt like she needed to sink her claws back into him. That's the kind of manipulative cow she is."

Becca spooned a bite of ice cream into her mouth as she muttered, "Wow."

"But you shouldn't write him off, Becca. I've known the guy for years and he's not a cheater. He's a good friend and a good teammate. Give him time to get his shit figured out."

Becca narrowed her eyes. "She's like a grown-up version of me. His ex, I mean. Seriously, I look like Barbie's little sister compared to her."

"No!" I protested just as Liam sat forward.

"Fuck no. She has those duck lips."

I eyed him with an appreciative smile. For a 6'3" soccer player that exuded testosterone and control at every moment, he was doing pretty well at girl's night. It was almost comical thinking of him beating up Josh the week before as he sat on my bed eating M&Ms and discussing relationship woes with us.

We all leaned back onto my pillows, talking about Penn and helping Becca feel better about the situation.

Liam gave her some advice on how to best deal with Penn. It was similar to what I'd been thinking. He told her that Penn needed to come to her and she needed to back off for a few days and let him realize what an idiot he'd been. We kept talking until the three of us were starting to nod off. I'm not sure who eventually fell asleep first, but we ended up sleeping like that: Becca rolled to the side in her footed pajamas and me, still in my slinky dress, with Liam's arms wrapped around me. His cologne swirled through my dreams.

It's strange how the little things end up illuminating your feelings for someone. Seeing Liam walk into my room with a bag of candy and alcohol for my best friend made me fall just a little more off the deep end for him.

Hopefully I was equipped with some floaties.

Chapter Twenty-Four

Liam was gone by the time Becca and I finally got out of bed the next morning, but I knew he had an early start. Apparently there was a press conference and some team photos before his game later. I was excited about the prospect of seeing him play.

I was in my bathroom brushing my teeth when Becca came in, eyed me wearily in the mirror, and handed me her phone.

"I don't know how I feel about it yet, but here," she warned. The image that greeted me felt like a punch to the gut. I leaned forward and spit out my toothpaste, wiped my mouth, and dried my hands with stoic precision, before turning and grabbing the phone out of her hand.

Sadly, in those few seconds the photo hadn't disappeared. I zoomed in and tried to quell the anger threatening to surface.

The photo was from last night. Depicted in a tight frame there was Liam and Penn with Penn's ex girlfriend and another girl that looked like an exotic-looking model. Penn was by his ex-girlfriend and Liam was standing beside the model. The caption below mentioned something about two LA Stars with "their dates" for the evening.

"I've already seen that photo on a few other sites," Becca explained, pulling the phone back from me and ducking out of my room without another word. I had no clue how she felt about it. For all I knew, it was the final nail in Penn's coffin.

I leaned forward onto the sink and let my head fall. I'd been so concerned with the media pestering Liam and I that I hadn't considered how crappy it would feel if Liam was actually reported to be with *another* girl. I shouldn't have cared. What did it matter if people thought that Liam was dating this girl? But I *did* care. I was angry that he was with another girl after I'd left. Did they dance? What made the media think they were together? Or was it just this one photo misconstrued to sell magazines?

My initial instinct was to imagine the worst: he was cheating on me. I was just as foolish as Becca, and Liam was playing me. After all, experience had proved that when it came to relationships, my worst fears were usually correct.

I sat on the edge of my bed and I let myself scroll through the photos of him from the event on all of the tabloid websites. That one picture was the only one where he was standing with the girl. But, there were surprisingly quite a few of *him and me*. We were standing on the side of the red carpet, chatting in the ballroom, and wrapped around one another on the dance floor. All of the feelings from last night rushed back in like a crashing wave, and I knew I wouldn't hold that one photo against him.

I could either assume the worst or assume that Liam

was watching out for me, that he was better than Trey and Josh. He'd done nothing but prove his trustworthiness, and I wasn't going to punish him for something he had no control over. I knew firsthand how quickly the media could spin a story, so I closed the web page and shutdown my laptop. When I glanced down at my phone, I saw a text from Liam.

Liam: My agent just alerted me to a photo circulating that has me posing with Penn and some random girl. It's bullshit. That girl came up to our group when I was laying into Penn and the photographer came around to snap a picture. I was *not* with her. I can't talk now, I'm at a press thing, but I'll call you when I'm done.

Kinsley: No, Liam it's fine. You came to *my* house last night. I trust you.

Liam: This kind of thing will happen, but I'll always be honest with you. That shit with Penn is not how I operate.

I sighed as I read his text. I knew I did the right thing by ignoring the gossip. Liam had a big day ahead of him and he didn't need drama from our relationship adding stress.

Kinsley: I know what I signed up for, Wilder.

Liam: No regrets?

Kinsley: Not when I think about how you looked in that suit last night... ;)

Liam: Don't start. I'm about to have to speak in a few minutes.

Kinsley: So I shouldn't tell you that I'm about to hop in the shower? Oops, there go my panties.

Liam: ... you're coming home with me after the game tonight.

Kinsley: Maybe I have plans with the team after?

Liam: Had. Cancel.

I smiled at his smug confidence as I threw my phone onto my bed. I'd lied about showering. I was going on a run and then I'd shower and get ready for the game later. I dragged Becca out with me knowing the exercise would make her feel better. I had no clue where her head was at. She'd told me that Penn had called her several times since last night, and she'd ignored them all.

"I'm just not ready to talk to him yet. I keep going back and forth between being angry and sad, and I don't want to cry when I finally face him," she explained as we started our cool down after our run.

"That makes sense. Give yourself a little time."

She sighed and propped her hands on her head so she could take deeper breaths. "I just wish I wasn't going to see him at the game tonight."

"Maybe it'll be good," I pointed out. "You'll see him, but you won't be able to talk to him since he'll be on the field. You can prepare yourself for when you do actually come face to face with him again."

After that, I decided to keep my mouth shut. Becca was torn; she'd have to figure out what she wanted to do on her own and I'd support her decision no matter what. Unless, of course, she wanted to swear off men and join a convent. Nun robes were just a short slippery slope away from her current onesies.

• • •

"What's with the oversized purse?" Becca asked as we got out of her car at the soccer stadium.

I blushed. "Um, Liam wanted me to come home with him after the game. I'm not 100% sure that I am, but I figured I should be prepared just in case." I hadn't packed much, just a change of clothes. It all fit discreetly in my bag so that it *hopefully* didn't appear too desperate.

"He's a good one, Kinsley," Becca offered with a timid smile.

The rest of our team was waiting in the designated spot outside the stadium, and once everyone had arrived, Coach Davis led us down to our seats in our matching black shirts. The stadium was huge and already packed with crazed fans, but we were given priority seating just behind the player's friends and families.

We were close enough to the field to see the players from both teams warming up. I spotted Liam right away and I couldn't help feeling giddy and proud. Penn was warming up near him as well but neither of the guys had seen us arrive yet. Becca sighed and fell instep behind me so she couldn't be seen.

We all shuffled into our seats, but the instant we sat down, a line of little girls quickly formed to get pictures with us. They were aspiring soccer players and one girl even knew my name.

"When I grow up, I'm going to play soccer at ULA just like you." She beamed up at me as I signed her shirt.

"You definitely will. I can already tell you're a great athlete, and uh, you know… don't forget to eat your vegetables." I smiled and handed her back her Sharpie. I glanced up to the girl's mom that was standing a few feet away with her iPhone at the ready. "Would you like a picture?"

"Yes! Please!" the little girl squealed and wrapped one arm around my back. I smiled toward the phone all the while feeling like I was having an out-of-body experience. The fact that even just one girl knew my name and recognized me was something I'll never forget.

By the time the line of girls died down, the players were done warming up and they'd disappeared into the locker room to get game ready. I took my seat next to Becca after she'd finished signing one last autograph. She was wearing a smile that hadn't been there before the girls had come over. Maybe she finally had a break from thinking about the Penn debacle.

We didn't sit there for much longer before loud dance music started pounding from the speakers. The entire crowd jumped to their feet and starting shouting and clapping.

It was finally time for the players to make their debut.

The announcer introduced the opposing team to a mixture of cheers and boos, but then he took his time announcing the LA Stars team. Each starting player was named individually while their picture was flashed on all the jumbotrons. One by one the starters were called and they ran out from the locker rooms to a cheering crowd. Penn was named and the crowd kicked it up a notch. Becca's claps halted altogether. His handsome face appeared on the jumbotron, and I couldn't help but sneak a peek to see her biting her lip in contemplation.

Liam was the last player called. The announcer dragged his name out and the crowd's screams seemed close to shattering my eardrums. The ladies went wild, even the girls on my team, and when his face popped up on the jumbotron, my heart melted. He looked so handsome with his killer smile. I scanned quickly to where he was running out, waving his hand toward the crowd and turning in a circle to acknowledge all of the fans. He was the crowd favorite and most of these fans felt like they owned a part of him; they'd watched him carry the team through some intense games and he'd made them proud season after season.

I clapped and cupped my hands around my mouth so that my shouts would carry toward him. I was only four rows up from the field and the team's bench was directly in front of us, but he still felt so far away. He ran to his team and his eyes scanned the crowd, but he didn't find me before the announcer started the pledge, and then Penn and Liam took the field for the coin toss.

Becca leaned in. "It's so weird that I slept with him last night."

I eyed her playfully. "Hey..."

"Okay, technically you were in between us. But doesn't it feel surreal? People are literally going crazy."

"They're going crazy for Penn, too," I reminded her.

She did have a point though. It seemed crazy to be dating a professional athlete. I would have never even met him if our paths hadn't crossed because of ULA soccer. In a setting like this, he really did seem out of my league.

"I wish he didn't look so cute in his uniform," Becca complained about Penn. I couldn't take my eyes off Liam long enough to notice though.

After the coin toss, we all took our seats again and the first half started. The game was fun to watch because I recognized most of the players from various parties and events.

It was a really close match and both teams had only scored once during the first half. Then finally during the second half, Liam blazed past one of the defenders for the other team and scored with a clean shot that sent the goalie sailing across the net. Liam threw his hands into the air and pumped his fist. I hopped to my feet and cheered with the rest of the crowd, so proud of him for helping pull to team into the lead. When he ran over to the side to grab a drink of water, he spotted me instantly. It was the first time he'd found me in the stands and I felt my heart puttering wildly in my chest.

I jumped and waved, and his grin widened even further. He pointed up at me and I felt like a tween staring at her heartthrob onstage. A few of the ladies in the rows in front of us spun around to see who he was pointing at and my cheeks flushed. My entire team was squealing and I just shook my head and covered my cheeks with my hands. Most of my teammates had figured out that Liam and I were dating by that point, especially since he'd slept at the house last night, but it still felt like I was on display for everyone.

The second goal he scored, he did the same thing and this time the cameraman working the jumbotrons was quick enough to follow his finger. It didn't help that the announcer knew who I was. He announced me and the rest of my team to the entire stadium.

Cue complete meltdown from embarrassment.

After that, I secretly hoped that Liam wouldn't score another goal for the rest of the game. We'd win without it and I couldn't bare another flood of unwanted attention. Yes, that makes me slightly evil, but c'mon.

"I think every woman in this stadium wants to kill you right now," Becca laughed as I slid down lower in my seat.

I shot her a pointed stare. "You aren't helping."

When the full-time whistle blew and the LA Stars

won, the crowd celebrated and cheered. It was the perfect game to start their season off.

Coach Davis gathered us all together at the top of the stairs. "Let's go down to where the players convene after the game. I think it'd be fun to show our support for Liam and the rest of the team," she said, glancing quickly toward me with a twinkle in her eye.

We were not the only fans with the same idea. They had metal barriers and security guards in place outside the stadium. Fans could stand behind the barriers and wait for the players to head out after meeting the press and finishing post-game protocol. Our team was crowded close to the entrance, next to the players' family and friends. I recognized a few of the other women from the industry event the night before, but Penn's ex was nowhere in sight.

After a long twenty minutes the players started trickling out. Josh exited with a few of the other rookies, but he couldn't see me behind all of my other team members. Becca and I had strategically stayed near the back of the crowd, and I knew we'd made the right decision when Penn walked out looking handsome in a dark grey button-down and slacks.

His bag was thrown over his shoulder casually as he eyed the crowd with his dark brown stare. He kept walking until he saw our small group, and then his gaze landed directly on Becca. She stiffened next to me, but made no move to walk toward him. He paused off to the side and stood, clearly waiting for her. A few fans took the opportunity to get autographs from him and he kindly obliged, but his gaze never left Becca for long.

Jeez, even I was sweating under his stare. How could Becca resist even one more a second?

He wasn't going to give up and I secretly wanted to

give him a high five. If he wanted her to feel special and prove to her that his ex didn't matter, he was starting out on the right foot.

For an awkward ten minutes, Penn stood there, waiting for Becca and talking to fans, and Becca just stood by my side. Eventually Penn called for her and our teammates gaped at her. She shrugged and crossed her arms as if to say, *I don't know who this 'Becca' person is.*

I mashed my lips together to conceal my smile just as Liam finally surfaced through the doors. Oh good god. He was freshly showered and his hair was styled back. He had on navy slacks and a white button-down rolled up his forearms. He was devastatingly handsome and I couldn't pull my attention away from him as I watched him sign autographs and take a few photos. He slowly made his way to Penn even though the crowd was screaming for him to come closer to where they were.

He patted his friend's shoulder and whispered something that made Penn shrug.

Then finally his gaze found mine, and he winked, slow and devious, as if he couldn't help exuding pure sex appeal.

And there went my panties instantly in flames. Damnit.

I didn't care what Becca wanted anymore, I wrapped my hand around her bicep and pulled her forward until we were face to face with the boys.

"Great game," I said with a broad smile.

"Yes it was. Are you ready to go?" Liam asked, eyeing the security guard next to us so that he'd know to open the gate. A few of the other players were joining their families and girlfriends as well so it seemed like standard protocol. "My car's parked in the lot back here with the rest of the players'."

I turned to Coach Davis and saw that most of the other girls had already started to leave. "Are we all set, Coach?"

She cocked a brow and gave me a hard stare. "Be safe, Kinsley. We'll see you at practice Monday."

I smiled and gave her a nod before turning back to the group.

"Well, I'm going to drive myself home," Becca began. "Kinsley, have fun and call me tomorrow. Liam, great game. Penn, you can go to hell." She said it so bluntly that my mouth dropped open.

Wow, she really wasn't going to let him get away with last night. Good for her.

"Becca, we need to talk," Penn demanded with a hard stare. His brown eyes were locked on her and I didn't think either one of them was going to budge.

Liam shook his head and then reached over to take my hand. "C'mon, Kins, let's leave these two alone."

A security guard opened the gate for me after I hugged Becca goodbye. It was probably best that I was leaving with Liam. Becca needed to face Penn in private... so there'd be fewer witnesses of his murder.

Chapter Twenty-Five

"Are you hungry?" Liam asked as we stood in his kitchen eyeing each other over the kitchen island.

We'd driven to his house out in Malibu so that we'd have some privacy away from his other roommates at the LA Stars' house. Liam hadn't even asked if I was staying over. He'd assumed and I hadn't corrected him.

"No." I shook my head and crossed my arms over my shirt. "Are you?"

His eyes narrowed on me, and he shook his head. He was leaning back against the counter with his arms crossed just like mine. He looked intimidating in his slacks and button-down.

We were eyeing each other hungrily as he pushed off the counter and stalked toward me. He reached out for my hand and pulled me after him until we were heading into his living room. The shades were drawn, but a few lamps placed around the room cast the space in a soft glow. Liam led me further inside and then dropped my hand so he could turn some music on. Arctic Monkeys, "Do I Wanna Know?" streamed throughout the room.

I watched him drop the remote back onto the stereo and then he slowly turned. He was wearing a dangerous expression and I bit my lip as his eyes blatantly perused my body.

Neither of us said a word as he moved toward his couch. There were no arms on the side near him so he sat on the end with his hands clasped between his knees. He was hunched over, watching me.

"Strip for me, Kinsley," he murmured with a dark tone.

His command caught me by surprise and my breath hitched in my throat.

I eyed the windows over my shoulders, but no one could see in. We were completely alone. I'd imagined this moment since I first saw him, and now that it was here presented before me, I couldn't calm my nerves. I licked my dry lips and stared down at Liam. His brow was arched in a challenge and I let his gaze and the rock music seduce my movements.

I kicked off my shoes and socks, winking at Liam as I tossed them his way. He chuckled, but his stormy eyes never lightened.

I reached for the hem of my jeans and slowly unbuttoned them. Liam's gaze followed my hands as they tugged the denim down my legs. I kicked the pants aside and straightened back up. I'd selected my underwear very carefully earlier. The soft pink material was detailed with silky lace and it caressed my skin gently whenever I moved.

"The shirt, too," he demanded as I stood waiting for him to step closer.

"So demanding," I murmured cheekily.

I crossed my arms in front of my chest and pulled the ULA shirt over my head. Without its protection I was at the mercy of his gaze. I glanced down at my matching light pink bra. I could see my breasts through the thin material, and when I glanced up, Liam raised the edge of his mouth in a devilish smirk.

He looked like a fantasy come to life. His toned legs straining against his navy slacks. His strong forearms peeking out from his crisp white button down. Everything was perfectly in control. I wanted to make him drop the act. I wanted to make him groan my name and forget that he was the one in the position of power.

I reached behind me and fingered my bra clasp until the dainty material gave. When a cool whoosh of air caressed my breasts I knew there was no going back. I let the silky straps glide down my arms, and then I let the bra fall on top of my shirt at my feet.

"You're so goddamned sexy," he groaned with a husky voice.

I bit the edge of my mouth and soaked in his compliment as my fingers found the hem of my underwear.

"No. Come here," he ordered, standing up from the couch.

I paused and walked toward him, nervous of how I would react when he finally touched me.

"Lay back on the couch with your legs hanging off," he instructed. I did as he said. My brown hair fanned out around my face and a few of the silky strands cascaded down my neck and over my breasts.

He came to stand over me. His hands ran down my body, brushing my hair aside and cupping my breasts. He stole the air in the room as his fingers toyed with my nipples. I arched my head back and whimpered as he traced the outline of my breasts and then bent to mark the same path with his tongue. His mouth clamped over each nipple and I could feel dampness pooling in my silky underwear. I hated that he was still fully clothed. I felt like I was at his mercy. So I reached up and cupped him through his designer trousers. He was thick and hard against my small palm. I traced the outline of his length and licked my lips when I heard his shallow hiss in response to my touch.

He backed up, disconnecting my hand, so that he could unbutton his shirt and toss it aside. His sensuous muscles made him look aggressive, rugged, and untamable. His tattoos drew over the sharp contours and I wanted to reach my hand out and trace each black line.

His hands reached down to unbuckle his belt and I watched with rapt attention as he pulled the black leather out of the loops. His wicked grin told me he knew what I was thinking. I could feel my cheeks flush with color as he unbuttoned his trousers, but he didn't unzip them yet. He came to stand between my legs.

He was already taller than me, but when I was lying down, our proportions were thrown off even more. I felt small and helpless, especially when he reached down and peeled my panties down my legs.

I lifted my hips so that he could drag them lower and I knew he could see all of me from that angle. His gaze focused between my legs and he practically licked his lips as he bent down to have a quick taste. I wasn't prepared for his tongue and I bucked my hips as his lips hit my bundle of nerves. It was too much too soon, and I gently twisted my hips, trying to dull the intense sensation.

He wasn't having it. His strong arms pressed my thighs apart on the couch so that I was completely bared to him. He stared up at me as his tongue stroked up and down, working me into a frenzy of passion and lust.

I couldn't wait any longer. I dragged my toes up his trousers. He was rock hard and I wanted to know what he'd feel like deep inside me. I wanted to wrap myself around him and scream his name.

"Greedy little thing," he accused with a dark smirk. He swatted my foot away and took one more taste before standing back to his full height. He reached into his back pocket, retrieved a condom, and then finally pushed his pants and boxer briefs to the ground. I'd seen him before, but this angle magnified every single inch of his smooth skin. He expertly rolled on the condom and then he wrapped his strong hands around my thighs.

I squealed as he tugged my body to the end of the couch so that my ass was right on the edge. He separated my legs and bent his knees until he was positioned perfectly.

"Do you want this, baby?" he asked with a sharp tone.

I nodded instantly. It wasn't a question I had to consider. "Yes," I said, begging him to sink into me.

His stomach muscles clenched in tandem as he positioned himself at my entrance. I tried to take in everything at once. His bulging arms, his strong thighs, his divine lips, and his dark eyes that were focused directly on what was going on between us.

When he slid into me I moaned his name, and he didn't stop until he was pressed in to the hilt.

"Fuck," he growled, dragging the word out so that it rolled down my spine and made my toes curl.

Once he was in me, there was no going back. Liam wasn't a slow and steady type of guy. He was a world-class athlete whose body was made for professional level sporting events. I was learning in that moment that it was also made for professional-level fucking. He slid in and out of me, standing up and leveraging himself into me. The angle gave him so much control and I couldn't temper the soft cries that fell out of my mouth every time he pulled out and sank back into me.

He reached down and grabbed my arms. "Flip over, baby," he commanded. He lifted my body and spun me around so that I was on my hands and knees on the soft leather.

He immediately sank back into me as if he couldn't handle the few seconds of transition. His hands gripped the edge of my hips hard as he pounded into me again and again. I was losing my mind with each thrust and I was helpless to try and cling onto my sanity. He stroked me to the rhythm of his hips. I came hard, pressing back onto him.

"Oh, god, that felt so fucking good. I could feel you clenched so tight around me," he murmured, readjusting us again so that he was lying down on his back and I was sitting on top of him. It felt deliciously sexy to ride him like that. I liked being on top, commanding his pleasure like he'd just commanded mine.

I gripped his knees and pulled myself off of him slowly before letting my weight push me back down. I felt him shudder every time I did it, and his dark, husky groans fueled me forward.

"That's it. Push yourself down onto me. Ride me, baby," he ordered.

I did just as he said, slowing our pace to a maddening rate. His hands were gripping my ass hard enough to leave marks. He let me move up and down a few more times, but then I knew I'd pushed him too far. He gripped my hips and took the power back as he started pounding into me from below. I was forced to take it as he yanked my hair so that my back arched.

"Yes, right there," I told him as I felt him stroke the spot that threatened to make me scream. I felt wild and hot. Our heavy breathing intermingled. Our skin was slapping together in a symphony of delicious sound.

"Liiaammm..." I dragged as he continued to push into me. I knew I wouldn't last much longer. His fingers circled once. Twice. And then I was coming again, harder and longer than the first time. He kept pounding into me, chasing my orgasm with his own. Just as my pleasure was starting to wane, I felt him come, hot and hard inside of me. I knew that if he wasn't wearing a condom he would have coated me from the inside out. The idea made me shiver with lust.

"Kinsley," he groaned over and over again until finally we were laying there in silence. I'd fallen back onto him so that my hair fell around his neck. His chest rose and fell beneath me, carrying me up and down.

We laid like that until our breathing eventually returned to normal. It was clear a monumental road had just been crossed and neither one of us was ready to get up yet.

"I need another shower. C'mon," he said, sitting up and carrying me with him. My thighs felt like jelly and I laughed when I tried to stand.

"Here," he said, scooping me into his arms and twisting me so that I had my legs wrapped around his middle.

I laughed as he started walking us to his room.

"That was..." I began with a dazed expression.

"Fucking amazing," he filled in before planting a kiss on my lips.

I chuckled and agreed emphatically. He didn't set me down until the water was warm and even then he soaped me up and helped me wash my hair.

"So, not a fan of the standard missionary?" I joked as I wrapped a towel around my chest.

He eyed me mischievously. "Not when I've got a body like yours to work with," he winked. "Now, I'm starving... will you help me cook dinner?"

I trailed after him with a cool smile. "Only if you tell me 'Kinsley Bryant, you are the sexiest lay I've ever had. No girl can compare to you. Not even all the models that I've slept with'."

Liam paused and spun around to face me with an arched brow. "No other girl compares," he smirked, stepping closer to me and bending low so his face was level with mine. "They were fucks, you and I are on a completely different playing field, Kinsley."

I smiled cheekily before dipping forward and kissing him on the tip of his nose. Then I spun around him and spanked him on the butt. "Now feed me!" I joked, quickly running away before he could return the spanking.

I, of course, wasn't fast enough and he made my ass sting with a cocky grin and a flash of a sexy dimple.

While Liam pulled out a few ingredients for dinner, I found my phone so that I could call Becca. I was dying to know how things ended up going for her and Penn.

She answered on the fourth ring. "Can't talk right now, Penn is trying to weasel his way back into my good graces."

I started laughing hysterically. "Is he there right now?"

"Yes. I'm actually at his house in Malibu."

"Hey! We're in Malibu, too."

"Oh good, I might have to come stay there depending on how the next few hours go," Becca joked.

I pulled the phone away from my ear. "Becca says that she might crash here tonight."

Liam cocked a brow. "Hope she enjoys hearing you screaming my name."

My mouth fell open. "Oh my god. Becca if you heard that—"

I could hear her saying, *ewwww*, even before I held the phone back to my ear.

I laughed, "Sorry. He can't be tamed... he's just like Miley." I shook my head at Liam, but I couldn't wipe the smile from my face.

He flashed me an innocent shrug.

"You two are gross. I might have to stay here just to spare my ears from the madness," she said, and I heard Penn chuckle in the background.

"All right, well call me if you need me... and seriously, Becca, hear Penn out."

Liam yelled so she could hear him, too, "Yeah! Give my friend a second chance."

"Okay, okay. I'm hanging up now."

"Bye, Becs."

After I hung up, I sidled around the counter and started helping Liam with dinner. He'd given me one of his shirts to wear with my underwear and he couldn't seem to keep his hands from sliding under the cotton hem.

I'd stir the pasta and he would set his hand on ass. I'd cut some tomatoes for the salad and he'd have his arms wrapped around my waist, watching me work.

"You realize we *just* had sex, right?" I joked, twisting around to give him a chaste kiss. I felt his hard muscles against my shoulder as I spun back around. God, he was in good shape.

"You realize that, as your boyfriend, I'm allowed to appreciate how sexy you look wearing my shirt," he joked, before setting to work on the garlic bread.

"It feels weird thinking about you being my boyfriend," I admitted sheepishly.

"Why?" he asked, preheating the oven.

"I mean, I just watched one hundred thousand people chanting your name. Isn't that crazy? You'd think it would go to your head, but you're actually a really nice guy."

He laughed. "To be honest, I still feel like the same little kid spending day in and day out on the soccer fields near my house."

"Just a little more in shape," I winked, and he shook his head with a small smirk.

We finished prepping the rest of the meal and then sat down and ate at his breakfast table. I pulled the shutters open so that we had a perfect view of the ocean with the sunset. It was nice just being with him after the chaos of the past few days.

He was wiped out from his long day, so we cleaned up quickly and then cuddled on his bed. Everything felt so natural with us. Each step that should have been awkward was eased by Liam's confidence. Before I even asked for it, he'd pulled out a washcloth and spare toothbrush for me in case I'd forgotten mine. Which of course, I had. Then he had the covers on the bed pulled back so that I could just slip in next to him. I tried to tone down how giddy I felt as I cuddled into his side and inhaled his masculine scent. *Be cool, Kins.* My fingers dragged across his chiseled abs, adoring every single contour. *This is your life now. You are the person that sleeps next to this set of abs. Also, this set of abs is attached to a man that probably has some major neurological damage since out of all the models in the world, he's chosen you and your flat-ass.*

"Hey, I like your ass. It's not flat," he said right after I realized that my internal monologue had actually been an external monologue. "Also, I'm more than just my abs."

"Of course you are, babe. Of course you are."

Don't worry, abs. I'm actually here for you.

"Yeah, still out loud," he smiled, pulling me into his side.

Chapter Twenty-Six

"Liam. Liam! Are you still sleeping at this hour?" A cheery voice rang throughout the house as I drifted into consciousness.

Then I realized what I'd heard and I shot up in bed. Liam was still sleeping soundly next to me, but I'd definitely heard the sounds of a woman humming and moving about the house. Then I noticed the amazing smell of sizzling bacon drifted closer.

Was there a *woman* inside Liam's house and was she *cooking* for him? What in the world? Did he have a housekeeper or some kind of weird estranged lover that broke in every now and then and made him breakfast?

That actually wouldn't be so bad... free pancakes.

I turned toward Liam and shook him awake. "Hey, babe, wake up."

He moaned then blinked his eyes open.

"There's someone in your house calling your name. It's a woman and I think she's making breakfast. Do you have any crazy stalker fans that would do that?" I asked, only half kidding.

He squinted his eyes and then shot up suddenly.

"Oh crap. It's my mom," he said, throwing the covers off himself.

"Your *what*?!" I asked, my eyes growing wide.

He grabbed a t-shirt out of his closet and pulled it over his head. Did he *have* to cover up his abs? Wait no. I couldn't think about that right now.

I hopped out of bed and went to my oversized purse to get my clothes that I'd packed the day before. I had a pair of shorts and a summery blouse, so I pulled on the outfit quickly and tried to calm my nerves.

Let's recap. We'd just had some raunchy sex in his living room last night and now I was meeting his mother. And oh yes, I'd gone to bed with my hair still damp. I reached up to feel around the web of tangles that had at some point been my hair. On a scale of one to toe-up, I was probably looking similar to Courtney Love on a bad day.

How would this even work? Would he walk out first and then I would follow him fifteen minutes later and explain that I'd slept in the guest room?

"Oh, ha-ha, I always come over to Liam's house at the crack of dawn... no, of course, I didn't have sex with your son last night."

"I forgot she was coming into town." He eyed me with amusement. "I've been a little preoccupied."

I wiped my hand down my face and then ran to the bathroom so I could pee and brush my hair. Thankfully once I was done, I looked semi-presentable.

"Ready?" Liam asked when I'd returned from the bathroom.

I gulped. "Are we going down together? What are you

going to tell your mom? Does she know you have girls stay over?"

"I'm 25, Kinsley, not 15."

I rolled my eyes. That wasn't helping. He stepped closer and wrapped me up in a tight hug so that only my tiptoes were left on the floor. "Besides, she knows about you and she's wanted to meet you."

I pressed my lips into a thin line. Had he really talked to his mom about me? I remembered him mentioning her visit the other week. I couldn't believe we'd completely forgotten. I should have had it tattooed on me somewhere.

He loosened his grip and then took my hand to lead me toward the kitchen.

"Mom!" Liam yelled as we rounded the corner.

"Liam!" she exclaimed, turning from the stove and throwing her arms around her son. I pulled my hand out of his so they could have a private moment, but it only took her a second before she glanced up and saw me standing there with my hands clasped in front of me.

"You must be Kinsley!" she beamed, pushing Liam aside like he was yesterday's news and then stepping forward to wrap me in a hug. Citrus. His mother smelled like fresh citrus, and I took a deep breath as she enveloped me in her arms.

"Hello, Mrs. Wilder," I smiled when she released me. Her eyes scanned over me, not to size me up, but rather just to get a good look at me. She was an inch shorter than me with the same dirty blonde hair that sat atop Liam's head. Hers was mixed with a few strands of grey though. She was probably in her mid-fifties, but she exuded a youthful air and I think I fell for her instantly. I wanted her to like me.

"You have the best taste, Liam," she winked at me. "He gets that from me," she said before going back to tending the stove. "Do you like bacon and eggs, Kinsley? I've got some muffins going in the oven as well." The more she spoke, the more I noticed her slight English accent. It added to her charm.

"I love all breakfast foods," I said, patting my stomach. She beamed at me again and then I finally glanced toward Liam. He'd been resting against the refrigerator wearing a playful grin. I winked and stuck my tongue out at him before turning back to his mother.

"Do you need help with anything? I'm pretty good with eggs. Wait, let me rephrase that, sometimes I can scramble eggs without burning them," I offered.

"Could you start making some coffee? I was filling the pot when you guys walked in," she answered. I immediately started tending to the coffee while Liam grabbed the cream and sugar.

"How long are you in town for, Mom?" he asked, slinging his arm over her shoulder playfully. She hip checked him and then shooed him away so she could flip the bacon.

"Well I was supposed to be here yesterday afternoon so I could see your match, but my flight was delayed," she huffed and threw her hand in the air as if to say 'those damn airlines'. "So now I've only got three days left before I head home."

"You didn't miss anything special, promise," Liam assured her.

"I cheered extra loud when he scored, Mrs. Wilder," I winked, and they both laughed.

"Well as long as he had you there, he probably didn't miss me at all," she quipped, piling the eggs and bacon onto a big plate.

I set the table and Liam set out a carafe of orange

juice.

"You two need to eat up, you're both top athletes and you need your fuel. Especially you, Kinsley. You look like you're skin and bones," she said, pushing eggs onto my plate.

"I promise I eat a lot. I just run every day," I shrugged and started biting into my bacon.

Liam gave me a reassuring smile and then reached to hold my knee under the table. I think all parents have instincts to fatten up their kids. My grandmother would always shove cookies down my throat whenever we went over for holidays. If only I got cookies shoved down my throat everywhere I went…

"Well you two are quite the athletic couple," his mom smiled and munched on her breakfast, eyeing us with admiration. I had no clue how she normally acted, but so far I felt like this meeting was going much better than expected.

"Good morning, you filthy neighbors! Tuck away your naughty bits, Becca's on the scene!" Becca voice rang out as the back door opened. Liam laughed as I hid my face behind my cup of coffee. I'd be karate chopping her naughty bits as soon as we were alone. A moment later, she and Penn walked into the kitchen like they owned the place.

"Oh, oops!" Becca exclaimed, covering her mouth with her hand as she realized her mistake. "Is this a family breakfast?" she asked, pausing so that Penn nearly walked into her. "Ignore what I said about the…"

Mrs. Wilder scooted her chair back to cut her off. She probably didn't want to hear anymore about her son's naughty bits. "No, no! Join us! You must be Penn's friend," his mom said, standing up to greet Becca. They shook hands as Becca attempted to cover her flushing cheeks. Hah.

"Hey *neighbors*," I smiled, hopping up to get them plates.

Thankfully Mrs. Wilder had prepared more than enough food, and soon the five of us were all sitting around the table eating and chatting. I only attempted to kick Becca in the kneecaps twice beneath the table.

"So you girls play on the same team?" Mrs. Wilder asked Becca and me.

"Yes, ma'am." I smiled at Becca who was in the middle of taking a big bite.

"They must only recruit the pretty ones," she proclaimed, making us both blush. The boys agreed emphatically. I rolled my eyes at Liam and he just shrugged like he had no choice.

"Well Kinsley was recruited because they felt sorry for her," Becca joked, "you know for being…" she paused and signed the universal gesture for cuckoo. I jabbed her with my fork.

"Becca's actually the team manager. She just gets me water when I need it and cleans my sweaty jerseys," I quipped with a cheeky grin.

Becca gave me a pointed stare and held her fork up in a way that made it look like she was flipping me the bird.

"We actually have a game this week that my mom will be in town for," I said, turning back to Mrs. Wilder who was laughing at our little exchange.

"Oh, how fun! Let's hope her flight isn't delayed like mine was."

I laughed. "Well it's a short flight from Denver, so it shouldn't be too bad."

"What day's your game?"

"Tuesday," I said, realizing that was only two days away. How could time be flying so quickly? I couldn't believe I only had two days left until my first game, well technically it was a scrimmage, but still the media would be there ready to build me up or tear me down.

She clapped her hands together in glee. "I don't leave for London until Wednesday morning! I'll be at the game sitting in the Kinsley and Becca fan section."

Liam shook his head, but he was wearing an easy smile. "Mom, maybe Kinsley doesn't want your English butt there. You are very rowdy at sporting events."

She eyed her son with an exaggerated expression of disbelief. "Nonsense! I was only kicked out of one for your matches, but that referee clearly hadn't updated his prescription contacts in years. You can't blame me."

Becca and I cracked up. "You can definitely come, if you'd like to. It's at 4:00 P.M. over at the ULA stadium," I explained.

"Well, it's settled," she said, pushing back from her seat. "Now you guys finish up so we can go do something fun. If we stay around here, I'll just fall asleep. Jet lag is already catching up with me."

We did as we were told, shoveling the rest of our breakfast into our mouths and then loading up into Liam's car.

• • •

"So, you and Penn are back to normal?" I asked as soon as we'd left Liam's house after dinner. We'd spent the day shopping around Malibu with Mrs. Wilder. I tried to keep a close watch on Penn and Becca the entire time, but I couldn't tell how much they'd worked out the night before. They looked better, but she still seemed to have the upper hand. He'd sidle up behind her while she was looking at clothing and she'd twist out of his hands and flash him a devious wink. It seemed like they were playing a little cat and mouse game.

Becca rolled her eyes. "If by normal you mean completely dysfunctional, then yeah."

I laughed and reached to turn the music down.

"He begged me to go home with him after their game, so I followed in my own car and told him I'd stay for thirty minutes. Obviously, that didn't actually work out too well. He explained everything. Just as you had suggested, his bitch of an ex-girlfriend kissed him, which didn't excuse him entirely, but he swore he was over her. He finally sees her for what she is, and he made it perfectly clear to her that he had moved on."

"At least she wasn't at the game on Saturday," I mentioned, remembering how confident and smug she'd looked as were leaving the event on Friday.

"Yeah, I listened to him leave a message for their team manager telling him that she was effectively banned from that section from now until forever."

I covered my laugh with my hand. "Damn. He must be serious."

She nodded but kept her attention on the road in front of her. "He asked me to be his girlfriend, to make it official, but I said I needed a bit more time."

That was surprising. I doubt Penn had many girls turn him down.

"He didn't seem too deterred by that today," I joked, recalling all of the attention he'd bathed her in.

She smirked. "I swear I'm not playing games with

him. It's just that Friday night was terrible and I can't just forget about all of that within 24 hours. I think it'd do us both some good to slow down and make sure we really want this."

I narrowed my eyes in thought. "So you aren't sure if you want to be with him?"

Her eyes slid over to me quickly. "Oh, I would cut off my right arm to be with him, but he doesn't need to know that."

"Becca! You little tease."

"Oh please! He deserves it. He needs to know what he has."

I laughed and pulled out my phone to check my messages as Becca turned the music back up.

Liam: My mom passed out as soon as you guys left.

Kinsley: She can't hang.

Liam: She wouldn't stop talking about you. She was practically murmuring your name as she fell asleep.

Kinsley: I think I'm leaving you for her. I need a more experienced partner ;)

Liam: Turn around, I'll show you how experienced I am.

Kinsley: Becca's driving... no can do...

Liam: She really liked you. Can't imagine why...

Kinsley: It could be because of any number of my talents. Did she hear me whistle? I'm a pretty good whistler.

Liam: I could whistle you into the ground.

Kinsley: What does that even mean? You'd kill me with your whistling?

Liam: You should brush up on your idioms.

Kinsley: Maybe you can teach me? I'll be the student. Do you own a ruler?

Liam: Kinsley...

"Uhh, Kinsley," Becca interrupted my texting session with a scared tone. I glanced up to find that we were pulling onto our street... but it was almost impossible to maneuver toward our house. News vans were parked out front with paparazzi idling next to them.

"What the hell? Are they just waiting outside of our house?" I asked, slipping my phone into my purse and pushing up onto my hands to get a better look. The second the news teams saw Becca's car, they jumped into action. Paparazzi pulled off their lens covers and adjusted the zoom straight onto the windshield.

Becca slowed the car down enough so that she wouldn't hit any of them, but they were getting way too close. Had she been going the speed limit she would have run some of them over.

"Why are they here?" Becca snapped, pulling the car into the driveway. The paparazzi hadn't followed us onto the private property, but I turned around to find them lined up on the edge of the street like a row of vultures.

"Let's just hurry inside and we'll figure it out, okay?" I grabbed my purse and used it to shield my face as I ran for the door. Becca ran next to me and we didn't stop until we were safely inside with the door locked behind us.

"They were calling our names, Kinsley," Becca said with a hollow voice as she leaned back against the door.

"They've been here all day," Emily said. We looked up to find her making her way down the stairs with a few of our teammates in tow.

"Are you serious? They have nothing better to do than camp out front of our house?" I asked, tugging my hand through my hair.

Emily paused on the last stair. Her expression was bleak and her brows were furrowed tightly. "You don't know, do you?" she asked.

I snapped my gaze toward her eyes. "Know what?"

She frowned and pointed toward the large sectional placed in our living room. "C'mon. Come sit. It's not that big of a deal, but you'll want to just hear everything first."

Becca and I followed her over to the couch as my heart pounded in my chest. I could feel it fighting to be heard, even as I pressed my hand against it, trying to calm my nerves.

"What the hell is going on?" I asked, pacing in front of the couch.

"Tara went to the media. She spun the story in the worst possible way, and you and Liam are the biggest news in the country right now."

I could feel the blood drain from my face. "Wait? What?"

"Tara leaked the story of you dating Coach Wilder. The media is having a field day, spinning it like he was taking advantage of you and they're making you look like the bad girl of soccer. Like you wanted to seduce your coach or something."

"Fuck! You've got to be kidding me. Does that girl have nothing to do other than attempt to ruin my life?"

I was beyond angry, tipping toward blind rage. She couldn't leave well enough alone. I should have realized she wasn't done tormenting me.

"And you're sure it was Tara?" Becca asked from her perch on the couch. I hadn't even thought to ask.

Emily mashed her lips together. "She was linked with the story over and over again. It wasn't like she asked to be an anonymous source. She was interviewed and her photo was added to the story."

"This is such bullshit!" I yelled, thinking of the girls that had wanted my autograph yesterday. I was a role model to those girls, and now I was no better to them than all the other dumb celebrities dragging their own names through the mud. I didn't want to be like them. I didn't want to be the bad girl of soccer. I wanted to be known for my skills, not who I was sleeping with on the side.

"Tara can go fuck herself," I explained, moving toward the stairs.

Becca hopped off the couch. "Kinsley, are you—"

I held up my hand. "I'm going to go call my mom and see if the PR team my dad has is working on this yet or not."

Once I got upstairs, I opened my laptop and searched for the news stories. Article after article came up, each one worse than last. Slut of Soccer was the name of the worst article, posted by a salacious blog that half of America seemed to love to browse every day.

I didn't have time to let my rage boil. Tara thought she was messing with an innocent rookie, but I wouldn't stoop to her level. She wanted me to fight back and talk shit about her in the media because that way she could ride the fame as well.

I'd show her by doing the exact opposite. I wouldn't let this affect my soccer game. I wouldn't let this affect my relationship with Liam. And I sure as shit wouldn't lose a wink of sleep over that bully.

I called my mom as soon as I closed my door and explained everything to her.

"Don't worry. I was already dealing with it this morning. I didn't want to notify you in case we could get away with you staying in the dark," she explained.

"Can we sue her for slander?" I asked, pacing my room.

"Well, technically, the facts she laid out were true, albeit skewed in a very negative light. We can't control what people are doing with the story on social media. People want a blood bath; they want to slander you and Liam because some people get off on tearing others down."

I nodded and chewed on my lip. "I should have been smarter about this. I knew she was going to do something like this. I should have put out a statement before she could."

"There's no use worrying about that now, Kinsley," my mom argued, trying to calm me down.

"Mom, I can't even leave my house! There are paparazzi lined up outside!"

"I'll be flying in tomorrow and I've already booked a hotel with top notch security. You'll stay with me tomorrow night and we'll have security at your game so that you can concentrate on what's important."

I sighed hearing the details that she'd already laid out. Holing up in a hotel with my mom sounded like exactly what I needed. I wanted to pretend like none of this was happening. Once we made plans for the next day, I hung up and texted Liam.

Kinsley: FUCK TARA.

Liam: I just heard— calling my agent + PR team.

Kinsley: I'm so sorry

My phone buzzed in my hand with Liam's name flashing across the screen. As soon as I answered, his husky voice spilled out over the line.

"Don't you dare apologize. We'll get through this," Liam murmured.

I already missed him. Why had I chosen to leave instead of staying the night with him?

"I know. I just hate that our relationship seems to cause so much damage."

"I don't give a fuck what the world thinks, Kinsley. I'm so happy with you. I'm focusing on what's important. You and soccer. That's all I need."

I smiled despite the circumstances, recalling what it'd felt like to fall asleep in his arms the night before. He was right. I'd focus on what was important and ignore the rest.

"Okay. My mom's coming in town tomorrow and I'm staying in her hotel with her for the next two days."

"That's a smart idea. Text me the hotel and I'll have a security guard there as well."

I didn't argue. His voice was commanding and I knew that he'd feel better if I agreed.

"Okay. Go call your agent," I said, falling back onto the bed.

"Okay… and Kins," he paused and I heard him take a deep breath, "I really care about you."

I closed my eyes and soaked up his words. I loved him then. Of course, I loved this guy who would take on the world for me and asked for nothing in return. Well, besides my killer lovemaking.

"I know. We'll get through this. Sweet dreams," I whispered before hanging up. It was too soon for declarations of love and I wouldn't dare say it during a conversation that had anything to do with Tara. I'd wait for a much better moment than this. Like the next time we're riding through a meadow, naked on horseback.

Chapter Twenty-Seven

My mom assured me that the press release was sent late Sunday night, but the media was still relentless on Monday. There was a group of paparazzi waiting for me outside of the house, shouting questions and snapping photos when I left for practice Monday morning. We were forced to practice in an indoor facility down the road from our normal field.

Coach Davis asked me to stay after practice and explained that she and the team were behind me. She said the college sent out their own press release clearing my name and condemning Tara as a "conniving bitch". All right, maybe that's not a direct quote, but still, Coach Davis was on my side and she wasn't going to give up on me yet.

I was eating room service with my mom on Monday night when my phone rang. Liam's dimpled smile lit up the screen and I felt my heart flutter.

"Hey babe," I answered with a tired voice.

"Hey, are you at the hotel?" he asked while street

sounds drifted into the background.

"Yeah, my mom and I just ordered room service."

"Okay good, I'll be up in a second."

I glanced down at my robe and realized I still had wet hair from my shower.

"Oh... yeah ...okay, see you in a second," I said, hanging up and glancing over to my mom.

"Liam's coming up. I think he might be here already, actually," I admitted with a sheepish smile.

My mom's eyebrows shot up. "I get to meet the infamous Liam Wilder. How exciting," she winked, and then took another bite of her meal.

A few minutes later, a soft knock sounded at our door and I hopped up to go let him in.

As soon as I turned the handle I inhaled his signature scent. He'd just come from practice so his body wash mingled with his sweat and musk. It was oddly seductive and I almost jumped him in the hallway, especially after I pulled the door open and saw his appearance. His light brown hair was unruly and sexy, his soccer shorts showed off his tan, toned legs, and his workout shirt clung to his hard chest.

I unraveled a smile and jumped up to throw my arms around his neck.

The security guard stationed outside of our door cleared his throat and I started to laugh. I'd forgotten he was even there. Mostly because normal people don't have security guards.

"Well hello to you, too." Liam smiled and dipped down to give me a kiss. As soon as he pulled away, his eyes scanned over my shoulder to find my mother who'd stood up to greet him. I unwrapped my hands from around his neck and stepped back to eye her. I knew he was comparing how similar we looked in that moment. She had the same dark brown hair that I did, but hers was cropped into a short pixie cut. We had the same build, although I had a bit more muscle, whereas she was a little taller and more lithe.

I beamed watching her take Liam in. "I can't believe I finally get to meet you," she smiled, reaching out. "I'm Lydia."

He shook her hand and I thought I saw a little blush across his tan cheeks. "Hello Mrs. Bryant."

"My daughter has talked my ear off about you for the past few weeks now," she admitted, and then I was the one with flushed cheeks.

Liam's cool gaze slid toward me.

"She's exaggerating, I hardly mention you at all," I winked.

Liam glanced back to my mom wearing a cheeky half smile. "That's not surprising to hear. Your daughter is definitely in love with me, Mrs. Bryant. She hasn't told me yet, but she will soon."

My mouth fell open. No, it fell onto the ground and just sat there as I stared at Liam. My mom laughed and glanced over toward me with a knowing smile. I couldn't believe he'd just said that so... bluntly. And damnit, could the jerk read me that easily?

"Wow. You seem pretty confident about that, Liam," my mother joked, waving us over toward the table so we could finish eating.

Liam shrugged and I could feel his penetrating gaze on me. "I read that Mark Twain said all you need to succeed in life is ignorance and confidence. Kinsley can attest to my having both of them."

I laughed. "You can read?"

He shot me a playful wink before my mom mentioned, "You know that's exactly how it was when I met Kinsley's father. I think we dated for a month before he asked me to marry him. But we were young and reckless, only nineteen at the time."

I coughed and tried to ignore the fact that Liam was still watching me. I'd forgotten about the fact that my mom had married at my age. I couldn't imagine. How would anyone find the time? I was trying to go to the Olympics, not plan out matching bridesmaid dresses.

"Well rest assured Mom, you will not have a teen bride on your hands." I finally found my voice and smiled up at her.

Liam shrugged. "You just turned nineteen. We have about 300 days left to change that."

My mouth dropped again and I turned to face him. "You can't be serious right now."

He smiled and shook his head. "Nah, but I was serious about the love thing."

I shot him a pointed stare and then picked up my plate of leftover fries and handed it to him.

"Are you sure you're done?" he asked, pinching my waist playfully.

I swatted his hand away, but if my mom weren't watching us I would have pushed him back onto the bed and kissed him senseless. "Yup. Eat up. Did you just get done with practice?"

"Yeah. I'm exhausted. I won't stay long, just wanted to make sure you were okay."

"And he wanted to meet me," my mom interjected with a smile that looked exactly like mine. The apple definitely didn't fall far from the tree.

Liam laughed. "Of course. Mostly I came to meet

your mom. You were an afterthought." He winked and I shot him an angry scowl.

He swallowed up the last of my fries and put the plate back on the table. "I better get home or I'll fall asleep right here."

I frowned, not ready for him to go so soon. "Can I walk you down?"

"Not dressed like that," he noted, and I realized I still had my robe on. "How about we go to dinner after your game tomorrow with our moms? My mom wants to see you again before she leaves for London," he noted as he walked toward the door.

I clapped my hands together and my mom agreed before I even had time to answer. "That sounds great."

He bent to kiss my cheek and then murmured in my ear so my mom couldn't hear. "I'll be cheering for you tomorrow, Kins." His voice skimmed over my cheek and I pressed my lips together and nodded up at him. Our eyes locked and I soaked in one last moment of being near him.

Crap.

Was I ready for this? At 19 is anyone equipped to give their heart away? Wasn't I still trying to get to *know* my heart? Its likes, its dislikes? Liam was older and had probably sampled a whole plethora of girls before landing on me.

As I closed the hotel door, I felt a sinking feeling in the pit of my stomach at the idea that I was maybe getting in over my head. Being with a star athlete is the farthest thing from a normal, wholesome relationship. I didn't want the limelight or the stardom and being with Liam meant accepting everything that came along with him.

Adios, heart. Nice knowing you.

• • •

"You girls have worked hard for this moment, and you all need to remember that this is a practice run. Stay calm and focused on executing clean plays. This is a simple scrimmage, so let's get out there and show 'em what we've got!"

My team was standing in a huddle just behind the stadium door. We'd donned our new baby blue uniforms, warmed up, and came in for one final pep talk before the scrimmage started. I could feel my nerves brewing over, but I tried to squelch them. Becca and I were both starting today's match. Emily hadn't made the cut to start, but I knew she'd still get a lot of playing time. We all would. The point of today's game was to get accustomed to playing as a team, not for one of us to shine above the rest.

Becca gripped my shoulder and I shot her a nervous smile.

"Wildcats on three," Coach Davis instructed, and then counted down.

"Wildcats!" we all screamed together in unison, and then the door sprung open and we were running out onto the field. It was a beautiful day in LA. The sun was shining overhead and most of the smog from this morning had cleared so that the temperature was warm and inviting. I was already sweating from our warm up, but it felt good. This is what I loved. I lived for soccer games; those ninety minutes of head to head competition fueled my body like nothing else in life.

I ran alongside Becca toward to the sideline and looked up into the packed stands to find my mom sitting next to Mrs. Wilder. They looked cute perched next to one another, like they might have been friends for years. I waved to them both as they chanted for Becca and me. I didn't see Liam yet, but I knew he was probably still at practice.

There was a pile of people hoarding the media box, much more than there should have been for a preseason women's soccer scrimmage. I rolled my eyes and ignored them. There was enough riding on this game without the added stress of my failures getting plastered across the Internet.

Sofie and our co-captain stepped forward to do the coin toss, and then we took the field to cheering fans. I marked my position and shook out my arms, trying to loosen my muscles and calm my breathing. It was normal to feel nervous before a match, especially since I hadn't played an official game in months, but these nerves were in a league of their own.

I bent forward and gripped my knees, centering myself in the moment. The media would spin their stories however they damn well pleased, so there was no point in stressing about it. My eyes focused on the blades of grass bending beneath my cleat as my resolve began to build. This was *my* game. The media couldn't touch me here.

The referee blew his whistle and in a flash, the game began.

We'd lost the toss, but it wasn't long until our defenders assumed control of the ball and advanced it downfield. Everything fell into sync as it should have. I worked my way into open space so Becca could pass me the ball. Her pass hit me in stride, and I used quick footwork to evade a few defenders. I was in my element, slicing through double teams and dodging slide tackles, and

341

then I passed the ball to the next player. By half-time we were up by three and I was feeling confident. I'd executed well so far and my endurance was hardly being tested. All the late night runs and extra workouts were paying off.

I ran off the field to sub out and when I got to the side, I looked up to find Liam leaning against the field's fence. He looked just as sweaty as I did. I guess he'd rushed over from practice instead of showering. When he saw me glance toward him, he dipped his head and sent me a confident smile. There was no need to draw any more attention than that, especially with the media's lenses pointed directly at us. I shot him a quick wink and then turned back to my team in time to catch Coach Davis' waving us into a huddle.

The second half passed quickly, and other than one collision with a defender for the other team, I'd played a stellar game. It felt like a rush, coming off that field with a preseason win under our belt. Coach Davis was proud of us and I'd noticed that Becca and Emily had played great as well. I knew if we kept it up, we'd definitely be contenders for the national championship. I showered quickly and put on a fresh pair of cut-offs and a flowy tank top that I'd packed in my bag.

"Do either of you want to come with us to get dinner?" I asked Emily and Becca as we headed out of the locker room.

"Nah, Penn's picking me up," Becca said.

"I have a Skype date," Emily winked. She and her boyfriend probably kept Skype in business, but I couldn't blame them. I'd do the same thing if Liam lived across the country.

"All right, I'll see you guys later then!" I waved as we parted ways. They headed toward the parking lot and I turned to find my tiny cheering section waiting for me at the base of the bleachers. I couldn't help the smile from unfolding across my face at the sight.

"There she is!" Mrs. Wilder cheered, throwing her hands in the air. I laughed and shook my head as they all clapped loudly. They really were making a big deal out of this.

"For someone that hates being in the limelight you guys sure know how to put the attention on me," I joked, stepping up to the group and giving my mom a side hug. She squeezed me back hard before letting go. A bright camera flash caught the entire exchange, momentarily blinding me.

"All right, All right. Let's go eat and we'll *only* talk about what a stellar soccer player you are as we walk to the car," my mom promised.

I'd felt cheerful walking up to the group, but my endorphins from the game started wearing off as soon as I was reminded of the shuttering cameras. The paparazzi were completely impossible to ignore, even as I tried to push their presence to the back of my mind.

I hadn't searched my name on the internet since that night a few days ago, but I knew it wasn't getting better. As long as Liam and I were together, I would be in front of the spotlight, and I had to consider if I was doing the right thing. I was putting a lot on the line for a guy that was probably as ready to commit to a relationship as George Clooney was.

Chapter Twenty-Eight

Thursday evening, I was standing in Liam's kitchen starting on dinner. Both of our moms had left the day before, and we were finally going to get some alone time. He was due home from practice any minute, which is why I was moving around the room like a madwoman trying to get everything prepared.

I was making lasagna and a salad that my mom had given me the recipe for. My first idea had been to cover myself in rolls of sushi and let Liam eat them off of me, but Becca said she didn't want to picture my naked ass every time she tried to order a California Roll. *Some kind of friend she was.* I threw some cranberries and walnuts on top of the salad, and then popped the lasagna into the oven just as Liam opened his back door.

Show time.

I closed the oven and twisted around to spot him standing in the doorway. He'd showered after practice and was wearing worn jeans and a white t-shirt. I smiled down at my own wardrobe. I'd slipped on a pair of skinny jeans that I knew would drive him insane and a blue v-neck that was comfortable, but sexy.

His hair was still damp from the shower and he had one sexy brow arched at the sight before him.

"I'm preparing a feast," I announced with a flourish of my hand.

"I see that. It smells awesome," he complimented, dropping his workout bag and keys on the table and continuing toward me. "I like this sight as well."

"The mess?" I asked, gazing down at the cheese, pasta wrappers, and the cutting board with chopped up tomatoes and onions. There was tomato sauce spilled on the counter as well. Had I managed to put anything actually in the damn lasagna?

He stepped closer still, coming to stand right behind me so he could wrap his arms around my waist.

"No. You in my house when I get home from practice," he answered, eliciting a wave of goose bumps.

"It was fun, like I was playing house in someone else's kitchen," I shrugged. "I swear I'll clean all of this up."

He chuckled and spun me around so that my back was to the counter. "*We'll* clean it up. What's in the oven?"

"A lasagna," I answered, feeling his lips briefly make contact with my neck. It was enough to elicit a soft moan.

"How long do we have until it's done?"

I cocked a brow as his hand drifted beneath my shirt. "About an hour. I just put it in."

A seductive smile spread across his lips and I suddenly knew I was in trouble.

"Well, I've had almost a full week without getting to touch you and I'd like to make up for that," he said, lifting my shirt and skimming his hands upward, over my ribcage and breasts.

I lifted my arms up over my head and cast him a devious smile as he pulled off my shirt and tossed it onto the kitchen table. His gaze drifted down to the swell of my breasts peeking out of my black bra and his eyes narrowed slightly at the sight before him. *High five, Mrs. Victoria Secret.*

I dropped my hands to undo his jeans and then I pushed them down his long toned legs. Everything about him was worthy of worship, but those soccer legs made my sexual prowess shine. I let my hands drift over his thighs and back up, watching as he hardened beneath his black boxer briefs.

He was every ounce of man, and as I scored over his body, I realized that I wanted to be completely taken by him. He tugged his shirt over his head and then reached down to wrap his hands around my biceps, pulling me to my feet. I didn't have time to catch my footing before his hand was dipping down the front of my jeans. He unbuckled them and the zipper gave way as his finger sank into me. My mouth fell open, but no sounds escaped. He slowly withdrew his finger before sinking into me again.

"This is what I've been dreaming about all week," he murmured, dipping forward to steal a kiss. His lips were hungry and demanding; he possessed my mouth and I tried to keep up, but he overwhelmed my senses. He kept sliding in and out of me, slowly at first but then picking up the pace. I felt myself crawling toward an orgasm just as his thumb started spinning soft circles. He had masterful hands and the pad of his thumb might have been my favorite part of his entire body.

He withdrew his mouth from mine just as his fingers sped up their pace. He leaned back and watched my reactions to what he was doing like he was a voyeur. It felt sinfully sexy to have him watch me come. I licked my lips, trying to dampen the dry flesh, just as a shudder ran through me.

"Come for me, baby. Let me watch you."

My blue eyes met his grey stare and a spark caught fire inside of me. I came around his fingers, leaning back against the counter and moaning his name over and over again.

There was no time to recover. I was still feeling the echoes of the orgasm as he stripped off my jeans and panties and spun me around so that my hip bones met the counter. He flicked off my bra and shoved everything on the counter aside so there was room for me.

"Holy," I whispered as I felt him push himself against my exposed flesh. I'd never had a man take me the way he did. He didn't ask for permission. When we were making love, exploring each other, my body belonged to him like he had the sole rights to it.

"Bend forward, baby."

I gaped at his sexy command, but nevertheless, I felt myself bending forward. The cold granite countertop pressed against my breasts, but I didn't shirk away from the slight sting. I was too busy concentrating on his fingers spreading my entrance and appreciating my beauty.

He groaned behind me and then slid down onto his knees to lap me up with his tongue. I bit down on my bottom lip, but soft moans still escaped me. My fingers gripped the edge of the counter as he licked me slowly, dragging his tongue from the very base of my entrance all the way back up. He used his palms to spread my legs out even further, baring every ounce of my flesh for him. I thought my hands would break off the edge of the granite I was gripping down so hard.

"You are the fucking sexiest thing I've ever laid eyes on," he swore, leisurely stroking me up and down. I picked my head up off the counter and spun around to see him rubbing himself with one hand while exploring me with the other.

God, I wanted that image burned into my memory forever.

"Have you ever been taken this way before?" he asked with a controlling stare. His words were dark, but they sparked something inside of me that needed to hear them. I loved his easy confidence. His absolute ownership of the situation.

I shook my head no and he dragged his gaze up to my eyes.

"Hold onto the counter," he instructed as he removed his boxer-briefs. He was hard and throbbing. I could remember exactly how he'd felt the last time we'd had sex: like my body couldn't decide if he was tearing me apart or building me back up. I didn't care. I needed him inside of me again or I'd scream. Maybe I'd end up screaming either way.

He unrolled a condom and then positioned himself back against me from behind. One hand gripped my hip tightly, the other reached up and wrapped around my neck so that I couldn't turn away from him. I appreciated the support. My head started to feel heavy, but with his hand there I could watch him shove into me slowly at first, and then in one quick thrust, I felt all of him inside of me, spreading me open and crashing into my world.

"Oh my god, Liam," I moaned as he settled into me, not moving at first but letting me get accustomed to his size.

His eyes were dilated in lust and each of his features seemed even sharper and more in control than usual. His freshly shaven face gave way to his strong jaw-line, his chiseled cheekbones, and his perfectly pouty lips.

He slowly withdrew and I shuddered. I could hardly catch my breath and the position he had me in wasn't helping. Then he thrust back into me, hard, and I cried out. It was pure bliss.

It was all the goading he needed. He tightened his hold on my waist and started pounding into me from behind. My body rocked into the granite with each roll of his hips. His movements were so quick and controlled. There was no time to process each thrust before he was starting on the next. He was fucking me in every sense of the word and I felt my body blooming with lust and desire.

He picked up one of my legs and pushed it onto the counter. The movement forced a plate off the edge and it fell to the floor with a loud clap. Neither one of us cared as Liam continued to seduce my body.

He pulled me up so that my back was pressed against his front. His hand wrapped around my throat and I twisted around to steal a kiss. His tongue met mine as my hips bounced back onto him. The first shocks of an orgasm raced through me and suddenly I had to come. It was on the horizon and I couldn't let it wash away.

"Oh, don't stop. Don't stop," I begged as his hips met mine. Even when he thrust into me quick and hard, his movements were calculated and smooth, like he was using his hips to curl into me.

"Fuck," I moaned as one particularly seductive thrust rubbed directly against a sensitive bundle of nerves. I gripped the back of his neck as an orgasm overtook me. My stomach quivered and he groaned huskily into my ear, drawing out even more pleasure. He came just after I did. He'd hung on long enough, and when he spilled himself into me, I shuddered as the feelings threatened to consume me.

"Liam!" It felt like too much, like my body wouldn't survive the deliciousness of our lovemaking.

He fed off my desire, rocking his hips into me until we were both falling to pieces on the kitchen floor. Our bodies slumped down and I fell on top of him with uncontrollable, delirious laughter.

"I mean, seriously, that is not even fair. How do women walk away from you?" I asked as my head rested on his chest.

"They don't," he quipped, making my heart stop.

His words were meant as a joke, but I knew they were far from it.

They don't.

What the fuck had I been thinking, falling in love with a guy like him? Not two months ago I was swearing off the male race all together. I couldn't have found a nice, humble guy who was my age and didn't have sex like it was his life's calling? How stupid was I to put my heart on the line for the third time?

I laughed at the thought. That wasn't true; I'd never put my heart on the line with Trey and Josh like I was doing right now with Liam. Liam wasn't something you chose to do or not do; he was like a virus, invading your system and taking root without your permission. He did it to every female in the United States, and sadly, I was no different.

I pushed off the ground and shot him a small smile before heading toward the bathroom to wash up before dinner.

"Kins?" he asked, standing up and tossing away the condom.

I shot him a wave and kept walking. I felt tears burning the edge of my eyes and I realized that having that revelation directly after making love had been a bad move on my part. I always felt a little more vulnerable after mind-blowing orgasms. Maybe I just needed a few minutes to collect myself.

I could feel his presence behind me and I knew he'd catch up to me before I reached the shower. I hurried my pace as I walked into his bathroom. Then I saw the separate room with the toilet and ran straight for it. He couldn't follow me in there. I locked the door and sank down onto the seat folding my head into my hands.

He didn't knock right away. Maybe he wanted to give me the chance to calm down, or maybe he thought I was actually using the facilities. But when I didn't come out even after I'd flushed and stayed inside for a few more minutes, his voice drifted through the solid wood.

"Kins, are you okay?" he asked with such sincerity that it only made my tears even harder to push down.

"Yes... just *regrouping*," I answered honestly.

"Could you regroup with me? What's wrong, babe?" I could hear his body slide down the wall next to the door and I knew he wasn't going to budge until I came out.

"Will you be honest with me if I ask you something? Completely honest?" I asked, stepping closer to the door and resting my forehead against it.

"Yes. Just tell me what's going on. We'll fix it."

I took a deep breath and prepared my heart for the wrong answer.

"Am I being naïve to trust you? Seriously, Liam, you *have* to be honest with me, I can handle the truth... what I

351

can't handle is getting into another relationship with a guy who doesn't respect me enough to be honest."

He sighed on the other side of the door. "Kins, get your ass out of that bathroom and talk to me face to face."

I mashed my lips together in annoyance, but twisted the knob and cracked the door open. He was still gloriously naked, sitting on the ground, staring up at me with earnest eyes.

Once I'd cracked the door slightly, he reached forward, pried the wood out of my hands, and pushed the door open completely. I jumped slightly, but he shook his head as if to tell me to calm down.

"I am not Josh. I will not hurt you. I was joking in the kitchen. I'm just a normal guy, Kinsley. I want what any other guy wants: to have a girlfriend that he loves and who loves him in return. I want there to be trust between us, and I want us to be open with one another. We haven't reached that point yet. I know I have to work to undo the crap other guys have done to you, but please don't shut me out. I can't change your past, Kinsley."

I nodded and finally felt the tears streaming down my cheeks.

"I just felt scared and vulnerable lying on that kitchen floor with you. You could pull the rug out from under me whenever you feel like it... whenever you're ready to move on."

He reached up and pulled my hand down so that I collapsed onto his lap. Our skin was pressed together, hot and sweaty from our lovemaking, but I loved it all the same.

"I love you, Kinsley Bryant. I love you because you aren't afraid to go for your dream. I love you because you had the balls to ask me to show you my tattoos when you didn't even know me. I love you because you're so talented and yet so humble. You've been given this tremendous gift and you push yourself every day to become even better. You're inspiring to be around and I love you. Please, believe that."

I stared at his chiseled chest, rising and falling, and let his words marinate inside of me. After a few moments, I finally glanced up and flashed him a small smile.

"You didn't say anything about my rockin' bod or my quick wit..." He started laughing and shook his head, but I kept going despite my laughter. "Or my amazing talents in the bedroom, or my stellar whistlinggggaggghh—" he started tickling me and I couldn't speak over the laughter. I had to use every bit of strength to fend him off.

"Ahhh, STOP Liam Wilder. Right now!" I demanded, though he didn't heed my harsh tone. He picked me up off the ground and carried me toward the shower, depositing us both under the warm stream. He kept holding me, letting the water rush over both of us.

"By the way, I'm on birth control and I'm clean y'know... if next time we want to…?"

He kissed me before I could continue. "I got checked before we started dating, so yeah, no more condoms."

I smiled up at him. "Perfect. Let's go again."

He laughed and tossed water onto me. "You're insatiable, but I love you," he murmured, kissing my lips. "I love you," he said again, kissing each of my cheeks.

When I opened my mouth to tell him that I loved him too, he stole my breath with a kiss and I never got the chance. I think the sneaky twit did it on purpose.

Chapter Twenty-Nine

"Are you sure this is a good idea to look at this?" Becca asked as we huddled together over my computer on my bed. I was finally going to go online and see what was being said about me. I knew it was a bad idea, but curiosity was eating away at me and I had to know.

"No, this is a terrible idea, but since we've already closed the drapes and locked the doors, we have no choice."

"Yeah… that's not how that works, Kinsley," Becca laughed.

"There's no choice, Becca!" I added dramatically.

"Whatever, weirdo."

My life had completely flipped upside down in the past few weeks. I used to take my old life for granted. Going to the grocery store, to practice, out to eat—I couldn't do any of it anymore without a group of photographers hounding my every move. And I wasn't even doing anything interesting! Had I been leaving clubs at

2:00 A.M. with white powder dusting my nose, sure, maybe Instagram me, but carrying Whole Foods bags to my car did not seem interesting to me.

Which is why I had to see what they were posting about—why was I still so newsworthy?

Becca typed in one of the top celebrity gossip sites and we waited for it to load. The first few stories were about actual celebrities doing things that were actually semi-interested: cheating, partying, and spending their money frivolously.

Then my name popped up and beneath it there was a photo of Liam and me walking hand in hand out of Starbucks. I was prepared for the worst, so when I saw "America's Sweetheart Soccer Couple" beneath the photo, I gasped. They clearly had the wrong person; that photo didn't even show the real details of the situation. Beneath my stylish sunglasses I had zero makeup on, they thought my hair looked trendy because I hadn't washed it yet that day, and there had been a coffee stain on the front of my shirt, which the website had clearly photoshopped out. I was smiling up at Liam because he was making fun of me for being a klutz with my coffee. I mean, we were happy and we were a couple, but as far as being anything close to "America's Sweethearts"... they had it all wrong.

Becca scrolled down to the comments section and that's where all the real controversy was housed. There were thousands upon thousands of comments concerning whether I was good enough/hot enough/nice enough/stylish enough to be dating Liam Wilder. Becca didn't let me read them for too long, but the comments I had time to read tore me apart piece by piece. Some of the claims were just too ridiculous not to ignore. *"He should be with a blonde."*— *"He should be with a republican."* — *"He should date someone who is Jewish."*

"Wow. People are really opinionated about Liam's dating habits. Like hyper-opinionated. Why do they care if I use a certain kind of shampoo?" I commented as Becca flipped to another website.

"Probably to make sure you don't use a shampoo that tests their products on animals. They said they don't want Liam dating an animal abuser."

Oh good God. I wasn't killing monkeys over here.

The next site she pulled up had a photo of Liam and me out on the beach near his house. I remembered seeing paparazzi that day and Liam had wanted to go back inside, but I wasn't going to let them ruin our afternoon. Now, I wish I'd listened. Seeing my body in a bikini splashed across the Internet felt oddly personal. The photographs weren't even close to being pornographic, but it felt like I should get a say in whether they get to use photos of me in a bikini or not.

It didn't help that Liam was rubbing lotion onto my back, and the attraction between us was clear even through the computer screen. Had there been an audio clip alongside the photo I would have surely been moaning.

"Do you want to keep going?" Becca asked, eying me wearily.

"Just a few more," I said, knowing the sinking feeling in my stomach was there to stay, even if I stopped looking now.

I should have stopped.

Why the fuck didn't I stop.

The next few websites were clearly going for a different angle. All of them talked about the controversy that Tara had brought to the limelight: Liam dating me when he was my coach, our age difference, his womanizing past, and my seduction of him. All of it was complete bullshit. After all, the media had mostly crafted his past anyway, but it still stung to know that some people were judging me based on this information. And not just some people, *thousands* of people that didn't know me at all.

I was surprised to find quite a few new comments from Tara. It seemed that the threats from my father's lawyers hadn't shut her up and it enraged me to know that she was still out their spewing her lies.

"I'm going to talk to her," I stated, hopping up off the bed.

Becca sat up, her eyebrows pressed into her forehead in shock. "Who? Tara?"

"Yup," I said, reaching for my phone. I still had her number programmed in from when she was on the soccer team.

"Call Liam first, he'd want to know," Becca said, pushing off the bed and leaving the room to give me some privacy. I motioned that I'd just be a second. She motioned back with a crude jacking-off gesture. *Never change, Becca.*

I thought Liam might have still been at practice, but when he answered, my stomach dropped. Crap, I was going to leave a vague message to get myself off the hook... now I actually had to be honest.

"Hey babe, I'm just leaving the fields. What's up?" His voice was smooth and it almost erased all of my anger from Tara. But not quite.

"Hey. I think I'm going to call Tara and see if she wants to meet me for coffee or something..."

Silence hung on the phone line as I heard him fiddling with his keys and getting into his car.

"Why would you want to do that?"

I took a deep breath, collecting my thoughts into coherent sentences. "Because she's still out there leading a hate campaign against me and maybe if we meet up and talk, some of the things between us can be settled. She obviously didn't respond to my parents, but maybe I can figure out why she's doing this."

"For attention, Kinsley. She wants the limelight and you know it. She can't get there on her own, so she's dragging your name along with her."

I sighed. "Well I still think it could help."

He started his car before answering. "I'm not going to stop you, but I'd like you to go during the day and somewhere that will have a crowd."

"She's not a murderer, Liam."

"Maybe not, but she's certifiably insane, and I'd rather not have to worry about your safety," he sighed. "I still think this is bad idea..."

I paced across the floor of my room, thinking the plan through. "Okay. I promise to do that, and I'll keep you posted. Okay?"

"All right. Call me later. I wish you were going to be at my house when I got home."

I smiled against the phone screen. "I know, but Becca and I promised we'd spend some time together today. Tomorrow, I'm all yours," I promised.

"All right, love you. Good luck," he said before hanging up. My heart fluttered like it still did every time he said those words. I'd been counting. That was the tenth time he'd said it to me and it still didn't feel real.

The next phone call wouldn't be quite as easy. I scrolled through my contacts until I came to the "T's". Tara's name was first and I pressed send before giving myself time to back out. Each ring that passed seemed to last a lifetime, and I wondered if she'd actually pick up or not.

Then the phone clicked into the call.

"Kinsley Bryant." She dragged out my name like it was something disgusting stuck to the bottom of her shoe.

"Tara. Hi. Do you have a second to talk?"

She sighed with an exacerbated air. "Not really, but I'm already listening, so whatever."

Stay calm. Stay calm. "Okay, well I was actually calling to see if you would meet me for coffee tomorrow."

"Why the hell would I want to do that? You got me kicked off the ULA soccer team because you couldn't keep your slutty hormones under wraps."

All right. So she hadn't had a personality transplant since we last spoke. Bummer.

"Tara, I think we both know that you *want* to meet with me as much as I *need* to meet with you. Think of the photos they'll take of the two of us. I'll even sit outside so they get a good one of your face."

I was being a bitch, but we both were at this point.

"You think you're such hot shit, Kinsley. I'll meet you tomorrow, but only because I want to see that dumb expression on your face one last time."

"Great. I'll let you pick the place. Let's meet around three." Then I hung up before she could protest.

Dumb expression? I paused for a moment, realizing what I'd just done to myself and instantly regretting it.

"Becca!" I called, and a second later I heard her footsteps in the hallway. When she pushed my door open I turned to face her with a solemn voice.

"I'm meeting with the devil tomorrow at 3."

Becca narrowed her eyes, nodded, and then stepped into my room. "Welp, I guess we better watch the rest of

Game of Thrones tonight then just in case you get offed."

• • •

Downtown LA was bustling the next day so I had to park quite a few streets away. The Coffee Shop Tara picked was mostly empty which made it easy to spot her bright blonde hair as soon as I stepped up to the outdoor seating.

I was joking about sitting outside so the paparazzi could photograph us, but apparently Tara couldn't pass up a golden opportunity like that. It made me all the more happy that Becca had helped me curl my glossy brown hair. We'd picked out a cotton dress that I paired with a light, summer scarf and my favorite pair of designer flats. For once, the paparazzi would snap photos of me when I didn't look like crap after practice.

"Hi Tara." I smiled down to her as I walked up. She'd been scrolling through her iPhone, no doubt googling herself, so she hadn't seen me approach. The second she heard my voice, her ears perked and she shifted her vicious gaze to me. Tara was a prime reason to not judge a book by a cover. She looked beautiful and docile. Her sweet features masked such insanity beneath them that I couldn't quite figure out how she'd become the bitch that she was.

"Hello, Kinsley. Please take a seat."

I thought she was actually going to be polite.

"You're blocking the sun and I'm trying to get a tan while we get this over with."

Or not so polite.

"Right," I said, shifting down into the seat across from her and placing my purse on my lap. I pulled out my cell phone and ensured that the speaker was facing her before dropping it casually onto my lap.

"How have you been, Tara?" I asked.

"Cut the crap. What do you want?"

She really wasn't going to make this easy. I folded my hands over my lap. "I want to apologize for the way I acted. I should have never started dating Liam while he was our coach and had I chosen my actions better, you might not have been kicked off the team."

My apology was clearly the last thing she was expecting because her face contorted into an amused glare.

"Oh, please. Anyone of us could have dated Liam. You were just the first one to open your legs. So don't think you're so high and mighty because you sucked him off in the field house and now you think you're actually his girlfriend."

I could feel my eyebrows drifting toward my hairline. Welp, I guess we hadn't actually gotten away with that as smoothly as I'd thought.

Alriiiighty, then. On to plan B.

"Well, if you aren't mad at me about those things, I'm a little confused why you're still going after me in the press. I've seen multiple quotes from you that are aimed directly at me."

She rolled her eyes and tipped back in her chair as if bored with the conversation.

"I do what I have to do to stay in the public eye. I put a pause on the soccer crap and now I have a bit more time to devote to my career."

"Your career?" I asked, trying to keep my tone attitude free.

"Modeling and acting," she answered dully, as if I was a blubbering idiot for having to ask.

"Oh, that's awesome. I think you'd be great at that."

And I actually did mean it. She was dramatic, crazy, and beautiful. What better person to be cast as the villain in films than a person who actually played the role in real life?

"Thanks, but I don't care about your opinion."

I nodded and shifted my gaze to the street for a moment. Camera flashes caught my attention and reminded me about the task at hand.

"So then, if you're focusing on your career now, maybe we can come to an understanding..." I began.

"And what might that be?" She cocked her eyebrow with an incredulous look.

"You have to stop finding fame by dragging me down. The story will fade and eventually people will see right through it. Not to mention people will realize that I'm actually very boring and they won't care what I eat for lunch or how I take my coffee. This won't last forever so there's no reason to prolong the inevitable."

A sinful smile spread across her lips. "Kinsley. The beauty of free speech in this country is that I can say whatever I want, whenever I want. If I want to keep telling the press lies about you then I will because I don't actually give a fuck about you or Liam. I care about making it big. So this whole conversation has been a colossal waste of your time. In fact, I think you've just made it all the more fun to talk about you to the press because now I know that it's bothering you. Honestly, Kinsley, you make it just too easy."

I'll admit there was only a small part of me that had hoped that Tara would come to the light and change her ways. The other 99% of me took pride in the fact that I'd been right in masterminding my plan from the very beginning.

I reached forward and set my phone on the table so that Tara could see the recording screen. Then I hit pause and glanced up at her with a confident smile.

"You know, you think you're so brilliant, Tara, but what you're actually doing is against the law."

"Oh please, I'd love to see you try and take this to court."

I laughed and saw her perfect facade start to crack. "No. I don't plan on suing you. I don't give a shit about your money. What I'm after is public opinion. You see, yesterday I met with a lawyer and filed a restraining order against you. I outlined all of the facts that happened concerning your hazing and bullying, and then I had the other teammates and Coach Davis corroborate my story."

That was complete bullshit, but she totally bought it. Her mask had a giant crack straight down the center.

"But still, I thought that wouldn't be enough for you, Tara, because let's face it, you are the most psychotic bitch I've ever met. So then I set up this meeting today so that I could record you confessing to telling the media lies all in the name of becoming a star."

She scoffed. "As if, Kinsley. You think you've outmatched me, but you have no clue who you're dealing with."

"No one likes a bully, Tara, and now I have proof. So if you spew one more thing about me in the press, I'll release the tape and we'll see what America decides to do about it."

"They'll assume its fake," she protested, still clinging onto her confident air.

"Maybe they will, but your voice is pretty recognizable. And you know the funny thing about the media? They want the most *interesting* story. So what's better than an *accurate* story that's also *interesting*? So why don't you consider which would sell the most magazines? A headline that reads Kinsley Bryant Goes to Soccer Practice Yet Again... or Crazed ex-ULA Soccer Player Stalking and Harassing America's Sweetheart?"

I was not America's sweetheart, not even close, but she didn't need to know that.

A pregnant pause passed between us and I knew I'd finally broken through to her. While slightly off her rocker, Tara was still fairly intelligent and she knew I had her.

"I could just come back at you with something twice as big. I'll reveal more details about you and Liam," she said, grasping at her last hope.

"You could, or we could stop this entire show right now. You can walk away with a little bit of your dignity left and I could forget that I even have this recording," I said, pulling my phone off the table and dropping it back into my purse.

"You're just as conniving as I am," she spat, pushing to stand. Her metal chair scraped against the concrete.

"Maybe I am. Or maybe my claws just come out when someone backs me into a corner," I suggested with an even tone. I had no clue which path she would choose, but I had a good feeling that my talk got through to her.

She stood to leave, casting one last evil glare in my direction before heading away. The paparazzi's shutters went wild and I sat there for a moment, collecting the last few minutes in my mind, before retrieving my phone to call Becca.

"Kinsley! How'd it go? Are you alive or are you calling me from the other side?" Becca asked as soon as she answered.

I tossed my head back and laughed, feeling instantly

lighter now that I was done with that showdown.

"I really think she'll back off now, Bec. I won't know for sure until enough time has passed, but she'd be an idiot to not move on and forget about this."

"I hope so."

I glanced down at the time. "Hey, I'll call you back when I get to Liam's place. He's out of practice soon and I want to beat him home."

"Why?"

"You don't want to know," I laughed.

"Oh my god, ew. Are you going to like wait for him naked on the bed or something?"

"Becca! Stop! We have to have boundaries," I laughed, standing up and grabbing my purse.

She couldn't stop giggling on the other end of the phone. "Let me know how that works out for you." Then she thought better of it. "On second thought, don't tell me anything about it."

"Ha-ha. I'll see you at practice tomorrow."

"Bye, Kins."

I hung up the phone just as a camera flash blinded my eyes. I blinked, trying to ease the dark spots in my vision, and then glanced up to find a man standing directly in front of my table. Usually the paparazzi kept their distance so as to appear respectful, but this guy apparently didn't abide by those rules. His beard was long and unkempt and his eyes were wild. I could see sweat dripping down his forehead as he leaned closer.

I almost opened my mouth to say something to him, but I was already standing, so I decided to just leave it and head for my car. I spun on my flats and turned toward the exit, but the guy beat me to it. He walked alongside me, continuously flashing his camera so that I had to hold up my hand to block his shots.

"Please back up. You're too close... this is ridiculous."

"Just doing my job," he shrugged, and kept walking in front of me, his flashes momentarily blinding me one after another.

I hated the fact that my car was parked a few streets away still. I crossed my arms and kept my head down, but that didn't deter him. As soon as we were away from the coffee shop, he started asking me question after question.

"Are you dating Liam Wilder?—Have you slept with him?"

"I'm not answering any of your questions," I answered, trying to sidestep around him, but he was relentless.

"Did you like that he was your coach when you first met him?—Did he take your virginity?"

"You need to leave me alone!" I shouted, and picked up my pace. His questions were cruel and gross. They made my skin crawl and I wrapped my arms around myself even tighter. The man kept running after me and that's when I noticed how wild his movements were. This guy was clearly on drugs or well past drunk. No normal person would act like this.

"Hey! Just give me a fucking picture, princess," he said, reaching forward and grabbing my arm between his sweaty fingers. I instantly flinched back, trying to get out of his grasp, but I had too much momentum. When he released me, I flew back and slammed my elbow and head against the concrete. Pain pierced the back of my head as I cried out. Stars danced around my vision for a brief second as I squeezed my eyes shut, waiting for the pain to lessen.

Holy shit.

He grabbed me.

I shot up and tried to catch my bearings. I shouldn't have gotten up right away with a head injury, but my flight or fight instincts took over and I knew I couldn't just lay there. The man was already coming toward me again, so I reached in for my cell phone and tried to ignore the glimpses of blood I saw on my arms.

"I'll call 911 if you don't leave me alone," I screamed with a shaky voice as his dark eyes met mine.

"Hey! Leave her alone! Let her be!" A sweet voice yelled behind him. I blinked, trying to clear my vision. A group of women had just come out of a shop nearby and had probably seen the entire exchange. One of them was already on her cell phone.

"I'm calling the police," she told him. The man instantly shoved his camera into his bag and took off running past me.

"Sweetie, are you okay?" one of the women asked, turning toward me with a piteous expression. I tried to answer, but instead I just nodded as tears streamed down my face.

The woman connected to the police and I gave them details about the man's appearance as they crowded around me and patted my back. They calmed me down enough so that I could speak coherent sentences to the officer. After they had everything they needed, I thanked the women for their help and protested when they tried to walk me to my car. It was still broad daylight in West LA, no one other than a drugged out paparazzi would pay me any mind.

The second I was inside my car though, I called Liam and the tears overtook me again.

"Kins, good news I got out of practice a little early. I already showered and was about to head home."

I sniffled into the phone, trying to calm down enough

to talk to him.

"Kinsley? Baby? What's wrong?" His voice grew more scared and demanding the longer my tears prevented me from answering.

"Kinsley—Are you all right? Are you hurt?"

"Liam," I began, taking a big breath. "I was walking to my car and there was a guy trying to take my picture. He grabbed me and I fell back and hit my head—"

"What? Where are you?"

"—It's not bad." I reached back and felt my scalp, not realizing I was bleeding down my neck. "Oh, I guess maybe it is bad. I don't know."

"Kinsley— where are you?" he asked again with a sharp tone.

"West LA, near Sunset."

"Are you safe?"

"I'm in my car with the doors locked."

"Don't move. I'll come get you. Do I need to call 911?"

"No! No. I'm fine. I already talked to the police. I just... it freaked me out."

"Okay. You're okay. Stay on the phone with me. I'm only five minutes away."

I leaned my head back against the seat and closed my eyes, letting the sound of his breathing calm my erratic heart rate.

Chapter Thirty

"I just pulled up. Hang on, babe," Liam said.

I opened my eyes and peered in my rear view mirror to see him hop out of his car to get to me. I opened my door just as he came around to my driver's side. I'd mostly conquered my tears when I was on the phone with him, but now that he was here in person, wrapping his arms around me, I felt all the emotion rush back in. He pressed his hand to my neck, brought me into his chest, and held me for a moment, hushing me and rubbing my back with his other hand.

"You're okay. You're okay," he kept repeating until my crying slowed and I was mostly sniffling.

"You're still bleeding, we need to go get this looked at," Liam said, pulling his hand away to see the blood on it. I would have been grossed out if I wasn't concerned that I might need stitches.

"Are you hurt anywhere else?" he asked, eyeing me up and down. At first the adrenaline pumping through my veins had kept me from noticing any of the pain, but now I realized I had a few scrapes and bruises. My elbow was still bleeding and my palm that I'd used to catch myself was scraped up as well.

"Just some little cuts," I answered, "but my head hurts."

Liam clenched his jaw and nodded. "Let's go," he said, reaching around me to grab my purse and then half-lifted me out of my seat. He carried most of my weight as we walked toward his car. My feet worked just fine, but I knew he was just as scared as I'd been a few minutes ago. Maybe it made him feel better to help me.

We stopped at an Emergency Clinic on the way to his house and they gave me six stitches on the back of my scalp. They explained that head injuries bleed much more than other injuries, but we still needed to watch out for any symptoms of a concussion.

While I was getting cleaned up, Liam called Coach Davis and explained that'd I'd be sitting out from practice tomorrow and would let her know how I was doing. Honestly, once the scrapes and everything were cleaned up and I was back in Liam's car heading home, I felt much better. Exhausted, but better.

We were quiet most of the way to his house. Liam had his hand on my knee and he'd glance over or squeeze his fingers to make sure I was staying awake. I think I just felt tired from all of the tears. I was usually better about pain. After all, soccer was an intense sport, but a lot of the emotion and tears stemmed from the man's verbal abuse rather than the injuries.

"I keep hearing the man's voice," I admitted when we were a few minutes away from Liam's house.

"Was he asking you for a picture?" Liam asked,

eyeing me cautiously.

"He was demanding a photo— but he was also asking really personal questions about us. He asked if you took my virginity and if I liked that you were my coach... you know..."

Liam's hand gripped the steering wheel even tighter and I knew my confession didn't sit well with him. I had to tell him though, the paparazzi's words were slimy; I didn't want to keep them to myself and let them rot.

"That won't happen again. I'll make sure of it. Do you hear me, Kinsley? I'll never let him near you," Liam bit out harshly.

I nodded and glanced out the passenger side window. Liam couldn't be with me all the time, but I believed that he would keep me safe when he could, and that's all that mattered.

When we go to his house, he helped me out of the car and then led me straight to his bathroom. I leaned back against the sink and he slowly helped me out of my dress, bra, and panties. His touch was gentle and soothing against my skin, and I sighed into him, letting him hold my weight. He drew a warm bubble bath and then gently set me inside.

When I was comfortable lying in the bubbles, he kissed the top of my head and headed for the bathroom door. "Wash up. I'm going to start dinner," he said with a tight smile. I knew he wasn't over the events of the day yet, but neither was I.

"Liam—" I said, getting his attention. He spun around in the doorway, and for a brief moment, I let myself take in his handsome features: the sweet lips, the straight nose, the chiseled jaw.

"I love you."

He closed his eyes for a brief moment, as if soaking in

my words, and then he smiled and glanced back at me. "I love you, too."

It was over dinner that Liam asked me to move in with him. I was taking a bite of the spaghetti when he said plain and simple, "Move in with me."

My heart paused for a moment as I finished chewing. Then I glanced up at him as if he were insane. "Here?" I asked.

"It doesn't matter where. If you don't like this house then we'll find another."

That's not really what I had meant, but I couldn't comprehend his request.

"We've been dating for two months," I stated as if maybe he'd forgotten.

"Two and half actually, but it doesn't matter."

"Is this because of what happened today?" I asked, setting my fork down on the edge of my plate.

He sighed. "It has a little bit to do with that. I've wanted you here with me from the start. We have such busy schedules that it would just make sense for us to live together. When I'm not working or practicing, I want to be with you."

"But—" I couldn't even process all of my protests into one coherent list. I was too young, I had to live in the house with the other rookies, I would miss Becca, my parents would flip, and our relationship was still so fresh. Any of those were valid reasons, but I knew they wouldn't be good enough for Liam, and to be honest, a part of me, a very big part of me, thought they weren't good enough for me either.

"Can I think about it?" I asked with a gentle tone.

His gaze scanned over me, memorizing the planes of my features. "Of course. It's a big decision."

"And you're 100% sure about asking me? You won't regret it in the morning?"

The edge of his mouth tipped skyward and he shook his head. "No, so you can't use that as an excuse.

I smiled and then took another bite of spaghetti, hoping to pause the conversation until my head wasn't aching.

We finished the rest of our dinner and he cleaned up quickly while I went to lie down in bed. I loved Liam's bed. It was oversized in every way, with too many pillows and light airy blankets that layered on top of one another. I felt tiny when I climbed inside of it and most of the time I never wanted to leave.

A few minutes later he came in carrying two Ibuprofen and a cup of water for me.

"Here, take these before you sleep or you'll wake up feeling terrible," he said, handing me the pills.

"And it's okay if I go to sleep?" I asked, fearful of the fact that I could still have a concussion.

Liam nodded and brushed my hair back from my face. "The doctor said you could sleep normally."

I swallowed the pills as Liam crossed the room to change into his pajamas. He pulled his shirt overhead and tossed it into the dirty clothes hamper, and for a moment I could hardly breathe. It was a sight that I'd never get used to: tan skin covering contoured muscles fit for a professional athlete. I loved each ridge and didn't even bother turning away when he spun around and found me staring.

"You're supposed to be sleeping," he joked, dropping his jeans and tossing them aside so he could put his sleeping pants on. My eyes scanned down the front of him, drinking in the sight of him and trying to quell my raging hormones. I was tired and injured, you'd think that would be enough of a turnoff, but unfortunately nothing could turn me off about Liam.

"You're making it impossible to sleep," I said with a cheeky smile. I sat atop the blankets with my long legs crossed at the ankle. My sleeping shirt barely hit the tops of my tan thighs and Liam's gaze dragged down them, then back up to me.

He slowly walked toward the bed, forgetting his sleeping pants all together. I could already see his erection growing thick beneath his briefs and I licked my lips in anticipation of the next few minutes.

"How are you feeling?" Liam asked, glancing up at me with a mischievous air.

"Good," I replied. It would have taken a gunshot wound to take me out of the game at that point.

"And your feet? How do they feel?" he asked, stroking his fingers and palms beneath my feet and massaging my soles gently. I was slightly ticklish, but he didn't linger long enough to make me laugh. Once I nodded, he moved onto my legs.

"And your calves? Are they okay?" His eyes were growing darker, more intense, and I felt myself starting to breathe quicker, harder.

"They feel fine," I said separating my legs slightly so that he'd know I wanted him to continue. He grazed over my knees and gently massaged higher.

"Are your thighs injured?" he asked, skimming his fingers along the inseam of my leg and pushing my shirt up over the top of my panties. His breath hit the flesh just inside my thigh and my stomach quivered in response. The way his fingers dug gently into my skin made me whimper. He hadn't even neared his end goal and I was already close to losing it.

"Liam, that feels so good," I moaned as his thumbs inched higher up my thigh. I could feel his erection against my calf and I had to bite my lip to keep from pleading with him to hurry up. I didn't want to rush him, not when his touch was erasing every bit of sadness and pain from my day.

"Does this make you feel better, baby?" he asked just as his finger skimmed over the outside of my panties.

I arched my neck and whimpered toward his bedroom ceiling. My wound stung slightly, but the pain was nothing compared to the pleasure stemming from his finger.

"Yes, it makes me feel... go—good," my voice broke midway through my word as he pushed my panties aside.

"Lie back and spread your legs for me. I don't want you to move. You should be resting," he said just before his mouth pressed against me.

He'd told me to lie still, but he said nothing about gripping his hair and moaning for him to continue. I couldn't help but twist my hips and angle myself so that his mouth hit me at the perfect angle. His fingers and mouth worked in tandem to bring me to the brink of oblivion. I watched the seductive rhythm of his fingers sliding in and out of me for a moment before the sensations became too much and I had to clamp my eyes closed. Two more sweet strokes and then my toes were curling and I was crying his name without an ounce of inhibition.

He slid up and smiled sinfully toward me as he propped himself onto his knees. His briefs were tugged off and tossed aside in seconds, and then he resettled himself against me with smooth confidence.

"This is going to be slow and easy, Kinsley," he promised as he pressed himself into me gently. I wasn't used to the slow-and-sweet version of his lovemaking, but it had its advantages— like when his mouth found mine as he slid all the way into me. Slow and delicious. It was enough to make my head spin. I knew it was driving him wild as well. He held himself up and I wrapped my small hands around his biceps, feeling their power and weight above me.

His hips worked their magic and I reveled in the luxurious feel of his lovemaking. I laid back and tried to cling onto each delicious thrust until we were both coming and murmuring each other's names. Our voices mingled together as he kissed me and whispered 'I love you's' into my ear.

I don't remember drifting off to sleep, but sometime in the middle of the night, my pain medication wore off enough to jar me awake. The throbbing settled in like a hazy cloud. As I waited for the new pills to kick into effect, I contemplated the last 24 hours. If Tara backed off would anything change, or would I be splashed across the media no matter what? If I made the Olympic team I'd be thrust into the spotlight, but the fact that Liam was interested in me made me a whole lot more interesting to the rest of America as well.

I sighed and tried to push away the negative thoughts. The bed dipped around me as Liam rolled over and pulled me closer to his sleeping body. He did it subconsciously, and I couldn't help but smile. Maybe even if the media didn't back down, I'd be okay. I could get used to it just like every other person that chose to have a public career. And if not, I'd make Liam buy me a private island. Hmm, maybe that was the better option. I'd ban pants on the island. Only Calvin Klein boxer briefs.

Chapter Thirty-One

Liam and I hadn't made it out of bed yet when his cell phone rang the next morning. It wasn't early, nearly eleven o'clock, but since I wasn't going to practice we took advantage of the free time. Let's just say that by that point I felt thoroughly orgasmed-out. I think that's what you feel like when you hit nirvana. So yeah, Dalai Lama, I'm onto you.

We were watching morning TV and eating breakfast when he reached over to answer the buzzing phone. He mouthed "Penn" to me, so I nodded and kept right on eating. Sorry, but nobody's more important than blueberry pancakes.

"What's up?— she's okay, I know Becca was worrying, but she got stitches and she's healing up—she already called the police, but I'm going to force her to move in with me—no it's the perfect time, asshat, thanks for your support— yeah, she's right here, hold on."

He held the phone out for me, "Penn asked for you."

I scrunched my brows together, but took the phone nonetheless. What would Penn need to say that he couldn't just tell Liam?

"Hey Penn," I said, holding the phone up to my ear and continuing to cut my pancakes with my free hand. Priorities.

"Kinsley, I'm glad you're feeling better."

I smiled. "Me too. You should see the other guy though."

Penn laughed. "Oh yeah, did you give him a shiner?"

"Yup. No worries."

"Good to know I shouldn't mess with you—but hey, I wanted to ask for your help with Becca."

He piqued my interest and I glanced toward Liam to see if he knew what Penn was talking about. He shrugged.

"Sure, of course. What do you need?"

"Well, I'm sort of concocting this elaborate plan to ask her to be my girlfriend."

I laughed. "Aren't you guys past that? You've been dating for as long as Liam and I have."

Penn groaned, "Yes, but it's complicated. You know she turned me down when I asked her a few weeks ago. She was scared we were moving too fast and that I needed to work some stuff out—which I did."

"So now?"

"So now I want to add the title and make it elaborate and showy so that if she turns me down she'll feel terrible."

I couldn't stop laughing. "Soooo, you're basically guilting her into being your girlfriend."

"Hey—whatever gets the job done," he quipped.

"Well definitely count me in then."

"All right, I'm thinking about doing it this weekend."

"As in two days from now?"

He chuckled. "Is that a bad idea?"

I toyed with my fork. "No. We just have to be creative and quick. Or have you already thought of something?"

"I want to do something on the beach with roses and candles. I know it's super cheesy, but I want to make it over the top so that she'll remember it."

I was so happy for Becca. So happy that she found someone like Penn who wanted to go through all this trouble just for her.

"All right, Liam and I will do whatever you want… I can't wait to see Becca's reaction."

He laughed. "She's going to flip. I know it."

"Okay well, I'm going back to my breakfast, but I'll talk it over with Liam and let you know if we come up with any good ideas."

"Sounds good, thanks Kins, and hope you feel better."

I hung up and I handed the phone back to Liam.

"Did you hear most of that?"

He smiled and leaned forward to kiss my cheek. "Let's make Penn buy her a yacht so we can use it whenever we want," he joked.

"Yes! I'll tell him she only accepts 40' boats as gifts."

We spent the rest of the morning concocting plans on how to trap Penn into getting Becca really awesome toys. We decided a helicopter with the four of our faces on the side would *really* make her want to say yes to him.

• • •

Sadly, Penn shot down all of our extravagant ideas with phrases like "you guys are ridiculous", "No, we don't need to buy a house in Hawaii so that Becca will date me", and "stop calling me or I'll turn my phone off". Liam and I chalked it up to poor judgment on his part. I guess romantic roses and candles on the beach would have to cut it.

All day Saturday we were running around doing his bidding. We picked up chocolate covered strawberries and a bottle of Dom Perignon. We drove around looking for the perfect rose petals because they couldn't *just* be red. Becca also loved yellow roses, so Penn thought we had to get *both* red and yellow petals. *High maintenance couple alert.*

On the way home I could feel Liam glance over to watch me every now and then. It made my skin flush to feel his gaze on me, but I never gave into the urge to meet his eyes. He seemed even more serious about us since the incident with the paparazzi. He'd asked me that morning if I'd thought anymore about moving in with him. We'd even discussed it with Coach Davis on Friday. She was wary about me moving in with him so soon, but she'd agreed that the security at the house wasn't up to par for someone with as much media coverage as I was getting. It was probably safer for the girls living in the house, as well as myself, if I thought about moving somewhere a bit more secure.

The more I let the idea linger in my mind over the last two days, the more I wanted to throw caution to the wind and do it. I'd seen different versions of Liam, but there were still so many that I wanted to know and learn. I wanted the midnight-snack Liam with the disheveled hair. I wanted the lazy Saturday Liam that never changed out of his sweats, but looked freaking adorable anyway. The hot bastard. The only reason I hesitated was because of Becca and Emily. It was so easy to see each other when I could literally shout across our bathroom to get Emily's attention, and Becca was in my room more than I was. I didn't want to drift away from them or the rest of the girls on my team.

My thoughts were interrupted when we pulled up outside Liam's house. I'd have time to make a decision later. We carried everything inside and then went to find Penn who was running around like a wild man. You would have thought he was asking her to marry him at this point.

"Penn, seriously, everything will work out," I said just as my phone buzzed. I glanced down to see a text from Becca.

Becca: Freaking out a bit. Penn's been acting weird all day. He still hasn't called, but he just texted me and told me a limo was waiting for me outside. That's good, right?

Kinsley: Yes! No worrying!!!

I dropped my phone back down and we hustled down to the beach so we could relieve Penn of his duties. He went to shower and left Liam and me to light all the candles. No big deal, right? *Wrong*. Who thought candles on a beach was romantic? There's this mysterious force at the beach that never stops. Locals refer to it as wind, and it majorly fucked up our plan.

So there we were unable to light a single candle while we also attempted to protect the entire setup before Becca showed up. This was actually much harder than expected considering the seagulls assumed the rose petals were some kind of food. They kept swooping down and stealing petals, almost taking me out in the process and pooping on at least three of the unlit candles. Sorry Becca, hope you like your romance with a side of bird flu.

"You know we should at *least* get one of these strawberries," I pointed out.

Liam chuckled. "We can make chocolate covered

strawberries, babe."

My brows perked up. "You have the supplies?"

"Strawberries, chocolate, and Kinsley— yes," he winked. I shivered at the thought of melted chocolate and Liam in the same vicinity.

I was still attempting to light the first candle just as Penn came back down to the beach.

"She's five minutes away! You guys have to go!" he said, hurrying us along. In a flurry of movements, we picked up the extra lighters and trash and ran up onto Liam's porch without explaining the fatal flaw in his plan. He'd figure it out soon enough.

"WAIT! THEY AREN'T LIT," he yelled.

Liam glanced over toward me with a wicked smile. "Run!"

We weren't planning on watching the entire thing, but I had to see Becca's reaction when she stepped outside.

"I don't want to watch for long. It feels like we're invading their privacy," Liam said, sitting down next to me on the porch.

"I agree."

Liam's hand stroked my leg and goose bumps bloomed beneath his touch. If he kept it up, we'd miss the entire thing.

"Oh, she's here!" Liam said, pointing to where Becca was exiting the back of Penn's house. I could barely see her through the tall shrubbery that outlined Liam's porch. She was wearing the blue dress and she looked absolutely stunning. The sunset silhouetted her from behind and her bright blonde hair shone against the vibrant backdrop. She'd slipped her shoes off so she could walk in the sand,

and the second she saw the sight before her, her hands flew to her mouth and she froze. Tears burned the corners of my eyes as I watched her step closer to the ring of unlit, poopy candles.

Liam's arm stretched across my shoulders and he swept the tear from my cheek without saying a word. Penn was talking to Becca, but we couldn't hear what he was saying. I assumed he was telling her how much she meant to him. Then he paused his speech and Becca threw herself into his arms. I had to fight the urge to cheer for them. They were finally getting their happy ending and I knew they both deserved it.

"I'd assume that was a yes, don't you think?" Liam asked.

Penn and Becca were kissing, his arm was slung low around her waist, pulling her against him with fierce intensity. It was our time to leave.

"I think so," I said with a giant smile.

Liam mirrored my smile and then pulled me through the back door into his house.

"What about those chocolate covered strawberries now?" he asked as I finished off my glass of champagne.

"How about we skip the strawberries?" I asked with a suggestive gaze.

Chapter Thirty-Two

I felt the wind rushing past me as I pushed myself to pick up the pace. I was beating my previous times, but it wasn't good enough. My sprints needed to be faster and my skills had to be perfectly honed if I expected to make it onto the Olympic team.

I'd been training every day, harder than I had in my entire life, and I knew I had a fighting chance at getting an invitation for tryouts. There wasn't a woman in America training harder than I was. Becca would join me on most days, and we'd push each other past our limits. Everything had fallen into a routine. She was staying at Penn's house in Malibu more and more often, and I was leaving my things at Liam's house whenever I stayed there. We'd drive to practice together, stay after to continue training, and then head back to Malibu afterward. Liam and Penn would get home around the same time and we'd cook dinner, hanging out together a few times every week.

I hadn't officially decided to move in with him, but it

seemed like eventually I'd wake up one morning and all of my crap would be at his house. Liam thought he was being sly, transitioning various things slowly so that I couldn't protest. One day he'd cleared out half of his closet. The next, I had a few drawers in the bathroom to leave all of my stuff. Tomorrow, I'd have monogrammed towels and he'd say "Oh, weird how did those get there?" I wasn't finding the energy to fight him about it anymore. I'd start school in a few weeks and we'd have even less time together, so it made sense for us to live together. I think I just liked making him work for it a little bit. And yeah, the day I came home to find a slew of various make-up and every type of shower essential possible, I knew I was milking this cow for all it was worth. *Shhh.*

"All right!" Becca yelled, "I'm exhausted, that's enough for today."

I finished my sprint, running past the net and exhaling a heavy breath. I rested my hands atop my head as I started my cool down. We didn't have long before we had to head home and get ready. Liam and Penn were taking us out for Mexican food to celebrate the end of summer. All of our schedules would get crazier in the next few weeks. I'd either start school as planned or I'd *hopefully* receive my letter for the USA Soccer Association any day inviting me Olympic tryouts. *Fingers crossed. And maybe my toes, elbows, eyelashes, and legs, too.*

"I'm going to eat every single taquito they have on the premises," Becca declared as we headed off the field.

"That's disgusting."

She scowled at me. "Don't you dare judge me. I'm starving."

"Taquitos are gross. Let's order like ten plates of nachos."

"That's my girl."

• • •

The next two weeks passed as if time was moving at 4x speed. Everything beyond soccer, Liam, my friends, and family fell completely by the wayside. I forgot what TV was, I hadn't cracked my laptop open, and I swear there were cobwebs surrounding my makeup and high heels.

But I loved every second of it. I loved training alongside Liam after we both finished our team practices. He pushed me to become better, and I tried to do the same for him. I'd finally made the final transition to move in with him and I loved coming home to his house every day. I couldn't feel the exact moments when our relationship began growing into something more, but one night as we laid in bed recounting our days and cuddling around one another, I realized that this was it.

He was *it*.

I buried my face against his chest and I kept my thoughts to myself. After all, we'd only been together four months and I was still nineteen… a baby in the eyes of most people.

Early the next morning, I woke up to my phone vibrating on the nightstand beside Liam's bed. I rolled over and reached blindly for the traitorous device, hoping in vain that my spidey senses would kick in. Nope, nothing. I had to actually blink my eyes open like a real person.

Emily's named flashed across the screen and I groaned before answering.

"Emily? What's up?" I asked with a sleepy voice. Why the hell was she calling me so early? I'd see her at practice in an hour anyway.

"KINSLEY! You got a letter!" She squealed into the speaker so loudly that Liam shifted in his sleep next to me.

"What are you talking about? My mom sends me stuff all the time. Just bring it to—"

"No! Kinsley, you got *the* letter. It's from the USA Soccer Association. I haven't opened it, but it's a thick packet and I know it's your invitation!"

That sentence woke me up as if I'd just downed five espresso shots. My mouth fell open and my fingers loosened around the sleek phone. In slow motion I watched it clatter to the hardwood floor.

"Kinsley! Kinsley?!" Emily called through the speaker.

"HOLY SHIT!" I screamed, and jumped out of bed.

"What? Kinsley, what's going on?" Liam shot up, rubbing his eyes and trying to piece together the strange wakeup call. I was too busy dancing around his room to care that I woke him up.

"Liam! I got a letter this morning from the USA Soccer Association! Emily called—"

"Yeah… I'm still here by the way." I heard her muffled voice through the speaker of my phone and started laughing.

I ran back over and grabbed the phone. "Ah! Will you bring the letter to practice, Emily? I'll open it there."

"Okay. I'm so happy for you! I'll see you in a little bit."

"Thanks Em," I hung up, dropped my phone on the bedside table, and slowly turned to Liam.

He was sitting there shirtless with the comforter

bunched around his waist. His hair was sticking in every direction, but his smile caught my breath.

"You did it," he murmured with a scratchy voice.

I mashed my lips together to quell my emotions. "I don't know if it's actually the letter. It could be something else."

He dipped his head and gave me a little smirk. "Babe, you did it. They don't bother sending letters of rejection. If you got a packet, it's an invitation."

"Liam…"

His smile widened, and he tossed the blankets off his body before reaching for me. His fingertips caught my waist and I squealed as he pulled my body onto his.

"You're amazing," he whispered into my ear as he pinned my body to his.

I propped my hands on his chest so that I could look up at him. The smile he was wearing was so genuine that I had to suck in a quick breath.

"So amazing that I probably can't date you anymore."

"Mmm…" he murmured, pulling me closer so that I could feel the rumbling in his chest. "Are you going to trade up?" he asked before placing a kiss right behind my ear.

Hah.

I tried to think of a single person that I could trade up to… let's see… there was… nope. No one. Liam was it. He was the person at the end of the day made me laugh the loudest and swoon the longest. He kept me on my toes and I liked hanging out with him— chatting, working out, and cooking dinner just as much as I enjoyed having rockin'-out-of-this-world sex. No really, I'm talking about some *primo* horizontal tango action.

There was no trading up.

I'd scored Liam Wilder.

I let my body collapse onto his and smiled into the warmth of his neck. "On second thought, I think I'll stay right here."

He laughed before wrapping his arms around me. "I'm so proud of you, Kins."

"It doesn't feel real," I whispered into his neck.

He was quiet for a moment, and then finally he answered, "She believed she could so she did." He was reminding me of the ink inscribed over my ribcage. Ink that I stared at every morning as I resolved to work harder than I had the day before, to push myself past my limits, because in the back of my mind I thought that maybe I was just crazy enough to reach my dream.

And today, in that very moment, I realized that all of the work had actually paid off.

"I did it."

Epilogue

On the eve of my 20th birthday I sat in a plush limousine, watching the city lights blur together as we continued to drive toward downtown LA. So much had changed in the course of one year. I'd been on a rollercoaster ride and there was still no end in sight.

Becca and I had both been invited to try out for the Olympic team, and to our surprise, we'd both made it past the first round. And then the second... and then finally our names were the final two printed on the Olympic roster. We were by far the youngest on the team, and we'd had a lot to prove over the last few months. Practices had challenged me mentally and physically, but I didn't take a single moment for granted. I'd had to step back from the ULA team and put school on pause for the time being, but none of that mattered. I wanted to play soccer and I'd landed my dream of competing at the world level.

"Are you all packed?" Becca asked, stirring me from my thoughts. I glanced back inside the limo to find her and

Emily watching me with curiosity.

I shrugged. "I have a few last minute things to get, but yeah, mostly. I just need to remember to grab my passport."

"As long as you don't go too crazy at your party, you should be coherent enough to remember it in the morning," Emily laughed.

I smiled at her joke and thought about how much effort Liam had put into tonight. On top of preparing to leave the country, Liam had planned an early birthday party for me. He'd kept every detail under lock and key, even when I tried to seduce it out of him. The guy wouldn't crack, so I'd spent the day getting pampered with Emily and Becca, excited that there was a surprise waiting for me at the end of the limo ride.

"I don't think I'll drink at all, actually," I said, staring down at my bright red dress. It was flirty with stretchy fabric, a dipped neckline, cap sleeves, and a flared skirt. It cut off fairly short, but I knew Liam wouldn't mind.

"Yeah, same here," Becca agreed. We both had to eliminate anything deemed "unhealthy" from our diets almost as soon as we'd made the team.

"Wait, so now *I'm* the craziest one out of the three of us?" Emily laughed.

I couldn't help smiling as I thought back on the first night I'd dragged Emily to the LA Stars' party. I thought I'd corrupt her, but in the end, the three of us sort of evened each other out. I like to think she gave me a bit of her calmness and I lent her a bit of my wild side. Becca just gave us both a ton of bruises.

"Oh, don't worry, we'll party with you when we get back from Sweden," I winked just as the limo pulled up outside of a trendy club.

In a rush, an attendant ran forward to open our door

and escort us out onto the carpeted walkway. I glanced up to take in the scene laid out before me. The club was modern, with sleek white walls and ivy twining up around a mid-century iron sign that read Tiger Lily, the name of the club. Hanging candles replaced the need for interior lighting so that the atmosphere seemed more intimate as we stepped past the front doors.

I recognized all of my teammates from ULA as well as other family and friends. There were a few boys from the LA Stars team and I nodded when I saw Josh. We were in an okay place and I was happy to forget about the drama of those few months.

My parents and Liam's parents were chatting in the center of the room and I pressed a hand to my chest as a smile spread even wider. It meant so much to have them all there, especially when I knew how long the flight was from London to LA.

However, the best guest of all was standing directly between our parents, and once I saw him, I couldn't keep my happiness from brimming over. Liam looked handsome as always in a tailored black suit. His hair was styled back in a way that highlighted his sharp features and cleanly shaven face.

I knew he could feel my gaze on him because he glanced up just as I bit down on my lower lip. His grey eyes pinned me to the spot and I was left disarmed as he made his way closer. His smile grew wider with every step, and as he drew near, Becca and Emily fell away from my sides as if on cue.

"Remind me to never let you wear red unless it's in our bedroom," he smirked, taking my appearance in with a confident air.

"Like the dress?"

"I love the woman *wearing* the dress," he said, taking my hand in his. "C'mon, let me talk to you alone for a second."

"But, I haven't said hi to my parents," I protested half-heartedly. There'd be plenty of time to talk to them; right now I wanted to tear this suit off of him.

"They'll understand, c'mon," he said, tugging me through the club and down a side hallway. There was a single black door at the end guarded by a burly looking bouncer. Liam nodded to the man, and the bouncer unlocked the door and held it open so that we could walk through.

I scrunched my brows in confusion. "Wait, where are we going?" I asked.

Liam glanced back at me with a wicked grin, but instead of answering, he led me further up the dim staircase. I thought we'd end up on a second level, maybe in a VIP lounge or something, but instead he pushed through a heavy door at the top of the stairs with a sign taped across that read "roof access."

Light seeped inside the dim hallway, and in that moment, I realized this was much more important than a small chat. I swallowed past the lump in my throat as he continued to push the door open and then my breath froze in my lungs as I took in the sight before me.

He'd created a tiny slice of paradise up on that roof. Strings of twinkle lights danced overhead. Flowers of every color and variety overflowed in each direction; their fresh fragrance wrapping around me as Liam took my hand and pulled me outside.

I closed my eyes for a moment, letting him lead me forward and trying to calm my racing heart. When I blinked them open again, I glanced down toward the path of tea candles leading us toward the center of the roof—to the center of that little paradise.

That's where we paused, where Liam's dark eyes locked with mine. That's where I watched him slide down to one knee and that's where my hands flew to my face as I tried to stop the tears that were threatening to overflow.

It didn't feel real. None of it could be real because then I'd have every single thing I could have dreamed for.

"Kinsley Bryant..." he began as the tears streamed down my cheeks. "At twenty-six, I never imagined finding someone I wanted to spend the rest of my life with. Three months before I met you, I was looking for the next thrill, the next party, the next girl. And then I walked in and found you perched in my kitchen like the most beautifully confident creature I'd ever seen, and I knew you'd be a wildfire. You challenged me from the very beginning and I tried to resist you, but I knew even then that I wasn't going to walk away without you by my side."

He paused and I watched him slowly swallow down his emotions. Liam Wilder, tough as nails soccer player, was actually the biggest softie I knew.

"This past year I've watched you strive for your dreams, and I've loved standing alongside you every step of the way—"

His shaking hand reached down to pull out a small black box from the pocket of his suit.

"Liam..."

His eyes sought mine and I drowned in the absolute vulnerability of the moment.

"Marry me," he said, cracking the box open gently.

A soft, happy sob broke through my throat.

"I'm too young," I protested weakly.

He smirked and calmly shook his head once back and

forth.

"Marry me," he said again so confidently that I knew he was putting my heart under his spell.

"Liam…" I began, my mind racing to keep up.

He shushed me with another shake of his head. "I lied to you that first night I met your mom."

I scrunched my brows trying to recall the conversation he was drawing from.

"What? How?"

"That night I said I was joking about asking you to marry me in three hundred days. I knew then that I'd marry you. I could have asked you that very moment, but I wanted to give you time. I've waited three hundred days, but I won't wait an hour more."

"Yes." I answered so softly that the words didn't pass my fingertips covering my mouth.

"We'll take as long as you want. We can be engaged until you turn ninety-nine and you can't even walk down the aisle. I'll carry you or wheel you down. Just tell me you'll marry me."

Another happy sob broke through my barrier, and I fell forward onto my knees in front of him.

"Liam, I said yes. Yes. YES!" I laughed, throwing my arms around his neck. He laughed against my throat as his arms pulled me close.

I hadn't even glanced at the ring. Does that make me crazy? I would have taken twine tied in a knot if it meant I got to marry this man.

He wouldn't hear of it though.

"I want to see it on you. It took forever to find one that I knew you'd like," he said, retracting his arms and reaching to push the ring onto my finger. I could hardly keep my hand steady as he slipped the band past my nail and up over my knuckle.

It was a simple, rounded square diamond on a skinny band. It looked like the perfect combination between delicate and ornate.

"You did good, Wilder," I teased with a wink, finally able to speak without tears convoluting my speech.

"Thanks, *Mrs. Kinsley Wilder*," he said with a wicked grin, testing my future name out for the first time.

I narrowed my eyes playfully. "Hmm... how about Liam Bryant instead?"

"Hey," he laughed, wrapping me up in his arms again.

"No. No, wait. *Mr. Kinsley Bryant*. Yeah, I like the ring of that."

"You're dreaming."

"C'mon, this is the twenty-first century," I joked.

"Mhm," he said, nuzzling my neck so that his cologne and body wash temporarily invaded the intelligent part of my brain. "Let's just pick new names all together."

I smiled. "I'm not listening anymore. I'm too busy trying to contemplate the fact that you actually want to marry me."

"Believe it."

"Say it, just one more time, so it feels real."

"Kinsley Grace Bryant, you crazy beautiful loon, marry me so we can make hundreds of little soccer prodigies."

I laughed. "Done."

Epilogue to the Epilogue (because I can)

Liam and I went on to win silver and bronze at the Olympic Games. We were also awarded "Cutest Couple". The title was self-appointed. When I returned back to LA, I had a few offers from various professional teams around the country, including a club team in LA.

Becca lost her virginity to Penn in the Olympic Village. Yeah, those *rumors* about the village are true. Liam and I had to turn down an orgy invitation from a group of Russian gymnasts. This was mostly a geopolitical decision on my part.

Emily and her boyfriend suffered from an embarrassing Skype-sex debacle. Let's just say you might want to keep your shirt on until you confirm that you're video-calling your boyfriend and *not* his parents. "*SON OF A PREACHER MAN*"

Josh got the bimbo pregnant and the babies turned out to be little shits. Justice was served.

Tara ended up posing for Playboy and then landing her own reality TV show. I watch it religiously.

Acknowledgements

To every reader that takes a chance on an indie author, thank you so much. It means the world to me that you took a chance on this book.

To my family for all of their unconditional support, and especially to my father for showing me how to find the humor in life.

Mom, as always, your first round feedback is the most helpful. Thank you for laughing at Kinsley and Becca before anyone else.

Lance, you're THE BEST. Thank you for reading and tweaking this book. You are the funniest person I know and I loved getting your stamp of approval on this book.

Thank you to all my beta readers: Jenni Moen, Staci Brillhart, Stacey Lynn, Brittainy Cherry, Jennifer Beach, and Maree Hunter. Your feedback was wonderful and truly, truly appreciated! Thank you for putting up with my changes and talking me through this book. You all helped bring this book to life.

Thank you to my amazing editor over at Taylor K.'s Editing Services.

GIANT thank you to my amazing proofreaders: Jennifer Flory-Van Wyk, Gabby Warner, and Rebecca Berto. I'm so thankful to you all!

Thank you to Patricia Lee for sending me a piece of inspiration everyday leading up to this release. You're so thoughtful and I truly appreciated your support.

Thank you to all of my fellow indie authors (within Author Support 101 & Write Club). I don't think I'd have the energy to write without the help from all of you ladies. Thank you for providing support and a sense of community within a crazy world!

Thank you to everyone who accepted an ARC edition of this book and hanging with me for all the tweaks and changes!

Am I allowed to thank Amy Poehler? Because I am. Thank you to every funny woman out there who blazed the trail for women in comedy. I look up to every single one of you.

Other Books by R.S. Grey:

With This Heart

If someone had told me a year ago that I was about to fall in love, go on an epic road trip, ride a Triceratops, sing on a bar, and lose my virginity, I would have assumed they were on drugs.

Well, that is, until I met Beckham.

Beck was mostly to blame for my recklessness. Gorgeous, clever, undeniably charming Beck barreled into my life as if it were his mission to make sure I never took living for granted. He showed me that there were no boundaries, rules were for the spineless, and a kiss was supposed to happen when I least expected.

Beck was the plot twist that took me by surprise. Two months before I met him, death was knocking at my door. I'd all but given up my last scrap of hope when suddenly I was given a second chance at life. This time around, I wasn't going to let it slip through my fingers.

We set out on a road trip with nothing to lose and no guarantees of tomorrow.

Our road trip was about young, reckless love. The kind of love that burns bright.

The kind of love that no road-map could bring me back   from.

Recommended for ages 17+ due to language and sexual situations.

Behind His Lens

Twenty-three year old model Charley Whitlock built a quiet life for herself after disaster struck four years ago. She hides beneath her beautiful mask, never revealing her true self to the world... until she comes face-to-face with her new photographer — sexy, possessive Jude Anderson. It's clear from the first time she meets him that she's playing by his rules. He says jump, she asks how high. He tells her to unzip her cream Dior gown; she knows she has to comply. But what if she wants him to take charge outside of the studio as well?

Jude Anderson has a strict "no model" dating policy. But everything about Charley sets his body on fire.

When a tropical photo shoot in Hawaii forces the stubborn pair into sexually charged situations, their chemistry can no longer be ignored. They'll have to decide if they're willing to break their rules and leave the past behind or if they'll stay consumed by their demons forever.

Will Jude persuade Charley to give in to her deepest desires?

Recommended for ages 17+ due to language and sexual situations.

Made in the USA
San Bernardino, CA
22 January 2016